Grace Point is blessed. Her beauty is enchanting, a striking juxtaposition of land and sea backlit by warm southern light. More spontaneous prayers are inspired by her dunes, her shores, her bogs than are whispered in the pews of her clapboard churches. Even her storms—wrathful, raving furies that terrorize and kill—produce canvases of splendid, seething glory.

The second truth is this: Grace Point is cursed.

Zoe Barlow came to Grace Point seeking a haven. What she found was a home of darkness. . . .

GRACE POINT

"A novel of tight suspense . . . a kidnapped baby . . . fiery seduction . . . foul crime . . . blind alleys . . . sinister scandals."

—*Kirkus Reviews*

"Masterful . . . intricate . . . an eerie, highly charged novel of wounded relationships and long-hidden secrets." —*Booklist*

"Terrifying suspense in the Mary Higgins Clark tradition." —*The Purloined Letter*

GRACE POINT

Anne D. LeClaire

A SIGNET BOOK

SIGNET
Published by the Penguin Group
Penguin Books USA Inc., 375 Hudson Street,
New York, New York 10014, U.S.A.
Penguin Books Ltd, 27 Wrights Lane,
London W8 5TZ, England
Penguin Books Australia Ltd, Ringwood,
Victoria, Australia
Penguin Books Canada Ltd, 10 Alcorn Avenue,
Toronto, Ontario, Canada M4V 3B2
Penguin Books (N.Z.) Ltd, 182–190 Wairau Road,
Auckland 10, New Zealand

Penguin Books Ltd, Registered Offices:
Harmondsworth, Middlesex, England

Published by Signet, an imprint of New American Library, a division of Penguin Books USA Inc. Previously published in a Viking edition.

First Signet Printing, July, 1993
10 9 8 7 6 5 4 3 2 1

Printed in the United States of America

Grateful acknowledgment is made for permission to reprint excerpts from the following copyrighted works: "What Can I Tell My Bones?" from *The Collected Poems of Theodore Roethke*. Copyright © 1957 by Theodore Roethke. Used by permission of Doubleday, a division of Bantam Doubleday Dell Publishing Group, Inc. "Whales Weep Not!" from *The Complete Poems of D. H. Lawrence*. Copyright © 1964, 1971 by Angelo Ravagli and C. M. Weekley, Executors of the Estate of Frieda Lawrence Ravagli. Used by permission of Viking Penguin, a division of Penguin Books USA Inc.

For my daughter,
Hope D'Avril

Acknowledgments

Grace Point, the town and her citizens, exists solely in my imagination.

During the creation of this work of fiction, a number of people were helpful. I owe a debt of gratitude to Kay Longcope, Anne Packard, the detectives of the Harwich Police Department, and Nat Wordell.

Special thanks to Kate Miciak and Pamela Dorman for insightful editing; to my agent, Andrea Cirillo; to North Cairn for reading the manuscript in progress and offering valuable suggestions; and to Margaret for the many cups of tea and conversations about the mysteries of the human heart.

And thanks, always, to Hillary for his unwavering support.

The Valley was full of bones . . .
and lo, they were very dry.

Book of Ezekiel 37:1–2

Prologue

All Hallows' Eve

Emily's nose was running again. Her cheeks were flushed. Zoe picked up a Kleenex. Overriding her daughter's twisting impatience, she blotted the chapped skin beneath the tiny nose. Then, deftly stroking back the fringe of brown bangs, she checked for a fever. As her fingers touched the child's brow, she felt a deep, familiar fluttering, as fragile as the heartbeat of a moth. Whenever she touched one of her children, she felt this thrill.

Unaware of her mother's emotion, Emily pulled away to focus on the macabre collection spread out on the table before her. She knelt on her stool and pushed aside her crayons and paper. Dimpled fingers, sticky with cider, bypassed the fanciful assortment of ghosts, bats, vampires, and witches, and without hesitation claimed the wizard.

Examining the sorcerer with the earnest deliberation of a five-year-old, she delivered her irrefutable opinion: "He's the best." She traced a damp finger over his silver beard, his round body, and the stars that were flung over his glorious purple robe. She wanted to keep him for herself.

Zoe studied her daughter, a miniature of herself. They shared a heart-shaped face with delicate, fine-boned jaw and cheeks and the hint of a dimple hiding in the chin. They had the same slight body, glossy dark hair, and eyes so brown they were nearly black. Yet Zoe could not remember ever being as trusting as Emily was, or as open and confident. Unaccountably, her throat tightened. She held back the tears, knowing too well that her child already shared Jake's distrust of sentiment. There was a lot of him in Emily, too. Zoe still felt awed that the two of them had created this singular being, barely five yet already an individual. Her glance swept across the room to the oversized wicker laundry basket set carefully on the deacon's bench. Snuggled inside, her son, Adam, slept.

Aware her mother's attention had drifted to the baby, Emily spoke up, using her newly mastered language, a dialect in which every sentence was a self-centered command. "I can't see. Turn on the light."

"Please," Zoe prompted absently. Maternal tenderness slipped away as swiftly as it had come. "That's the magic word. Remember?" She glanced around the kitchen. Bottles of paint, brushes, scissors, scraps of paper, and a pot of glue littered the table. Stray kernels of popcorn lay scattered on the floor beneath Emily's stool. The countertop was sticky where mulled cider had been spilled. She would have to clean up before Jake came home. To her, it was creative disarray; to him, it was a mess. She glanced at the clock, wondering how the afternoon had passed so quickly. She hated these days when darkness came too soon and lasted forever. She picked up the empty mugs and popcorn bowl and deposited them in the sink, switched on the overhead light, and returned to the table.

She reached for the rubber cement and began to stick the ghoulish sketches onto small candy bars, her compromise for Halloween treats. She would have liked to have made caramel popcorn balls and candied apples for the trick-or-treaters, as her mother had when she was a child. That was when Halloween was a magical time, an evening when each child crept into the scariest corners of his imagination to confront the worst he could conjure up. Now children were mindful of terrors far worse than crossing a graveyard at night. Even the smallest child knew not to accept anything that wasn't tightly sealed, that each cupcake or piece of fruit must be brought home so a parent could check for tampering. "Tampering"—a gentle catchword to cover other, less benign phrases: a razor blade inserted beneath the rosy skin of a fall apple, poison mixed in a pumpkin-shaped cookie, drugs injected into an orange-frosted brownie.

"Why bother?" Jake had asked that morning when she began her sketches. "Just get a jug of change and let each of the monsters take a fistful. They'll only tear your drawings off to get to the candy. Casting pearls before swine."

Zoe couldn't have explained to this rational man that this was her small effort to hold on to the enchantment Halloween had once held, and perhaps to touch her own childhood as well—whose innocence, she was forced to acknowledge, was more imagined than real.

Which was the reality: the good times—the portrait of the close and loving family that we presented to the world—or the tiny mental snapshots of isolation and pain, of anger never spoken of? How could the remembrances of warmth and laughter mesh with the other, darker memories?

"You made him Mr. Barber, Mommy. He's Mr. Barber." Emily leaned forward on the table, and the stool rocked precariously beneath her.

"Careful, honey." Would Emily remember this day, this moment? Or would she recall a time she had been chastised, magnifying the punishment? And years from now would Zoe be like *her* mother, and insist that they were the happiest of families?

Emily's grin grew wider. Now she was the image of Jake. "It's Mr. Barber."

"Who, Emily? *Who* is Mr. Barber?"

"The wizard. You made 'im look like *Mr. Barber.*"

Zoe leaned across the table to peer at the robed figure she had created. Emily was right: the face of the paper wizard looked just like their elderly neighbor.

With growing apprehension, Zoe looked over the other Halloween figures, but Emily was ahead of her, identifying in the pen-and-ink sketches of witches and ghosts friends and neighbors, shop owners, townspeople, and fishermen. Zoe wiped her suddenly sweaty fingers on her jeans. It had been unintentional, her subconscious at work.

God. What will Jake say? Will he see it, too? Maybe not. Her heart sank as she looked again. How could she have missed it? A diabolic bat was the girl at the drive-in window at Seaman's Savings Bank. The fiendish vampire was Mr. Gomez, the owner of Grace Point Hardware. Miss Turner, the nearsighted librarian, was transformed into a pumpkin peering at the world through bifocals. A fisherman's weathered face had been superimposed onto a one-armed scarecrow. A community of goblins: was this how she really felt about Grace Point?

"Who is this?" Emily—laughing at the wonderful game her mother had devised—held up a cutout of a witch. Black button eyes stared out of a shrewd, wizened face. Zoe studied the witch and frowned. This one she could not recognize. And yet—something stirred in the depths of her memory—in some way, the witch was familiar.

Emily was caught up in the game. "Do me," she demanded. "I want you to draw *me*. And then do you and Daddy." She ignored Adam.

Zoe sighed. She rotated her head, stretching tight muscles. The color in Emily's cheeks was hotter, her eyes brighter, and she considered vetoing the evening's trick-or-treat excursion. It would be a battle, and she knew that Jake, believing her overly cautious, would side with Emily. She surrendered silently. "All right, Sunshine, I'll make you a clown. Just like you're going to be when you go out with Daddy tonight."

"No." The one word was said with the force of a natural ruler. Zoe studied her daughter. *Where did the fierce sense of self come from—me or Jake? From both of us, in honesty.* "I don't want to be a clown."

"Look, Sunshine, *you* decided you wanted to be a clown. Just like the one in the circus book Daddy brought home. Remember? We talked about it all week. Your costume is ready." Zoe picked up the footed flannel sleeper from the stool by her side. She had just finished transforming it that morning. Bright multicolored patches decorated the arms and legs, and bells jingled on the toes of the feet. Pert ruffles encircled the collar and cuffs. Zoe bit back impatience. "You'll be the best, funniest clown in the world."

"Don't want to be a clown." Emily's lower lip trembled.

"Look, Emily, I'm sorry if you don't want to be a clown, but it's too late now. Next year, you can be something else, but this Halloween you're stuck with it."

"No." Brown eyes locked; neither pair was willing to relent. Zoe broke the contact first on the pretense of picking up the glue and scraps of paper. *I'm an unnatural mother. It's got to be unnatural to dislike your own child.*

The phone rang and Zoe grabbed it, knowing even before she heard his voice that it was Jake.

"Happy Halloween. How's my favorite witch?"

His voice warmed her, washing away the guilt. "I'm fine." Her eyes swept to the clock. Dinner. She hadn't even started it yet. "But I'd be even better if you'd stop at Stougie's on the way home and pick up a couple of mushroom with pepperoni." It was the second time this week she had asked him to bring home pizzas. Next week she'd cook every day. Real meals, with fresh vegetables. His favorites.

"I'd love to, Zoe, but that's why I'm calling. I still have several customers here, and it'll be a while until I close up. I was going to tell you not to keep dinner hot or anything. I'll grab something when I get home."

"No problem. I'll just scramble some eggs." There was a brief silence while both of them kept back their thoughts. He didn't say that Emily had had scrambled eggs for dinner three times that week. She didn't ask why he didn't close up at five like other stores, or mention that customers always knew they could walk in at closing and he'd keep the bookstore open as long as they wanted, even if they were only looking. And she bit her bottom lip to keep from asking if his help was still with him in the shop.

"Got to run, okay? Give Emily a kiss and tell her I'll be home before six. Okay?"

Zoe looked across the kitchen at their daughter and saw in Emily's pursed lips that she hadn't forgotten their disagreement. "Your daughter is lucky she doesn't get a swat on the behind," she told Jake, "never mind a kiss."

Across the table, Emily pretended not to hear her mother's remark, but her tiny mouth tightened.

"What's wrong?"

Zoe recognized the impatience in Jake's words. He often served as referee, and she knew he felt she didn't always handle conflicts with Emily well. Determined not to sound petty, she continued, "She just decided she doesn't want to be a clown."

"For heaven's sake, Zoe, she's only five. You can whip something up. Remember what Dr. Warner said? She's feeling left out. Pay special attention to her, spoil her a little. Just until she gets used to having the baby around."

"Easy for him to say. He's not the one who has to whip up another costume."

He heard the fatigue in her voice and softened. "Listen, love, hang in there. Just give me a few minutes to throw two biddies out the front door and I'll be right home, bearing gifts—or at least two pizzas."

His swift support strengthened her, and resentment faded. "Thanks, Jake, but I'll be all right. You go sell the two biddies the most expensive books in the store and I'll take care of things here."

"Hang in there." He paused. "I love you, Zoe." He whispered the words into the phone, embarrassed as always by affection expressed aloud.

"I love you too, Jacob Barlow. Truly I do." It was an old line, part of a private joke from the tender days of their courtship, and magically it swept away fatigue and worries.

"And I love you, *Liebchen,*" she sang to Emily as she hung up the phone. She crossed the room to give the child a hug. Jake was right. "We haven't got a lot of time, but if you don't want to be a clown, what did you have in mind?"

For an instant the child held back, wary of her mother's sudden acquiescence; then she grinned, her smile open and trusting. She squirmed out of Zoe's grasp and slid off the stool. Running on her tiptoes, she dashed to the toy box and pulled out a book. Zoe recognized it instantly: *The Nutcracker.* Jake had given it to Emily last Christmas, and it was still her favorite story.

"Her." The book opened to the page automatically. "I want to be her." The child's voice was soft with wonder. She crossed the room and placed the book on her mother's lap.

Zoe stared at the Sugar Plum Fairy and laughed. "You're not going to make this easy, are you?"

Emily caressed the pirouetting dancer longingly, imagining with her sticky fingers the stiff, scratchy tulle, buttery satin, cool sequins. "Please." The single word held volumes of longing.

Zoe recognized on her daughter's face the desire to be magically transformed, if only for one night. "Well, I just remembered something that might be perfect. Up in the attic there are some boxes of stuff I had when I was a little girl. I think there might be a dress I wore in a recital when I was nearly your age."

Emily tugged at her hand, urging her to hurry.

Zoe crossed to the wicker basket and stared down at her son. He had been sleeping for most of the afternoon, and if he woke and cried, she wouldn't hear him in the attic. But she worried about taking Adam from the warm kitchen to the unheated attic. Her face softened. *So serious, my little man.* She smoothed her fingertips across his forehead as if to erase the little frown he wore even in sleep. The faint sweet smell of him wafted up from the makeshift bassinet, along with the slightest sour odor; he had spit up on the sheet. Gently, Zoe adjusted the flannel so that the yellow stain no longer brushed his skin. His shallow breath whispered across her fingers, but he did not stir.

Emily, even as an infant, had thrashed in her sleep; but Adam barely moved when he slept. In the first days after his birth, Zoe would wake in the night and lie listening, fighting panic. Finally she would dash to his crib to reassure herself that he was all right. He was such a *good* baby. When she looked up again, she saw Emily watching her, patiently, quietly, with an expression impossible to read.

The awkward basket slowed her passage up the first flight of stairs. Before Zoe reached the landing, Emily was already halfway up the narrow treads that led to the third-floor attic. Zoe paused for a moment, struggling to change her hold on the basket, which was wedged between the banister and the wall.

"Damn." When a wave of cold air swept down from the door Emily had just opened, she debated leaving the bassinet at the landing.

"Hurry up, Mommy!" Emily disappeared into the darkness of the attic. Zoe pushed upward, struggling with the basket and praying that all the jostling wouldn't wake Adam.

She had not been up here in months. The musty air was frigid, and already she regretted her decision to bring the baby along. She set the basket down near the door and tucked the flannel blanket around him. Picking her way between boxes, she switched on the bare bulb that swung gently on its chain, casting dim shadows on angled walls and odd pieces of furniture, bringing cartons, trunks, and boxes in and out of its faint light as it swayed. Some of the stuff shoved beneath the eaves predated their move to the house—junk abandoned by previous tenants and summer renters, cartons that she and Jake had never gotten around to sorting out. Added to that was the detritus from their separate, single lives.

She looked around helplessly. She had no idea where the box holding the odds and ends of her childhood lay. There were spider webs on the rafters and mouse droppings on the floor. Already her hands felt soiled. "Just wait a minute, Emily," she started, but the child had disappeared. "Emily?"

Emily darted into the shadows, poking and prodding at cardboard cartons. She reappeared, holding out her pudgy hand. "Look."

"Emily." Zoe struggled to keep her voice calm. "Put that down. Put that down this instant."

There was no fear or disgust on the toddler's face, only curiosity, but she obediently dropped the mousetrap. It fell to the floor with a muffled thud. Shuddering, Zoe nudged it aside with the toe of her sneaker. Even through the fabric of her shoe, she felt the stiffness of the long-dead mouse shackled by the sprung wire bow.

"That's dirty, do you understand? It's filthy and could make you sick. I want you to wash your hands just as soon as we go downstairs. Okay? And keep your fingers out of your mouth. And don't touch anything else." Even as she spoke, Zoe strained to pick up the sound of muffled scamperings. She glanced at Adam's basket. The air seemed damper now, even colder. Apprehension turned to anger. *Why the hell couldn't Emily have been happy with the clown costume?*

Emily started to sniffle. Desperately, Zoe renewed her search for the carton. Finally settling on one that looked familiar, she pulled it closer to the circle of light and opened the flaps. A small box, gift-wrapped and still unopened, lay on the top. An envelope was taped to the pale pink paper. Intrigued, Zoe flicked it open and pulled out the enclosure.

Emily took advantage of her mother's preoccupation to return to her inspection of the attic. Quietly she slipped between a Hitchcock chair—one leg inexpertly mended with tape—and an ancient, scarred leather suitcase, to explore behind a garment bag that hung from a rod beneath the eaves.

The writing on the card was faint. "For Emily," Zoe read. Somehow, in the excitement of new motherhood and the move to Grace Point, it—alone among the scores of gifts she had received when Emily was born —had been misplaced for five whole years. She ripped off the wrapping paper and saw a tiny bonnet, obviously hand-knitted. She picked up the card again, turning it over to check for a signature, but there was none.

"Mommy." Emily's cry brought her back. "Mommy, come look. See what I found."

"Emily. Emily, where are you?" The moonless night pressed against the solitary window, soaking up the light of the swaying bulb. Zoe's eyes searched the shadows.

"I'm right here." Emily's impish face appeared from behind a stack of boxes. "Come here. Quick, Mommy."

Zoe stood, tensing as the prickling rush of blood flooded her legs, stiff from kneeling. How long had she been bent there? Surely no more than five minutes. Adam rustled in the basket.

"Come look. See what I found. It's a present. Can I open it? I found it. Can I?"

Gurgling noises floated from the basket as Adam stretched awake. Zoe walked stiffly toward the baby, bending so she would not bump her head on the roof beams. She heard the crackle of paper behind her. What has Emily gotten into? "Don't open anything, Emily," she said sharply. "How many times have I told you not to touch things that don't belong to you."

Zoe picked up the baby. His hands had worked free from the wrapped blanket and felt chilly to her touch. She snuggled him to her breast, warming him with her body. The dampness of his diapers spread through the blanket to her sweater.

"Emily. Emily, come on out. We've got to go downstairs. Your daddy will be home soon. Come on, hon." There just wasn't time to find a costume now, and she steeled herself to deal with a tantrum. The silence unnerved her. She reached for the length of the light cord. Pulling the bulb toward the spot she had last seen Emily, she swung the cord over a hook. Still holding Adam, now fully awake and hungrily gnawing at his fist, she ducked behind the boxes.

Emily was crouched beside a large open trunk; the appliquéd pink heart on the bib of her overalls was smudged with dirt and her nose was running again. She was bending over two old-fashioned hatboxes—one round and one octagonal—that she had taken from the trunk. The lavender octagonal box was propped against her knees.

Zoe winced at the heavy must of age and decay and snuggled Adam tighter, shielding him against it. The trunk had a domed top and a floral fabric lining that was shredded in several spots. She was amazed that Emily had been able to open it. Inside, there was a mildewed gray leather suitcase bound by buckled canvas straps, and a third hatbox. Each of the two boxes Emily knelt by contained a package wrapped in newspaper. Zoe could see that the paper was very old. Later she would recall that her first thought had been that the carefully wrapped packages were dishes of some kind, platters scrupulously packed to protect them against breakage.

Before she could stop her, Emily tore the brittle paper away from the parcel in the octagonal box. For one long, paralyzing instant, while Zoe dumbly stared at the contents, every sound, smell, sight was magnified.

She heard the little mouselike noise of Adam as he sucked on his fist, smelled the stale attic air and the ammoniac odor of wet diapers, felt the weight of her son in her arms, saw—this was the worst—Emily's curled, fat fingers reaching toward the thing.

"Don't touch." She struggled to get the choking, whispered words out.

"What is it, Mommy? Is it a puppy? Did someone put a *puppy* up here?"

Zoe's arms tightened around her infant son.

" 'Cause that's mean." Emily's face turned toward hers, babyish, scared. "Isn't it mean, Mommy? To put puppy bones up here?"

Zoe stared at the curled skeleton, knowing it wasn't a puppy, and *knowing*—measuring by her own yardstick, the baby cradled in her arms—that the object at Emily's knees had been only days old when it had been tightly swathed in paper and stored in the attic trunk. *Dear God.* Her eyes darted to the round hatbox, the other newspaper-wrapped package. Another one. She stared at the third hatbox and the mildewed suitcase in the trunk. *How many more are there? Three? Four?* She fought for control. *Dear God in heaven, what happened in this house?*

PART ONE

Pain wanders through
My bones like a lost fire.
What burns me now?
Desire, desire, desire.

—*Theodore Roethke*

Chapter 1

Rosalina

The four coffins were heavy. The fishermen bent under their weight, sweating in the sweet April air as the procession—a long, dark serpent of sorrow—wound its way up the hill from St. Peter's to the Catholic cemetery. The priest walked alone at the head.

His name was Father John Mallory. He was sixty and had a frail build and the pale complexion of a scholar or a prisoner. As he drew closer to the graveyard, he struggled with a mounting sense of inadequacy. He knew that the families of the dead had asked to have their former priest back for this day. "Father Mallory is your pastor now," the bishop at Fall River had told the four grieving widows. "He will conduct the mass."

Dust from the sand-packed road covered his shoes and filmed the hem of his normally immaculate cassock. He could not help recoiling. Instantly, he prayed for forgiveness. What, after all, was a little dust on one's shoes in the presence of death? Shamed, he listened to the labored breathing of the pallbearers behind him.

The twenty-four grim-faced men, six for each coffin, did not look up; each gripped his burden with callused, white-knuckled hands and kept his eyes focused on the heels of the man in front of him.

The Viera widows—bewildered, black-garbed women grown old in a day—and the Viera sons and daughters—seventeen frightened, hot-eyed children robbed overnight of childhood—followed. They clung together, isolated from the other mourners. Yet it was not propriety alone that segregated the four women and their children from the rest of the procession, but the chasm created by their intimate, hideous kinship with death.

Relatives trailed behind the widows. Then came the townspeople, a sad procession many yards long. Despite its size there was an eerie silence about the cortege. The stillness was broken only by the scuffing of feet on the narrow road, the rasping breath of the pallbearers, and, occasionally, a woman's muffled sigh. As they walked, the mourners listened for the sound of the surf breaking on the shore, but they caught only the rustling of the April wind as it blew through the pine and scrub oak flanking the road. No one wept. There had been plenty of that in the past few days. Now all that was left in the wake of shock and grief was for the town to bury her dead.

Rosalina Santos walked with the relatives near the front. She kept her eyes focused on the third coffin and the short, powerful man who marched at one side: her husband, Joaquin, in the suit he'd bought for their wedding. The jacket stretched over the corded muscles of his back and shoulders. In spite of her sorrow, a smile touched her lips as she remembered how he'd complained that morning about the stiff shirt. He could be so stubborn, so like a little boy. His dark hair—the same rich color as hers—grew long at the nape of his neck, curling down over his starched white collar.

As she walked, she kept her gaze locked on her husband, both to gather strength from him and to avoid looking at the knot of women who followed behind the caskets. Particularly Isabella. Rosalina did not want to have to look at her friend now.

Suddenly, a commotion ahead diverted her attention. One of the younger Viera children stumbled and cried out for his mother. She watched as Isabella, Manny's wife—*Manny's widow*—scooped him up and brushed his forehead with a kiss, then hurried to catch up with the others. Guilt pierced Rosalina. She was terribly sorry for Isabella, for all the widows and their children; but in some deep, secret place, she felt removed from their grief.

Oh, of course she had cried. The first day, when Joaquin had come home hollow-eyed and grim, she'd wept until her head ached. She'd clung to him, crying into his thick chest while he comforted her and rubbed her neck and shoulders with his rough-palmed hands. But she still had Joaquin. *He* would not be caught by the treachery of the sea. He was too good a fisherman for that. She would not wear widow's weeds. He—*they*—were invincible, protected by a force she could neither name nor understand, but one that she accepted without question. She thought of it as the force of their love. She returned her gaze to his back and kept it locked there. In her head, she hummed the little tune she had made up when she was in ninth grade and first in love with him. *Joaquin and me, Joaquin and me. We'll be together for eternity*. She skipped a half-step so that her feet walked in time with his.

As the procession entered the gates of the cemetery, the path narrowed and the women edged closer. Rosalina's hand brushed against Leona's arm, but her mother-in-law stared ahead. On her other side, Antone's wife sighed heavily and whispered to her son, who was squirming impatiently in her arms. Rosalina reached for him.

"You don't mind?" Dolores asked as she handed him over. Rosalina shook her head.

The boy quieted immediately in her arms. He tucked his face in the curve of her neck and wrapped his sturdy little legs around her waist. His skin was sweaty from the long walk. "I wuv you, Auntie Wosa," he whispered into the collar of her coat.

"I love you too, Tony-Pony." That was true. She adored the boy. She made up games for him and baked tiny bread-dough men with raisin eyes for him, dough men just like her mother had made for her. "You'll be such a good mother," Leona told her meaningfully whenever she saw Rosa playing with her grandson.

Still keeping step with Joaquin, Rosalina hugged the toddler closer.

Even in April, the graveyard had not lost the unkempt, barren look of winter. Frost-killed geraniums, long dead, lay on their sides, their clay pots cracked and broken. Faded, tattered flags fluttered on a few mounds, and ribbons—scarlet at Christmas, now washed out to a watery pink—held boughs of evergreens stripped of their needles. Lichen covered the sandstone grave markers like copper-colored stains, obliterating the engravings. Some of these monuments—stones carved with the names of Gaspa and Perry and Mendes, Costa, Roderick, and Alves—were massive and had cost more than the fishermen they honored had earned in months.

As the procession crossed the yard to the Viera plot, the mourners walked in the stark shadows cast by the towering stones. An oversized statue of Jesus as a shepherd. Mary bowing at the foot of the cross. Crucifixes and kneeling angels. They passed the marker of John Oliver, who had been buried just two weeks before. The plot was bare except for the carnations and roses that lay brown and limp beneath the headstone.

JOHN OLIVER
BORN OCTOBER 21, 1855
IN OLHAO, ALGARVE, PORTUGAL.
DIED APRIL 12, 1940
IN GRACE POINT, MASSACHUSETTS.

Old John had lived a full life, unlike the men they came to bury now.

Leona Santos muttered softly as the old priest began to speak. Everyone, not just Leona, wished Father Jim could be reading the service today. He wasn't a stranger, like this priest. For many years, Father Jim had eaten with them, christened their children and taught them their catechism, married their youth, and, when the time came, buried their dead.

By the four fresh graves, Father Mallory was reciting the names of the Viera brothers. John, Joseph, Manuel, and James. It sounded like an incantation. The little priest's voice rose, merging with the sound of the wind in the pines. The names were strange, foreign: Eel Pot, Sonny Joe, Manny, and Squash—those were the men Rosalina had known.

And Fat Tony. Her gaze dropped to the coffins, and she wondered if she was the only one who thought of the fifth brother now.

Fat Tony had not been found.

After the storm, the rest of the fleet had gone out to the weir grounds and trawled the churning waters. They'd found waterlogged planks that were the remains of the trap boat *Cathy Belle,* and in the ruins of the fo'c'sle they'd found the bodies of Eel Pot, Sonny Joe, Manny, and Squash: Fat Tony—Anthony—slept in another, watery grave. Hollow-eyed and grieving, his widow still lay in bed.

The voice of Father Mallory rose. He held an open Bible, and the wind riffled the tissuelike pages back against his pale, soft fingers.

While the priest read, Rosalina looked at Joaquin, willing him to look at her. He continued to stare at the open graves, his lips moving in soundless prayer. Little Tony was asleep in her arms now. To her right, Jackie wept softly. The boy was young—seventeen—and not yet a fisherman, and so had not been chosen to be a pallbearer like his brothers and father. Leona stepped in front of him, shielding him from her husband's sight so that Victor would not see their youngest son crying.

At last the priest finished reading. Rosalina raised her eyes and watched as he stepped toward the families of the dead men. The silence in the graveyard grew as he looked into each face, turning first to the widows, then to the children. Something in his manner caused even the smallest Viera youngsters to grow still.

"Do not be discouraged," he finally said. "Our Lord must have loved fishermen dearly . . ." He paused and allowed his gaze to drift from that small knot to the rest of the gathering, looking into masculine faces weathered by the wind, sun, and sea and womanly ones aged by grief and fear. "He must have loved them dearly because He chose His first apostles from among them."

Three of the widows began to weep.

The priest raised his hand in benediction. *"Requiescant in pace."*

The Viera widows sat in folding chairs at the front of the Portuguese Fishermen's Hall. With solemn dignity they received the women's tight hugs and the men's clumsy embraces. Many of these men—cousins and uncles and friends of their husbands—shoved thick envelopes into their hands. With movements as smooth as a magician's, the widows took the envelopes and made them disappear somewhere beneath the folds of their long black shawls.

The Viera children, freed from the constraints of the cemetery and their mothers' arms, crowded the food tables. They reached for the sweet-potato pastries, rolled cakes, fried dough, and sticky confections, wiggling impatiently whenever an adult bent over to wash them with a sad glance or touch their heads. Except for the oldest, shock had already left the children's faces.

At the urging of their mothers, each of them took a turn going to sit with old VoVo, who sat in a corner, swathed in rusty black, like a *bruchas,* a witch. Her lips were pursed, moving, as if she were chewing words, but no sound came out. Hidden beneath the folds of her heavy dress, her hands moved like moles. A Paternoster, ten Aves, a Gloria Patri. A Paternoster, ten Aves, a Gloria Patri. The beads slipped silently between her fingers. She frightened the youngest children.

"Hello, VoVo," they echoed. She stared at them with bright and hollow eyes, and they squirmed with eagerness to escape.

The mourners paid her their respects, as they had the widows, but they did not try to console her. There were no words one could say to the old widow. Not content with taking her only son years before, the sea now had claimed her grandsons as well.

As Rosalina waited in the line that filed by the seated widows, she tightened her grasp on Joaquin's fingers. The line inched forward, and at her turn she bent and brushed each of the women on the cheek with her lips. She did not let go of her husband's hand.

As they approached Isabella, she stumbled and instantly felt the touch of Joaquin's palm on her back, guiding her forward. Silently, she kissed her grieving friend and then stepped back. She wanted to say something but could not think of any words. At last their eyes met. The two women, barely twenty, stared at each other. Rosalina looked away first, terribly afraid that Isabella was able to read her thoughts: *Thank God I still have my Joaquin.* When she dared look again, all she saw on the young widow's face was pain.

Joaquin stooped over and hugged Isabella.

"He was a good man, my Manny. Never a better man." Her fingers locked onto his forearm.

Joaquin slipped his left hand from Rosalina's grasp and took the widow's cold hand in his. "He was the best," he said. He knelt so that his eyes were level with hers. "If there is anything we can do, anything you want, you let us know. Anything, you understand?"

"A wonderful father. A wonderful husband." Isabella wept openly. "You ask anyone about Manny Viera, they'll tell you what a wonderful man he was. You know that, Joaquin. You know what a wonderful man my Manny was." Drawn by her sobs, the other women surrounded Isabella, stroking her hair.

"What am I going to do? Oh, dear God, what am I going to do, what am I going to do without my Manny?" She was wailing now. Words flowed from her mouth like blood. She rocked back and forth, hugging her arms to her heavy breasts. Down the line of widows, the contagion of grief spread. One by one, like a row of crockery plates sliding off a shelf and shattering on the floor, the other widows began to weep. Even Sonny Joe's wife, who had not wept at the grave, had not wept since they brought his body home, began to sob, her fierce composure cracked.

Rosalina backed away. Noise rang in her ears with a hollow echo: children chattering, women sobbing. She was dizzy with the heaviness of death and with the paralyzing fear that the widows' grief, their bad luck were somehow infectious. "Joaquin," she whispered.

"Rosa, are you all right?" Concern darkened his face. "Do you want to sit down?"

She looked around the hall. Across the room from the widows and the other women, the men had gathered to talk and drink, Joaquin's father and brother among them. They passed a bottle. Jackie, Victor's youngest, sat alone at one side of the room.

Seeing Victor with Antone or Joaquin, even a stranger would know he was their father. Yet Victor Santos was handsomer than either of his older sons. He was a swarthy man with shrewd, fast-moving eyes and hair that was still as black as it had been at twenty except for a pair of perfect wings of white at each temple. He bore two imperfections—a scar that lay like raised string on his jaw and a gold tooth that glistened when he smiled—but they only added to his dark good looks. Once, years ago, he'd posed for the artist Hawthorne, who had seen in Victor Santos the bloodline of a pirate or a prince. That he was the first in his family to have been painted by an artist was a source of pride to him.

Rosa looked at the other men in the circle. Her eyes locked with one and she flushed. Konk Baptista was staring at her, his look sharp and knowing. Once, before she married Joaquin, she had overheard Konk telling another fisherman that she looked just like her mother. "Cut out of the same bolt, those two are," he'd said, and both men had laughed. *I am not like my mother, I'm not,* she had wanted to scream. But the men's words and laughter had haunted and frightened her, as if they knew something about her she herself didn't know.

"I want to go," she said to Joaquin. She wondered if he knew the other men talked about her. "Please. I want to go home."

He looked around to see if the widows had heard, but the sound of their wailing washed over everything else. "You just sit for a while. You'll feel better."

"No. Please, Joaquin. I need to go home."

"We can't. How would it look? They were my cousins, Rosa."

"Please, Joaquin." She looked up at him through lashes wet with tears.

"Let me get Dolores. Or Mama." He pleaded with her, his voice low, still afraid they would be heard. "They'll help you."

"No. I don't want them. I want to go home. I think I'm going to be sick." She would die if she couldn't get away from this place of death and knowing glances.

Finally he said, "I'll ask Papa if it's all right."

"Why do you have to ask him? Just take me home. Please, Joaquin." Her dark eyes blazed in her face.

Her husband hesitated, his eyes flicking back and forth between Rosa and Victor. "Just wait a minute, okay? Let me ask Papa."

Beneath lowered lashes, Rosalina watched as he approached his father. Joaquin never talked to her about how he felt; he was careful with his words. But one night shortly after their wedding, he had told her he knew he wasn't his parents' favorite son.

"Don't say that," she'd protested.

"It's true," he'd answered. "Antone is my father's favorite. And Jackie is my mother's."

She had not disputed him. She had seen Leona's eyes soften whenever she spoke of her youngest son; and Antone was, after all, the firstborn.

"It's true," he'd continued, "but it doesn't matter. Do you know why it doesn't matter anymore? Because I have you, my Rosa. Now I have you." But she had known that it did matter.

When Joaquin approached, Victor Santos stepped aside, making an opening in the circle of men so his middle son could join them. Antone stood at his other side. Victor stretched out his arms. He grasped his sons' necks with his huge hands and squeezed, drawing them closer. Across the room, old VoVo fastened her eyes on his back. As if he had been caught doing something shameful, he released his grip.

Joaquin felt the warmth on the nape of his neck. He accepted the bottle from Antone. He knew Rosa needed him, but he wished he could stay here for hours, talking and drinking and washing the bitterness of death from his mouth. The wine flowed down his throat to his stomach, heating him; but it was not as warm as the patch of skin where his father's hand had been.

The conversation picked up again. "Them boys was good fishermen," Joe Ducks said. "Good fishermen, but crazy." He took the bottle from Konk Baptista. "Crazy to be out in a storm like she was." He and Baptista had brought up the bodies of the Viera brothers in their nets.

"Shit, Joe Ducks, who you calling crazy?" Victor Santos's voice was hard. "You've been caught out in weather worse than that. All of us have. So don't you be going around saying things like that. How'd you feel if the women heard you talking fool talk like that?"

"Don't mean nothing," Ducks said, and passed the bottle to Victor. "They just shouldn't've been out in that storm."

"Joe's right," Frank Gaspa added. "It was their own fault. And the *Cathy Belle* needed repair. Everyone knows that."

The fishermen murmured agreement, shifting awkwardly, unable to look at one another. What boat in the harbor didn't need repairs? But it was better to lay the blame somewhere—the boat, the men, anywhere but the sea.

"Well, just don't let the widows hear you calling their dead husbands crazy." Victor Santos tilted the bottle back and drank deeply, then passed it to Joaquin.

Joaquin handed the bottle to Antone without drinking. "Rosa's not well," he said to Victor. "She wants to go home."

"Tell your mother. She'll take care of her. Woman's stuff."

"Here." Joe Ducks returned the bottle to Joaquin. "Let women handle your Rosa."

"I think she's really sick. She wants me to take her home."

Antone jabbed his brother's shoulder. "Little Rosa wearing the pants now? Well, I'll tell you one thing—you'll never see my Dolores telling me what to do. She knows better than that."

"Hey, Joaquin, how long you been married? Two years?" Johnny Limbs took the bottle. "You jump for little Rosalina now and soon she'll have you hopping all day and night."

Joe Ducks laughed. "It's all night he'll be hopping, that's what I say." He reclaimed the bottle.

"She says she's sick, but I bet you're the one who'll end up in bed." Konk grinned and poked his finger in

Joaquin's ribs. It was his turn with the wine, and he drank deeply.

"Better get a bun in her oven before long, or she'll have you too worn out to fish," Joe added.

Konk held the bottle out to him, but Joaquin did not take it. He could feel the burden of Rosa's gaze, could feel the heaviness of her need to leave, could feel it cooling the spot on his neck. "I'll be back," he said. "I'll just bring her home and come back as soon as she's settled." He could not meet his father's eyes.

"Jesucristo," Victor muttered.

Rosalina inhaled deeply, sucking sweet air into her lungs. She tucked her arm through Joaquin's and pressed against his side. "I love you, my Joaquin," she whispered. *Joaquin and me, Joaquin and me. We'll be together for eternity.*

The weight of the afternoon—the funeral, the freshly dug graves, the line of widows sitting on their wooden folding chairs—diminished with each step she took away from the hall. Already she was feeling better. She began to chatter. The more she talked, the more silent Joaquin became. When he didn't seem to hear her last question, she repeated it, tugging on his arm.

"I just don't understand, do you? How could she say he was so good to her? Everyone knew they fought like cats."

"What are you talking about?"

"Isabella. The way she was going on like Manny was a god or something. Everyone knew they fought."

"Don't say that, Rosalina."

"It's true. She talks like he's a saint now."

"Rosa, don't."

"But she told Dolores that he beat her. Dolores told me. Has she already forgotten that?"

"Manny was a good man."

"Just 'cause a man dies doesn't change how he was.

You can't pretend now that he wasn't mean, 'cause he was. Sneaky and mean as a water rat." Her face was set in a stubborn look, masking a phantom fear that took hold in her throat.

"He was my cousin." Joaquin stared straight ahead.

"Want to know something else? It's a secret. Dolores told me this too. Isabella told her." Her voice broke slightly. "She's going to have a baby. She's going to have a baby and Manny didn't even know it." She wanted to say more, tell him how unfair it was; but his brooding silence enveloped him, shutting her out.

The fear grew larger now, gathering form. "Are you mad at me, Joaquin? Joaquin? Please, don't be angry. I didn't mean anything by what I said about Manny." She waited for him to speak. "Please, Joaquin. I love you. Don't be mad." She stopped and tugged on his arm so that he would have to stop too. Her eyes brightened with tears, and she pressed the length of her body against his. "I love you. And I need you." It was the truth. Suddenly she was overcome with desire for him. She felt her need break through the wall he had erected and awaken hunger in him as well.

He kissed her, harshly, then reached for her hand and tugged her after him. They ran, her breath burning her throat. "Come on," he breathed once. "This way. It's shorter." He stepped off the sidewalk and pulled her after him, crossing one narrow street and then another. They ran past shops—closed because of the funeral—past the town hall and still more stores, past the shadows cast by Bayes' Sail Loft. Music and laughter flowed from the huge building. An artist leaned from an open window and called her name, but neither she nor Joaquin heard. They raced down an alley to the edge of the water. He stopped long enough to let her slip off her shoes so she could run faster on the sand. They passed dozens of houses. Some of them were empty. In others, the lights glowed brightly and startled faces looked out and watched as the couple raced past their windows.

Their cottage was dark. Before the door had even closed behind them, he began undressing her. Her chest rose and fell against his fingers as she fought to regain her breath. Her ribs burned from running. She wanted him then more than she could ever remember. His hands were rough, quick. His mouth was bruising, and she met it with a force of her own.

They could not wait but sank down on the floor. She wanted to feel him inside her—feel the life of him, feel life itself. It was as if that were the only way to keep them safe. The need to wash away death was urgent.

The idea came from nowhere. *This would be the time.*

She felt the rightness of it. She opened her lids and saw that Joaquin was wide-eyed too, staring into her eyes. She did not have to ask if he understood. She knew he did. Two years of waiting, twenty-four months of hope and anticipation followed by bitter disappointment, no longer mattered. This time they would make a baby. The knowledge added a new dimension to her lust. Her nails bit into the hardness of his shoulders and back, the smoothness of his buttocks. As she urged him to hurry, her voice sounded like a stranger's.

Chapter 2

This is the history and the truth of Grace Point.

It is located at the tip of a peninsula. This shaft of land, a vestige of the final stage of the Pleistocene epoch, is fashioned into the shape of an upraised arm. The limb attaches to the mainland at the shoulder, grows thick through the bicep, bends at the elbow, then runs straight at the forearm until it ends at the clenched hand: a militant arm thrust out into the Atlantic, challenging the sea. The fist of this peninsula—so boldly and foolishly defiant of Poseidon, of Nereus and Neptune, of every glorious and mythic god ever granted dominion over the sea—the fist of this arm is Grace Point.

There are no stones in the soil of Grace Point. The glacial bedrock that forms the rest of the peninsula ends at her borders; beneath her streets there lies no granite or gneiss. This place was forged not by ice but by the wind and sea. Beneath one's feet, the dunes shift.

If one arrives by boat, the town seems to rise up out of the deep, a leviathan exhaling a damp and ancient breath that hints of many things: sulfuric gases compounded in salt marshes, decaying flesh of shellfish dying on the shore, salt spray drying on wharfs. Town and sea feed off one another here. Long gray fish piers run out into the bay; and rotted stumps, far out from shore, are vestiges of aged wharfs. Low tide reveals worm-eaten ribs of wrecked boats caved in on the briny, furrowed sand.

Two truths prevail in this town.

Grace Point is blessed. Her beauty is enchanting, a striking juxtaposition of land and sea backlit by warm southern light. More spontaneous prayers are inspired by her dunes, her shores, her bogs than are whispered in the pews of her clapboard churches. Even her storms—wrathful, raving furies that terrorize and kill—even these produce canvases of splendid, seething glory. Fishermen—dark, princely men named Souza and Silva, Ferreira and Dias—crossed the ocean from their homelands in the Azores to fish her waters thick with cod and haddock, hake and menhaden. Artists were seduced by her haunting, barren beauty, and by her light, the same clear, meridional light as in Barcelona, Cannes, and Rome. Both fishermen and artists are nourished by this beauty, and aroused by the danger it masks.

The second truth is this: Grace Point is cursed, like a magnet that draws dark filings of rage. Go back—ten years, twenty, eighty, two hundred—and read the register, a deadly accounting of betrayals and murders, crimes of mind and crimes of passion, acts of revenge and savage emotions, whispers of mutilated bodies decomposing beneath the rotting roots of beach forests and moldering in bogs.

Like an onion, the town is secretive, stratified; her true identity is masked beneath thin concentric layers. Peel away the membranes and at the heart lies fear. Countless muted terrors—great and small, real and imagined—seize her inhabitants in their grasp, mirroring each man's weakness, his secret dread: failure, betrayal, or poverty; loss, heartbreak, and, always, death. Perhaps this is true of all places, yet it is especially so of Grace Point.

Twin terrors overshadow all others.

Fire is the first. Even in their sleep, the inhabitants of Grace Point listen for the scream of the icehouse whistles, the shriek that will waken them to a nightmare of flames.

With the single exception of the four concrete ice-houses and a fish-processing plant, the town is constructed entirely of wood. Her gray, cedar-shingled houses huddle shoulder to shoulder, their back doors opening to the narrow streets, the fronts facing the sea. A century ago, fourteen homes in the west end burned to the ground before the blaze could be contained; and at the edge of a wharf, an old sail loft went up in smoke even while the seawater lapped at the supporting pilings. Thirty-seven people died in this fire, six of them infants.

The other fear—so deeply ingrained it is never spoken of—is the fury of the sea. Time is reckoned here by the dates of great storms. The dead of Grace Point are buried not only in the ancient, iron-fenced ground atop Pilgrim's Hill and in the cemetery down the road from St. Peter's Catholic Church, but also in deep-water graves.

Visions of these frail bones lie buried in the heart of Grace Point, visiting her sleep and shaping her days. The reality is this: The sea gives a living to the people of this town and in return she takes a few away. It has always been this way.

There is one more truth about this town. All seaside towns are haunted. Grace Point is no exception.

The pier is alive with the sibilant sounds of midnight. Rats scurry over weathered planks. Water laps at pilings.

Old Scaggs lifts his head, ignores the rats. He knows it is something else that has roused him. He trembles and clambers awkwardly to his feet. As a pup, he lost his left hind leg the night Jesus Lopes, the cook at the Sunken Dory, nearly killed him in a drunken, kicking rage. The black dog waits, filtering out the normal nighttime sounds of the harbor, straining to hear again the noise that woke him. The hair on his back and haunches is raised, but he does not bark.

On Front Street, the monkey, a capuchin, awakens in the storefront of Izzy's Secondhand and Souvenir Shop. His name is Baby; he has an old man's face and quick little hands. Dressed in a child's ballerina skirt, the pink tulle limp and soiled, he rolls from the rag pile that is his bed and presses close to the plate glass window. His wet, unblinking eyes stare into the darkness.

While the townspeople sleep, the dog and monkey in turn follow the wraithlike form as it moves toward the harbor. The silhouette bends and weaves. Is it one body or two? Is it a man shadowboxing? Perhaps a drunk? Or a couple locked in a tuneless tango? It doesn't matter. The animals will not speak.

At last Old Scaggs returns to his shelter by the harbormaster's shack, and when he sleeps again, he whines deep in his throat. After a while Baby leaves the window and slips back to the pile of rags. He crawls beneath them, reaching for one of his toys. He hugs the stuffed bear tightly, rocks back and forth, and does not sleep.

Chapter 3

Rosalina stood by the curtain that separated the storefront from the bakery kitchen and watched her father. Even when he washed the bowls and pans, he moved through the kitchen silently. His arms were white up to his elbows with flour dust. He did not know she was there.

As a child, Rosalina used to drag a stool over to the counter and sit for hours while he baked. There was magic in the way he worked—a magic her mother had not possessed. When Anna Roderick helped her husband with the special holiday breads and cakes, she had to read from a recipe card. And when she added ingredients, she had to use the set of tin utensils stored in the deep drawer by the sink. Carefully she'd spoon sugar or flour into the metal cups; meticulously she'd level off lard with a knife.

Not her father. With sure, flowing movements, he'd dip his arms into the oversized canister and scoop up flour by the handful. He'd take pinches of baking powder and soda and salt and sift them into the dough, always knowing the proper proportions for the *trutas, bolos, suspiros,* and *malassadas.* The father of Rosalina's early childhood made music when he baked. The father of the adult Rosalina still had the instinct in his hands and head, but he no longer whistled or hummed when he worked. Now, watching as he moved around his kitchen wearing his silence like a penance, Rosalina mourned the father of her childhood. Now he bent over his work space, mixing, stirring, pushing and pulling the dough on the slab of marble, working currants and spices and nuts into the satin-smooth dough. Occasionally, while he was kneading, the dough emitted a soft sound, as if all the words the baker held locked in mind and muscles had worked through his fingers, passing into the flour and yeast to escape finally in a whisper of a sigh.

Rosalina was six when her mother left them. That's when the music went out of her father. The bellowing anger, too. He had been a passionate man. A giant man, so large that the strings of his apron barely tied around his waist. Now he was so thin, he wrapped the apron strings twice around before tying them in a bow over his flat stomach. When Anna Roderick left, it was as though she had taken with her her husband's sound and substance.

In her wake, Anna had left her only daughter a legacy of shame. Rosalina felt she was in some way responsible for her mother's desertion. She used her will to try to bring her mother back. She made a series of bargains with God. When she was seven, she vowed to stay awake all night with the understanding that if she did, her mother would be in the kitchen cooking oatmeal in the morning. In the dark, long after she'd heard the creaking of her father's feet on the stairs, the regretful sounds of his mattress giving way beneath his weight, she would sit up, fighting the heaviness of her eyes, pinching herself with cruel, relentless fingers. When the pinches no longer worked, she'd pile books and wire coat hangers in her bed, so that they would wake her if she nodded off. As a last resort, when even the corners of books felt comfortable, she would climb out of bed and sit on the cold floor. She always fell asleep, and her mother was never there in the morning.

Sometimes, when her father was in the bakery and she was alone in the house, she would tiptoe into her parents' room and open the door to the sloping closet beneath the eaves. Carefully she'd remove a dress from its hanger, crouch on the floor, and bury her face in it, breathing in the smell of her mother. She was always careful to put everything back just as she had found it. But one day she discovered all her mother's clothes gone. Shocked, as if her mother had been taken from her twice, she never dared ask her father what had happened to the clothes.

The year she was nine she promised God she would go without a single one of her father's cookies if He would simply bring her mother home. She went eight months—all through the Thanksgiving and Christmas holidays and the celebrations of the New Year—without taking a bite of even one spicy, raisin-studded cookie. It was like giving up something for Lent, except she did not tell Father Jim about these covenants, afraid they might be a sin. Her mother did not return. Soon after, Rosalina learned why Anna Roderick had deserted her husband and young daughter. From that day, she felt her mother's shame as if it were her own. She stopped praying for her return.

But today, for the first time in years, she missed her mother just as she had as a child. She squeezed her eyes shut, willing her mother to appear. As if from a bank of fog, a picture emerged. First she caught the shape of her mother's body, her hip and thigh outlined against the fabric of her skirt. Strong. Vibrant. Then the smell, talcum powder and nutmeg. Sweet. Spicy. Then her low voice, made for laughing and singing. She remembered her mother's silly songs, with words that rhymed but had no meaning, songs that delighted a young child. Suddenly she pictured her mother dancing, as clearly as if she were watching a movie. She must have been around four or five when the music woke her. Rubbing her eyes, she'd stumbled to the living room. Her mother was dancing, her father watching from a chair. Even now Rosalina could remember the gleam of pride in his eyes. And her eyes had been shining. She'd sung along with the music. *Da-da, da-da, da-da di-da da-da.* Her arms swung wildly, her legs flashed while her feet danced the complicated steps with abandon.

The memory faded. Rosalina stepped away from the curtain. The impulse to go into the kitchen and talk to her father evaporated. She could not share the fragile, glorious hope that grew inside her with this silent, dour man. It would be bad luck.

Returning to the front of the shop, she wiped the counter and looked up at the clock hanging on the wall over the display cabinet. Three-forty-five. It had been at least an hour since the last time she had gone to the pantry to check. No need to go, she thought. Nothing had changed in the past hour. Retreating to the childhood game, she began making deals with herself. In fifteen minutes, it would be time to leave. If she waited until she got home, she would be all right. If not, the news would be bad.

Only ten more minutes to wait until she could go home. She wiped the sides of the cabinets, placing fresh doilies on empty plates, readying them for the piles of sweet and fragrant pastries that her father was baking. Her breasts felt tender. Heavy. She was sure she felt wet between her legs.

Finally she could wait no longer. She slipped into the narrow closet that served as a pantry, let the cotton sheet that separated the alcove from the storefront fall behind her. She felt lethargic, as if her body floated under water. In the front room of the bakery, the bell that hung over the door jangled. She hesitated but could not go back now. Ducking behind the huge sacks of flour and sugar, she hitched her dress up, positive she felt blood.

"Rosalina?"

Moving quickly, she slipped her panties down to her knees, afraid to look.

"Rosalina? You here?"

She recognized the voice. Dolores. Quickly she checked, then closed her eyes and sank against the wall in relief. No blood. No spotting.

It had been three weeks since the night of the funeral. She was two weeks late. She had never been this late before. She pulled up her underwear and straightened her skirt and apron. Then she went to face Dolores.

"So. What do you think, Rosa? Do you like it?" Squinting at her reflection in the window of Collingwood's Drug Store, Dolores cupped her palm against her scalp, sculpting the newly marceled waves with careful, preening touches.

"Sure." She counted the days on her fingers one more time, as if they were the stations of the cross. "It looks swell."

"Really?" Dolores turned slightly, trying to catch a glimpse of her profile in the window. "You really like it?"

"Really. Where's Little Tony?"

"I left him at his grandmama's. I thought I'd go crazy if I didn't get away. I mean, I love him and everything, but he drives me crazy. You know, from the side I think I look a tiny bit like Lombard. What do you think?"

"A little." Rosa felt like laughing. Everything was beautiful, even Dolores's funny new hairdo. She turned toward the docks and inhaled the breeze coming in from the harbor. She sucked the salt-heavy air into her nostrils, past the thickness in her throat, down into her lungs, into her abdomen. "Come on. Let's go."

She opened the beveled glass door and walked into the drugstore, stepping lightly. She had been walking softly all day, a superstitious dance.

The drugstore was nearly empty. Maria Perry was working behind the counter, and Rosalina felt Dolores nudge her in the ribs, but she made a great pretense of ignoring Maria. Still, she could see the girl flirting with two coastguardsmen. She hung over the counter as she placed their hot fudge sundaes before them.

Seeing the men, Dolores froze for a moment, like a deer catching the scent of wolves. She pretended not to notice the servicemen, but her voice became artificially high, and as she led the way to a booth near the back, her walk was exaggeratedly feminine. "If you could be anyone, who would you rather be," she asked Rosa, "Lombard, Jean Harlow, or Bette Davis?"

Aware the two men had swiveled on their stools to follow their progress, Rosalina did not answer. She wished Dolores would lower her voice.

"Come on," prompted Dolores. "Which one?"

"None of them." Really, she thought, she wouldn't think of trading places with anyone, not even a Hollywood actress. She was Joaquin's wife, and that was everything.

"None?" Dolores was incredulous. "How can you say that? I'd switch with Lombard in a minute. Do you really think I look like her?" Again she ran her fingers over her hair. "Lombard isn't her real name, you know. It's Peters. Jane Peters. I guess if little Miss Peters can become Carole Lombard, then Dolores Santos can do it, too. Can't you just see me? At Hollywood parties?" She twirled on the wood floor, her arms encircling an imaginary dancing partner. Rosalina slid into the booth.

Dramatically, Dolores changed her stance and sighted along the barrel of an invisible shotgun. "Or skeet shooting. Lombard's a real good skeet shooter. I read that in *Life*. There was a picture of her and Gable." She dropped her arms and rubbed her shoulder absently, then flopped down on the bench, tossing back her freshly waved hair.

Maria approached their booth with her order pad. "Whatta you want?" She directed the question at Dolores, ignoring Rosalina.

"*Rosalina* and I will have two butterscotch sundaes. You do know Rosalina, don't you?"

"Nuts or whipped cream?" The counter girl kept her eyes on her pad, but her voice betrayed her anger.

"Both. And don't forget the cherries."

"Ugly as a dogfish," Dolores laughed, when the waitress left. "No wonder Joaquin wouldn't take her even when she threw herself at him."

"You're terrible," Rosa whispered. "She's not that bad-looking." She could afford to be nice to Maria now; she could even feel a bit sorry for her. At last, she dared to daydream, to wonder if the baby would be a boy or a girl.

"I bet he's great in bed," Dolores said.

"Who?"

"Gable. You can bet his ears aren't the only thing that stick way out."

Rosa's cheeks grew hot. She looked around to see if the two servicemen had heard, but they were bent over their sundaes.

Dolores fussed again with her curls. She gave Rosa's long, raven hair a quick glance. "Maybe you should get your hair done, too."

"You mean cut it?"

"Yes. And have it permed."

"Joaquin would kill me if I cut my hair."

"Screw Joaquin. It isn't his hair, is it?"

The breath caught in her throat. "Does Antone like yours?"

"Screw Antone, too." Dolores's mouth tightened. "He doesn't own me." She patted her fingertips over her curls. Her red polish was chipped. "There is only one man I'd let own me. Gable. If he asked me to, I'd even shave my hair off." She bent her head toward Rosa's. "Why, if he wanted me to, I'd even shave down there."

Rosa reddened furiously.

"I heard some men like that."

Rosa checked the servicemen. They were still eating their ice cream. "Shhhh. They'll hear you." She leaned in closer. "You're making that up."

"Honest. I swear." Dolores giggled. "And get this. Some women shave so they have a heart shape there."

"You're joking." Dolores was always telling her things like that, and it made her feel funny. Flushed. Dangerous.

They smiled like conspirators while Maria brought their sundaes. There were no cherries on the whipped cream, but Dolores didn't notice. "I'll tell you something else," she continued after the waitress left. "But you've got to promise not to tell anyone."

"I promise."

"Not even Joaquin?"

"Promise." They were whispering now, the ice cream forgotten.

"I did it once."

"What?"

"Shaved myself. There."

"You didn't." Rosalina giggled.

"Honest."

"God. What did Antone say?"

"He hated it." Dolores's lips tightened. "He said it was too scratchy. And that I looked like a plucked chicken."

"A plucked chicken?"

"Yeah. A chicken. You know. Cluck, cluck." They both began to laugh, and the two men at the counter looked over.

"But I told him it was better than looking like a man did, all purple and wrinkled. Better than looking like that thing—you know, that thing hanging off a turkey's neck."

"You told him that?"

"Gobble, gobble. You bet I did. What's it called, anyway? What about you? Would you shave off your hair for Joaquin?"

Rosalina felt uncomfortable again. Would she shave for him? The idea made her feel squeamish, hot. Anyway, didn't they shave you when you had a baby? Isabella Viera had told her so after she had her first child. For an instant, she was tempted to tell Dolores that she was pregnant, but she would tell Antone, Antone would tell Victor, Victor would tell Leona, and everyone would be angry she had told Dolores first. The father should be the first to know. Because she could not share her secret with Dolores, Rosa felt a wave of generosity. Impulsively she reached over and squeezed her arm affectionately. Dolores cried out sharply and twisted away.

"What's wrong?"

"Nothing."

"Did I hurt you? What's the matter with your arm?"

"It's nothing." Dolores shrugged off her concern. "I banged it against the closet door last night. Just stupid. Say, do you wanta go to the movies tonight? You and me and Joaquin and Tony?"

"I don't know," Rosa hedged. She had planned to tell Joaquin about the baby tonight, and she didn't want to share him with anyone. *Joaquin and me, Joaquin and me.* "I'll have to see what Joaquin wants to do."

"Joaquin wants what you want. You know he'll do whatever you say."

"That's not true," she replied.

"Sure it is. Tony says—"

"Well, hello, gorgeous." The two coastguardsmen stood by the booth.

Rosa froze and focused her attention on the melting sundae. The whipped cream had turned into a sickly yellow liquid. She swallowed a mouthful of butterscotch. It coated her tongue with sweetness, so sweet she felt sick. She was aware of Maria Perry watching them from behind the counter. Dolores looked boldly at the men.

The younger of the two—a blond with a gap-toothed smile—spoke. "Hi. You two alone?"

"Looks that way, doesn't it?" Dolores said.

Rosalina kicked her beneath the booth.

"So." The blond was grinning now. He hitched up the belt of his dungarees and bent toward Dolores. "Know what I said to my buddy here when you walked in? I said, 'Too bad my porch swing don't swing like that.' "

Dolores laughed. "Takes a real man not to fall off a swing."

Rosa tried to lash out again at Dolores; but her sister-in-law had moved her legs, and her foot only hit the wood booth. She fumbled with her napkin and wiped her mouth. "We've got to be going," she said.

"What's your hurry? We haven't even introduced ourselves yet."

"I'm married."

The blond laughed. "Well, isn't that a coincidence. So's my buddy here. A perfect match."

Taking that as a signal, the second man leaned in and rested his hand on the back of the booth. It was so close to her face that Rosalina could see traces of engine grease beneath his fingernails. He smiled at her. His teeth were bad, and she guessed that was why he let the blond do most of the talking.

"Get lost."

"Hey, come on—no need to be unfriendly. We just want to buy you girls a Coke. Nothing wrong with that, is there?" The smile was gone from the blond's face, and his friend removed his hand from the booth back.

"Just get lost."

Dolores opened her mouth to speak and Rosalina kicked, finding her shin this time—a quick, hard kick that made Dolores gasp. "You make me sick," Rosalina said. "You think you can come in this town and take over, like you own it or something. Well, we're not interested. So just get the hell out of here."

"It's your loss, sugar. No skin off our backs." They swaggered away, and Rosalina heard one of them say "Bitch." The other laughed.

"Rosa—"

"Just shut up. Don't say anything."

"Why are you so mad? They were just kidding. They didn't mean anything."

"I'm not mad. Dogs get mad, people get angry."

"All right then. Why are you so *angry*?"

"I hate them. All of them."

"Oh, they're all right."

"You shouldn't talk with them."

"I was only having a little fun."

"You're married, Dolores. Or did you forget?"

"Jesus, Rosa, I wasn't going to go to bed with them."

"You shouldn't talk with them."

"Rosa?" Dolores hesitated, studying her sister-in-law's face. "Is it . . . is it because of your mother? Is that why you hate them?"

Rosalina looked down. She laced her fingers together and pressed them over her abdomen.

"Is it?"

"She has nothing to do with it."

"Well, what's the problem, then? What's wrong with flirting a little?"

She wished Dolores would shut up. Talk of her mother scared her. It scared her the same way Joaquin did when he took her in the boat way out beyond the jetty, to where the water turned black. When she looked over the gunwale, it frightened her so she could scarcely breathe, but she couldn't stop looking. "Want to go swimming?" he'd joke. He'd pretend to throw her overboard. She'd shriek, but part of her wanted to go, to see what it was like. That scared her more than anything.

"Well? Tell me, then. What's wrong with a little harmless flirting?"

"Is that all you think about, Dolores?"

"Well, don't you? Tell me a secret. Have you ever kissed anyone else but Joaquin?"

"Of course not."

"Haven't you even looked at another man and thought about what it would be like to kiss him? Or sleep with him? Maybe not a man you know, but someone like, oh, I guess, someone like Gable. Or Flynn. Don't you even wonder what it would feel like?"

"Never." Dangerous waters. She was not like her mother. She was *not. Joaquin and me, Joaquinandme.* "Besides," she added. "Joaquin would kill me if I even looked at another man."

"Joaquin would never hurt you."

"Well, he wouldn't stand for me to look at another man. I know that." She glanced over toward the counter, but Maria Perry was running water into a sink of dirty dishes and couldn't hear them. "Remember Frank Cabral's wife? Well, before they were divorced, we saw her one night in the alley by the Lost Dolphin Cafe. She was kissing a man, one of the summer men —an artist, I think. We never told anyone, but Joaquin got so mad just seeing her. He told me he'd kill me if I ever fooled around. And you should have heard him, Dolores. He really meant it." She fell silent, remembering. "I would kill you," he had said. She had looked to see if he was fooling, but his face had been so dark and serious that she had shivered. "He loves me so much. I don't think he could stand the idea of another man touching me."

A faint scratching sound came from the booth behind her. "Dolores—" She whispered across the table. She could smell pipe tobacco. "Dolores, there's someone sitting in the booth behind me."

"So what?"

"But he must have been there the whole time. God, do you think he heard us?"

"So what if he did? What did we say that was so horrible?"

"You know." She blushed with the memory. "You know what you said about—about shaving down there."

Dolores shrieked with laughter. "Good enough for him. He shouldn't have been listening."

Horror and laughter welled up in Rosalina. "Oh God. Do you think he really heard what we said? Let's get out of here. At least he hasn't seen us. He doesn't know who we are."

She slid over in the booth, but before she could get up the door flung open, slamming back against the wall so hard the glass rattled. A young boy stood framed in the doorway.

"Watch it!" Maria yelled. "Watch your step, Dominick Alves, or you'll be paying for new glass for that door. It ain't cheap, neither."

The boy stood as if paralyzed, gasping for breath. His face was white and his eyes were wide with excitement.

"Down at the pier—" He danced from foot to foot. "Down at the pier—" He was whiter now, as if he were going to be sick.

Doc Collingwood came out from behind the pharmacy counter. Rosalina and Dolores were standing now. The man in the next booth also stood—so close he could have touched them with an outstretched arm—but they had forgotten him. They stared at Dominick as if hypnotized.

"Down at the pier," he repeated. "They've found a body down at the pier."

Although the police had cordoned off the end of the wharf, a crowd already pressed against the rope, straining to catch a glimpse of the body that lay in the pool of water on the dock.

"Who is it?"

"Do they know who it is yet?"

The questions swirled in the air, filling it with a buzz like angry bees. Dolores ducked and dodged, pulling Rosalina along with her as she pushed her way to the front of the crowd for a better view.

"A woman. I heard it was a woman." The voices seemed eager. Rosalina hesitated, but Dolores dragged her along until the rope pressed against their thighs.

"Shit," Dolores said. "We're too late." The body on the wharf was covered with a sheet. There was another, heightened buzz from the crowd as the men lifted the body onto a stretcher and began to head toward the ambulance. When they were almost in front of Rosalina, the corpse's arm flopped off the stretcher. The exposed arm, slender and pale, bobbed in step with the stretcher bearers. The hand was deathly white, the fingers slightly curved as if in slumber. The nails were polished a bright red. Rosa watched the seawater drip down the smooth inner arm, down the curled fingers, the crimson nails, off onto the wharf.

She pressed her palms to her stomach, wishing for Joaquin's arms around her. Then she felt the hot fluid rush between her legs. Shamed, she thought at first she had wet her pants. Then, she realized without looking that it was blood that dripped in hot red drops down her leg—just as the seawater dripped from the cold, white fingers of the dead woman.

She was cold—so cold she feared she would never be warm again. Joaquin lay beside her, his body fitting to the contour of hers, his chest to her back, his groin pressed spoon-fashion to her buttocks, his legs wrapped around hers. She felt the heat rise from him like waves, but she shivered. The small of her back ached, but she did not move, did not ask him to rub it.

All evening her throat had ached with the need to

cry, but she had not given in. Her head throbbed now from the suppressed tears. Her eyes burned with them. Later, after she was sure he was asleep, she would cry.

"Rosa? Rosa? Are you okay?" He adjusted his arm so that his hand cupped her breast. "Rosa, it's okay." His voice was gentle in the darkness. "I know you're disappointed, but it doesn't matter. Honest, it doesn't."

She concentrated on breathing. Deep, feigned breaths of sleep.

"I still love you. I don't care if we can't have children. It's all right with me."

The lie lay between them in the night.

Maybe it's not me. Maybe it's not my fault. Maybe it's you. The words screamed with a wild, white brilliance in her mind. Then, as quickly as they had been born, they died. To think such a thing was madness.

"I love you, too," she whispered without moving.

After a while, his arm relaxed and fell away from her, and his breathing deepened. But now that she was alone, the tears would not come.

Chapter 4

Clumps of barnacles and rockweed ringed the high-tide mark on the pilings. The air of ebb tide—a pungent, sulfuric smell of salt and decay—rose from the newly exposed shore. The sawhorses and ropes that just yesterday had cordoned off the area were gone. No evidence remained of the corpse that had dripped seawater onto the plank decking.

Over at the icehouse, hunkered down, backs leaning against concrete as they drank strong coffee, the crew took a cigarette break. Their chatter buzzed through the air. Overhead, gulls soared and scolded. An elderly man—a rod over one shoulder, a bucket of bait in hand—shuffled along at the edge of the pier, his pant legs rolled up to expose ropy white calves mapped with varicose veins. He whistled cheerfully. The sound unfurled from his pursed lips like a brazen, gaudy streamer of song.

Rosalina didn't know what she had expected, but she knew there should be some lingering traces of the tragedy. It was all just so . . . just so normal. Life went on. *Life went on.*

The dead woman had been a stranger. A transient, they said, who arrived before the tourist season in search of a summer job. There was talk of suicide, but already the town's interest had waned. A report would be filed, the case all but formally closed. The idea that one could disappear here—*could die*—and no one would care depressed Rosalina.

She watched as the elderly fisherman approached the wooden ladder attached to a piling. Old Scaggs was in his path, chewing on a ham bone long ago cleaned of meat and marrow. Juggling bucket and pole, the fisherman skirted the dog and climbed down into a skiff. He settled weather-bleached oars into oarlocks and rowed smoothly through the quiet harbor. Outside the icehouse, the workers drained the last of their coffee, ground cigarette butts out beneath their feet, then filed back to work. A cloak of serenity descended, a soft and golden peace. Even the water beyond the breakfront lay calm. It was as if the dead woman had been some sort of sacrificial offering to the gods of Grace Point, and now satisfied, these deities laid beneficent, guardian hands over the town.

Rosalina wondered if towns could have sacrificial victims, some dreadful penance paid so there would be no more untimely burials at St. Peter's cemetery, no more widow-making storms at sea. And if so, would she be willing to enter into such a covenant? Would she agree to any sacrifice if it kept her Joaquin safe? If it protected her from a widow's grief like Isabella's? Automatically she said an Ave Maria and made the sign of the cross. But the wicked truth crept in anyway, slipping in through her prayers. *I would do anything to keep Joaquin safe.* The idea was new, yet felt as familiar as the smell of the sea.

She hurried from the pier, eager to distance herself from these disquieting thoughts, eager to continue on to the sail loft. But the words echoed fiercely. *I would do anything to keep Joaquin safe.* They rolled in a militant meter that beat time with her feet. *I would do anything to keep Joaquin safe.* Then new notes joined the staccato litany. *And I would do anything to have our child.*

Her feet came to a standstill; the words flooded her mouth. She felt them liquefying on her tongue, pressing against her teeth. She *tasted* them. Finally, she gave her oath to the gods of Grace Point. *I would do anything to have our child.*

The cry of a gull broke her trance. This is crazy, she scolded herself. Crazy. She began walking again. Of course no omnipotent spirits swirled in the air. Holy Mother Mary, what would Father Jim say if he even knew what she was thinking? By the time she reached Bayes' Sail Loft, she was breathless.

Until the 1920s, the Sail Loft, a wood-framed building shingled with weathered cedar, had been a shop where immense canvas sails were cut and sewn. Then Ben Bayes had returned from Europe with visions of a space where artists and writers could work and live, and bought the building. Partitions now divided the huge interior into individual studios for painters and sculptors. Several smaller rooms on the first floor—dark rooms with none of the precious northern light—were reserved for writers. A narrow exterior staircase, as steep as a ladder, gave access to the second-floor studios. A catwalk rimmed two sides of the building. During breaks between classes and work, artists sat on this balcony, faces lifted to the sun, smoking or sleeping, drinking coffee or—in late afternoon—cheap wine or beer. Odd items of laundry—time-bleached slacks and shirts, cotton shorts and paint-spattered smocks—hung over the railing. Battered espadrilles and pairs of gaping canvas shoes, their laces long lost, littered the decking.

The air was cool in the building. The chill of winter still clung to the concrete floor of the first level, where it would linger until the sweltering days of July. Unmindful of the cold, Rosalina darted up the stairs to the second floor and slipped behind the curtain in the corner that served as the model's dressing room. Lengths of rich fabric and an assortment of costumes —white peasant blouses, colorful scarfs, things Ben Bayes had picked up over the years—hung from a rod.

Tams and berets, felt cloches and straw boaters spilled out of a basket on the floor. A wall shelf beneath a framed mirror was littered with hairpins and ribbons, combs and a brush. Tangled strands of long blond hair twisted through the bristles of the brush.

Rosalina picked up a bright shawl from the stool where she had dropped it after the last class and rubbed the textured cloth between her fingers. It felt foreign, exotic. She wrapped it around her shoulders. She swung her hair back, caught it in one thick strand, then twisted it and deftly pinned it high on her head. After a last quick check in the mirror, she entered the studio.

Just as she would recognize her father's bakery if she were blinded and led there, so would she know the Sail Loft by its smell, an acrid blend of turpentine, oils, and mildew that stayed in her nostrils for hours after she had left. Over it all hung the scent of kerosene from the heater.

As she crossed to the model's stool, she avoided the artists' eyes, still shy. They were as alien as the scarf draped over her shoulders. Some of the time they acted like children, quarreling over the positioning of their easels and vying for Ben Bayes's attention, but other times she overheard them, and their arguments over Picasso's *Guernica* and the German Blitzkrieg confused her. Those times she felt like an ignorant youngster at a gathering of very sophisticated adults, as if they expected more of her than she had to give. They made her feel like an outsider in her own town.

Ben Bayes was the most formidable of them all. Everything about him was oversized: his height; his full, gray beard and curling halo of hair; his rounded belly, which pushed against his flowing smock. He was bigger than her father. His hands were as gnarled and thick as a fisherman's, with square fingernails that were cut straight across. Paint clung to his cuticles. A bolt of scar tissue traversed his forearm—the result, she'd heard, of a drunken night in Paris. Rosalina was attracted to the spiral of energy he radiated and repulsed by the violence that seemed to hover around him. She feared his power.

Whenever he came to the bakery, she used to duck into the back room, begging her father to wait on him. As if Ben knew this, he would bellow out for her. "Come on, little Rosalina, little Rosa Rugosa. Don't make your father leave his work. I don't bite, you know." He would so charm her silent father that the baker would come out of his kitchen retreat and give the artist a bag filled with day-old pastries and loaves of bread.

And then, one day years later, Bayes asked her if she would model for his classes at the Sail Loft. Of course she had refused. In Grace Point, rumors burned like dry driftwood about what went on at Bayes' Sail Loft. Artists' orgies. New Yorkers. At the center of all the stories was Ben—and his wife, Louise, a slight, intense woman with flaming red hair, who created giant sculptures much bigger than herself. Rosalina decided not to tell anyone, not even Joaquin, about Bayes's request. But after he'd left, she'd run to the mirror, lifted her chin, and imagined how artists might paint her. Then, feeling suddenly silly, she had returned to her work.

The next day, Bayes went directly to Victor Santos. Victor, recalling his own days modeling for the famous Hawthorne, agreed that Rosa could work two days a week at the Sail Loft.

She'd had to check with Joaquin and with Father Jim, but these were merely courtesies. Victor Santos had already decided. As proud as if he were Rosalina's father—or her husband—he had bragged to the other fishermen about his beautiful daughter-in-law who would be posing for Ben Bayes.

"So how's my little flower, my Rosa Rugosa, today?" Ben swept in the door, bellowing his greeting, and all eyes turned first to the master and then to Rosalina. Not waiting for her answer, he made minute adjustments, rearranging the folds of the shawl, pulling a tendril of hair forward so that it curled over her cheek. He took particular care with the forearm and hand that rested on the high stool at her side, spreading her little finger from the others, arching her two middle fingers. Then he edged her hips forward until her buttocks were barely leaning on her stool, giving her the long look that he sought. His touch was light, impersonal, but even so Rosalina shivered. She could smell the nicotine on his fingers. No other man but Joaquin was ever this close to her.

Finally satisfied, Bayes nodded and tapped his walking stick twice on the floor. There was a rustle of sound, as if a collective breath—long held—had been released. The class began.

Modeling was not as easy as it looked, but from the first Rosa was good at it. And under the glow of the artists' compliments, she grew better. Complaining about the other girl, who could not hold the poses, they praised Rosa, telling her she was like a statue. Even Bayes, congratulating himself on recognizing her talent, told her she was a natural. She could stay motionless for a long time or, if it was called for, could flow from one position to another like a dancer. After the first week, at least during the time when she was working, her self-consciousness disappeared. Reality dissolved into a fantasy world of her own creation. The artists did not know her as Joaquin's wife or Victor's daughter-in-law—or the daughter of Anna Roderick.

Occasionally she'd find an excuse to return to the studio after class, when she could be alone with the portraits. She took her time then, studying the many images of her as they dried on the easels, as a means toward a deeper understanding of herself. Sometimes Rosalina saw partially finished portraits of the other model, the one the artists complained about. The girl was not Portuguese, and Rosalina thought the wild, blond-haired creature was beautiful. Something about her reminded Rosa of a mermaid—perhaps the full breasts and thin hips, or the fact that she modeled nude, something Rosalina would not even consider.

The ambiance of the studio, like the weather—or Ben himself—changed from day to day. Some mornings Ben's students were lighthearted and gossiped or told jokes. Other times they were intense, quiet, with undercurrents of anger and frustration. While they painted, Ben walked between the easels, offering encouragement to some and to others only criticism, suggesting a particular refinement of line or shade. One or two he left alone. Some artists flattered Ben, looked for his approval like pets; others challenged his every suggestion.

Today the mood was subdued, and Rosalina was glad. She drifted off into daydreams, pastel visions of herself and Joaquin and the child they would surely soon have. If it was a boy, she decided, he would be a fisherman like his father. By then Joaquin might have his own boat, and the two of them could fish together. Joaquin would be a kind father, as loving to their son as he was to her, not withholding like Victor Santos. And if the child was a girl? Of course, she would want her to find someone wonderful to love, someone just like Joaquin. And she'd want her to be happy. Not like Dolores, who was always pretending she was someone else, or that she was married to a movie star. The child would be pretty, of course; maybe she would even grow up to model.

Rosalina smiled at the thought. Maybe Ben Bayes would want mother and infant to model. Wouldn't Joaquin adore that? This idea of a painting was her secret. She had started hiding a portion of her wages in her bureau. She hoped to be able to buy one of the portraits of herself to give to Joaquin. As excited as she was, sometimes the growing pile of money in her drawer made her feel guilty. It was the only secret she had from Joaquin.

The door shut behind her, and the sound pulled her from her reverie. The artists looked up, then glanced toward Ben. He never allowed anyone—not even Louise—to disturb him during a class; it was one of his cardinal rules. She waited while Ben crossed the room, waited for the sound of his roar.

"Well, God damn it. Well, God damn it." Each sentence was punctuated by the sound of his walking stick striking the floor. "If I'm not drunk, I must be dreaming. You rum-drinking son of a bitch, I thought you were dead."

The artists had stopped painting and were openly watching the scene playing out behind her. Rosalina longed to turn around but was afraid to break her pose. Laughter exploded—Ben's and another's. A man's.

"Jesus Christ. Jesus Christ." She heard them embrace and the hearty sound of palms slapping backs. "When did you land in town?"

"Yesterday." The voice was deep, faintly accented.

"Yesterday, and this is the first time I see you? Has Louise seen you yet? No? Well, she'll have my hide hanging from one of her sculptures if I keep you up here. And we'll both draw and quarter you if you don't explain why you're alive when we heard you had died in Spain. Or was it Paris?"

Without a word to the students, he led the stranger out, and the door closed on the echo of their laughter. The work proceeded halfheartedly, as if Ben Bayes had taken with him all the energy in the room. The minutes dragged by.

When Ben finally returned to his class, Rosalina knew the stranger was with him even though he was silent. And she could feel his eyes on her. Her muscles grew tense and tired. She longed to move; the pose was no longer easy or natural. Her throat grew dry. There was a pitcher of water on Ben's desk and she stared at it, longingly. But she could not walk across the room with the stranger watching her. Her skin began to feel itchy, as if it didn't fit her body. She wondered if Ben would ever call for a break.

Also aware of the stranger, the students began to talk, laughing and teasing as if to draw his attention. She could almost read their minds: *He must be important if Ben is letting him stay in the studio during class.* If the stranger felt any curiosity toward their work, he did not show it. He was content to stay leaning against the wall by the door, not even bothering to glance at the canvases of the students nearest him. For his part, Ben was more critical than usual. He stopped at the easel of a woman who did delicate, misty paintings and threw up his arms in disgust. "Is this the best you can do? You waste my time, do you understand? You are wasting my time with this drivel." The artist flinched, and after Ben walked away, she wept silently. Rosalina had never seen Ben be cruel before. She knew he was showing off for his friend. It made her angry, and she disliked the stranger instinctively. Her anger gave her the strength to speak.

"I need a break. I'm thirsty."

Ben looked at her in surprise and arched an eyebrow. In all the weeks of posing, she had never asked for a break. She waited for his outburst. Instead he threw back his great head and laughed. He struck his cane three sharp raps, his signal for a break. With relief, the artists moved from their easels, except for the student who still wept.

Purposely, Rosalina did not look at the stranger when she crossed to the water pitcher. She would not let him bother her, would pretend he wasn't even there. She wrapped the shawl tightly across her chest and held her head high, but her knees were trembling. He was still staring at her. She knew he was. The weight of his gaze felt like hands on her body.

She drank the water thirstily, struggling to regain

composure. From the corner of her eye, she saw that the man was dark, slender against Ben's great girth, and tall. He had a narrow mustache, like Gable's or Errol Flynn's, but he was too old, and his face too thin, for a movie star. Joaquin was much better looking, she decided—stronger, too. Ben's friend looked soft. The thought made her smile and sustained her during her walk back to her stool.

"Hey, Rosa, my Rosa Rugosa." Ben's voice stopped her before she could assume her pose. "Come here. I want you to meet someone." Grinning, Ben clapped the stranger on the back. She understood instantly that the two men had talked about her when they had left the room. For the first time, she didn't trust Ben at all. "Come on. Come on over and meet my friend."

The stranger's smile was the expression of a person who knew a secret. Trapped, she crossed the room.

"Fenris, this is my little Rosa. Rosalina Santos. Isn't she lovely? Now you can see why she is my favorite model." Ben did not have to direct his friend's attention. The stranger had not taken his eyes off Rosa.

"Rosa . . ." Ben bowed slightly, a funny, mock-courtly bow, and took her small hand in his great one. "Rosa, may I introduce one of the great writers of the western hemisphere. Fenris Boak."

So he isn't an artist after all. What is he doing here? Why did Ben allow him in the studio? What kind of a name is "Fenris" anyway? His hand covered hers, the skin smooth, not like Joaquin's at all. He held it too long and she pulled away.

"Hello," she murmured.

Ben was watching them.

Fenris Boak's eyes narrowed and his smile grew broader. She knew he was laughing at her.

Now she could see that his eyes were a cool clear blue, but changeable, with depths like the ocean water. The mustache was thin, carefully trimmed. His lips were thin too, like a girl's. The Mexican shawl felt scratchy against her neck. She felt exposed, vulnerable, and she disliked the man for making her feel that way. Now she knew she couldn't model with him watching her. She wasn't safe with him there watching. *Joaquin and me, Joaquin and me. We'll be together for eternity.*

"I've seen Rosalina before, although we didn't have a chance to meet." Boak's voice, like his eyes, had many levels.

What was he talking about? She turned to Ben. "I can't do the afternoon class. I meant to tell you earlier. I have to help my father in the bakery." The lie was out before she knew it. "It's Jackie's graduation tonight." She felt safer now. "I have to help get things ready for his party."

Before Ben could say anything, she fled. As she ran down the stairs, her feet barely touching each tread, she yanked hairpins from her hair and pulled the shawl from her shoulders. She tossed it in the basket on the floor, not even bothering to fold it. She was almost outside, had almost made her escape, when she heard his voice calling her name. She whirled around.

"Was it something I said?" The laughter still shone in his eyes. He slouched against the doorjamb. He wasn't blocking her way. She knew she could get by him if she wanted to, but her feet were frozen. Now she saw that he was older than she had first thought, in his forties at least.

"Want to have a Coke? Or a cup of coffee? You must be thirsty after this morning's work."

I'm married. What do you want from me? Leave me alone. "No, thank you," she said. "I'm late. My father will be waiting for me." She walked past him, edging to one side so that not even the cloth of her skirt would brush against him.

"Miss Santos . . ." He waited until she was several steps away.

It's Mrs. *Santos. Mrs. Rosalina Santos. I'm married. My husband's name is Joaquin Santos. He is much stronger than you. And better looking too. And his smile, my Joaquin's smile, is kind, not like yours at all.* The words died on her lips. "What?"

"It's a wattle." Still that infuriating, arrogant grin.

"What is a wattle?"

"The thing on a turkey. The red, wrinkled thing that hangs down on a turkey. It's called a wattle."

She was on the street outside the Sail Loft before she understood what he was talking about, and then she could have died.

Chapter 5

Zoe

There were four bodies in the trunk. No, not bodies, Zoe reminded herself; what she had found today were skeletons. A trunkful of miniature, dry, pearl-white bones.

Filtered light from the hall leaked into the bedroom. Hours ago, her eyes had become accustomed to this dim curtain of light, and she stared now at the familiar shadows of her room: the outline of her easel, barely visible in the small alcove; the blue, brushed-velvet wingback chair; the looming pine wardrobe and matching bureau; the tall basket of beach grasses by the window; the nightstand. Jake.

She raised herself up on one elbow and looked down at her husband. He was sturdy, good-looking. Her rock and anchor. Yet tonight, asleep, without his glasses, he looked infinitely vulnerable. He lay on his back, his left hand curled in a fist next to his cheek, like one of their children.

She watched him breathe, listened to his soft snoring. He slept deeply, unmoving, maddeningly untroubled by nightmares, by terror-filled dreams about the fleshless bones of babes, or by the horror that death had entered his home.

She shifted in the bed, pulled aside the blanket, swung her feet to the floor. The wood was cold, but she did not stop to put on slippers. She crossed the hall to Emily's room, hearing the child's stuffy, open-mouthed breathing. The smell of Vicks Mentholatum filled the air. She stood by the bed for several minutes, watching her daughter just as she had her husband. Except for the ragged breathing, the child slept peacefully. The pink comforter trailed onto the floor, and she tucked it around her daughter, folding it back from her face. Then she bent and kissed Emily's smooth cheek—warm, but not feverish, she noted with relief. As she stooped over the bed, she saw the brown bag by the pillow. She picked up the sack of Halloween treats and placed it on Emily's bureau, then tiptoed from the room.

Adam rested on his stomach, knees drawn under him so that his diaper-thick bottom was raised in the air. Fine brown hair, silken as down, capped his head, and she reached over the edge of the crib and stroked it. This touch did not assuage her need. When she picked him up, he woke and gurgled briefly. His face wrinkled into a frown; then he sighed and snuggled against her, the scowl gone as quickly as it had appeared. He was such a good baby. *Like the babies in the attic. Had they been good babies?*

She froze, willing these thoughts to disappear, to leave her in peace. Still cradling her son, she left the nursery.

The kitchen was a mess. Two pizza boxes—the contents cold and nearly untouched—lay on the counter. The popcorn Emily had spilled still littered the floor and table. All of the candy bars adorned with her Halloween sketches remained on the table. No takers this night. The little children in costumes had stayed away, frightened perhaps by the flashing lights, the police cars, the ambulance. Emily—a very subdued Emily, who had worn the clown costume without complaint—had gone to a few houses with Jake. For her sake, they had tried to pretend things were normal. Or rather, Jake had; Zoe was too shaken and too numb. The medical examiner, before climbing the stairs to the attic, had given her a tranquilizer.

A half-dozen coffee mugs were scattered on the countertop. Several of the policemen had taken cream with their coffee, and a small pitcher was still on the table. It probably had already soured.

The normally cozy kitchen felt unfamiliar and strange tonight. The weight of the house—the deadweight of the attic—pressed down on her. Anger took root in her chest. She almost trembled with it, wanting to yell or strike out at someone, to fight. Holding Adam tighter, she crossed to the rocker and sat down. The chair creaked as it arced back and forth. The squeaking came from the base of the chair, the curved slat on the left-hand side, and she concentrated on it. Back and forth she rocked, pushing off each time with her bare feet. Her toes curled tight from the cold floor.

The creak sounded only on the back tilt, a low, reassuring sound, and she rocked slowly to and fro, to and fro, as if the chirking would eventually lull her, too. Adam slept on. She cupped her hands over the warm fullness of him, but even her son could not erase the haunting image of the tiny dead bodies.

Four of them, three in the hatboxes and one in the moldy gray suitcase. And an orange rubber envelope that was cracked and crumbling, with a long tube screwed to its stopper. A douche bag. This had seemed almost more obscene than the bodies.

The skeletons had been carefully wrapped in newspaper, naked in death. That seemed horrible to Zoe too: that they were without flannel gowns or undershirts or even diapers when they had been bound up in newspaper, packaged like some kind of garbage to be thrown away with the day's trash. She started to cry, sobs that burned her throat.

"Zoe?" Jake, his brown hair tousled, wore a sleep-dazed look. He had not put on his glasses, and he squinted slightly. "Zoe, honey, are you all right?"

She stared at him as if he were a stranger. Unable to stop her tears, she continued to rock. The creaking sounded louder now. He crossed to her, stooping awkwardly by her bare feet. At her breast, Adam did not stir.

"Emily woke me up," Jake said. "She was having a nightmare." He looked at her, helpless in the face of nightmares. "Perhaps it was Halloween."

"It wasn't Halloween."

"Come on, hon, come back to bed. Here, let me take Adam back to his crib. Does he need to be changed?"

She did not answer.

"Listen," he said, "you go on up and try and get some sleep. I'll take care of the baby." He reached for the sleeping infant. But she pulled back from him, tightening her hold on Adam.

"No."

He hesitated, trying to gauge what was happening. "Okay. It's okay. You cold? Want me to get you something to put on your feet?" His voice was calm, as if it were perfectly normal to find her in the kitchen at three in the morning, holding their son and weeping. When she did not answer, he went to the living room and returned with a mohair throw, which he tucked snugly around her and Adam. This time she did not shrink away from him.

He crossed to the deacon's bench and sank down. "You want company? I mean, do you want to talk about it?" He combed his fingers through his hair while he waited for her to answer.

Her voice was harsh. "They were here all this time. All this time we've been living here, they were here . . . in this house."

He did not ask who "they" were.

"I can't stop thinking about that. We were *living* here with them."

"They're gone now, Zoe. They aren't here anymore. It's going to be okay."

She stared at him. She knew the police had taken

everything away: the trunk; the faded hatboxes; the mildewed suitcase; the sheets of newspapers, torn by her hands; the foul, crumbling orange bag. They had removed the skeletons last, because they had to be transported by ambulance—it was the law, the medical examiner had told her—and the town's only ambulance was delayed on an emergency run to Boston. It had been nearly eleven before her home was relieved of its dreadful secret. But Jake was wrong: the touch of death remained.

Creak . . . creak . . . creak. She rocked slower now. "Did you see the newspapers?" she asked.

"Briefly. I heard one of the men saying they were old. Nineteen forty," he said. Her tears had stopped and Jake relaxed. She looked almost peaceful now, wrapped in the peach throw, rocking their infant son.

"They were from here, you know." *Creak . . . creak . . . creak.* "They were pages from the *Grace Point Sentinel.*" She shivered and rocked on. She saw Jake grit his teeth against the grating sound of the chair.

"I mean," she continued, "it seems worse, somehow, because of that. It's too close. It would be better if it had been *The New York Times*. Or the *Boston Globe.* Or even the New Bedford paper. Do you know what I mean?"

A tentative grin flickered across Jake's face. "Personally, it sounds more like a *National Enquirer* story to me."

"God damn it, Jake, that's not funny. That's not one damn bit funny."

"Sorry."

"I mean, Jesus, how could you even say that?"

"I said I was sorry, Zoe. I was just trying to lighten up, put the whole thing in some kind of perspective. It's not as if we knew who they were or anything. We're talking about something that happened before you or I were even born."

"God. How can you say that? I mean, I can't believe

you'd joke about this." Her voice grew shrill. "I mean, Jesus, Jake, there were four dead bodies—four *babies'* bodies—in our attic, and it doesn't matter if they've been there fifty years or five days." Adam stretched against her stomach, the little scowl again creasing his brow. She lowered her voice. "You can't make things go away by joking about them," she continued bitterly. She bit off other, unspoken words, afraid of where the conversation was going.

Jake stared down at the floor, unable to meet her eyes.

"I'm sorry," she said.

"No. You're right. I'm sorry."

Their unspoken history lay between them like broken glass neither dared walk on.

Aren't you afraid? she wanted to ask him. *Aren't you just a little bit scared?* Instead she said, "Have you called your sister?"

He stared at his hands, then shrugged helplessly. "No." After a minute he rose and began to gather the coffee mugs. He rinsed them and stacked them in the dishwasher. He sniffed the cream, then dumped it down the drain and placed the pitcher in with the dirty cups. He pulled the plastic wrap from a drawer and carefully packaged the cold pizza in individual portions—three slices each—and put them in the freezer. Taking a damp sponge, he wiped off the countertop.

"Can I get you anything? Tea? Coffee?"

She shook her head, waiting, watching him work. The only sound was the creaking of the rocker. "Jake?"

"What?"

"I'm sorry. I didn't mean it, what I said before. I'm just upset."

"No. You're right. I shouldn't have joked about it."

While she rocked Adam, he cleared the table, picking up the crayons and scraps of paper, the pens, scissors, and glue. "I'll phone Jeanne in the morning," he finally said.

"And I'll call Tory." The thought made her tired. Her mother preferred to deny the existence of any unpleasantness. Rocking, she watched while Jake swept up the popcorn Emily had spilled.

When he was done, he stood for a moment, again gave that helpless half-shrug, then crossed to her. This time she let him take Adam.

"There were four of them, Jake."

Something evil had occurred in this town—in this house. A long time ago, but it reached across the decades and touched her and her family. She didn't think she'd ever feel absolutely comfortable in this house again. "How could four babies just disappear? Disappear without anyone wondering what happened to them or who they were? What in the name of God was going on here fifty years ago?"

He bent and kissed the top of her head.

She watched him walk from the room with Adam. *Why can't we talk?* she wondered. *Even about this. Have we become so terribly afraid of making waves?*

With Adam no longer in her arms, she felt colder. She shivered. *What had happened in this house?*

Chapter 6

The phone woke them in the morning. Zoe pressed her face against the pillow and felt the mattress shift as Jake got out of bed. When he picked up the receiver, she heard the raspiness of sleep still in his voice.

"Yes. This is Jake Barlow. . . . Oh, good morning, Deputy."

Zoe was fully awake now. She lay absolutely still, concentrating on Jake's conversation. Her mouth felt dry and stale.

"No, fifteen minutes will be fine. . . . No, it's not inconvenient at all. . . . Of course. Yes, I understand." His voice was smooth, cordial now, with no trace of sleep. "I'll put the coffee on.

"That was a deputy from the county sheriff's office. He and his partner are coming by in fifteen minutes."

"I heard," she said, already on edge. "What do they want?"

"More questions, I guess. I'll shave and start the coffee while you're dressing."

"Why did you do that?"

"What?" Jake took a pair of jeans out of the closet and pulled them on.

"Invite them to have coffee." Having the police in their home was a reminder of all that she wanted to forget.

"I don't know. It seemed polite. Nothing wrong with it, is there?"

"I just don't know why you're being so nice to

them." She was becoming more and more ill-tempered, but she could not stop. Behind her anger, fear gnawed.

"Look, Zoe. It's seven-thirty in the morning. I always have coffee in the morning." He selected an oxford-cloth shirt. "Two sheriff's men are going to be here. I invited them to join us. What's the big deal? Besides, if we're going to find bodies in our attic, we might as well stay friendly with the police."

"It isn't funny, Jake."

Jake stood in front of the closet, silent in the face of her attack. They stared at each other across the cozy cream-and-blue bedroom. Zoe had worked hard to make this room a place of refuge and peace. *I'm scared,* she wanted to cry, but could not bring herself to say the words aloud.

Jake crossed to the bed. "It bothers me, too, Zoe. But it happened and it isn't going to go away, so we may as well learn to live with it."

But how can you shrug it off so easily? Just like before. Why is it that you can always detach so easily? Of course, she did not say these words. "Before" was a mine field she would not walk through again.

"I know you think I'm being callous," he continued, "but a sense of humor will help us get through this. Okay?" He bent over and tilted her head up until their eyes met, and then he kissed her.

The terror receded and the bedroom was returned to her, once again a haven. "Okay," she murmured into his chest.

"Just try to remember. It has nothing to do with us. We are bystanders, honey. That's it." He leaned over to give her another kiss.

"I love you," she whispered.

"I love you, too."

"Mommy!" Emily's shout broke the spell.

"Another country heard from." Jake brushed his lips against her hair and then headed for the door. "You want Emily-duty or the coffee?"

"I'll take care of her."

He was in the hall when she stopped him. "Jake?"

"What?"

"Use coffee beans from the freezer. The French Breakfast roast." She grinned up at him. "If we're going to bribe the police, we might as well use the finest."

"A joke. Zoe made a joke." He turned and reached to lift his daughter, who stood in the doorway. Her hair was matted from sleep, and traces of clown makeup still marked her face. "Did you hear that, Emily, my girl? Your mother just made a joke." He stopped short of lifting her in his arms. "Whoops. What's this? You better go see your mother."

As soon as she was alone with Zoe, Emily started to cry.

"Emily, honey. What's wrong?" She held her arms out toward her daughter, but Emily did not budge from the doorway.

"It was an accident."

"What, honey? What was an accident?"

"I'm not a baby."

"What was an accident?" Zoe repeated. She swung her legs out of bed and crossed to give her daughter a hug. Then she smelled urine and understood. Concern for Emily overcame her initial exasperation. "No, Emily, you are not a baby. You're a big, beautiful girl. And accidents happen, even to big, beautiful girls. Come on. Let's go into the bathroom and run a tub for you."

Emily sniffled back her tears. "Can I have some Mr. Bubbles?"

"Absolutely."

She sat on the edge of the tub while Emily bathed, never more than an arm's length away. She was all too aware of how easily a young child could fall in the slippery tub.

She took up the face cloth and soap. "Look up at

me, hon. Let me wash your face. You've still got red clown circles on your cheeks from last night."

Emily turned her face toward her mother, squinching her eyes so tightly shut that her nose wrinkled. "Don't get soap in my eyes," she said.

"Promise." Gently, Zoe scrubbed the little face. Then she wrapped Emily in a bath sheet and carried her back to her room. The child smelled sweet and clean.

"Okay, pumpkin. Let's get you dressed."

She held out a pair of panties and Emily stepped into them. Docilely, she held her arms over her head so Zoe could pull on an undershirt. It was too small, and she had to tug it over her daughter's head. Emily was growing so quickly it was difficult to keep her in clothes that fit. She chose a long-sleeved cotton shirt with ruffles at the neck and bibbed overalls from the dresser. From downstairs, she heard Jake's voice and then deeper, unfamiliar ones. The sheriff's men. She felt jittery. Moving quickly, she ducked in to check Adam. Mercifully, he still slept. With Emily at her heels, she returned to her own room and pulled on a pair of jeans and a T-shirt. Then she went back to the child's room.

She stripped the urine-soaked sheets from the bed. The bedpad needed laundering as well. A plastic sheet protected the mattress, and she was grateful for the precaution. Although Emily had not wet the bed in nearly a year, Zoe had left the plastic there, just in case.

She dumped the sheets in the laundry basket, which she set in the hall to remind her to bring it down to the kitchen.

Emily watched silently while she worked. "I'm not a baby. It was an accident." Her voice quavered.

"Accidents happen to everyone, Em."

"Even to you?"

"Even to me."

Emily absorbed that thought quietly. She trailed her mother so closely that Zoe kept bumping into her.

"Is that what happened in the attic?" the child asked in a little voice. "Was it an accident?"

Zoe caught her breath. "We don't know what happened there yet, Emily. That's the policemen's job. It all happened a long time ago and it has nothing to do with us. Now let's go down and get some breakfast."

She was astonished at how much she sounded like Jake. She took her daughter's hand in hers, picked up the laundry basket with the other, and started down the stairs. *Jake is wrong,* she thought. *It does have something to do with us.*

The deputy sheriffs were not in uniform. One stood silently by the door. The other was sitting at the table. The kitchen was fragrant with coffee.

Jake gestured toward the two men. "Sam Riley and Daniel Cole. They're from the county sheriff's criminal investigating unit. They were here last night, too."

Sam Riley nodded but continued to slouch against the door frame. He was short and struck Zoe as soft. His clothes were sloppy, and his shirt looked like it had been left in the dryer too long.

At the table, Dan Cole rose. He was slender, well-groomed, and very masculine. As he stood, he hitched his thumbs in his belt and gave his slacks a tug over his slim hips. The gesture was a cowboy's, an instinctive male swagger. Zoe's dislike was immediate.

As she pulled Emily's stool to the table and busied herself getting out cereal, bowl, and spoon, Zoe was aware of the deputies' eyes on her and aware as well that the two men missed nothing that went on in the room.

Emily had gone to her father. She rested her head on his lap and stared up at the strangers. Cole reached inside his jacket for a pack of cigarettes, and Zoe had a quick glimpse of a holster. Emily saw it too, and her eyes widened.

"Emily!"

The child jumped at her mother's sharp tone. Deliberately, Zoe lowered her voice. "Come on, honey. Let's get you some breakfast." Before Em could protest, Zoe scooped her up and set her on a stool across the table from Cole.

She poured two glasses of juice. When she turned around, she was conscious of Riley's gaze on her body. The room was still chilly, and she knew her nipples stood out against the thin fabric of her T-shirt. A flannel shirt of Jake's was hanging from one of the hooks by the back door. Riley stepped aside as she reached for it. She pulled it on, tying the tails in a knot at her midriff with curt, stiff movements.

Cole fingered the pack of Winstons. "Y'mind?"

Zoe hated it when people smoked in the same room with her children. She could picture the poisons turning their fragile lung cells from pink to brown. She waited, hoping Jake would say something, but he was silent.

Cole lit his cigarette and dropped the match in his saucer.

A pad with several scrawled lines lay on the table in front of Jake. "Just a few notes," he said in response to her look. "They want us to think of as many people we know who have lived here or rented here. They're going to check with Bill and Norma Casey." The Caseys were real estate brokers.

She nodded.

"And they say they'll be back with some men from CPAC," he said. The acronym rolled glibly from his mouth.

"CPAC?"

"The crime unit from the state police," Cole explained. "They'll need to go through the attic." The idea felt like a violation.

Zoe wished he had not mentioned the attic in front of Emily.

"The bones are on the way to Boston, the state lab. We're pretty sure they're—" He stopped short. His eyes brushed over Emily. "We're sure they're h-u-m-a-n remains," he said, "but we won't be certain till after the autopsy." He flicked ash in the saucer next to the dead match. "We've had a call from one reporter already, so the sheriff's set a press conference at the town hall for ten."

"Reporters?" Her voice twisted.

"He'll try to keep you and your family out of it. It's pretty clear from the dates on the newspapers that all this happened before you two were born. There's no reason to release your names at this time."

"We appreciate that," Jake said.

Cole shrugged. "We'll try, as I said—do the best we can to contain the reporters. But they can be pretty persistent, and a small town like this . . . well . . ." He gave another shrug. "You understand what I'm saying. I can't guarantee anything."

Jake nodded.

Cole reached for the list of names in front of Jake and then rose. "Well, I guess we've bothered you enough for now. We'll be back with the CPAC unit around two." On the way to the door, he stopped by Emily's chair. "You know, last night I saw someone who looked an awful lot like you. Could she have been your twin?"

Emily shrank back from him. Her eyes darted to her father for reassurance.

"I'm not kidding," Cole continued. "Just last night. In this very room. You don't have a twin, do you?"

"No." The word was tiny.

"Yep. Just like you, except this person was a clown."

Emily's eyes narrowed in suspicion; and then, in understanding, a grin split her face. "That was me."

"No!"

For the first time since she entered the kitchen, Zoe smiled at Cole.

"It was. I was a clown. Wasn't I, Daddy? For trick or treat. I was a clown."

"Well, you sure had me fooled." The deputy winked at Jake over the top of Emily's head.

Cole was near the door when his partner spoke. "If you don't mind, I'd like to ask a couple of questions."

Zoe froze. The fear again licked at her chest. Riley. She saw then that though his rumpled look gave him a harmless appearance, his eyes missed nothing.

"When did you move to this house?" he asked.

Zoe looked at Jake. He was returning Riley's gaze, and his face was clear, guiltless.

"A little over a year and a half ago," he answered. "If you're looking for the exact month, it was May of '89."

"I see." Riley turned to Zoe. She forced herself to meet his eyes, steeling herself for his questions.

"I'm just curious, Mrs. Barlow," he began. His tone was light, but it felt menacing to Zoe. "How did you and your husband happen to move to Grace Point?"

She could not answer.

"Mrs. Barlow?" Riley prodded gently. Cole's eyes were on her, impassive, probing.

"Why are you asking us these questions? The medical examiner said the babies were probably put there nearly fifty years ago. That's before we were born. It can't have *anything* to do with Jake." She stopped. "Anything to do with *us*," she amended lamely.

Riley waited.

She looked at Cole, as if for help, but he was watching his partner. The room was quiet. Emily slid off her stool and buried her face in her mother's knees. Zoe pulled the child onto her lap and hugged her close, glad of her daughter's warmth in a kitchen grown suddenly chill. "Well, I . . ." she faltered. Her eyes appealed mutely to Jake.

"Deputy Riley." Jake smiled, the disarming grin Zoe knew so well. "Is that right? Is it Deputy? Or Mister?"

"Mister is fine. Or you can call me Sam." Riley returned Jake's smile with an easy one of his own. The tension that had slipped into the room vanished.

"Sam," Jake said, smoothly, "do you have any children?"

"Not yet," Riley said. "I guess it would be a good idea to get a wife first."

Cole chuckled at this, but Zoe tightened her arms around Emily.

"Well," Jake continued, "before we moved here, Zoe and I lived in New Haven, Connecticut. Are you familiar with New Haven? No. Well, it's a fairly large city. Believe me, a city is no place for a child to grow up. We wanted to raise our children in a small town. A place by the sea. Some place safe." If he was aware of an irony in this statement, he did not show it. "Grace Point seemed just about perfect. I guess you don't have to be a parent yourself to appreciate that."

Sam Riley nodded. He looked at Jake and then at Zoe and Emily. "You have a nice family here, Jake. And a baby, too, I understand."

"A son. Adam."

"Well, I can see why you'd want to protect them." He backed toward the door, and Dan Cole followed. His hand was on the knob when he turned back. "Like I said—just curious."

"Not at all," Jake said. "Glad to help. Anytime."

Zoe stared at the pudgy deputy. She knew absolutely that he was the one she had to fear.

"Do you want me to stay home today?" Jake asked.

"No. You don't need to."

"You sure? It's Debra's day on. She can cover. It hasn't been that busy."

"I told you, it isn't necessary." Her voice was sharper than she had intended. Neither of them mentioned Riley's questions. She got up and opened the kitchen door so the lingering smoke would air out. On the way back to the table, she picked up the saucer Cole had used as an ashtray and took it to the sink. Her nose wrinkled in distaste while she rinsed it.

"I'm cold," Emily said. "Shut the door."

"Please," Zoe reminded. "Say 'Please, shut the door.' And I will in a minute, Emily. I just want to get the filthy smoke out of here." The righteous tone in her voice reminded her of Tory.

"After breakfast I'll call Tory," she told Jake. "But even if she has kept any of the old leases—and you know Tory, she doesn't even keep her IRS returns for more than a year or two—they'd only go back ten years or so. Do you really think there's any reason we have to drag her into this? Fifty years ago, she was just a baby herself." She shook her head. "Do they think they can track down something that happened so long ago? God, Jake, it seems impossible."

"God, Jake," Emily repeated, her voice as solemn as her mother's. "God, Jake. God, Jake."

Zoe turned to admonish her daughter, but before she could say a word, Jake grinned at the child and reached over and tousled her hair. "You'd better be praying when you say that, pardner," he said casually.

Emily grinned up at her father. "God, Jake," she said again.

He swooped her up and tossed her into the air. Her arms and legs flopped like a doll's, and she shrieked with delight. "Again," she demanded when he stopped.

"On one condition."

She grinned at him, trusting.

"The next time I hear you speaking to God, I want to see you on your knees by your bed."

"Okay, Daddy," she agreed. "Now do it again."

A flash of jealousy stung Zoe. Jake was so good with Emily, so natural. He always seemed to hit the right note.

Soft, gurgling noises crackled from the intercom speaker that hung on the wall by the refrigerator. "Adam," Zoe announced, grateful for the distraction. "Would you put a bottle on to heat while I change him?"

She took her time with her son. He lay on the changing table and smiled up at her, making his infant noises while she slowly cleansed him and sprinkled him with powder. She was careful with the talcum, not using too much. She had read in an article that it could be dangerous for babies to inhale the dust. Then she bent over and nuzzled her face into the sweet, soft creases of his neck, cooing nonsense words into his skin. She felt his tiny fingers grabbing at her hair. She pulled away and stared down at her son. If anything happened to him, she knew she would die. The thought of him being hurt . . . sick . . . dead . . . brought tears to her eyes.

Cole had said the policemen would be returning that afternoon. She imagined them in her kitchen, walking through her halls, filing up and down her stairs on their way to and from the attic. She could smell the smoke from their cigarettes. The idea of leaving her house while the police invaded it made her feel vulnerable, but the need to protect her family from the intrusion was stronger than her urge to stay.

Moving quickly, she fastened the tapes of Adam's diaper and slipped a clean nightshirt on him. Cradling him against her breast, she left the room.

In the kitchen she said to Jake, "I've changed my mind."

"About what?" While she had been upstairs, he had

made hot chocolate for Emily, and Adam's bottle was waiting.

"About your going to work. I want you to stay with us. I thought maybe we could take a drive. Maybe go to New Bedford. We could shop the outlet stores there. The kids both need winter clothes. And Emily's undershirts are so small they hardly fit over her head."

He opened his mouth to protest, but he saw the determination on her face. She did not need to tell him she was escaping.

"Great idea," he said cheerfully. "Tell you what. While you're feeding Adam and getting stuff together for the trip, Emily and I will take a ride down to the bank, drop off some money for Debra in the store, and then swing by the police station and tell them to let Cole and Riley know."

"Why do you have to tell them? God, Jake. They didn't tell us we couldn't leave town, did they? I mean, we aren't suspects, for heaven's sake."

"Easy, Zoe. I'm just stopping by to drop off the house key so that they can get in."

Please stay away from the police. "We'll be ready in a half hour," she said.

She finished feeding Adam and washed the breakfast dishes. Jake had not yet returned. Eager to escape the silence of the house, the weight of what had been in her attic, she bundled her son in blankets and went outside to wait. Shards of smashed pumpkins littered the length of the sidewalk in front of the house. In neighboring yards, swags of toilet paper hung drunkenly from tree limbs and sodden wads of it lay along the curb. Down the block, the windshield of an old station wagon was embellished with shaving cream. Yet Halloween seemed a long time ago.

She sank into the porch glider. A tenant had left it behind, and somehow she just hadn't been able to throw it out. She had painted it bright blue, but rust bubbled beneath the fresh enamel.

A car approached, but it was not Jake. *Where was he?* A motion, more sensed than seen, caught her attention, and she turned to the narrow road—alleyway, really—that flanked their home. At first she saw nothing, but then she caught sight of the man, half hidden in shadows. He stared in her direction and she shrank back, but soon she understood that he was staring not at her but up at her house.

He was old. Stooped. He was smoking. In fact, it was that motion, match lifted to cigarette, that had caught her attention. She continued to study him. He was hatless. Soiled Levi's were tucked into his rubber boots. Over them he wore a ripped and faded denim coat. To her artist's eye, there seemed something off-balance about him. Then she understood. The right sleeve of his jacket hung limp. Empty.

Where was Jake?

The old man caught sight of her then, and their eyes locked. Even at that distance, she saw the anger in his face. She inhaled sharply and tightened her hold on Adam, causing him to squirm. Her gaze darted quickly to the street to check for Jake.

When she looked back, the one-armed man had disappeared.

Chapter 7

Dan Cole descended the steps of the Grace Point town hall, opened the passenger door of the sedan, and slid in next to his partner. Sam was still where he had left him forty-five minutes before, slouched behind the wheel eating a Milky Way.

It was only ten and already Sam had gone through three candy bars. By the end of the day, he'd have eaten at least a dozen of them. Dan picked up the wrappers and dropped them in the litterbag that hung from the radio dial on the dash. A heart attack waiting to happen, that was his partner. Frustrating thing was, he hadn't gained an ounce in the four years they'd been partners in BCI, though he was hardly trim.

"Here's what we got," he said, flipping open his notebook. "Okay, looks like the Barlows are clean. Just like he said, they moved here eighteen months ago. He owns a bookstore. She's a housewife and an amateur painter. They've got two kids, a baby and a five-year-old. No relatives in town. He's on the planning board. She does volunteer work at the Cetacean Stranding Center."

"The what?"

"Cetacean Stranding Center. They work with the aquarium in Boston. They aid whales, dolphins, and seals stranded on shore. Keep 'em alive."

"Shit," Sam said. "The Ce-ta-cean Stranding Center. Do-gooders. Enough to drive you crazy. Shhhheee . . . it."

Dan ignored this outburst. He had heard it before. "About a hundred volunteers with a paid director. Only twenty real active volunteers. The Barlow woman is apparently one of them." Sam unwrapped another candy bar. "Go easy on those things, will ya? The whole car's beginning to smell like a candy factory. I swear, you know what Jenny told me when I got home last night? That I smell like chocolate. I'm not kidding you."

Sam kept eating. He looked through the windshield, surveying the street. Dan went back to his notebook.

"Okay, before the Barlows moved in, the house was empty for a couple of years. No reports of any vandalism or break-ins. Before that, it was rented to summer tenants. And before that, a couple from New Hampshire ran it as a boardinghouse. The Salt Spray Inn. Straight, not gay. Respectable. Rented to tourists, not kids. They had it for fifteen years, then threw in the towel and retired to Florida. I've got someone trying to call them. Don't think they'll have much to give us. Fifteen years. Even with the two years it was empty, two years of summer people, and the year and a half with the Barlows, that only brings us back a little over twenty years. Still, who knows? Maybe someone will remember a tenant who brought in a trunk."

Dan flipped to another page in the notebook. "Before this couple from New Hampshire—name's White. Did I tell you that?—okay, before them, place was vacant winters and rented out summers to tourists. We've got the realtor checking it out, but it looks like a dead end there, too. Most of the leases are long gone." He made a note on the page. "I've got them checking with the registry of deeds, but the selectmen's secretary—fat, nosy old bird—she said the house used to belong to a family named Santos and before that to a guy named Roderick. A widower, deceased. Ran a bakery there in the thirties."

"Jesus Christ!" Sam exploded. "Will you look at that?" He slid upright out of the slouching pose. He stared at a couple walking toward their car. The pair strolled, arms around each other so tightly their hips swayed in rhythm as they walked. "Fucking queers," Sam sneered. "I'll tell ya, this fucking town gives me the creeps."

"You're a bigot, you know that, Riley?" It was perhaps the hundredth time Dan had made this observation. "You know what Jenny told me yesterday?"

"Yeah. She said you smell like candy."

"She was watching 'The Oprah Winfrey Show' and it was about married couples where each one was the exact opposite of the other one. A woman seventy-two married to a guy thirty-six; a tall black chick married to a short white guy; a straight-ticket Republican married to a flaming liberal Democrat—couples like that."

"Should be against the law. I'll tell you this—if my daughter married a black guy, she'd be gone."

Dan had heard that before, too. "You don't have a daughter."

"Well, if I did."

"So Jenny says," he went on, " 'You and Sam shoulda been on that program. You two are the oddest couple I've ever seen.' "

"So who you wanta be, Danny? The big nigger bitch?" Sam glowered at the gay couple as they passed by the sedan.

Dan looked over at his partner. Jenny was right. The two of them made the oddest pairing in the whole bureau. He voted independent but if pressed would probably claim kinship to Democrats. Not too extreme. He was meticulous about his dress, watched his diet, drank decaffeinated coffee, kept his smoking down to five cigarettes a day, worked out in the sheriff's office gym (though it was stretching some to call it a gym—it was just an old file room that a bunch of them had outfitted with free weights). He wasn't conceited, but he was proud of his pecs. And his lats weren't too bad, either. He had a careful, thorough approach to his work, and he was a dogged investigator. He could follow a trail—find clues others overlooked. He had a gift for assembling the pieces of the puzzle.

Sam, on the other hand, was a junk-food junkie who couldn't care less about his clothes or his pecs. An ex–Marine staff sergeant, he was an intolerant, closed-minded chauvinist who specialized in black-and-white thinking on all social issues and had probably voted Republican since he was in the cradle. The original Neanderthal man. He was sloppy at paperwork and bored by what Dan thought of as the puzzle-piece assembling part of the job. He hated legwork.

The thing was—and admitting this stung—this Milky Way–fed, opinionated, lazy lump had a weird sixth sense that clicked in when confronted with a crime. Unlike Dan, he didn't *need* clues. He had the instincts and intuition Dan lacked. They made a great team.

"I tell ya," Sam continued, "there is something sick about this place. I sure as hell am glad I don't live here. You take a look at any of the stores?"

"Not yet."

"Do yourself a favor. Don't bother." He snorted in disgust. "There's this leather shop down the street. In the window they got this mannequin—a guy, right?—a guy all dressed in leather, and there are handcuffs on his wrists. And overhead, they got whips suspended in midair. *Whips.* It's enough to make you sick. The way they got this stuff right there on Main Street . . . Damn perverts. It's like there's something in the air here."

Dan turned to another page in his notebook. Sam was right: there was something in this town that bred violence. "You're going to love this, then. I got this from the old town reports." He read from his notes. "Back in '39, there were four murders, one suicide—guy, twenty-seven, hung himself—twelve dogs killed, and eleven people committed as insane: six to Taunton, one to the psychopathic ward of Boston Hospital, two to Westboro State Hospital, and two to Wrentham State School. In '40, there were four committed for being insane, three murders—one a fractured skull, one a knife, and the last a gun. Eight dogs killed. Wonder why they killed the dogs? In '41, we got a drop in dogs killed, down to five, only one murder, and three people arrested for participating in an immoral show." He looked up. "It sure seems strange. I mean, the population of the town isn't that big."

"What the hell has all that got to do with the case? Dead dogs. Christ." Sam slouched back in the seat, fingering a fresh Milky Way.

"Just seemed interesting." He flipped to another page in his notebook. "Well, here's what we got. Medical examiner confirmed the bones are human. Can't give us much else yet. But get this. He's running tests to determine their sex and age. He got hold of a pediatric radiologist from D.C. who can establish the age from X rays, and there's some book called *Forensic Fetal Osteology* that he's using. It's a bible in the field. It was published by the University of Budapest in Hungary, but they've got hold of an English translation."

Sam's head was resting against the headrest, and his eyes were closed. Dan could not tell if he was asleep. He sighed and went on. "The trunk and hatboxes are on their way to Washington, to the FBI lab."

Sam did not open his eyes. "Who called those clowns in?"

"The state police. But they're not going to participate in the investigation. We're just using their labs. They've got lasers to locate latent fingerprints—" he stopped and checked his notebook—"and will also use tests involving an electron microscope scan and neutron analysis."

"Clowns," Sam repeated.

"They've lined up an entomologist at the Smithsonian to examine the insects they found in the trunk. Maybe it will help determine what season the babies were put there." He loved that kind of detail, the pieces of the puzzle. It was the essence of being a detective.

"So that's it so far. I told the chief we'd call in again before we go back to the Barlow house." He flipped his notebook shut and set it on the seat between them. Suddenly he felt depressed and tired, a feeling that usually hit him midway through a case. It was not a good sign to have it so soon. "What's your take on this one, Sam? How do you think those skeletons ended up in that trunk?"

"You know what I think?" Sam did not bother to open his eyes. "No matter what those clowns find with their lasers and neutrons and scans, I think we don't stand a prayer in hell's chance of solving this one. We'll bust our butts digging up information about something that happened more than half a century ago, and in the end it'll be a waste of time. This one's going in the great unsolved crime file. That's what I think."

Dan sighed and checked his watch. Almost time for coffee. For a minute, Dan let his head fall back against the seat and closed his own eyes. The knowledge of the inevitable washed over him: during the next hard days and weeks—hell, maybe even months—he would be the one who broke his butt, did legwork until his calves cramped chasing leads that wouldn't pan out, spend sleepless nights staring up at shadows on the ceiling, trying not to wake Jenny and watching the details of the case play out against the dark like a never-ending movie. He, not Sam, would trace every soul who had ever lived at 204 Main Street, Grace Point. He would follow through on everything the forensic guys could come up with, spend hours interviewing everyone who had lived in the town fifty years before, and fill his notebook with details about dogs who had died five decades ago. And every step along the way, he'd have to listen to his partner gripe about a hopeless waste of time. But in the end—and he knew this so surely he'd be willing to bet Jenny's life on it—in the end, Milky Way Riley would be the one to identify the babies.

He sat up and retrieved the notebook from the seat. Restlessly he turned the pages, reviewing his notes. His gaze fell on one brief paragraph. "Here's something. Don't know why I took this down—can't have anything to do with this case."

Sam Riley opened his eyes.

"I guess I had babies on the brain. That's why I noticed it."

His partner waited.

"Just one of those funny coincidences. Here we are trying to find out what happened to four babies nearly fifty years ago and there's a case just over a year ago."

Riley's posture shifted slightly.

"July of '89. A kid was kidnapped. Eight months old. The case was never solved. Mother's name was Oliver—Sara Oliver. Ring a bell with you? She was vacationing here from Pennsylvania. A lot of talk about it being a nasty custody battle with the husband and speculation he had nabbed his own kid. Never solved. Like I said, nothing to do with the Barlow case." He shut the notebook again. "You ready for coffee?"

Riley stared out the window. "You got any connections in New Haven?"

"What do you mean?" Dan asked.

"Do you know anyone there? Anyone who can get some answers for us?"

"On the force?"

"Yeah."

"New Haven? Let's see. Yeah. There's one guy I went to school with. Last I knew he was working there. I don't know if he still is, but I could try."

"Call him."

"Why?"

"The Oliver baby? The one that was kidnapped?"

"Yeah?"

"Kind of a funny coincidence."

Dan knew his partner didn't believe in coincidence. "What's funny?"

"The kid was nabbed two months after Jake Barlow moved to town."

PART TWO

Bone of my bone, flesh of my flesh . . .

—Genesis 2:23

Chapter 8

Rosalina

Twisted streamers of purple and gold hung from the gym ceiling and decorated the walls, but crepe paper was not able to camouflage the lingering scent of sweat and sneakers or erase the echo of shrill whistles and youthful laughter. How many times had this scene been played out? The familiarity of it—the smell of young bodies, of stale sweat, of varnished floors and dusty books—comforted those who waited. All, that is, except Leona Santos.

She fumbled nervously with her purse. A drop of sweat formed on her forehead, and she wiped it away. Her fingers smelled like onions, and the odor mingled with the perfume of the corsage pinned to the lapel of her dress.

She leaned forward, restless with the waiting. Stains of perspiration crept out from the armpits of her good black dress, shiny from repeated ironings. She wanted to slip her feet out of her shoes—the toes pinched and the leather cut into the swollen flesh of her instep—but she was afraid she wouldn't be able to get them back on again. She had been on her feet all day, cooking for the party for her adored son Jackie—so much food to prepare, so many people to feed. That was the least of her worries. Cooking for the Last Supper would have been easier than what lay ahead. She looked at Victor; his eyes stared forward. His collar was crooked, but she knew he would be irritated if she reached over and straightened it, so she turned her attention back to her purse.

Victor hated secrets. What had she been thinking of to keep one such as this from him? In fact, just before they'd left the house, she'd almost told him. Fear had silenced her—and hope, too, that somehow her secret would turn out as wonderful as she had dreamed. Restlessly her hands fidgeted with the straps of her purse, then moved on to the clasp. *Click, click, click.* Over and over, unaware that she was doing it, she opened and closed the clasp. She felt sick with the waiting. *Click, click, click.* Maybe it wasn't too late. Victor had folded his program and tucked it, unread, in the pocket of his jacket. Furtively she unfolded her own folder, and her gaze fell without hesitation on Jackie's name. John Manos Santos. Her heavy finger retraced the letters. Her son. Her wonderful, talented Jackie. Victor would be proud of him tonight. Proud of him at last. Sighing, she refolded the paper and resumed fussing with her purse. *Click, click, click.* Would the procession ever begin?

The clicking was driving Victor crazy. He wished Leona would calm down. It was only a graduation, for Christ's sake. They had been through enough of them already. He couldn't remember her ever being as nervous as this before. Not even for Antone's. Victor remembered how proud he had been when his oldest had graduated. Christ, the boy had been a wild one. Always in trouble. A man, that one. Twice the man of either of his brothers.

Then Joaquin. Joaquin was all right. He worked hard and he was a good boy, not a man like Antone, but still a good boy. But Jackie . . . well, Jackie . . . Victor's hands tightened on his knees. It wasn't that Jackie was bad, exactly, just that he was weak. Sometimes, God forgive him, Victor felt it would have been better if Jackie had been a girl. Some of this he blamed on Leona. She spoiled the boy. Always had. Since the moment after his birth when he was brought to her to nurse, she'd treated him differently.

But Victor believed, too, that part of the weakness he saw in Jackie he had been born with. There had been three before him—Antone, Joaquin, and the baby who had died—and Victor believed that a man's sperm weakened with each child he sired. There were times when he felt fortunate that Jackie hadn't turned out to be an idiot, a mongoloid like Joe Ducks's youngest.

The sound of instruments tuning up flowed from behind the gym's closed double doors, and the audience turned expectantly. The wide doors opened and in one motion the people stood, each craning his neck to catch a glimpse of the one person he had come for. The orchestra entered first. Its members, a little flustered at all the attention focused on them, hurried down the center aisle and took their places on the left of the stage.

Leona panicked. Where was Jackie? Why wasn't he with the rest of the orchestra? Then she saw the empty seats—seven of them—and realized that the senior members would come in with their class.

Grinning self-consciously, the students took up their instruments and looked at their leader. He waited until he had their attention, then raised his arms. Raggedly they began to play the processional. Once again heads turned toward the rear. Members of the graduating class marched in, two by two. They stared ahead, their expressions strained, trying to look solemn, but they were unsuccessful in keeping the grins from their faces. The girls walked proudly in their long blue robes, as if they had practiced for this moment and would not ruin it now, but the boys shuffled in embarrassment, their shoulders hunched beneath the robes. They held their heads stiffly, as if afraid the tasseled caps would fall off.

Leona edged forward. There he was. *There he was.* Keeping her gaze fixed on him, she followed her son's progress as he walked to the stage with his classmates.

Leona again read the program, although she knew it from memory by now. She sighed impatiently, waiting. John Silva walked to the podium. She remembered when he was a toddler, in diapers. Now here he was a man, the president of his class. She settled in and tried to concentrate on his speech.

"Thank God I'm an American . . ." the boy began.

Click, click. Click, click. Her fingers moved quickly over the clasp. Her stomach hurt and her throat ached.

At last the boy finished and sat down, flushed from the applause. The next speaker was Ruth Costa. Leona didn't even try to listen. She looked at Jackie, but he was watching his classmate deliver her speech. He seemed calm enough. Wasn't he nervous? Not that Leona didn't have nerves enough for two of them.

Finally the girl took her seat. Leona didn't have to look at her program. Now that the moment was here, she wished for a few more minutes. Her palms were wet with sweat. Holding her breath, she waited for her son to stand.

Jackie took his time, as if he sensed the drama of the moment. The auditorium grew hushed. He crossed the stage and took his instrument up from one of the empty chairs in the orchestra. He took a deep breath, closed his eyes for a moment—only a moment—and then looked up. Proud parents turned their gaze from their own offspring to the slender boy, standing before them, so young, so vulnerable. Then he raised the violin to his shoulder. The conductor nodded. Leona murmured a prayer.

The first notes were faint, barely more than a whisper, as fragile as a filament of silk and so soft that the people bunched together on the bleachers at the rear of the gym were unsure whether or not he had begun. Then the music grew, magnifying, expanding, spinning out as the bow skimmed the strings in pure and confident strokes. The townspeople leaned forward. The beauty of the music filled the air, touched their skin, became part of their breath, part of them. They inhaled it, feeling its power in their brains and in their muscles and in their souls. Women wept, and men who had not cried at the funerals of their own fathers felt their throats thicken with tears.

Leona sank back in her chair, her fingers quiet on the clasp. Everything disappeared except her son and his music. She knew now that the sacrifice—pennies and nickels pinched from the food money, the stress and strain of keeping the secret safe for three long years—had all been worth it for this moment.

The notes and measures were etched in her memory. Hour after hour—time stolen when Victor was out fishing—the sound of Jackie's music would catch her during some household task. Then she would freeze, concentrating. While he practiced, she'd keep the beat with a slight nodding motion, her head his metronome. Sometimes she would soundlessly sing the words while he played. *Ave Maria, A-ve Ma-ri-a.* Other times she would just follow the notes.

Listening now, Leona knew that he had never been better. The music was at once tender and bold, triumphant and sorrowful. A prayer that spoke of passion and pain and the mysteries of the human heart. She feasted on her son. He was beautiful. His hair—*when had it grown so long?*—curled softly against his head. Only he was no longer her son. He was his music. It was as if God had sent them an angel this night. She closed her eyes, and her heart swelled with pride.

In shock, Victor could not believe his eyes. He forced himself to look up at the stage and at his son. When had they done this? *How* had they done this? His hands trembled.

He remembered the arguments, the weeks filled with bitter fights that ended with him shouting and Leona pleading. "No son of mine is going to play some goddamned girl's instrument," he'd sworn. "Let the boy play a trumpet if he's got to play anything." The betrayal cut so deep it hurt him to breathe.

Two rows in front of him Manuel Pina took out a white handkerchief and wiped his eyes. Behind him, he heard someone blowing his nose. His son was making people cry. *Jesucristo. Jesucristo.* Victor knew Rosalina and Dolores were crying, but he didn't dare look at Joaquin or Antone. He was afraid of what he might see. He looked at his wife. Rivers of tears rolled down her face, dropping off her jowls and onto the bosom of her black dress. He clenched his jaw. Her expression frightened and confused him. This stolid, ordinary woman, this plain and aging creature who smelled of onions and dying roses, wore a look of rapture he had never seen in their thirty years of marriage, not in church or in bed. She looked . . . she looked like some kind of goddamned saint.

He clenched his hands together to keep from striking her. It pained him to look at his son. *Christ, his hair is so long, he looks like a girl.* He ached for the song to end, for his son to sit down—his son who was sitting in the girls' section of the orchestra, who was playing a girl's instrument, his son who was making people cry. His son who had deceived him and mocked him with this deception. He was filled with fury and with shame.

Leona had exchanged her shoes for slippers. An apron covered her dress, and she felt like herself again. Her face was flushed, and she gave a practiced glance around the room, now crowded with aunts and uncles, neighbors and friends. Satisfied that everyone had a drink in hand and a plate piled high with food, she poured herself a tiny glass of port. After all, this was a celebration.

"Where is he? Where's Jackie? Where's my little brother who has surprised us with his secret?" Antone's voice was loud. He already had had too much to drink.

"He went to the beach with his class to set off firecrackers. He'll be here soon," she said. She knew tomorrow Dolores would arrive with sad eyes, Little Tony in her arms. But for tonight she blocked out her eldest son's drunkenness. For once Antone was not going to be the center of attention.

"Fireworks, the devil," Victor said as he crossed the room to pour another shot into Antone's glass. "If the kid's got any hair on his chest, he went there to drink. That's what you did, right, Tony?"

Victor's good cheer puzzled Leona. She had anticipated and feared his anger. But when he had seen and heard Jackie playing like an angel, Victor must have understood why she'd had to go against his wishes. This one time.

Tony laughed. "Me and Manny, we got so drunk, we puked for two days."

"Jackie isn't like that," she said.

Victor's face tightened, but before he could speak, the door opened and Jackie entered. No longer in his graduation robe, he had rolled his trousers up to his knees, and sand clung to his bare feet. He carried the violin case.

Leona went to him at once and embraced him. "You were wonderful," she whispered against his cheek. Her eyes shone with tears.

He hugged his mother in return. "Thank you, Momma. Thank you for everything." Then he looked over her shoulder and saw his father by the table, talking with Tony. Before he could cross to him, he was overwhelmed by adoring aunts and female cousins who kissed him noisily and proud uncles and male cousins who clapped his shoulder.

Jackie listened to the respectful compliments and returned the embraces, and all the while he waited. Still his father did not come, did not give a word of recognition or praise. The craving grew, winding through his stomach with fingers that burned and tightened.

Leona, too, watched and waited. So, she thought, it is not going to be so easy. Victor's pride has been wounded. Finally she could stand it no longer. On the pretense of passing a platter of sweet rolls, she approached her husband.

"Go to him," she said.

He did not answer.

"He is waiting for you, Victor."

"He has plenty of attention. Let him be satisfied with that." He could no longer conceal the anger, but he kept his voice low. This exchange was between husband and wife.

"But he is waiting for you. Can't you see that?" The smell of her rose corsage lodged in her throat, too sweet, cloying. "Go to him, Victor. Tell him how proud you are of him."

"Why?" The word was a cry from his heart. "You think I should be proud of him, proud that he played like a girl?"

"People cried when he played." Her voice filled with wonder. "Do you hear me, Victor? They wept when your son played."

"Leave me alone," he answered. "Take care of your guests and leave me the hell alone."

Watching the exchange, Jackie did not need to hear the words. Smiling, nodding politely to relatives, still clutching the handle of his violin case, he slipped from the room. Dolores and Rosalina were in the kitchen cutting cakes and talking. They called to him as he ran past, but he did not stop. Shaking so badly that he had to set the instrument case down, he gulped the night air. Then he sank down on the steps and dropped his head in his hands. *Why does he hate me? Why does he hate me so much?*

Behind him the screen door open and closed. "I

thought you might be hungry," Rosalina said. "I brought you some sandwiches." She set the plate on the step beside him and then, after a brief hesitation, she sat on the top stair. "The song was beautiful, Jackie."

He leaned his head back against the railing and stared up at the stars. He longed to be as distant as the constellations.

"We were all so proud of you."

His silence frightened Rosalina. "Jackie? Are you all right?" She wanted to draw him back down again to this old wooden porch and the steps with the peeling paint. "I mean it. It was just the most beautiful thing I've ever heard. It made me cry."

The sounds of the party flowed through the open window. Men's voices rose above the others: "Pete and Little Joe signed up today." "Army or Navy?" "Navy."

Rosalina shivered. Joaquin had never mentioned enlisting. Her husband never even talked to her about his friends who had joined up. Did he wish he was free? No, it couldn't be. He loved her and wanted to be with her. He did not want to join someone else's war. She turned back to Jackie.

She took a half sandwich from the plate and handed it to her husband's brother. "Here. Eat this. You must be hungry." To her surprise, he took it, then a second one. It made her feel better to see him eat. "Do you want something to drink? Punch or coffee?"

He shook his head. He wiped the crumbs from his fingers, and then he reached out for the case by his feet. He unlatched it and picked up the violin. The old wood shimmered like liquid in the silver light. He stroked the instrument, running the pads of his fingers lightly along the curves. "He didn't like it," he said. "He didn't like my playing." He was talking more to his violin than to Rosalina, but his hurt was so deep it washed over her.

"He liked it," she said. "I'm sure he liked it. Everyone did."

"He hated it."

"Don't pay any attention. What does he know?" Still, she lowered her voice, afraid the blasphemy would be heard through the open windows.

"It's always like that. Tony and Joaquin. Tony and Joaquin." He held the violin tighter. "That's all I ever hear. He wants me to be like them, and I can't."

She was uncomfortable with his shared confidences. The folds of her white cotton dress moved against her skin as she stretched her legs out on the steps. The tips of her shoes nudged the open case. "Would you play something for me?"

He shook his head and made a move to replace the instrument in its case.

She reached out and stopped him. The hardness of his forearm beneath her fingers surprised her. "Please."

Their eyes met. She was startled by the pain she saw in his eyes. She had thought of him as a child for so long, but in his face she saw a man's pain. It was the first time she had ever thought of Joaquin's younger brother as a man. "Please," she asked softly.

Slowly, Jackie lifted the violin. His left hand curled around its neck, and the fingers pressing against the strings were strong and confident. *It is as if he were making love.* She was immediately embarrassed by the thought. Then the music began. It was nothing like the piece he had played at graduation. This was sensuous, yearning, a song that spoke to the heavens and held the promise of summer and youth. How had he learned to play like that?

She felt the music fill her, and she wanted to sway with it, to stand and slip off her shoes and dance barefoot on the earth, to feel the damp grass against the soles of her feet and the summer air against her bare arms and shoulders and legs. She drew her legs up and hugged her knees close to her chest.

Abruptly the music changed, became darker. The notes churned in some hidden part of her. She was angry at her husband for reasons she couldn't understand. The yearning, followed so quickly by hunger and anger, confused her. What was wrong with her? Now she wanted Jackie to stop playing. She closed her eyes, trying to shut out his music. It held too much power, awoke too many feelings in her, feelings she neither understood nor welcomed. Hidden in the shadows beneath them and behind them was the face of Fenris Boak.

All the while, the music continued, rushing in like a tide held too long at bay.

Before the echo of the last notes had faded, Victor Santos's bellowing broke the spell. "Jackie!" he called.

Joy crossed the boy's face. "Did you hear that? He wants me now." The grin spread, transforming the shadow of the man he was becoming back to a young and eager boy. Still grasping the violin in his hand, he strode into the house.

Victor waited in the dining room. He motioned for Jackie to put the instrument down on the table and then passed a tumbler of wine to him. His gestures were overly precise, the careful moves of a man who has had too much to drink.

"Congratulations, Jackie."

Jackie beamed.

"Your brothers and I welcome you to the crew of the *Sea Bird*."

Victor raised his glass high, motioning with his free arm for the others to join him in the toast. He swallowed all the wine. A river of burgundy trickled down his chin. "Come on, boy. Drink up. Welcome aboard."

Leona's glass, like Jackie's, was untouched. She opened her mouth to speak, but Jackie cut her off.

"Thank you, Poppa, for asking me, but I'm not going to fish."

"Of course you're going to fish." Victor refilled his

glass. Purple drops of wine stained Leona's best lace tablecloth.

"I'm not going to fish. I have a job."

"You have a job?" Astonishment flooded Victor's face. "What the hell do you mean, you have a job? You went and got a job without asking me?" He spun to face Leona. "I suppose you knew this? Is this another of your goddamned *secrets*?" He spat the word out. "Well, forget the job," he ordered Jackie. "You hear me? You already got a job, with me—me and your brothers."

Uncertain smiles froze on the faces of the others.

Jackie flushed with embarrassment. "Can we talk about this later, Pa?"

"There's nothing to talk about. You're going to fish with me."

"No, Poppa, I'm not going to fish. I don't want to."

"What is it? It's not good enough for you, is that it?"

Leona reached a hand out, her fingers splayed, as if they could snare the words and stop them. "Don't, Victor—not now . . ."

"Keep out of this. You've done enough damage, you and your secrets. This is between my son and me." He turned to Jackie. "For as long as I can go back, all the Santos men have been fishermen. It's in our blood. It's what we know how to do. It's our history—you hear me, *our* history." His anger drew everyone into the room. Dolores came from the kitchen, Rosalina from the porch. Shamefaced and mute, as if his fury were directed at them, the others watched.

"Maybe that's because we never tried to do anything else." Jackie's eyes were dark with pleading. "You're a good fisherman, Poppa. You and Tony and Joaquin are all good. It's just like you say. It's in your blood. But it isn't in mine. I don't know why. Isn't it enough for you to have Antone and Joaquin with you?"

Antone stepped up to Victor and tried to put his

arm round his father. "Let him go, Pa. He's a good boy. So he don't want to fish—we don't need him anyway."

Victor shook the arm off. "Mind your own business, Tony. This has nothing to do with you. This is your fault, Leona. You were always too goddamned soft on him. Hiding behind my back, the two of you. Well, you've turned my son into a girl and I hope to hell you're happy."

"It's not her fault, Poppa. It's me. I just don't want to fish."

It was the first time any of his sons had dared to defy him. The boy's calmness enraged him. He raised his fist. Leona inhaled sharply, but Jackie did not flinch.

"Don't, Victor. Let him be." She was crying now.

Victor stared into his son's face. He saw defiance, but he saw too a flicker of something else: he saw he had fallen in his son's eyes. Pain bolted across his chest, so sharp he wondered for a moment if he was having a heart attack. He wanted obedience, and he wanted to wound his son as deeply as he had been hurt. With the same fist he seized the violin. The strings creaked in protest. Brandishing the instrument like a club, he repeated, "You're going to fish. You understand? Tomorrow morning, you're going to get up and you're going to fish with your brothers and me. You're going to be a *man*."

"No."

Victor fell back a step in confusion. His eyes clouded like those of a cornered bull. "You say no to me? You say *no* to your father?" The echo of his heartbeat pounded in his ears and filled his head with the sound of the surf crashing. "I'll teach you to say no to your father." He brought the violin down, swinging it against the doorjamb. The sound of splintering wood exploded in the silent room.

Spent, his face smooth and clear of anger, as if the

outburst had never taken place, he turned his back on his wife and son and left the room.

The boy knelt in the doorway and stared at the ruined violin. He did not cry. Moving slowly, as if there were more damage that could be prevented if only he was gentle, he reached out and carefully picked up a shard of varnished wood. Leona was weeping. Rosalina, too, wept. She clung to Joaquin, burying her face in his shoulder. At last Jackie held all the pieces. He cradled the broken body in his arms, hunching over it as if he were holding an infant. Leona moved toward him, but he ignored her and left the room.

Rosalina thought that forevermore—even in her dreams—she would hear the dry savage sound of the violin shattering. It sounded like the splintering of bones.

Chapter 9

The story of how Victor Santos had destroyed his son's violin spread swiftly throughout Grace Point. Over the weekend, it was told at the docks and on the decks of boats, told again in kitchens and across the tops of scarred barroom tables. As they rehashed the story, the fishermen grew indignant, taking on, as if it were their own, Victor's fury in the face of Jackie's insubordination. It became a cautionary tale: *This is what happens when sons defy fathers. This is what happens when women keep secrets from their men.*

In the recountings of that weekend, one aspect remained constant. When reciting the story, no one mentioned the sweetness and power of the boy's violin. It was as if already they had forgotten the moment during the high school graduation when Jackie's music had made them weep.

Victor looked over to where Leona busied herself at the sink. Usually she sat across the table from him and drank her coffee while he ate the breakfast she had prepared. It was a habit as old as their marriage, and he had come to count on this moment of predawn companionship as part of his daily ritual.

"Got any more syrup?" He needed her to look at him.

She crossed the kitchen without a word and refilled the pitcher. He flinched from the grief he saw etched on her face. He ached for her to sit down, but he couldn't ask her to. He was afraid she would refuse.

"Joe's boy signed up. Army. Fool thing to do." He sliced a triangle from the stack of pancakes and swiped it through the pool of syrup. He shoved the forkful into his mouth and began cutting another. "If Roosevelt does get us in a war—which he won't—the whole lot of them will be called up soon enough." He took a swig of coffee, washing down the cakes. "No sense in volunteering. Joe tried to tell that to the boy, but he wouldn't listen."

Her back offered no response. The punishing silence wore on.

He swallowed another mouthful, but the pancakes were beginning to sit heavily in his stomach. He pushed the plate away and reached for more coffee. Suddenly confused, he closed his eyes and rubbed his fingers over the scar tissue that corded his jaw.

He was a good husband—a damn good husband. She had no cause to carry on this way. He took care of her, always had. There'd been times in this town when a number of the kids didn't have shoes to wear to school. But by God, there was always food in Victor Santos's kitchen and shoes on his kids' feet; even when the fishing was lousy, he'd managed to bring money home. A couple of times, years ago when he'd been desperate, he'd even risked his neck rum-running, and she'd been glad enough then to take the cash without questions.

He drank his coffee and continued to catalog his virtues. He took a drink or two—who didn't?—but he didn't come to bed drunk every night like some husbands did. And Leona's bed was the only one he came to. Not that he hadn't had the opportunity, with more than one sad-faced widow. They were clever about it; they unnerved him with their cunning. They worked through his wife. "Josephine Perry needs some help putting up storm shutters," Leona would say to him as she cleared away the supper dishes on a cool October night. "I told her you'd be happy to help out." He'd start to refuse, but she'd cut him off. "She's all alone. It won't take you long, Victor. It's the least you can do." And so he'd take his hammer and head for the Perry house. Working quickly, he'd put up the shutters. Then—he could count on it—Josephine Perry would offer him a drink. She would accent the invitation with a coy motion, a young girl's gesture that looked foolish from one her age. He'd always stayed clear of the Josephine Perrys. There were too many widows in Grace Point. He'd see the hunger in their eyes, feel the desperation in their fingertips, and know they were nothing but trouble.

Then there were the summer women, as much a part of July and August as high-course tides, crowded streets, striped bass, and blues. Half the men he knew slept with them. When he tied up at the end of the day, they would be waiting at the pier, bending over to ask about his catch. From where he stood on the deck of his boat, his eyes were level with their bare legs. Their voices were gay and flirtatious, not winter-widow sad, but when he looked up he saw the same hunger. Still, he found these women tempting in a way the widows could never be. He saw something exotic in their cotton shorts and their sandals and the toenails they'd painted bright pink.

Oh, he'd looked at them, all right. You can't blame a man for looking, can't blame him for drinking them in, or for dreaming.

How he'd dreamed about them! He'd filled his life with dreams about these smiling women with their soft, tanned bodies and long legs that went on forever; dreamed about their perfect little toes, toenails gleaming wetly like seashells from a foreign land. He imagined doing things with these women he could never do with Leona. He dreamed about licking the honeyed curve of a high-arched foot, tasting the faint saltiness of summer mingling with the sweetness of woman's flesh; dreamed about taking one of those tender, rose-tipped toes into his mouth and sucking on it like it was a nipple. These dreams fueled a lust that he took to his bed on heavy summer nights and drove him to mount Leona's thick body with an urgency he never felt in winter. But he was always faithful; he was proud of that.

In the silent kitchen, the power of these memories aroused him. Looking at Leona's back, Victor regretted all those opportunities lost. Was this what being a good husband finally got him? Forty years down the drain because of a goddamned fiddle. That was what lay at the bottom of her silence, her righteous, punishing silence.

She had no right to make him feel guilty. After all, she was the one who had joined with Jackie against him. It was her fault. By God, it was time she learned who was the boss. The muscles of his thighs bunched, and his hands tightened into fists.

At that moment, they heard the sound of feet upstairs. The footsteps crossed the ceiling. Leona paused in her work and closed her eyes, as if in prayer, and then busied herself setting another place at the table. Her gaze passed over Victor's plate, the breakfast half eaten, but she said nothing. Now he averted his eyes.

He had not spoken to his son for two nights, but he could not believe the boy's defiance would continue. Odds were he was not going to work for Dominus Roderick at the bakery. Odds were he'd be joining his brothers on the *Sea Bird*. He waited with growing dread for his son to appear. These were not odds he would like to lay money on.

Victor felt Leona looking at him. He raised his head and their eyes locked. An entire conversation passed between them in that instant, and the fight went out of him. *If anything happens to my Jackie,* her eyes vowed, *if anything happens to him on that boat, I swear, as God is my witness, I'll never forgive you. Do you hear me, Victor Santos? I swear, I'll never forgive you.*

It was this promise, shining out from her eyes, hardening her mouth, which, more than anything, told Victor that even if his son gave in and went fishing, he had lost.

He spat the words in a fury of defeat.

"Tell him he's to work in the bakery." He shoved his chair back so hard it toppled over. "I don't want him on my boat. You understand? He hasn't the heart or guts for it. He isn't man enough. There's no place on my boat for one like him."

She came to him then, and the gratitude in her eyes shamed him.

"Thank you, Victor," she said. She reached a hand toward him, but he ignored it. Now his silence was as cruel as hers had been.

Fenris Boak was not in the studio. Rosalina knew it the instant she entered the room, sensed it even without looking around. She felt as if she had been holding her breath all morning and now could breathe freely again. Her mouth softened. "Thank you, Virgin Mary. Blessed Mary, Mother of God, thank you," she whispered.

She slipped into a pose at once so natural and attractive that Ben nodded approvingly. Without even stopping to adjust the line of her arm or the fold of her scarf, he began pacing the room, watching as her face materialized on the canvases of his students.

I was being silly. He's a writer, not an artist. I probably won't ever have to see him again. But as the class wore on, she grew edgy. Twice Ben spoke to her and she did not hear him. She jumped when he touched her shoulder.

"Daydreaming, Little Rosa?" he asked kindly.

I will forget about him, she willed. *He has nothing to do with me. He is rude and conceited, and if he bothers me again, I will tell Joaquin.* But at the break, she asked Ben Bayes in a voice she tried to make casual, "Is your friend still here?"

"Fenris?" He looked surprised. She rarely showed any interest in the studio or the artists. "Fenris is here for the season. He is working here, writing a history of the art colony here at Grace Point." The big man studied her face, and there was an expression in his eyes that made her wish she could take back her question. She felt she had given part of herself away.

"Little Rosa," Ben continued, "you are a very good model and a sweet girl. You are beautiful. Like the *Rosa rugosa*—the beach rose, heh? And maybe, like the beach rose, you are untamed. Growing in sandy soil. Yes," he said almost to himself, "he would see that." His voice became gentle, and she was reminded of the way her father used to be. "Fenris is an old friend. He's a good writer, and I have known him for a long, long time." He paused, as if weighing whether to say more. The break was over and the students were returning to their easels. Ben adjusted her shawl with his powerful, paint-stained hands, moving the folds so they fell softly around her shoulders, and he spoke as if to a child. "Forget Fenris, Little Rosa. He is my friend, but sometimes he is not a nice man."

Rosalina's cheeks stung as if she had been slapped. She was furious with herself, furious with Ben for the rebuke. What must he think of her? She looked around, then realized that running would only make things worse. She would pretend the conversation had never taken place. After all, Ben knew she was married. And if Fenris Boak did come in, she swore savagely, she would not so much as look at him. She spent the rest of the class thinking of Joaquin's favorites of all the foods she cooked.

"Good-bye," she called to Ben as she left the studio,

her tone carefully casual. "See you on Friday." Then, just to show that she had totally forgotten about their conversation, that she held no grudges, she added, "And Poppa said for you to stop by the bakery and pick up some loaves of bread."

Now she would go home and cook one of those meals for Joaquin. She would buy a bottle of wine. She would set the table with the two crystal glasses her father had given them on their wedding day. And even though he was tired and often did not see the nice little things she did, he would notice the wine and goblets. "What's so special?" he would ask. "Every day is special with you, Joaquin," she would answer. And then he would kiss her, and she would laugh and twist away because the day's growth of beard would scratch her face. But her eyes would hold a promise for later.

As she walked down the stairs from the studio, she began to plan. The meal *would* be special. She would even steal a little from the portrait money hidden in her dresser and buy two chops. She would fry them with port and apples, and the fragrance of fruit and sweet wine would greet him even before he opened the door.

She lingered in the dressing room and took her time combing out her hair. She started to braid it and then decided to leave it brushed out, the weight of it full and heavy on her shoulders. She heard Ben's students leave, their chatter echoing in the loft as they left. She listened as the artists who lived in the Sail Loft called out and made plans. Some were heading for the beach; others agreed to meet at Willie's for a drink. You better go too, she told her reflection in the smudged mirror. You've got to run home and get some money if you want to buy two perfect chops before the market closes. Her reflection stared back steadily. A nimbus of hair glowed like a dark halo around her head. The building echoed with the silence.

She left the dressing room and went down the stairs. Her feet fell softly on the treads. The first floor was dark. The writers' studios were here. She looked around guiltily, as if she were trespassing on forbidden territory. She felt lightheaded, dreamy, hypnotized. The door to the last studio was open, and she walked toward it as if magnetized. He'd be with the others at Willie's. He'd just forgotten to switch off his light.

Once when she was eight, she and Isabella had sneaked back into the church after Saturday-night confessions and hidden beneath a pew. They had wanted to see how Father Jim acted when he didn't know anyone was watching. They had crouched in the dark for an hour, until their knees hurt and their feet fell asleep. There was a delicious sense of naughtiness and risk about the adventure—and a feeling that a secret might be revealed. But in the flickering candlelight, all they saw the priest do was pray before the altar. She remembered wondering if his feet also were asleep, but he had not moved. She felt that dangerous naughtiness again now.

As she approached the doorway, she heard a woman's laugh. The sound paralyzed her. Fenris Boak looked up at her in that instant.

The blond model's blouse was unbuttoned. Rosa's eyes fell to the girl's exposed breasts. The model saw her now, but she made no move to cover her nakedness. The girl's chest was pale and spread with freckles. Her breasts were full and the nipples huge and erect. The areolas were pink, a rich, rosy tint, as if they had been rubbed with rouge.

Fenris Boak left the model and crossed to the door. He did not hurry, and the girl did not move to cover herself. Before he closed the door, he stood for a moment and looked at Rosalina. And then he smiled.

She spun and ran from the building. The sun was harsh on her eyes and she raced down the street. Unseeing, unhearing, she ran. She did not remember running home. Sweat coated her back and ran down her ribs. She felt soiled, corrupt, as if she, not the model, had been naked before his eyes. She could have wept with the shame she had carried into her home.

Her bathing suit, still damp from her last swim, hung in the side yard, and she jerked it from the line. It smelled faintly sour. Standing in the kitchen, she stripped with hands that trembled. She changed into the suit quickly, yanking it over her hips.

Barefoot, unmindful of the stones that bruised her instep, she ran to the bay. The water was so shallow that when she dove in, she struck her knee on the sand. After a while, her shoulder and thigh muscles knotted with the effort, but she did not stop. Her hair, unbound, clung to her neck and shoulders and face, plastering her skin like brown dulse. She swam until she could no longer think, as if exhaustion could clear her brain.

She was far out from shore when she saw the object floating toward her. At first she thought it was an overturned dory or a piece of furniture, something nearly as large as a kitchen tabletop. It was almost close enough to touch before she saw that it was a sea turtle, bloated and long dead. Recoiling, she went under, swallowed a mouthful of bay water, surfaced, and spat it out. It seemed to taste of disease. She needed to float, to catch her breath and build up some strength, but she did not want to stay near the reptile. It was so close now that she could see rust-colored barnacles on its carapace, the ancient, wrinkled head, opaque eyes protruding. Then she envisioned, as clearly as if it too floated nearby, the body of the drowned woman the fishermen had snared in their nets a week ago. Fear lodged in her breast like a cramp. Her sobs and ragged breathing mixed in with the sound of the surf. Her calves knotted, but she swam through the pain. Fear swam with her, but it was not fear of death. Giving herself over to the dark suddenly felt very familiar, as if she had done it before. It was some other nameless terror that drove her toward the shore.

She was ten feet from the water's edge when her

feet touched bottom. She sank down on her hands and knees and crawled the last distance. In that way, like a beaten dog, she struggled from the sea. Her limbs trembled so badly she knew it would be a long time before she could trust her legs to carry her. She lay on the beach until her hair, sticky with salt, had dried in the sun and the nausea had dimmed to a memory. Her body felt as if it had suffered an electric shock.

Her bedroom was cool and dark. She peeled off her suit, leaving it at her feet in a damp pool. Her reflection shimmered in the dresser mirror. She walked closer, watching as she approached herself. Her knee was bruised where she had struck it on the bottom of the bay. She reached a hand up and touched the pale, untanned skin of one breast. *Joaquin and me, Joaquin and me.*

She brushed a forefinger lightly over her nipple. She had never noticed how small her nipples were. Like a child's. *Joaquin and me, Joaquin and me. Joaquinandmejoaquinandmejoaquinandme.*

"I am never going to the studio again," she whispered. "I don't care what Ben Bayes says. Never again." She stared at her own scared face, then shivered and turned from the mirror. Her nipples were too dark. Too small.

Chapter 10

Zoe

Questions surfaced in the middle of the night. Zoe rolled over and looked at Jake. The specter of New Haven would not go away. It was as if the ghosts of the babies hidden in their attic, reawakened, would let no other phantom rest. *New Haven.* Distance and time had helped, but could she and Jake ever completely recover from the damage done there? How much had already healed between them, and how much was simply a veneer that would not bear testing? Finally—and this question was one she had struggled with for months—could she ever totally trust Jake again?

Could she learn to truly forgive him? And if so, would her forgiveness be granted for the sake of Adam and Emily, or simply because she was afraid of being alone? Sometimes, whatever the reasons, forgiveness seemed too much to expect of her. Beside her, Jake slept on, oblivious. When she closed her eyes, memories of New Haven returned.

The barbecue on the Stuarts' patio was at that stage where words grew soft at the edges, consonants blurred by gin and tonics. Men took off their sports jackets, and several of the women slipped out of their heels and padded about barefoot on the sun-warmed flagstones.

Jake didn't want to leave. Zoe, ankles swollen and back aching, waited until after Alice Stuart had served pie, then, pleading exhaustion, asked him if they could leave. She saw his mouth tighten with disappointment, but he left without protest. Too tired to talk, Zoe rested her head against the back of the seat while he drove home. She couldn't remember being this exhausted during her first pregnancy. Jake drove silently, and she was relieved.

At the apartment, she checked on Emily while he paid the sitter. She was asleep before he returned from driving Laurel home. She didn't hear him come into their bedroom, didn't wake when he got in the bed.

In the morning, he brought her a cup of tea before he left for school. Then he tucked in Emily, fed and dressed, beside her with some toys. Zoe smiled up at Jake. He was such a good and loving father. At times like this she could imagine an entire brood of children. He bent and kissed them. "My women," he said in a possessive John Wayne drawl that made her smile and Emily giggle. Beneath the bedclothes, she felt the heat of Emily's small body warming her. She was the luckiest woman in the world.

The phone rang soon after. She remembered later the chill that had gripped her as she listened to the detective reporting Laurel's complaint. She reached Jake at school, before he had begun to teach his first class. He came home immediately.

"She's lying," she began before he had time to speak.

"Yes," he'd replied.

"Why?" Her voice cracked with anger. "Why would she lie?"

"I don't know."

"There was that business last fall. Remember? She had a friend over when she was sitting and they had a beer."

He said nothing.

"Remember?" she pressed. "You lectured her, but we never told her mother. Could it have been that?

Could she have resented that all these months?"

Jake removed his glasses and polished the lenses with the corner of his shirt.

"We'll have to fight this, of course," she continued. "Maybe we should have a lawyer here when the police arrive."

He fiddled with his glasses.

His calmness in the face of her own growing worry unnerved her. "Well, aren't you going to say anything? Aren't you even angry?"

Jake sank in his chair. His words, when he spoke, were barely audible. "Zoe? Zoe, we have to talk. . . ."

A bolt of fear sliced her chest. If she could have stopped his words then, she would have.

"Laurel wasn't . . . she wasn't lying."

"No." The denial was instinctive.

"Zoe, listen. . . ."

She was sick to her stomach, too stunned to cry. Jake stood and reached for her, but she recoiled.

"Zoe, please. Listen."

She fled the room. When the police arrived, she stayed upstairs in their bedroom. She did not come down until long after they had left.

It was a sleepless night. After her tears were spent, she lay with her arms wrapped around her swollen belly, her mind going round and round until her head ached. What would she do? Leave Jake? Take Emily and leave? And go where? Home to her mother? She had escaped from her mother's home once. She could not return, no matter what. She felt heavy, weighed down by sorrow and pregnancy and fear. Pregnant. How could she do it on her own? But how could she stay with Jake? The thought was abhorrent. She couldn't stand to look at him.

At dawn she fell into a fitful sleep. When she woke, she felt old, changed. Neither marriage nor the act of childbirth had robbed her of her girlhood, but it was lost now.

She faced Jake at breakfast. "Tell me what happened."

"Now?"

"I want to know."

"God, Zoe. I . . ."

She could see he had not slept. He was pale, unshaven, with lines drawn deep from his nose to his lips. She saw then what he would look like when he was old, and for one flickering moment she felt herself softening. This weakness frightened her, and when she spoke, her voice was harsh.

"Tell me all of it so I'll know what I have to deal with."

"I," not "we." He noticed her choice of words, and some frail hope he had brought into the kitchen with him died. He sank down into a chair. "It's no use talking about it," he said in a monotone. "You couldn't understand."

"Don't." She heard the scorn in her voice. "Don't tell me I *couldn't understand.*"

"Zoe, please . . ."

She stared at him coldly.

"I love you, Zoe. I love Emily. You have to know I do. You have to know that."

His hands were spread, fingers splayed, on his knees. Unbidden, the image of them on Laurel Blake's breasts flashed in her mind. A wave of something akin to hatred swept over her. "Then tell me how the hell you could feel up our baby-sitter if you were so filled with love for me. Tell me *that,* because I don't understand any of this."

"It just happened. I was driving her home and she was talking about her mother. Her mother drinks." He looked up as if asking for help with the story, but her face was stony. He rubbed his eyes.

"So what happened?"

"She was just talking. She told me about her boyfriend. They had had a fight. Well, I don't know . . . she just looked so small and so lonely and hurt. She looked at me and, honestly, I really don't know what happened, Zoe. I just wanted to comfort her. I thought she was going to cry. So I pulled over the car and gave her my handkerchief and I don't know how it happened, but I kissed her."

Zoe couldn't breathe. She wanted him to stop now.

"I kissed her and . . . and she didn't pull away. She kissed me back, and I touched her breast. That's all. I swear that's all, Zoe."

"That's *all*?" Her chest hurt.

"I can't explain, Zoe. It was all so confusing. I didn't mean anything by it. I'd been drinking at the Stuarts'. Maybe that had something to do with it."

"Please. Don't blame what happened on the party. It's as bad as lying."

"I was lonely, Zoe. That's all I know. I was as lonely and fucked up as Laurel looked, and it just happened."

"So you were lonely and fucked up. What's that supposed to mean? That you couldn't talk to me?" She drew her breath in sharply. "Was it sex? Is that what this is about? Is it because I'm six months pregnant and we haven't had sex? Is that why?"

"It isn't sex."

"Well, what the hell is it, then? Explain it to me, because I just don't understand a goddamn thing about it."

"I can't explain it because I don't understand it myself. It's like a nightmare. It just happened," he repeated.

"Things don't *just happen,* Jake."

"Well, this did. There was one moment when I was alone with someone who was vulnerable and lonely, and suddenly I realized I was lonely, too. I just wanted to touch someone. To be held."

"I would have held you. What was wrong with asking me?"

His eyes were dark with pain and he didn't answer.

"What? You couldn't ask me? So somehow this is my fault now?"

"No. It's not your fault," he said. "God, Zoe. I love you. I'd do anything not to hurt you. Anything."

They began the horror of learning how to navigate through a nightmare. How to go on.

It had been Zoe, not Jake, who had gone to Laurel's mother and pleaded that the charges be dropped. She stood before the woman, conscious that her pregnancy helped her cause.

Two days later, she had miscarried. Her doctor told her that it had nothing to do with the stress she was experiencing, and she tried to believe him.

And then they had moved. Zoe had insisted. They could begin again somewhere else—away from New Haven and the memories. Her mother owned an investment property Zoe had never seen. Swallowing her pride, she asked Tory if she and Jake could rent or buy that house. She faced her mother's scorn and listened to her deride Jake. In the end she got her way. They moved to Grace Point. But the healing had not begun with the move. It began with Adam's birth. Only then did the pain in her chest go away.

Gradually the memories faded. The bookstore they bought proved a success. Fixing up their new home brought them together. Watching her husband care for Emily and Adam warmed her. Jake was a loving father who adored their children. And if his boundless common sense and always-logical mind occasionally irritated her, his steadiness grounded her and made her feel safe. And, at times, it was almost possible to believe that New Haven had never happened.

* * *

So they could learn to forget, but could she learn to forgive, Zoe asked herself again. Beside her, Jake still slept.

She slid out of bed and crossed to the window. The moon cast a ribbon of silver on the bay waters, and she shivered in its icy light. Weary, she rested her forehead against the cold glass. Just as she closed her eyes, she caught a shift in the alley below. She stiffened.

Her vision adjusted to the night darkness, and she scanned the shadows until she picked out the figure. In the dark, his features were not clear, but she *knew* who it was: the old fisherman with one arm. Her fingers tightened on the windowsill.

"Jake?"

He did not wake.

Her whisper became more urgent. "Jake?"

She chanced a quick look toward the bed, but her husband slept soundly. "Jake, damn it, wake up."

His deep, heavy breathing did not vary.

She looked down on the alley. The shadows were flat, lifeless. Whoever had been keeping vigil by her home was gone. To make sure, she waited until her legs grew stiff and her feet chilled. When she crawled back into bed, Jake reached for her in his sleep. His body was warm. For an instant she thought about waking him, telling him, but Jake would think she had been dreaming.

She woke crying.

"What is it? Zoe, honey? What's wrong?" Jake smoothed the tears from her cheeks with his thumb. As quickly as he wiped them away, more tears streamed down her face. He tried to wrap his arms around her, to cradle her against his chest, but she pushed him away. *Adam was in terrible danger.* As she woke, she understood this with every cell in her body.

"It's Adam, Jake." She was so afraid it hurt to

speak. "Something's happened to him." She rushed toward the nursery.

She flipped on the overhead light in Adam's room, but knew even before looking that he was gone. She heard a low, terrible moan, unaware it came from her lips, and stared at the empty crib.

Jake brushed by her and bent over the crib. She closed her eyes, fighting the panic that threatened to overtake her.

"It's all right." Jake's voice brought her back. "He's here. He's all right." He picked up their son and carried him to her. "See. He's all right. You were having a nightmare."

"I thought he was gone," she whispered, still chilled with the terror that had consumed her.

"He crawled up near the bumper pads. That's why you didn't see him. He's fine. See."

She took her son and held him close. She looked down at his tiny face, checking it carefully. He was wet, and she carried him to the changing table. He woke and stretched his chubby legs out while she put a dry diaper on him, but he did not cry. She cradled him and rocked him until he fell asleep again, and only then did she return him to his crib and tuck the blankets around him. She waited a moment to make sure he was really sleeping, and then let Jake lead her back to their room. In bed, he held her and gently rubbed her back and shoulders in slow, soothing circles.

"Are you okay now? Do you think you'll be able to sleep?"

"I'm fine," she said.

"You sure?"

"Really. I'm okay."

But she could not forget the sight of Adam's empty crib.

Chapter 11

Agnes Farmer woke in the middle of the night. Her neck was stiff; the faint, familiar bite of the beginning of a bursitis attack nipped at her right shoulder. The air in the bedroom was cold. Now, sitting up, she could feel the draft sweeping in from the hall. "Cripes," she said.

She reached out to turn on the lamp on her nightstand, and the pain in her shoulder sent a ripple of shock the length of her arm. It was times like this she missed Charlie. If he'd been here, she would have nudged him awake, let him bring her aspirin and the heating pad for her shoulder, maybe a cup of warmed milk to help her get back to sleep. And he would have gone to see the old lady. But Charlie had been dead twelve years now. She'd have to do it.

Moving gingerly, she switched on the light and got out of bed. She pulled on her robe, belting it snugly, and slid her feet into her slippers. Even the tip of her nose felt cold. "Cripes," she said again.

The hall was colder. Agnes hunched against the chill, absently rubbing her shoulder to ease the ache. "Senile old fool," she muttered. "Senile old fool. This is the last time. I can't be having bursitis all winter because of her. I'll have to get rid of her." Building up a head of steam, she approached the shed room at the end of the hall.

The room had been Charlie's idea. He had added it on to the side of their house one spring, and every summer after that they had rented it to college girls who spent the season in Grace Point working as waitresses—until the day she'd come home from her job at the Laundromat and found Charlie in bed with one of them. A redhead. He'd always been a fool for redheads. Not really his fault, the way the brazen little chippie threw herself at him. As far as Agnes knew, it was the one and only time in their marriage that he'd slipped. Better than a lot of men. Even so, the shed room stayed empty after that. Handy for storage. The year Charlie died, Grace Manor burned down, and they'd had to find housing for all the old people. Heaven knows she needed the extra money, so she'd taken in one of them. Twelve years now, old Birdy had been staying in the shed room. Lord, how time flew by.

She wasn't much trouble. Ate like a bird—that was why Agnes called her Birdy. And Lord knows, she was quiet. No radio or television. She just liked to sit by the window and knit. A knitting fool, old Birdy. Each Saturday morning—string bag clutched in her hand—she would toddle to the thrift shop and, for a quarter or two, buy moth-eaten sweaters, pawed-over knit hats with holes in them, castoffs from old women just like herself, women who had died and whose families couldn't bear to throw out their clothes—no matter how tattered—and so brought them by the bagful to the thrift shop.

Agnes was amazed at the sentimentality of people. They believed that throwing out the clothes—nearly rags, some of them—of the departed was in some way dishonoring them. Not her. Not Agnes Farmer. When Charlie had gone, she took one suit, his best one, his only one, and brought it to the funeral home for him to be buried in. The rest she'd boxed up and brought to the dump. Her niece had helped her. "What about Uncle Charlie's shoes?" the girl had asked. "The dump," she'd replied. Who on earth, she had wondered, would want to wear a dead man's shoes? When she went, she hoped they'd just sweep through her drawers and closets and get rid of it all. The thought of someone else wearing her blue pantsuit, or one of her slips, for heaven's sake, gave her the creeps. So everything of Charlie's had gone. Except for one shirt. She had saved a white, long-sleeved shirt worn soft with age and washings. Even now, she didn't know why she had set it aside, but it still hung at the rear of her closet.

Birdy loved the thrift shop. Each week she would return home to her shed room with the string bag stretched full of the cast-off clothes of dead women. The next day, she would sit in her chair and patiently unravel the garments, rolling the salvaged yarn into balls of faded maroon, gray, navy blue, or a speckled combination of the three, occasionally joined by a deep purple or green skein. Then she'd knit. Booties. Tiny hats, skullcaps for little heads. Doll-sized sweaters. Blankets, small squares worked in a pattern marred by holes and irregularities where tired eyes and hands had missed a stitch or an elderly mind had lost count of a row. Babies clothes fashioned out of the colors of old women.

In her own way, Agnes thought, old Birdy was rather sweet. The only problem was the cats. She took in stray cats, tried to hide them—under the bed, next to the stacks of booties and sweaters and carriage robes, in the closet, even in the bureau drawers.

Usually Agnes caught them right away, but sometimes Birdy kept them hidden until the smell wafted down the hall. On damp days, the whole end of the hall stank with the old lady's cats. Agnes would rant and scold and threaten to throw the old lady out, but then Birdy would cry like a child and promise never to do it again, and Agnes just didn't have the heart. Even at her most exasperated, she had to laugh at the irony of a Birdy bringing cats to her nest.

The cats were less likely to get Birdy evicted than her need for fresh air. Not just fresh—cold. The old lady loved the cold. It was a miracle, really, that she hadn't caught pneumonia.

Agnes pushed the door open. The room was frigid, so chilly she felt it through her robe and nightgown, and the ache in her shoulder deepened.

The old woman was sitting in the dark. In the moonlight that streamed through the open window, Agnes saw that her eyes were closed. "Birdy," she shouted.

Birdy opened her eyes. She stared out into the night. Agnes crossed the room and closed the window, banging it shut with more force than necessary. Her shoulder shouted its protest. The old lady took no notice. She continued to stare out, lost in a world far beyond Agnes's reach. In spite of the cold, she wore only a nightgown, thin from use, and her feet were bare. Gnarled and contorted by bunions and corns, with toenails yellow and ridged, they were the feet of a poor and aged woman.

Crazy old fool, Agnes thought. "Land sakes alive, dearie," she said aloud. "You'll catch your death, sitting there that way with the window wide open."

The old woman didn't respond.

"Woke me up, the cold did. Probably get another bursitis attack and you'll probably get double pneumonia. And then what? Answer me that." She raised her voice, as if the old woman were deaf, which she wasn't. The old fool might be crazy, but her hearing was as sharp as Agnes's. Still, she leaned in and hollered at her. "What are you doing sitting up all night in the dark like this? Someone see you sitting like this, they're as like to think you're crazy as not," she shouted at the silent old woman. Agnes had a mean streak, and it surfaced in the face of Birdy's obstinacy. "You know what they'd do, don't you. Take you off to the nuthouse! Is that what you want?" She was rewarded by a flash of fear in the old lady's eyes. Satisfied, she backed off. "No. No, of course it isn't. So here now. Let's get you in bed. Imagine, sitting here like that in the cold. Here.

Into the bed. That's a dearie." She maneuvered the woman into her bed and pulled the blankets over her.

I swear I don't know why I keep her on, she said to herself as she returned to her own room. *Maybe it's time I sent her out. Let someone else worry about her.* She had relatives somewhere, some other state, or so Agnes had heard—a daughter or a niece. All well and good for them, far away, not having to take a bit of care of the old woman. Young people were like that now. Happy as not to have someone else take care of their old ones. Couldn't be bothered with them. Well, maybe it was time they took some responsibility. See how they liked her living with them. Her with her cats and icy night air chilling the whole house. Course it was the beginning of the month. The old woman's social security check would be coming in any day now. That sure took the sting out of it.

In the shed room, the old woman called Birdy lay quietly, straining to hear the sound of Agnes closing her door, the creak of her mattress as the landlady climbed into bed. She waited a few extra minutes to be sure it was safe. Then she got out of bed. She went to the window and opened it. Just a crack this time—not enough to bring Agnes back. She pressed her cheek against the cold glass pane. She *liked* the cold. She was used to it.

She sat back in her chair by the window, waiting. Silence pressed against the darkness in her head, but she was patient. Gradually, the song returned. She hummed snatches of it—pieces of a tune from long, long ago. At first only the notes came through, for she could not remember the words. If she hummed it long enough, the words would come.

She rocked slightly from side to side with the rhythm that rolled in her head. *Baby.* That was one of the words. It was coming now. She remembered that word.

Cradle. That was another one. *Rock my sweet baby. Rock my sweet baby.* What was next? *On the treetop.* Yes, that was it, but now the darkness started creeping in on the edges of her brain. *The cradle will . . . The cradle will . . .* She swayed faster and faster. *The cradle will . . .* Faster and faster she moved in the chair, no longer rocking, but jerking back and forth. A faint moaning sound escaped from her lips. *The cradle will . . . The cradle will . . .*

. . . fall.

Then her brain went black.

Chapter 12

Rosalina

Dom Roderick got up from his rocker by the window and switched on a lamp. He crossed to the kitchen and, using just the light that leaked in from the living room, refilled his glass with port. It was his fifth drink, and his hand was unsteady. Wine stained the already soiled tablecloth. His apartment was over his bakery. There were five rooms: a small kitchen, a storeroom, two bedrooms—one just an alcove off the kitchen, really—and a living room that fronted the main street. A musty odor hung in the air, the fusty smell that clings to the place of a person living alone and not particular about cleaning.

Usually he limited himself to four drinks each night, but tonight he was restless. The baker could not stop thinking about Jackie. He had only hired the boy because Rosalina pestered him into it. Aptitude for baking, he knew, was not something one could be taught. One had to be born with the ability, and he had no desire to baby-sit an apprentice who thought these things could be learned. Dom also possessed an alchemist's paranoia about the tricks of his craft and was hesitant about having someone else share his kitchen. No one, not even Rosa, knew the secret of using whiskey in *trutas,* or the proportion of butter and lard in the *boles de folha* that made them so meltingly rich.

On the boy's first day at the bakery, Dom had treated him poorly, hoping he'd quit. He'd made Jackie wash the pots and pans and then, saying they were still greasy, had thrown them in the sink again. He had accused the boy of spoiling a batch of cookie dough by putting in too much salt, even though this was not true. The boy accepted all this with sweet-tempered silence. At the end of the day he had given Dom money to pay for the batter he had ruined with too much salt. Dom was shamed.

By the end of one week, he'd begun to tell himself that it had been his own idea to hire Jackie. Although he would never let on to the boy, he was pleased with his work. Like Dominus Roderick himself, Jackie had no use for conventional measuring tools and added ingredients with his hands, sifting with his fingers pinches of spices and powders. He didn't need to glance at the clock to know when the sweet dough was ready to punch down; he seemed to know as if the dough were part of his own flesh. He was a hard worker, too. He did more than his share, washing sinkfuls of pans and bowls, scrubbing the countertops cleaner than they had been in months, sweeping up the veil of flour from where it lay on the floor, all without complaint.

Dom began to take pride in Jackie's skill, in the little changes he made in their products. Pastry leaves adorned pie crusts; glazes shone on the breads; intricate swirls and flowers decorated the cakes. The *trutas* had never been flakier; the *sprecíones,* never moister; the *suspiros,* never more delicious. All of this made Dom warm to the boy. But there was something else as well.

Years before, when Anna Roderick left, Dom retreated from the rest of Grace Point, dividing his time between this apartment and the bakery kitchen below. The isolation suited him. It became a refuge from the pity he saw reflected in the eyes of others, as well as a form of self-punishment. In the presence of Jackie's mute sorrow, his own long-buried grief surfaced once again. Dom had not gone to the high school graduation, but he had heard the story about how Victor Santos had destroyed Jackie's violin. He thought Victor Santos was a fool. If he had a boy, he would want him to be like Jackie. All his life Dom had wanted a son. He had wondered, in the first tortured weeks after Anna was gone, if things might have been different if they had had a son instead of a daughter.

Thoughts of his daughter brought only painful memories. Once, in a time he could barely recollect now, he had loved Rosalina and taken joy in her beauty, which so closely mirrored her mother's. All that—all fatherly pride and delight—had hardened and died when Anna had left. He grew silent around his daughter, watching, watching, alert for the signs that she was like her mother in more than appearance.

Dom poured another inch of wine into his glass and switched off the table lamp. Like a playgoer attending the theater—or a dark recording angel—he returned to his seat by the window as he did every night. Sounds floated up on the heavy summer air. Music from the New York Cafe, drunken arguments from the Sunken Dory, women's laughter, dogs' barking, and scraps of conversation rose to this vigilant witness in his dark and silent room. Through the hours of the night all he heard only reinforced his disdain and despair.

Movement below caught his attention, and he leaned forward and parted the curtains for a better look. A couple, clinging so tightly the two seemed like one, entered the alley across the way. Dom watched while the man pressed the woman against the side of the building and ground his hips against hers, half hidden in the shadows. With swift, jerky motions, the man hitched the woman's dress up about her waist and pulled her underpants down past her knees. When she stepped out of them, they shone like a spot of milk on the street. Then the man unbuckled his belt, dropped his pants, and lifted the woman up. Greedily, she wrapped her legs around his waist, her exposed skin glowing like phosphorescence.

As he watched their awkward, thrusting movements, the baker thought of dogs mating. The sight did not arouse him. He might as well have been observing a man taking a furtive piss in the alley. When the couple came back out onto the street, he recognized Joe Silva's daughter immediately. "Cunt," he said aloud. Her underpants lay forgotten in the alley. He wanted to lean out the open window and scream after the girl. "Cunt. Whore. Stupid bitch, you forgot your panties." A wave of satisfaction passed over him as he imagined their shocked faces looking up, but he just watched until the couple had disappeared into the night. He reached for his glass of port and took a long swallow and then, like a sentinel who would someday be called to testify, returned his attention to the scene below. Love, betrayal, anger, lust. Drunks, whores, lovers, sailors. From his window seat, he saw everything, and nothing surprised him. He knew which husband was cheating with which man's wife. He knew which married man used the cover of midnight to creep to and from the home of Josephine Perry. He had watched queers weaving arm in arm down the sidewalk, seen them, too, make use of the alley across the way. Like the rest, they believed the night hid their sins. They were fools. While the baker watched, all of man's delusion and folly were revealed to him. Iniquity abided in this town, but it did not daze him. Dominus was a man conversant with evil.

Joaquin was asleep. Almost as soon as he had withdrawn from her, he had rolled over on his side and within seconds he was snoring. The sheet was twisted at the foot of the bed. Rosalina considered reaching down and pulling it over her husband, but she did not want to raise her body. Carefully, so as not to wake him, she pulled the pillow from beneath her head and bunched it up so that it was double its normal thickness. Then she lifted her hips and wedged it beneath her buttocks. Her pubic hair was sticky from their lovemaking, but there was not yet any wetness on her thighs. She bent her knees and let them fall slightly apart. She gazed up at the ceiling and imagined the river of his seed reversing within her, flowing back, deep into her body, settling in her like a tidal pool remaining in the flats after the tide recedes.

Sweat from lovemaking dried on her body, cooling her, and she wrapped her arms around her chest, hugging herself. Lying like this—nude, arms holding tight to her chest, hips elevated—she felt as though she were engaging in an ancient, mystical rite. A priestess. *Or a sacrifice.* She shivered and concentrated on their baby. She knew, she absolutely knew, she would become pregnant tonight.

As Joaquin snored, she shifted her weight slightly so that she was half lying on her side. She was glad he was asleep, for she wouldn't have moved the pillow if he had been awake. Once she reached over and stroked his forehead, gently so as not to waken him.

"I love you," she whispered. The wind blew outside, and the curtains billowed. She felt the summer air on her skin and she shivered. The touch of the wind stirred thoughts she could not face in her dreams, let alone in her waking hours. The face she had banished from her consciousness smiled down from the ceiling. She shut her eyes, but the face was still silhouetted against the blackness of her brain. She moaned and tossed. The cotton pillow slip felt wet against her leg. Even with her hips raised, fluid had leaked out. Moaning again, she slid off the pillow and cradled her body around Joaquin's, slipping her leg over his, sliding her calf up toward his buttocks. He did not stir. She wanted to protect him, to keep him safe. And she wanted him to protect her. She clung to him, as if the substance of him could erase from her mind the image of Fenris Boak.

When she finally slept, she dreamt not of Boak but of her mother.

Chapter 13

Although it was only nine A.M., heat had settled on the town like a cloak. Rosalina ducked into her sister-in-law's house, happy to escape the oppressive sun, her shirt sticky with sweat.

Dolores looked awful. The humid weather had turned her permanent into a frizzy mess, and stale lipstick smudged her mouth. Her worn chenille wrapper gaped at the throat, revealing breasts already beginning to lose their firmness. Rosalina estimated quickly that she must have gained at least ten pounds in the past month.

"Jesus. Will you look at this?" Dolores lifted a sodden sweatshirt off the counter. The slime of gurry stained the sleeves, the fishy smell permeating the room. "How many times do I tell him to leave his stinky shirts outside? Honestly. He drives me crazy." Holding the garment at arm's length, she opened the back door and draped it on the porch railing. "Men," she sputtered as she slammed the door, "they're worse than kids. Don't you just get sick and tired of picking up after them?"

"I don't know. Joaquin isn't so bad." Although she'd never say it, Rosalina didn't think Dolores had a lot of room to complain about Tony. She wasn't the world's best housekeeper.

"You know what I hate the most?" Dolores continued. "Washing his laundry. His dirty underwear. His socks. It really gets to me. You know what I mean?"

"Hmmmm." Rosalina felt disloyal to Joaquin when Dolores complained about husbands.

"Dolores?"

"Yeah?"

"Joaquin says two more of the men joined the Navy."

"So what's to worry about? As long as Joaquin isn't the one putting on the uniform, what do you care?"

"That's just it. When he talks about someone that has joined up, he sounds—I don't know—like he'd like to be going himself."

"Joaquin?"

She nodded, miserable.

"Is that what's got you down? Well, you can stop your worrying. He wouldn't go."

"I wish I could really believe that. You should hear him when he tells me about Joe Ducks's boy. He sounds hungry. That's it, almost hungry."

"I'm telling ya, you've got nothin' to worry about. Pa wouldn't let him."

Rosa was not reassured. "I don't know. Pa couldn't stop Jackie when he didn't want to fish. How could he stop Joaquin?"

Dolores's laugh was raspy from too many cigarettes. "Joaquin isn't Jackie," she said.

Stung, Rosalina wanted to defend her husband, but she wasn't sure Dolores had intended any insult. She fell into silence as her sister-in-law padded barefoot across the kitchen to turn off the gas beneath the coffee pot and set out two cups. She took a pack of cigarettes from the pocket of her robe, shook one free and lit it, then moved a pile of laundry off a chair. The chenille strained over her thick hips, but as she moved about her kitchen, she seemed to dance. This was what Rosalina couldn't understand about her sister-in-law. Even overweight, her hair mussed, and her face puffy from sleep, Dolores still believed she looked like Carole Lombard.

Unaware of Rosalina's silent appraisal, Dolores poured their coffee and sat down. She put out her cigarette, but within seconds lit another. Her hands toyed with the match, and she looked up at the clock twice. "Listen," she finally said, "I've got to get going. Bring your coffee into the bedroom and we can talk while I get dressed."

"You go ahead. I can come back some other time," Rosa answered, but Dolores was already heading down the hall. Reluctantly, she followed. The house seemed abnormally quiet. "Where's Little Tony?"

"At Helen's. He stayed there overnight."

Window shades cut the morning light out of the bedroom. In the semidarkness, Dolores moved gracefully. She stood in front of the bureau, her back to Rosalina, and slipped off her robe. She held up a puff from the jar of talcum on the top of the dresser and dusted her body. Fine white particles of powder floated through the air like mist, settling on the floor and furniture. "So what's going on?" she asked over her shoulder. "There's something else on your mind." As she moved about the room, her bare feet left a mosaic of footprints in the powder that dusted the floor, like diagrams of a complicated dance step.

Rosa sighed. She didn't know how to begin. She watched as Dolores tugged a girdle up over her hips, a bulge of flesh rolling over the top of the elastic. She really has gained weight, Rosa thought. Unconsciously, she smoothed a hand over her own hips.

Dolores fastened her bra and reached for her slip. It slid over her head and shoulders. Then she unscrewed the lid of her cold cream, dipped two fingertips into the jar, and quickly dabbed the cream on her face. With little circular, scrubbing motions, she spread the cleanser over her skin, then tissued it off. The smell of the cosmetic mingled with that of the talcum powder, a skin-sweet, intimate smell. The familiar smell of women, so familiar Rosalina grew weak. She sighed and leaned back against the doorjamb, as long-buried visions surfaced.

A child again, she was curled up on her mother's bed watching her mother dress. Even now she remembered her mother's daily rite with the cold cream, making the sign of the cross. A blessing with cream: forehead, chin, cheek, cheek.

Rosa shuddered and pressed her hands against her eyes. Why? she wondered. Why now, after all this time, is she haunting me? It seemed Rosa had thought more about her mother in the past week than in all the years since she'd gone away. Finally the words that had been lodged in her throat all along came out. "Do you remember my mother?"

Dolores was working on her hair now, taming it back into her Lombard look. There was a growing impatience to her movements.

"Dolores?"

"What?"

"Do you? Do you remember my mother?"

Dolores turned from the mirror and stared at Rosalina. Finally she nodded.

"What was she like?"

Dolores took a second before answering. "Pretty. Pretty like you."

"What else? What else do you remember?"

Dolores returned her attention to the mirror. She applied rouge, then spoke in choppy half-sentences as she put on her lipstick. "I don't know. She was always . . . she was always . . . sneaking us cookies." She pressed her lips together and blotted the lipstick against a tissue. "That made your father so mad. 'How we gonna have any profits, you keep giving cookies away to those kids?' he'd say. But she would just laugh and sneak us all another one."

Then, caught up, Dolores sank down on the edge of the bed. "Yeah, that's right. I remember her laugh. It was really contagious, you know—made you laugh just hearing it." She smiled at Rosalina. "Of all our mothers, I liked her the best."

"Why?"

"I don't know. She was so alive, like—" Before she could continue, a knock at the door broke the spell. "Shit," she said softly, then louder, "Come on in." Hurrying, she pulled a floral print dress from the closet and yanked it over her head. "Does this look all right?" she asked anxiously.

"You look great."

Isabella stood in the doorway, carrying a wicker basket. "Hi, Rosa."

"Hi." Rosalina stumbled over the word. Haunted by a vision of the black-garbed, haggard widow, aged and tainted by death, she had avoided her friend since the funeral weeks before. But a pretty, gaily dressed woman stood in the doorframe. Her hair was pinned back on one side of her head and fell forward in a thick curtain of waves on the other. Behind the exposed ear, she had tucked a wild daisy. Unsure of what to say, Rosa finally stammered, "I've been meaning to come and visit you."

Isabella brushed her words aside with an impatient gesture. "God, aren't you ready yet?" she said to Dolores. "We'll be late."

Rosa caught the look of warning Dolores shot at Isabella.

"Where are you going?"

"Just on a picnic," Dolores answered quickly. "We're just going on a picnic."

"We have a date," Isabella said. Her eyes flashed with defiance. "We're going on a picnic with some sailors."

"Now you've done it," Dolores moaned. "Now we'll have to listen to a lecture from Saint Rosalina."

"You're joking. You aren't really going, are you?"

"Don't make such a big deal out of it. I mean, it's not like we're going to *do* anything. It's just a picnic."

"But you're *married.*"

"Don't be such a prude. Besides, what Tony doesn't know won't hurt him. We just want to have a little fun. Jesus, you're such a stick, Rosa."

Rosalina turned to Isabella. "And you?" Outrage sharpened her voice. She felt betrayed in some way. "What about Manny? How could you?"

"Manny's dead."

Rosa could see nothing of the grieving widow in her face. "Manny isn't cold in the grave yet," she said cruelly.

"Manny's dead," Isabella repeated. "Did he take care of me? Did he worry about me, about what would happen if he died? That's a laugh. He left me nothing. You know what the son-of-a-bitch insurance man said when I went to see him? He said Manny took out a sickness and accident policy so big it would take the top of your head off, but no life insurance. You know what Manny told the guy? Manny told him, 'You think I'm gonna work so my wife will be a wealthy widow when I die? I don't need no life insurance.' Stupid son of a bitch. He could at least have thought of the kids."

"There's the fund."

"The *fund.*" Isabella spit out the word. "A pittance that won't keep clothes on our backs." A shadow darkened her eyes, and for a moment Rosalina saw the fear and hurt beneath her friend's anger. "It's not just the money, Rosa. My bed is empty. You can't know what it's like. Well, I'm not going to stay a widow all my life, dried up like the rest of them. I'm alive, Rosa. I'm not going to be buried with Manny. A new ship came in last night, and the sailors want some fun. We want some fun. What's the harm? Manny's dead. I can't hurt him. And we're all going to be dead soon enough."

Isabella's words chilled Rosalina. Then her gaze dropped to Isabella's stomach. The folds of her dress fell over the faint mound where her pregnancy was just beginning to show. "But you're pregnant."

"Come on, Rosa," Dolores said softly. "Lay off. It's just a picnic. No big deal."

"It's wrong," she said stiffly. "You just shouldn't go."

Before Isabella could respond, Dolores grabbed them both in a hug. "You want to come with us? Be our chaperone?"

"No." She felt like crying. "It's wrong. Don't go. Something will happen. It's a sin and you'll be punished."

"Listen, Rosalina, you know your problem? You don't know how to have fun. For years now, you're scared stiff you're like your mother. You don't say it, but everyone knows it. Well, the truth is, you're not like her at all. *She* knew how to have fun."

Rosa's face grew white. "You're right. I'm not like her. And I'm glad. I hate her." She slammed the door behind her and ran. But her words followed, echoing, swirling, pressing down upon her. *I hate her. I hate her. I hate her.*

Doc Cook stood on the dock, his wife, Lillian, at his side, and watched the destroyer approach the harbor. The gray warship was a fitting symbol of this summer —a season, it seemed to him, when the gods of fortune had deserted the town, abandoning her as if this were the price they were exacting for gifts so generously rendered in the past. A season of madness.

Perhaps it's the heat, he mused. This year there had been no alleviation. Even the southwest breeze, which usually brought welcome relief in from the ocean, was absent. When the boats unloaded a prize catch, fish rotted even before it could be iced down and loaded on the railcars for New York and Boston. In the bars and down on the wharves tempers flared, and he had more than his share of cuts and bruises and broken arms to tend to.

There were also the news reports of the growing war in Europe. He, along with the other citizens of Grace Point, followed the newspaper headlines about German troops garrisoned in Paris and Belgium and watched the grainy newsreel pictures of the blitz over Britain. Nervously the townspeople speculated about whether F.D.R. would be able to keep the country out of it. Even if they wanted to forget about the war, they couldn't. Every week hulking battleships moored outside the harbor, and sailors in summer whites strolled the streets on shore leave.

There was, too, an eerie quality to the summer. It might have been because the death of the Viera brothers had heralded the season. Or perhaps the ghost of the young woman who drowned off the pier had grown restive. The doctor was uncomfortable with this thought. On the certificate he had put down suicide as the cause of death, but rumors of murder persisted. Her body had been buried in the part of the town cemetery reserved for paupers. At night, lying in bed, the doctor would hear the throb of music underscored by laughter, and it seemed to him that this wild beating was the pulse of Grace Point.

The destroyer was closer now, and the doctor shook his head at the row of white along the rails: uniformed seamen crowding close for a glimpse of their new port. Without taking his eyes off the ship, the doctor muttered to his wife, "You know, Lily, nine months from now, I'll be having an awful lot of work I hadn't ought to have."

Chapter 14

Rosalina leaned against the wall outside the studio, fighting lightheadedness. No lunch on top of too much coffee—no wonder she was dizzy. She shrank from the curious stares of the art students and ran down the stairs without waiting for her head to clear. Her pulse raced in time with her feet. On the last few steps, she forced herself to slow down.

"Hi." Fenris Boak was waiting by the dressing room.

"Hello." She was proud of the firmness of her voice. He was blocking the narrow hall, making it impossible to pass without brushing against him. He was so close she could see the stubble of beard on his chin and pockmarks on his cheeks. His dark hair hung lankly over his forehead. How could she have remembered him as handsome?

"I've been waiting for you."

She felt her cheeks flush, but didn't answer.

"How did the modeling go today?" He was acting as if they had known each other for a long, long time.

"Okay." She couldn't look at him.

"That's good." He continued to smile down at her. "I thought maybe you'd like to have a Coke with me."

"I can't. I need to get home. To start dinner for my husband." There. She had said it. *My husband.* Now he knew for certain she was married. Protected.

"Just for ten minutes. For business, really. I need to hire a model and Ben suggested you."

"I thought you were a writer."

"I'm a photographer as well as a writer. I was hoping I could talk you into posing for me. It would only take a day, possibly two."

What about the other model? Why don't you ask her? She froze the words before they escaped.

"Come on—just a Coke. I promise I won't keep you long. We'll simply talk about the job. You'll be home in plenty of time to cook dinner." His smile was cocky. Infuriating.

No. The word was so easy to say. *No.* Not too prim, not too unfriendly—just polite and firm. *No. No, thank you.* She was not like Dolores and Isabella. And she was definitely not like her mother.

"Okay," she said.

She saw at once that he took her answer for granted, as if they had already come to some understanding. He reached out to take her hand. She let it lie in his, quiet and submissive. Instead of leading her outside, he turned toward his studio. She hesitated briefly, but if he felt this shrinking—if it traveled the length of her arm and through the muscles of her hand to his—he gave no sign of it. "It's cooler here," he said as he pushed the door open.

She had never been inside his studio, only seen it from the door that day. She shivered. She should not have come. Her hand was still cupped in his, and awkwardly she withdrew it.

The small room was half the size of her own bedroom, and crowded. She looked around, her eyes flitting over the furnishings. She saw the bed, the small bureau, the overstuffed armchair, the typewriter, stool, and table. And everywhere books, overflowing the bookcase, heaped on the floor and in piles along the wall, even on the seat of the armchair.

Fenris dumped a half-dozen paperbacks from the cushion of the armchair. "Have a seat," he said. "I'll be back in a moment."

The smell of him, of stale pipe tobacco, lingered. She listened as he walked down the hall to the kitchen shared by all the Sail Loft artists, heard the muted sound of the icebox door as it slammed shut. She sank into the chair and rubbed her hands over the upholstered arms. The fabric felt oily against her fingertips. She tried not to look at the bed. It was unmade, the sheets rumpled, the pillow dented where his head had lain.

Nervously she got up and stood in front of the bookcase and, tilting her head, scanned the titles: *The Forsyte Saga, Ulysses, Tropic of Cancer, Studs Lonigan, Finnegans Wake, Heart of Darkness.* She had never heard of any of these books. She looked toward the door, wondering what was taking him so long. She twisted her fingers and fidgeted with her wedding band. Her gaze returned to the unmade bed. Resolutely, she turned back to the bookcase. Two books—*Waiting for Lefty* and *Golden Boy*—were by the same writer, a man named Odets, but she had not heard of him. *Tender Is the Night. Lord Jim.* They sounded like they might be poetry. She read on. Wedged next to a hefty volume on the Russian Revolution by a man named Trotsky was a book called *The Daring Young Men on the Flying Trapeze.* Why was he interested in the circus? Then, on a book so new the dust jacket was still uncreased, she recognized a title. *The Grapes of Wrath.* It was a movie with Henry Fonda.

She moved on to another shelf. The next line took a moment to register. *Paris by Boak.* Boak? She pulled the book from the case. His picture was on the back of the dust jacket. He was leaning against a streetlight, his face shadowed, and he looked nearly handsome. She turned the book over. It was a volume of photographs. A brief biography was printed on the flyleaf. She absorbed the information: prize-winning photographer, work appeared in *Look* and *Life.* He was famous.

More anxious than ever, she read on. She'd thought

he lived in New York, but he was from Minnesota. Wasn't that somewhere near Ohio? She tried to picture the map on the wall of Mrs. Steele's sixth-grade classroom, but it wouldn't come clear. Geography and math had been her worst subjects.

Opening the book, she found no pictures of the Eiffel Tower. Instead it was filled with photographs of people. Beggars. Students. Old men and women. A nun walking down the street with a loaf of bread tucked under her arm. Dirty-faced children. Some, like the hollow-eyed man injecting a needle into the crook of his arm, were shocking. Others had a sadness to them. Sad old women sitting on park benches, their thick legs stuffed into coarse stockings like sausages. Toothless, wise smiles. A black man standing in a doorway, hunched over a saxophone, smoke swirling around his head like a halo. The photo that most fascinated her was of two French sailors arm-wrestling. Tattoos covered their arms. A snake, magnificent in detail, slithered up the arm of the younger sailor, entwining itself around wrist, forearm, and bicep. Its fangs seemed to disappear into a woman's bare breast that decorated his shoulder. On his chest, he sported a grinning skull in a top hat.

She shuddered and looked at the young sailor's face. About Joaquin's age, he seemed much older, as if he had gone many places and done things she could only wonder at. Her gaze returned to the snake tattoo.

"Like it?" He was watching from the door.

"I can only stay a minute," she said, closing the book.

"Yes, I know. You have to go home to get dinner for your husband." He crossed to the desk and poured the Coke into two glasses. Then he took a bottle of rum from the bottom drawer and, without asking, splashed some into both tumblers. She took the glass when he handed it to her. She knew she shouldn't have any hard liquor on an empty stomach. He watched her as she took a sip. It tasted sweet, reminding her faintly of the fruit-studded cookies her father made at Christmastime, but it burned her throat and lay heavy in her stomach.

He picked up a bag of peanuts from the top of his dresser and offered her one, which she refused. Would he notice if she didn't finish her drink? She would leave as soon as they discussed the job. She'd already decided not to model for him. When he sat down on the unmade bed, she wished he had chosen the chair. She could not look him in the face. She was shy with the knowledge that he was famous, and shy, too, because they were alone in his room.

Using one hand, he picked out a peanut and cracked it between his thumb and forefinger. "You're pretty quiet."

"Am I?"

"Most women talk all the time. It's quite attractive, your silence. Mysterious."

She blushed. A circle on the crown of her skull throbbed with a pulsing, liquid beat. She was very aware of his every movement: the way he tilted his head when he drank from his drink and then ran his thumb over his slender mustache, as if to wipe away any drops that might be there. A short-sleeve shirt revealed arms more muscular than she would have thought. His fingernails, filed straight across, were very clean. She wondered if he had them manicured. She had heard that some men—gangsters and rich men and movie stars—did. He smelled faintly of spice, like the kitchen in the bakery. For a brief moment, she was both glad and regretful that Joaquin did not smell of spice.

"What does your husband do?"

The question caught her by surprise, as if he had read her mind. "He's a fisherman."

"Do you have any children?"

"No." She lowered her eyes and rolled the glass between her palms. It was slippery with condensation. "I don't want any yet." She felt his eyes on her and wondered if he knew she was lying. She remembered how she had lain the night before with her hips held high on a pillow.

"Do you like to model?"

"It's all right." She absolutely would not model for him.

"Cynthia says the artists and students like you. They say you're good."

"Who's Cynthia?"

"The blonde, who models for Ben."

The picture of the girl's naked breasts, their large, pink nipples flashed before her eyes.

"She says you won't model nude."

"No."

"Why not?"

She squirmed, avoiding his glance. She ached for him to change the subject. Talking with him was not like talking with Joaquin. It was like navigating over shifting, hidden shoals. Dangerous, yet exciting. There was less than half the rum and Coke left. As soon as she finished it, she would leave.

"I don't want to."

"You should. You have a beautiful body." He got up and crossed to her, offering her a shelled nut, holding it close to her mouth. The gesture was too intimate. *I'm not a child. I can shell my own.* She opened her mouth and he fed her the nut. His fingertips brushed against her lips. Tendrils of smoky ice stirred in the lining of her stomach. The rum churned uneasily.

He was cracking another nut. Afraid he would offer it to her again in that unspeakably intimate way, she got up and took a shell from the bag and busied herself cracking it. He returned to the bed and watched her.

She wandered around the room. There was a picture on his bureau, and she bent over it. A woman and a boy sitting on the steps of a wide wooden porch returned her gaze. The woman was thin and looked tired—a plain woman. The young boy was thin, too. They sat side by side but did not touch. The boy looked a little like Fenris, a younger Fenris, smiling. But the woman stared out at the photographer as if confronting her soul. There was an intelligence in her eyes and a grimly uncompromising set to her mouth. "Is this your mother?" she asked.

He leaned back against the wall and pulled one leg up on the mattress. "My wife."

"Your wife?" She was mortified.

"And my son."

"I didn't know that you were married." The words were out before she could stop them.

"Oh, yes," he said. "I'm married."

Of course he was married. Why shouldn't he be? There was a little twisting in her chest—the rum on an empty stomach. Her mind chattered fiercely. It was good that he was married, she thought. It was safer. She could feel him looking at her, but she looked again at the haggard face, trying to connect this woman with Fenris. She was surprised a famous writer would have such an unpleasant-looking wife. Unconsciously, she compared herself with the woman. This made her brave, as did another sip of her drink. "What's your son's name?"

"Lawrence. After his grandfather."

There was something about the way he said the name that made her think the boy had been named after his mother's father, but she didn't ask, any more than she would ask him what his wife's name was. She didn't want to know.

"You like books," she said, indicating the room. She felt foolish as soon as the words were out.

"Do you?"

"I liked your book," she said shyly, surprised at herself.

"Did you?" He laughed and reached for the book. Flipping it open, he turned to the picture of the sailors and held it up for her to see. "Even this one?"

So he had seen her revulsion. She wasn't safe at all. She looked down at the decorations that marked the sailors: "Why do they do it?"

"The tattoos?" He shrugged. "The first time they were probably drunk. After that, who knows? Maybe they don't even know. It's an ancient art. In some cultures there are religious overtones to tattoos. Some believe they have power and are used to frighten enemies. Like war paint. Others believe they're an art form. Once, in Paris, I saw a man who had the Eiffel Tower tattooed on top of his head."

"You're making that up."

"No, I'm not. He had a miniature of the tower right in the center of his bald spot, a perfect replica. I wanted to shoot his picture, but he wouldn't let me."

The idea that a man would undergo such a process—needles injected into the skin of his head—made her weak. "Do you think it hurts?"

"I'm told it hurts a great deal. The pain, I think, is part of the appeal. Like a primitive rite of manhood. Men, drunk or sober, get tattoos as proof of their virility. For women, of course, it is another story."

"Women get tattooed?"

"Someone I knew in Paris—an artist—gave one to his girlfriend."

"A tattoo?" She couldn't keep the horror from her voice.

"A butterfly. Where only he would see it."

"That's terrible."

"Is it? She was his woman. She wanted his mark on her. That's my theory. As visual proof that she belonged to someone, so she had an identity."

"I'd never do it."

"Never?" He smiled. "Never, little Rosalina?" He was laughing at her. "Never say 'never.' "

When he looked at her, she felt he was seeing something in her no one else ever had, not even her husband.

She wished with her soul she had never come with him. The rum and Coke churned in her stomach.

"Joaquin . . ." she began. "Joaquin will be waiting for me. I have to go now."

"It would be rather special, don't you think," he asked, as if she had not spoken, "having a man put his mark on you?" He got up from the bed and crossed toward her. "I've often envied my friend in Paris. Imagine a woman who loved you so much, who belonged to you so completely that she would wear your mark. I would like that very much." His voice was soft.

She thought of his stern-faced wife, tried to imagine her with a tattoo.

He stood close enough now to stroke the inner part of her forearm with a fingernail, tracing so lightly over her skin that she shivered. She recoiled from his touch.

He took the glass from her hand and crossed to the desk. "Yes. I think my woman should have a tattoo."

He put their glasses down. The sound of the tumblers on the desk top was like a door closing. She knew even before he touched her that this was what she had been afraid of. She was intoxicated by his breath, the smell of tobacco and rum. And she was hypnotized by his eyes. She closed her eyes, as if that could end the spell. He kissed her. She was trembling, but he did not hold her or offer support. Still kissing, weak with the kiss, she leaned against him. He ended the embrace, took hold of her arms just above the elbows, and held her away. Her eyes were still closed.

"Open your eyes," he said. "When I kiss you, open your eyes and look at me."

"No." She was ashamed.

"Open your eyes when I kiss you, Rosa." His voice was deep, and she was faint with the sound of it. She wanted him more than she had ever wanted Joaquin, which shocked her. She could not trust herself to speak. She shook her head.

"You will, you know. Oh, little Rosa, you will do things you never dreamed of."

His words terrified her. "I have to go." Before he could say any more, she turned and left the room. Her lips tingled, burned, stung. She rubbed them fiercely with her fist, as if she could rub away the memory of his touch.

"I love you, Joaquin," she whispered aloud as she walked swiftly from the Sail Loft. She sent her message to him on the breeze. "I love you. You are the only man for me." Sweat sheeted her breasts and temples and the inside of her wrists, and the top of her skull throbbed with a pulsing beat. The sweetness of the rum rose in her throat.

She was sick by the side of the road. Just like a wharf dog, a stray who ate too many bad fish, she stiffened her legs and vomited. But she knew if she threw up all day and into the night, she could not get rid of all that roiled inside of her.

St. Peter's was dim, even in midday. In the pews by the confessional, old women bowed, the fabric of their dark dresses shiny where they knelt. They looked alike, these old women in black cotton kerchiefs who prayed over their rosaries, as if they belonged to an ancient order of nuns. They were always the first in the pews at confession.

Rosalina bent her head, concealing her tear-stained face from these old ones whose eyes, even when closed, missed nothing. The beads of her rosary rolled through her fingers. Sweat wept along her spine. It was hot in the church, and the air was heavy with the smell of old flesh and incense and wax, thick with the muted murmurings of prayer. The whispered words, in Latin, Portuguese, and English, melded into one language, a sorrowful undersong of supplication and contrition.

One by one, the parishioners got up and went to

the confessional. Old women, Rosalina thought—what transgressions could they confess? She felt the weight of her mortal sins.

St. Peter's was a church of fishermen. Though casual about attendance, the fishermen were generous. The mural behind the altar was a seascape in which a boat tossed in a tempest. The sky and sea were so stormy, it was difficult to know where one left off and the other began. Along the sides of the church, all the stained-glass windows that towered over the pews depicted sea scenes: Jesus walking on water; Jesus teaching from Peter's boat; the shipwreck of Saint Paul on the isle of Malta; Christ calling Andrew and Peter, making them fishers of men; Christ calling James and John to leave their nets and follow him; Jesus teaching on the shore of Galilee; Jesus blessing the fishermen as they tended their nets. Everywhere Rosalina looked, it seemed that gaunt-faced men were looking upon her. She felt the burden of their judgment as she walked to the confessional.

"Bless me, Father, for I have sinned." Her voice was harsh from weeping, and from fear. "It has been two weeks since my last confession, and these are my sins."

"Begin."

The rosary was damp in her hands. "I have lied . . ." How many lies? The toll mounted in her head: Joaquin, her father, Leona and Victor, Ben Bayes. She was soiled with her lies. "I have lied five times since my last confession."

The little priest waited. His palms, too, were wet, as if he dreaded her revelations as much as the penitent did.

She did not rush the words, would not spare herself even that much, but repeated the sin slowly, deliberately. "I have kissed a man not my husband and have committed adultery in my thoughts." She paused. On the other side of the screen, the priest shifted position.

"For these sins, and for the previous sin of impure thoughts, I am deeply sorry."

Father Mallory cleared his throat, his fingers trembling slightly. He longed to be back in his study in Fall River, happily bent over his books. That was where he belonged. He had always been proud of his skill with math and his several languages, and he had been punished for his sin of pride. He smiled at the irony. It was his proficiency in Portuguese that had led to his being named priest in Grace Point. He sighed heavily. As sure as he was of his skill with verb tenses and the laws of mathematics, he was far less confident navigating the muddy waters of men's souls. "Do you seek spiritual instruction?" His voice was soft, almost sad.

"No, Father. I am deeply sorry for this sin."

"And you promise not to repeat this sin, nor to put yourself in the occasion of sin?"

"Yes, Father."

"Say two Hail Marys and make a good Act of Contrition."

The phrases, such a familiar part of her life, came fervently, as if this were the first time she had said them. "Hail Mary, full of grace! The Lord is with thee; blessed art thou among women, and blessed is the fruit of thy womb, Jesus. Holy Mary, Mother of God, pray for us sinners, now and at the hour of our death. Amen." She prayed for forgiveness and longed for the sanctifying grace to sweep her soul. Wasn't that what Father Jim had told them in catechism—that confession was Mary sweeping their souls clean of sin?

"O, my God, I am heartily sorry for having offended thee, and I detest all my sins, because of thy just punishments, and because I dread the loss of heaven and the pains of hell. . . ." From the other side of the screen, like the low hum of the surf at night, came the priest's absolution. Tears thickened her voice. She continued. "But most of all because they offend Thee, my God, who art all good and deserving of all my love. I firmly resolve, with the help of thy grace, to sin no more and to avoid the near occasions of sin."

"For your penance you will say the stations of the cross every day for a week."

"Yes, Father."

"Go and sin no more."

The organ was playing when she left. Old Mrs. Alves was practicing for the Sunday mass.

Chapter 15

Dom Roderick woke before dawn, although for the past week Jackie Santos had been opening the bakery and starting the ovens, allowing him to sleep a little later and go down to the kitchen at five instead of four. Downstairs, the coffee would be brewed and waiting on the burner. The fat would be heating in the fryers, ready for the first batch of *malassadas*. The dough for the yeast breads would be covered with linen towels in pale yellow crockery bowls and already beginning to rise. By the time he descended the stairs, the bakery would be warm and filled with fragrance, a hushed and welcome refuge where he and the boy would work side by side in silence. Only their hands would speak, a sibilant, rich language of pastry and sweets.

No, no reason at all for him to get up this early, but old habits die hard. Dom rose from the sofa and, joints stiff from the lumpy cushions, shuffled off into the bathroom. He couldn't remember the last time he had slept in his bed like a normal person. *A normal person.* He wondered if in all creation there was such a creature. Sighing, he reached for the box of baking soda, sprinkled some into the palm of his hand, and began brushing his teeth. His mouth felt sour from the wine of the night before. He cut himself shaving, a bad omen.

He was on the back stairs when he heard the sound. He stood a moment in the predawn darkness of the stairwell and listened. So eerie, the sound raised the hair on his neck and arms, and it took him a moment to recognize it as music. The song—a humming, really, a humming pitched high and tight like held-back tears in the back of the throat—was coming from the kitchen, spreading into the hallway like fog. He shivered, then continued down the stairs, quietly now, his feet soundless on the treads, a spy in his own bakery. Through the doorway, he saw Jackie.

The boy stood by the big black ovens, his back to the door. His hands, white with flour, were suspended in the air; his chin was tucked tight against his shoulder, resting on the imagined wood of his instrument's neck. His bow hand moved gracefully, longingly through the air, pulling notes from the fictive strings. The nimble tips of his left fingers bared down against the invisible fingerboard. He swayed as he hummed. He played every measure, every sweet and pain-filled note of the song. When at last the piece was finished, the boy let his arms fall to his sides and stood motionless. Then, with a sob that was torn from the same deep place in his throat where the humming had been born, he dropped his face into his hands and wept.

Soundlessly, Dom retreated back up the stairs to his apartment. When, minutes later, he made his way to the kitchen, he was careful to call out a greeting. The boy was cutting lard into flour, and there was no sign of tears on his cheeks, no ghost of music in the air. The baker crossed to the coffee and poured himself a cup. "Want some?"

"No, thanks," Jackie replied. Granules of flour stuck to his chin and along one cheek.

Dom drank his coffee, then tied on his apron. He took his place at the counter. As he rolled out dough and peeled and cored apples, Dom found himself stealing looks at the boy. The more he thought about it, the more it seemed that he could still hear the thin, yearning sound of the song. He wanted to say something to the boy, offer some consolation, but he did not know how.

He had finished the pies when the idea came to him.

Without explanation, he left the kitchen and climbed the stairs to his apartment. For a moment, standing in his living room, he had misgivings. Maybe it was a dangerous and daring deed he would soon regret. But the boy's song echoed in his brain, urging him on. He crossed the room to the carved, claw-footed sideboard where the object rested, half hidden beneath a moth-chewed, multicolored shawl edged with a tangled fringe.

He wrestled the bulky object down the stairs. Breathing heavily, the baker set his prize in the far corner of the kitchen on a pine table near the shelves that held the bowls and pans and pie tins. It was still covered with the fringed square of silk. Without a word, he went again up to his apartment, this time returning with a crate.

Jackie watched all this with his mouth open in surprise. It was the first time since he had come to work for the baker that he had seen Dom smile. Not just smile—grin.

With a flourish, Dom removed the cloth. Jackie's jaw dropped even wider. Pleased, the baker took up the metal crank and inserted it in the side of the machine. He selected a record from the crate, carefully removed its protective sleeve, and slipped it on the turntable. Then he wound up the machine. The music of violins, only faintly scratched, flowed from the horn. Jackie shut his eyes and drank in the music like a man dying of thirst.

Work was forgotten. When the first record was finished, they listened to another. Then another. Jackie selected the next one, flipping through the stack in the wooden box. Cole Porter, Gershwin. Arturo Toscanini and the New York Philharmonic. Jascha Heifetz. Cab Calloway, Benny Goodman, and Bix Beiderbecke. *Rhapsody in Blue.* He was astounded by the size of the collection. Later, the boy would try to imagine this dour, silent man listening to these records alone in his room at night.

He put on a Jerome Kern record and cranked up the Victrola. The music played loudly. Shyly at first, as if somehow they were revealing too much, they hummed along with the music, the older man's voice a register lower than Jackie's sweet tenor.

They returned to work. Dom rolled out cookie dough and Jackie drizzled glaze on the top of warm breads. While he pushed the pin back and forth on the counter surface, the baker hummed, and as he hummed, he thought. He found himself thinking about the sleeping alcove in the apartment overhead, the empty space going to waste.

At the moment he decided to offer it to the boy, a bell tinkled in the front of the bakery. The song died in Jackie's throat, and Dom, too, stopped humming. They stared at each other guiltily, as if they had been caught in a crime. Again the bell rang.

"We are not open yet," Dom said gruffly. "Whoever it is will come back."

The bell rang again, a shrill, impatient summons. Jackie went into the shop front.

Dom listened to Jackie's low murmur and that of another man. All he could hear was indistinct muttering. Jackie returned but said nothing.

"Who was that?"

"Someone from the Sail Loft."

"What did he want?" Probably bread, he thought. Those artists were always wanting more stale bread.

"Rosa."

"Rosa? My Rosa?" A chill crept into his fingers and assaulted his bones. In the background, the phonograph played. *Dat ol' man River* . . . The words revolved in his brain.

"Yes."

"Was it Ben?"

"No. Someone else. A man I did not know."

What did a man, a stranger, want with his daughter? The chill spread to his stomach. "She's not here," he said angrily.

"I told him that."

"And he went away?"

"Not until I gave him her address."

"You gave him her address?"

"He wouldn't leave until I did."

"That's all he said? That he wanted Rosa?"

The color in Jackie's cheek was high. "No," he answered.

The phonograph needed winding. *It jussst keeps rollinnn'* . . . , it moaned.

Dom waited for the boy to continue.

"Can I . . . can I leave work a little early tonight?"

"Leave early?" Dom looked at Jackie. The boy had come in early and left later than he was supposed to every day since he had begun work. Yet the request made the baker angry.

"There's a party . . ." the boy began.

"You don't have to explain," Dom cut in, so that he wouldn't have to hear any more.

"It's at the Sail Loft. At Ben Bayes's," the boy continued, as if apologizing, but excitement sharpened his voice. "All the artists and their friends are going to be there. Rosa's friend asked if I want to go too."

"Of course. Go. Have fun. You work very hard." Yet Dominus could not keep the stiffness from his voice. The record on the Victrola was finished, and the needle ran back and forth over the last groove with a clicking sound. He went over, lifted the arm, and abruptly turned the machine off.

His back still turned to Jackie, the baker made the sign of the cross. Evil had entered his shop.

Every morning of the week, as soon as Joaquin had left for the dock, she had knelt by her bed and said the stations of the cross. *Every morning of the week.* She turned to the figure in the doorway. "What do you want?"

"I was worried about you. Ben said you were too sick to model."

"Yes." *Every morning.*

"You don't look sick. In fact you look pretty healthy."

"I'm better now." She wondered if he could tell she had been crying. "How did you know where I live?"

"They told me at the bakery."

"You went there?"

"The boy there told me where to find you."

"He is my husband's brother." She let her eyes flick to the left and then the right, checking the windows of the houses across the street. Frantic with fear and guilt, she felt as though everyone in the town were suddenly watching her home. *I have done nothing wrong,* she told herself, *I have done nothing wrong.* But she could not rid herself of the feeling that she had invited Fenris Boak to her door as surely as if she had sent him a message, summoned him by the power of the dreams in which he appeared every night, attracted him by a potent scrap of paper. It had been madness to take the page from the atlas at the Grace Point Library. What would he think of her tearing out the state of Minnesota and hiding it in her closet? Her heart thundered so, she was sure that he could hear it.

"He said he was your brother-in-law. He's pretty."

"Girls are pretty, not boys."

"Some girls are very pretty." He stroked the line of her jaw with his forefinger.

Her eyes darted back to the neighboring windows, and she stepped back. She knew what the townspeople said about women who invited men to their homes.

He was smiling at her discomfort. "Would you like to go for a ride?"

For the first time, she noticed the green De Soto by the edge of her walk. "I can't."

"Sure you can."

"I can't." She hesitated, then plunged on. "I promised Father Mallory."

"Father Mallory?"

"The priest at St. Peter's." It slipped out, and she saw at once, even before he began to laugh, that the admission was a horrible mistake.

"Are you so afraid of me, Little Rosa?"

"I am not afraid of you."

"Of what, then? Yourself?"

"Nothing. I fear nothing. Certainly not you."

"The priest—this Father Mallory you made your promises to—do you fear him?"

"Of course not."

"Well, then, if you have nothing to fear, you must come for a ride with me. Surely there is nothing sinful in an innocent ride with a friend."

The stations of the cross. Every morning of the week. She remembered this as he opened the door of the De Soto.

They headed back up the peninsula. Before they had even crossed over the town line, he reached out and took her hand in his. She did not know what to do about his hand and finally decided to stare straight ahead and pretend his fingers were not entwined with hers.

The feeling of his hand around hers reminded her of his kiss in the studio. She was terrified he would do that again. She darted a sideward glance at him. He drove confidently, one hand casually on the wheel.

He caught her looking at him and grinned. Then he pulled her closer, rested his hand on her thigh. She didn't know what to do about this, either, so she continued to pretend it was not happening.

They were at least fifteen miles out of Grace Point when he slowed and pulled off the road. She could smell the ocean even though it was hidden from view by a dune.

He reached under the steering wheel and turned the ignition off with his left hand, leaving his right still on her thigh. He turned and grinned at her. "Ready?"

"Ready for what?"

"To take some pictures." He leaned over the seat and picked a camera up from the back floor. When he lifted his hand, the place on her leg where it had rested felt damp and cool.

Without waiting he started across the sand, and she had to run to catch up. She smelled the whales before she saw them.

"Jesus. Would you look at that," he said.

Just beyond the low-tide mark, nearly twenty whales lay like berthed boxcars in the sand. Scores of men wove in and around their mammoth bodies. A line of balloon-tired trucks parked to one side looked like miniatures next to the whales.

"A pod came ashore last night." Fenris walked closer but she held back.

She'd never seen a whale harvesting before. Two years ago, just after they were married, Joaquin had worked on one. He had earned ten dollars a day while the job lasted, and come home half drunk, his clothes stinking so badly they'd had to burn them. She remembered how excited they had been with the extra money.

The men were divided into crews. One group sawed open the heads. They had stripped to their undershirts, and the muscles of their arms and shoulders glistened with sweat. Their clothes spattered with gore, they swore as they hacked away, cursing their dull blades. Over by the trucks, downwind, two men sharpened knives on grinding wheels. The whetstones never stopped spinning. A young boy, no more than ten, carried the newly honed knives to the whale butchers, then returned to the sharpeners with dull ones. He was kept so busy he had to run.

Another crew, using baggage hooks, pulled the oil-filled melons from the skulls. It took two men to lift and carry each one to the truck. They staggered in the soft sand. She watched as two of them paused on their way to the truck and posed for Fenris. The gleaming, oil-filled melon swayed from the hooks in the space between them.

She was nauseated by the odor of dying whales, sickened by the sight of the slaughter. But worst of all was the noise, a haunting sound of whale tails beating against the beach while men hacked open their heads. The thumping of the animals' tails sounded like a herd of wild horses galloping along the beach.

This was her punishment. This horrible scene was her punishment for coming with Fenris Boak. She walked into the smell of carnage, letting it envelop her. It was the worst thing she had ever smelled in her life. Fenris came back and gave her his handkerchief. She tied it over her nose and mouth. The cloth held the scent of pipe tobacco, but the terrible stench still filtered through.

Rosalina had never seen a whale before. The smallest, still huge, lay in a shallow pool. She approached it, awed by its size. As she drew closer, she saw that one wet whale eye stared right into hers. Accusing. She bowed before the denunciation. Then she saw the eye turn sorrowful, too sorrowful to beg or blame. A drop of water leaked from the corner of its eye, a single, sad tear from the single, sad eye. She turned away, suddenly ashamed. She wanted to walk away from the animal, but instead she knelt in the tidal pool and reached out with her hand. She began to pray.

She was crying when he found her in the car. The rear tires spun noisily in the sand when he pulled onto the road. He offered her no words of comfort. He did not head back to Grace Point, but she didn't notice. They drove with the windows wide open, and still the smell of the whales permeated the car. She could not stop crying, but she wept softly, without sound. It was all mixed up in her head: the memory of Fenris's hand on her leg; the nightmarish vision of the harvesting; the young boy running through the sand with the newly sharpened knives; the sound of the whales' tattoo on the sand and the greedy cries of seagulls.

He pulled into a narrow dirt road that led to the edge of a beach forest. She continued to cry while he unlatched his car door and held it ajar with his foot. He reached across her, unlatched the glove compartment, and took out a silver flask. He drank deeply from it, then handed it to her. She took a swallow of rum. She was already beginning to associate the sticky-sweet drink with him. She took a second swallow, but it did not take the taste of the dying whales from deep within her throat.

"One of the whales was crying. I saw it. It was crying. It knew. It knew it was going to die."

" 'Whales weep not,' " he said, so softly she could barely hear.

"What?"

He took another swig from the flask. "A poem," he said. He started reciting, his voice tired, raspy. She knew he was saying it for himself, not her.

> . . . whales in mid-ocean, suspended in the waves of the sea
> great heaven of whales in the waters, old hierarchies.
>
> And enormous mother whales lie dreaming suckling their whale-tender young
> and dreaming with strange whale eyes wide open in the waters of the beginning and the end.

It seemed, then, the most natural thing in the world to let him hold her. She kissed him back, urgently, with a passion that would defy death and dying. He drew away and slid out through the open door, pulling her after him. He knelt in the sea of yellow grass, wild and brittle from lack of rain, and she knelt with him.

He began undressing her. "Help me," he said. Hands trembling, she slipped off her skirt. After she was naked, he took off his clothes. He lay next to her on the ground, kissed her again. The dry blades of grass pricked at the naked skin of her legs and back. She began sneezing, and he kissed her until she stopped. "Open your eyes," he said.

She looked at him. They were so close she could see his eyelashes disappearing into tiny pores on his eyelids and faint pink veins radiating from his pupils into the whites of his eyes. Confusion swirled. She was all mixed up: the taste of rum in her throat . . . the feel of his hands on her body . . . his eyes looking so deeply into hers that she felt she could drown in them.

He kissed her again. When he rolled over onto her, his weight was welcome. He did not have to tell her to keep her eyes open. She drank him in. From the beach forest, she heard the sound of a hawk overhead, its call mingling in her head with lines of poetry. She lifted her body to meet his, opened to him in a way she never had to Joaquin.

She walked through her home, looking at the familiar belongings: the used furniture from Victor and Leona, wedding gifts displayed on the dark walnut sideboard in the living room. She wandered into the kitchen. Supper. Joaquin would be home soon, and she would have to have his meal ready. She was in a daze, like an accident victim.

In the bathroom she stared at herself in the mirror over the basin. She could not look into her eyes and dropped her gaze to the rust-colored stain in the sink.

She had tried to get it out, but the iron in the well water stained everything, even their clothes.

She bent over the bathtub and turned the faucets on full, stripped, and stepped into the tub. She did not turn the faucets off until the water was up to her chest. There would be no hot water for Joaquin when he came home, but she could not think of that now.

Her body felt sore. The skin around her brown nipples was red from his teeth. She closed her eyes and scrubbed herself with a coarse cloth, rubbing until the flesh of her face and belly and thighs was pink and tender. She pulled her feet in close so that her knees jutted up. She wrapped her arms around her legs and hugged her knees close to her chest. Her hair fell forward, swooped past her face. The smell of him was in her hair. She tilted her face to the side and inhaled. No, she was not imagining it. *Even in her hair.*

She unclasped her hands and slid down in the water, letting her hair float out in the bathwater. She slouched lower, felt the water edge up onto her face. Lower and lower. The warm water circled her ears, chin, forehead, and cheeks. Still she sank. She kept her eyes open, unblinking, as if to wash the lenses of everything she had seen. She was totally submerged, and everything was blurry. She thought she was crying but could not tell if tears were mingling with the bathwater. Like a whale, suspended in the waves of the sea.

"Rosa?"

The sound of Joaquin's voice came down into the bath. She sat up, chilled despite the steamy water.

"In here." It was too soon to face him. "I'll be right there, okay? I'm almost done." She stepped out of the tub. The air felt cold on her flesh, still pink from scrubbing. She wiped the mist off the mirror and stepped close, examining her breasts. Jesus. What would Joaquin say? The marks Fenris had made still showed. She turned around and studied the reflection of her back. It was scratched from the stalks of dry grass.

She wanted to pray, but she felt she had lost that right. She dressed and went to face her husband.

He sat at the kitchen table, a bottle of whiskey in front of him. He did not look up at her.

"Hello, Joaquin," she said, afraid he would see that she was trembling. She saw then that he was drinking. He knows, she thought. Fear closed her throat.

"Rosa," he said, "come here."

She stood at the sink.

"Come here. Let me hold you. Please."

She stiffened. "You need dinner. Aren't you hungry? I'll make dinner for you."

"I'm hungry for you, Rosa."

He crossed the room and took her in his arms. She held her breath, waiting for him to strike her. Surely he could smell the scent of Fenris on her.

He pulled her into the bedroom and took her onto the bed. "I need you, Rosa. I need you so much."

It was dark in the bedroom. *He is my husband,* she told herself as she got undressed and slipped beneath the bedsheet. She closed her eyes. *He is my husband.* But she hated him for needing her.

PART THREE

Break the bone and
suck out the substantific marrow.
—*François Rabelais*

Chapter 16

Zoe

In the morning, Emily had another "accident." Grimly, Zoe pulled the sheets from the bed and threw them in the laundry basket. Emily, unusually subdued, watched silently from across the room. Zoe grasped her by the arm and took her into the bathroom. Then she ran water in the tub and set the child in it.

Emily's lip started to tremble. "Don't be mad at me, Mommy. I didn't mean to have an accident. Don't be mad at me."

The child's tears shocked Zoe out of her anger. She was distressed to see that the imprint of her fingers showed red on Emily's arm.

"Oh, Em, honey. I'm not mad at you. Honest." She pulled the child from the tub and held her close, mindless of the water soaking through her sleeve to her skin. She held her daughter until the tears ebbed, then wrapped her in a towel and returned to the bedroom. Still holding her, she sat on the edge of the bed and rocked her, rubbing Emily's back, as if warming herself. "I'm not angry with you," she repeated. *I'm afraid,* she wanted to say. *I'm afraid because I think that you are wetting your bed because you, too, remember what was in the attic. I am afraid because I want to protect you and I can't. And because I am so afraid, I am angry. But I am not angry with you, dear child; and now because I have made you cry, I am ashamed.*

But she said none of these things. "I'm not angry with you. I'm just tired." Gently, she dried and dressed

Emily, relieved that the finger marks had faded. "Now you go down and Daddy will get your breakfast while I get the baby up. Then Daddy will walk you to Mrs. Lake's, and when you come home you can help me make cookies. Okay?"

"I don't want to go to Mrs. Lake's today. I want to stay with you."

"But you like Mrs. Lake's."

"I don't want to go."

"Why?" Zoe's mind raced. Had there been some problem neither Mrs. Lake nor Emily had told her about?

" 'Cause. I just don't."

"Is everything all right at school?"

"Yes." Emily stood looking down at her feet. She picked at her thumbnail. "I just don't want to go."

"Well, we all have to do things we don't want to, Emily. Now hurry up or you'll keep Daddy waiting."

The child worked nervously at the skin of her thumb. "I'm scared," she whispered.

The words stopped Zoe cold. In that moment, she wanted to give in to Emily's fears, and to her own. She wanted to keep her daughter by her side, as if she could thereby protect her. She sank to the bed and lifted Emily onto her lap. "Okay, Em. Listen to me. What is our phone number?"

"Four-five-five-oh-six-one-seven."

"That's great, Em. Now I want you to go to school, but if anything makes you afraid, you ask Mrs. Lake to use the phone and you call me and I'll come and get you, okay? Promise."

The child was still in her lap.

"Besides," she said, "isn't this your week to feed the bunnies at school?"

Emily slid off her lap, blessedly diverted, in the wondrous way of children. "Can I bring a carrot?"

"Two carrots. Ask Daddy to get them for you. Now let's get moving or you will be so late the bunnies will be cross-eyed from hunger and wondering where you are." She was relieved to hear her daughter giggle.

"Silly," Emily said. "Bunnies don't get cross-eyed."

Zoe kissed her daughter and sent her down to the kitchen. But the echo of Emily's whispered "I'm afraid" reverberated in the room. How long would it be before Zoe would stop waking at two in the morning to check on her sleeping children; how long before haunting visions of the bones of babies and visits from the police receded from her thoughts; how long before Emily stopped wetting the bed; how long before the house would be hers again?

She showered, dressed, and went in to get Adam, who still lay scrunched up at the head of his crib. At the bottom, Winnie-the-Pooh and Paddington Bear stood sentry, button eyes gleaming in the morning light. She reached out and petted their furry heads. Then she picked up her son, warm with sleep-sweat. She hugged him and kissed the sweet curve beneath his ear.

In the kitchen she found that Jake had left the coffee warming for her. As the idea of tending the school bunnies had healed Emily, so was Zoe restored by feeding her son. Spooning the oatmeal into his rosebud mouth was like feeding a bird. If she wasn't quick enough with the next portion, he stuck his fist in his mouth, and soon oatmeal was smudged across his face, on his fingers, in the wisps of hair over his ears. Between each spoonful, he smiled up at her with his happy, toothless-gummed grin.

"You little funny-bunny," she laughed back at him.

When he was finished, she wiped his face and hands and then crossed to the deacon's bench and laid him in the basket with a warmed bottle. For a moment, things were back to normal.

She heard Jake's whistle as he returned from walking Emily to school. She heard him stop by the door, could picture him picking up the newspaper from the porch. She got up and poured him a cup of coffee. This was part of their morning ritual. After he brought Emily to school and before he went to the bookstore, they spent a half hour reading the paper together and drinking coffee. Then he was off to his world and she to hers. She sat down and waited, realizing his whistling had stopped.

When he came in, he was reading the headlines.

"What is it?" She already knew. He spread the paper out on the table between their coffee cups. The story was on the front page under a bold heading that shouted HUMAN BONES FOUND. With growing dread, Zoe read on:

> Mystery surrounds the discovery of skeletal remains at an undisclosed location in Grace Point Tuesday night. According to Deputy Sheriff Daniel Cole, assigned to the case from the county sheriff's department, the remains, which are believed to be human, will be examined today by Dr. Richard Belliveau, county medical examiner.
>
> Cole would say only that the bones are believed to be the remains of "individuals," indicating that they belong to more than one body.
>
> In a press conference held yesterday morning at the Grace Point Town Hall, Cole said the investigation, which is being conducted jointly by the Grace Point police, the State Police CPAC unit and the County Sheriff's Office's Bureau of Criminal Investigation, is in the primary stages, and further information will not be released until later.
>
> Belliveau said he would be examining the remains today and he expects to call in a full-time forensic pathologist to take over the case if they are determined to be human. "This is a little over my head," he said.
>
> Cole would not release the location where the bodies had been discovered, the exact time, or by whom. Unconfirmed reports indicated that the remains were of two individuals and had been found in an attic trunk in a Grace Point home. It was also speculated that the remains were of children.

Jake leaned back and picked up his cup. "Well, it's not as bad as it could have been. At least they kept our names out of it."

"For now." Zoe took a sip of coffee. It was cold, and she crossed to the sink and dumped the rest down the drain. "Emily wet the bed again."

"Poor kid." Jake was already engrossed in the sports page.

"That's two days in a row," Zoe said, her voice carefully even.

Picking up her signal, Jake lowered the paper. "You think maybe it's because of her cold?"

Zoe returned to the table and sat down. "I think it's what happened in the attic," she said firmly. "And I think that's why she said she was afraid to go to school. How was she? Any problems dropping her off?"

"She didn't fight it. She was afraid to go to school?"

"That's what she said."

"Well, she went. It was probably just another Emily stage."

"I think she's reacting to all that's happened. The bones. The police. All of it."

Jake opened his mouth, then paused.

"What is it?"

"It's nothing, I'm sure. Just her imagination."

"What?"

"Well, before I left her, she told me she wasn't afraid of the witch."

"What witch?"

"That's what I asked her, and she said the witch that put the bones in the attic."

"Jesus, Jake. You don't even tell me? You come back here and read the paper as if this was just another day." She pushed back her chair with a jerky motion and pulled on a sweater.

"Where are you going?"

"To get her. Where else? She must be scared to death, can't you see that?" she asked angrily.

"What I see, Zoe," Jake replied, "is that the more normally we can behave, the quicker Emily will let go of any fears she might have. If we go running to take her out of school, she'll figure she really does have cause to be afraid."

Zoe stopped at the door. "You really think so?"

"Yes. I do."

"Maybe you're right." She had overreacted and been quick to anger. Since New Haven she'd found it too easy to be angry at Jake.

"And I think we should sit down and talk to her tonight, try and reassure her about witches skulking around in the attic."

Of course. Maybe there were no witches in the attic, but there was *someone* skulking around their home: the one-armed man. "Jake—"

Zoe was cut off by the phone. It was Dan Cole. She pictured the deputies. Cole was the thin one who smoked. "Yes?" she said.

"We've got a little problem," the deputy began. "One of the reporters—guy from the *Globe*—he's been busy, asking questions around town, seems he got wind of the ambulance run Tuesday night, looked at the log at the firehouse, saw your name and address."

Zoe shot an anguished look at Jake. Her hand tightened on the phone.

"He's pretty persistent. Now we didn't want to release the information yet, but this fellow is pushing pretty hard. I just wanted to warn you, we are going to be giving out your name this morning."

"You said you'd keep us out of it." Adam began to cry in his basket, and she motioned for Jake to pick him up.

"I said I'd try."

"We don't want our name in the paper. This has nothing to do with us."

"Don't worry. We'll make it clear that other than finding the bones, you are not involved. Still, once your name is public, you'll be getting calls. They start to bother you, give me a call. Some of these reporters are as pesky as greenheads on a pile of dung."

"The bones." Is that how they already referred to the babies? "What should we say?"

"You might want to prepare a statement, something so that you won't be caught off guard." He laughed softly. "It can be overwhelming, ten or fifteen reporters—radio, newspaper guys, television, the wires."

"A statement," she repeated inanely. A picture from television news—of microphones shoved in the haunted faces of survivors of fires, plane crashes—flashed into her mind. Greenheads.

"Just some brief sentence to get them off your back. You and your husband might think about getting a lawyer. Just say nothing, refer them all to your attorney."

"A lawyer," she said weakly. "Doesn't that sound like we're guilty or have something to hide?"

"Hell no. You're just protecting yourself. Getting them off your back. That's what I'd do if it was me."

"Do you know any more about the . . ." She hesitated, unable to call them babies, unwilling to call them bones. "The paper said a doctor was examining the—ah, the bodies. Does he know any more yet?"

"Well, they're human, we know that much." Cole's tone was lively, that of a detective facing a challenging mystery. "A pathologist at our office is working on sex and age now. We'll keep you informed."

She hung up the phone and turned to Jake, who was busy changing Adam's diaper. "That was Dan Cole. He's giving out our name. It's going to be in the papers. He said we should be prepared for calls from reporters."

"Do you want me to stay here with you?"

"No, I'll be okay. He said we should think about getting a lawyer. Someone to run interference, I guess."

"That's a good idea." Jake didn't even look up. "I'll

stop in to see Teddy Ryan on the way to the store. I'll have him give you a call."

Jake fastened the last tab on the diaper and picked up Adam. Cradling his son in one arm, he crossed to hold Zoe with the other. "We'll be all right," he whispered into her hair. "It has nothing to do with us. Just hang tough, honey—it'll pass. We'll be all right."

The morning dragged by. Zoe went about her chores, but her thoughts churned. *Who were they? How had they come to be in the attic? Who were the mothers of the four infants, and what had become of them?* She couldn't imagine how it would feel to know your baby was dead, hidden in a hatbox, never given a proper burial. She wondered if the mothers still lived in Grace Point and whether they'd read today's headlines.

She gave Adam his bath, then propped him in his high chair and fed him some mashed bananas. Full, dry, and happy, he gurgled and watched while she moved around the kitchen. She was wiping the counter when she saw the candy bars, which had been pushed back out of the way, behind the sugar canister. The faces of ghosts and witches, goblins and bats—faces from Grace Point—stared up at her mockingly. Halloween seemed ages ago. Impatiently, she began to gather up the candy. Then she gasped, her hand suspended over the weathered features of one familiar face. An old fisherman, masquerading as a scarecrow—a scarecrow with one arm. She drew back as if scalded. The face was that of the man who stood in the alley and watched their home.

Where had she seen him before and why had he been watching them? She crossed to the window and looked out, half expecting to see him, but the alley was empty. She traced a finger over the sketch. Somewhere in the past she had seen his face, imprinted it on her memory. But she knew she hadn't seen him lurking outside her home until after the babies had been found. Still holding the drawing, she went to the phone, then changed her mind. Before she told Jake or anyone else, she would find out the identity of the one-armed man. Any action was better than sitting and waiting for the police to finish their investigation.

She pulled on her jacket and bundled Adam up. Just before she left the house, she pried the drawing of the scarecrow off the candy bar and slipped it in her pocket.

At the mouth of the harbor, the waters churned, spitting froth. The draggers pitched and rolled at their moorings. On the *Sea Witch,* Davie Long and Bill Packett worked on gear. Piles of nets, rank with seaweed, lay underfoot. From time to time Davie would look out at the choppy sea beyond the breakwater and swear. Bill had witnessed Davie's impatience before and said nothing. Just a kid, Davie was. He had a lot of growing up to do, but he was a damn hard worker, he'd give him that. For his part, Bill did not regret the day ashore. Plenty to do on the boat. The fish would be there tomorrow or the next day. Davie would come to understand that. Bill turned his attention away from his mate and back to his tasks at hand. So much to do on a boat and never enough time to get it all done.

"Excuse me." The voice was light, the tone tentative. Both men heard it, but neither looked up from his gear.

"Excuse me. Sir?"

Bill caught a glimpse of the woman out of the corner of his eye. She was standing near the edge of the wharf, one hand atop the oil-slick ladder as she bent toward the *Sea Witch*. "Sir?"

She wasn't bad-looking. Decent body—damn decent. He could see that even though she was carrying a baby in some kind of pouch strapped around her neck. It was the kid as much as the body that decided him. He looked up at her.

"I wonder if you could help me," she began.

Behind him Davie stirred. "Just bet you'd like to help her, hey, Bill?" he muttered softly.

Bill could see the girl had heard his mate. Her cheeks reddened, and she tightened her arms around the baby.

"I'm looking for someone," she continued.

His face neutral, Bill spat over the gunwale. He could see that she was older than he had first imagined. Not a girl at all. Probably in her thirties. One of the newcomers. Time was when he knew everyone in Grace Point, but not anymore. "That so?" he said.

"An older man. Maybe sixty or seventy, I'd guess. About five ten."

His gaze traveled over her body. He wondered if she was nursing the kid. He'd had a woman one time who was nursing, let him have some too. He'd laid at her breast and sucked like a baby. Made him hard just remembering. "Not much of a description," he said. Behind him, Davie laughed.

"I think he's a fisherman," she said.

She *thinks*. He spat again. What the hell was he—the Yellow Pages? A Chamber-of-fuckin'-Commerce guide?

"And he has one arm. Here—" She juggled the baby to her side and slid her hand in her pocket. She held a piece of paper toward him. "He looks kind of like this."

A light of recognition flitted quickly over Bill's face, and he narrowed his eyes. "Whattaya lookin' for him for?"

She was sharp all right. She had caught the flash of recognition, but his question had stopped her.

"To paint," she said after a minute. "I'm an artist. I've seen this man once or twice around the town and thought I'd like to paint him."

"Jesus," Davie swore. He was staring at the drawing the woman still held toward them. "What the hell does Old Joe have anyway? Old geezer like him."

Bill shot a glance at his mate, and Davie fell silent. He turned back to the woman. She was lying about wanting to paint Old Joe, he'd bet a day's catch on that. He narrowed his eyes and looked the woman over again. Christ, he thought, if Joe's old lady heard he was foolin' around, she'd have his one good arm in a sling before he knew what was happening.

"Do you know where he is?"

Well, if the old man got himself into a scrape, he'd have to worm his own way out. "You'll find him out on Town Road. His place is on the right, just before the turnoff to the dump."

"Does it have a name in front or something?" She put the slip of paper back in her pocket.

"You can't miss it. It's the only trailer out there."

"Thanks."

"Old Joe likes the young blood," Davie said as they watched her walk away, "but I sure as shit can't see what the young ones see in him."

"She's not so young." Bill's eyes traveled over the retreating legs. Not so young, but not so old, either. "And who knows? Maybe she does just want to paint his picture." He returned to his gear.

"Oh, sure," Davie replied. He raised his voice. "Hey, lady, if Old Joe disappoints you, you come on back. You come on back and *paint my picture.*" He rolled his hips with the last three words.

She didn't turn around, but Bill could tell by the way she got all tight in the shoulders and ass that she had heard.

"Stow it," he said to his young mate.

Zoe concentrated on the road, as if it would keep at bay the memory of the men at the wharf. The fishermen's rudeness, their hostility, had shaken her more than she was willing to admit. This was not the first time she had encountered the coarse sexuality of men, nor was it the first time since she had moved to Grace Point that townspeople had treated her like an outsider; but this time it had seemed so personal. She glanced across the seat at her son. Usually when she had Adam with her, people were kinder. But it hadn't softened the fishermen at the pier.

She flicked on her blinker and made a left turn onto Town Road. Her hands tightened on the wheel and she resolutely turned her mind away from the men on the *Sea Witch* and to the task ahead. Meeting Old Joe, whoever he was.

In her dozens of runs to the dump, she had never noticed the trailer. A rusted hulk with a door and two windows it sat on blocks. Strips of tape used to mask the fault line of a crack crossed the larger of the two windows. An overturned rowboat, planks rotted through, lay close to the walk. Off to one side, a larger boat raised on salvaged trap poles was listing dangerously to the left. A dozen lobster pots, useless from age, blocked the path to the trailer door. Clutter—old batteries, furniture, fishing gear—littered the yard. Everything wooden was peeling or weathered gray. Everything that was metal was rusted.

Swallowing her misgivings, Zoe pulled into the ruts that served as a driveway. The only sign of life was the laundry flapping on the clothesline: two pairs of work pants, a half-dozen sets of underwear, and three plaid shirts, all men's. The shirts, sleeves full of wind, dipped and waved at her.

When she turned off the motor, she heard the howling of two German shepherds that had crawled out from beneath the dory. Only the short chains around their necks kept their front legs from touching the car, but even so, she shrank back. The dogs were thin and mean, with hungry red eyes, and they lunged again and again, each time jerked short by the chains. Somehow, mercifully, Adam slept.

The trailer door opened and a man appeared on the

step. She recognized him at once. He snarled at the dogs and kicked out at them. He caught one in the hind quarter and it yelped. Both dogs slunk back underneath the rowboat. The man with the face of her scarecrow walked toward the car.

Quietly, so as not to wake Adam, she slipped out of the car. The echo of barking hung in the air.

"What you doin' here?" He did not move from the steps. She crossed the yard.

Beneath the rowboat, one of the German shepherds snarled deep in his throat. "Shut up, you bastards," he growled to the dog. His eyes did not leave her face.

Zoe's mouth was dry, but she knew she must not betray her fear. "I wanted to talk to you."

"Git away. Go back where you came from. You hear me? Get the hell away from me."

"I just want to know why you come and stare at my house."

The dogs started snarling again.

As if that were a signal, the door to the trailer opened. The woman standing in the doorway was no older than Zoe, but she was gray-faced with poverty and fatigue. Once she had been pretty, but now her features had thickened. Her large breasts hung heavy and shapeless beneath her shirt. "What's she want?" she whined, her voice as colorless and tired as her skin.

"Git back inside."

"Joe—" she began.

"Go on," he said. He snarled the order over his shoulder as if he were talking to one of the German shepherds. "This has nothin' to do with you."

The woman retreated.

"You," he said to Zoe, "you git out of here. You hear?"

"Why were you in the alley last night? Is it because of the babies?" she blurted. "Do you know something about them?"

He was close enough now for her to see a thin scar

beneath his unshaven beard, close enough to see the slight widening of his pupils.

"Git the fuck outta here." His eyes were mean, but she saw fear in their depths as well, and she gained courage.

"I haven't come here to cause you trouble," she said firmly. "I promise."

"Did she send you? Go back, you hear—go back and tell her to leave me the fuck alone." The shirts on the line flapped behind him, mocking him. "Go on, now. Git out."

"Her?" Zoe persisted. "Tell *who* to leave you alone?"

His mouth opened, then contorted with rage; he did not answer. It took her a moment to realize that he was staring at her car. At Adam. His face was twisted with hate, and spittle shone wetly at the corners of his mouth. She moved instinctively, cutting off his view of her son.

The motion broke his spell. "Git out," he screamed. "Git out. Git off my land. Goddamn you, you bitch, git off my land."

The shepherds came to life, baying and straining at their chains. Fumbling, she opened the car door and slid inside. With shaking hands, she pushed the door locks down and twisted the key in the ignition. She had to get Adam away; he'd begun to cry.

She pushed the gas pedal to the floor and threw the car in reverse. The engine died. "Slower," she whispered. "Slower." She could not erase the hatred she had seen on the man's face when he'd looked at her son. She inhaled, forcing herself to be calm.

Outside, the man named Joe was white with fury. He screamed—at her, the dogs, the gray-faced woman who had reappeared at the trailer door. Even through the car windows, Zoe heard his fury. Heard the dogs whimper as he struck out at them. Heard the woman as she cried, "Joe, what's wrong?" The dogs escaped from their rowboat retreat. Enraged, the old man kicked a lobster trap. Two, three times, he lashed out at it. With the last blow, he shattered its ribs.

This one splintering sound rose above the madhouse din. It sounded to Zoe like the cracking of bones.

Chapter 17

Old Joe.

Zoe smoothed out the crumpled drawing of the scarecrow and studied it. Now she had a name for him. Old Joe. And now she knew, absolutely *knew,* that this man was linked to her grisly discovery in the attic.

Tell her to leave me alone.

Who did he think had sent her to see him? Who had so enraged him? And frightened him, for Zoe had seen fear beneath the rage. She crossed to look out at the alley, but she knew that he would stay away from her now. Well, she would have to make another trip out to the trailer on Town Road. Remembering the fury of the dogs, she shuddered.

From the deacon's bench Adam smiled up at her. He had quieted down almost as soon as she had pulled away from the trailer, and had soon reverted to his usual sunny self. She bent over and kissed his cheek. He made a small, gurgling Adam sound, and she smiled as she untangled his tiny fingers from her hair.

She would not bring him with her next time. Nor would she tell Jake about the man. Not yet. He wouldn't understand her need for more answers, because he didn't feel the same about the babies in the trunk. To him it was a simple accident of fate.

The pealing of the church chimes broke in on her thoughts. Quarter of twelve. She had to hurry or she would be late picking up Emily. She scooped up Adam and carried him to the front hall and set him in the carriage. She wedged the door open with one foot and maneuvered the buggy outside. Then she closed the door, taking the time to double-check the lock.

Swathed in blankets, Adam watched the play of sun and shadows dancing on the hood. The carriage was large, black, old-fashioned. She had found it in the basement when they moved in. "It's an antique," she'd told Jake proudly as she scrubbed it inside and out. "Or at least a collector's item."

At Mrs. Lake's nursery school, she joined the throng of waiting mothers. There was none of the casual banter this morning. The silent women pressed close to the school yard and waited for their children. They, too, had read about the skeletons in the morning headlines.

The children spilled out of the nursery school. Eagerly Zoe sought Emily, picking her out at last. Across the yard, Emily walked side by side with her friend Elizabeth Bower. The two little girls chattered on, oblivious of their waiting mothers.

Zoe took advantage of the last few moments before Emily noticed her to study her face, but all she saw was a sunny, laughing child. She could have wept with relief. Maybe Jake's right, she thought. I'm overreacting.

Emily ran up to her. "Mommy, can I go to Elizabeth's for lunch and to play? Please? Can I?"

"I don't think so, honey. Not today."

"Please. Mrs. Bower said I could. And Elizabeth wants me to. Please."

"What about your nap?"

"We'll rest at Elizabeth's. Honest. Please? Please say I can go."

"Don't whine, Emily." Fighting for time, Zoe longed to refuse. She wanted Emily home. But she forced herself to banish the fears that held her, prying them off as she would fingers encircling her wrists. She would not—*would not*—inflict them on Emily.

"All right," she agreed. She bent over and hugged

her daughter, but Emily squirmed out of the embrace, eager to be off. Zoe held her by the shoulders. "Now, I'll call Daddy and he'll pick you up at the Bowers' on his way home. Do you hear me, Emily? Daddy will pick you up." The child jiggled beneath her fingers, bounced on her toes. "And don't forget the nap. Promise? And be good."

Freed at last, Emily danced off to where Elizabeth and her mother waited on the other side of the school yard. Over their heads, Jane Bower waved at her. She cupped her hands to her mouth and, smiling, shouted, "Okay if Emily comes over?" The words were nearly lost in the clamor of children. Zoe nodded and returned the wave. She stood with the carriage and watched while Emily walked away. Her daughter never looked back.

Without the laughing children, the silence was full. As Zoe turned the carriage toward home, Adam smiled and gurgled. "Well, old man," she said, "look's like it's just you and me."

The old carriage rolled along the sidewalk; its rubber wheels whispered. She inhaled. The warm air carried the faint, salty taste of the sea. She looked down at Adam. The bonnet and netting shaded his face. She reached under the net and pulled the carriage robe up close to his chin, tucking him in carefully. She thought about practical things: she would prepare monkfish for dinner; she'd call Jake and tell him to pick up Emily at the Bowers'. But within minutes her thoughts returned to the old man. Old Joe. Joe who? She didn't have a last name. She'd check with the town clerk. Suddenly, she stopped and pivoted the carriage on its rear wheels until she was headed in the opposite direction. Suddenly she wanted to see Jake. To tell him about Old Joe. Not shut him out. She did that too often, to punish him. It was time to go on, to learn to forgive.

* * *

She stared at the square sign on the door: the clock face with the hands pointing to twelve and one, the words "Be Back At."

Strange, Jake seldom closed the store during the day. She wondered if he had decided on the spur of the moment to surprise her and go home for lunch. The thought brought a smile to her face.

Still smiling, she turned the carriage and headed home. She hadn't gone half a block when the smile—and all color—faded from her face. Shading her eyes against the sun, she squinted into the distance. *It can't be.* The slight, lithe figure with the curtain of blond hair swinging strode down the sidewalk, her back to Zoe. *It can't be. It can't be.* There were hundreds of young girls with blond hair cut blunt so it swung like that.

She forced herself to breathe. The girl rounded the corner and Zoe fought the urge to rush off in pursuit. Her mind was playing tricks, nothing more.

Adam was still asleep when they arrived home. She turned the carriage around and, rocking it on its back wheels, pulled it up the porch steps and into the front hall. The tiny scowl she knew so well flickered across his face; then he was at peace again.

There was no note on the kitchen table, no sign that Jake had been home. The kitchen clock said one-fifteen. He must be back at the bookstore. Only his voice would wipe out the phantoms awakened by the sight of swinging blond hair. She picked up the phone and dialed. Seven rings. Twelve. Fifteen. She looked again at the clock. Sometimes when he worked alone and wanted a break, he closed the store. Zoe tried to remember if this was Debra's day off. They seldom took a break at the same time. After the twenty-seventh ring, Zoe hung up. Her hand was still on the receiver when the phone rang. She jumped as if stung, then snatched it up. "Hello? Jake?"

"Zoe? It's me, Jane."

"Oh. Hi. I thought it might be Jake. I just tried to call him to tell him to pick Em up on his way home, but the line was busy." *Why did she say that? Why lie?* "Jane?" Concern tightened her throat. "Is anything the matter? Is Emily all right?"

"She's fine. She and Elizabeth are having some milk and cookies and then they're going in for a nap."

"Oh. Well, I hope she isn't too much for you."

"Emily? She's a living doll. She's a pleasure to have. Elizabeth loves the company. That's why I'm calling. The girls want to know if Emily can stay for supper and then overnight. We'd love to have her. She can sleep in some of Elizabeth's pajamas and go to school from here tomorrow. It's no problem."

She pictured Emily standing by her bed. The wet sheets, the tears. "Another time, Jane. She's just getting over a cold, and I don't want her getting too tired. You know how they are when they sleep over. Maybe next week."

"Okay. Listen, Zoe, don't bother Jake. I'll drop Emily off later on."

"You sure you don't mind?"

"Not at all. I have to go out to pick up a few things at the market, and I'll drop her off then. Late afternoon okay?"

"Fine."

After she hung up, Zoe checked on Adam. He was still asleep. She wandered from room to room, at loose ends. Twice more there was no answer at the bookstore.

At last, she climbed the stairs to her bedroom. Leaving the door open so that she would hear Adam when he woke, she crossed to the alcove and stood before her easel. She pulled back the curtains of the window, hitching them up on the rod so her view was unobstructed. Grace Point lay below. The alley was empty. She looked down on the narrow street, on the shop fronts that lay shoulder to shoulder. In the horizon, the bay sparkled. The surface was green, but underneath, dark, nearly black waters roiled.

When she picked up her brush, she felt herself uncoil. She began unhurriedly, allowing her hands to become accustomed to the act of sketching. It had been weeks and weeks since she had stood at the easel. She was out of shape. People seldom understood how physical painting was. One had to be in condition for it. Bit by bit the work drew her in, until she was no longer in her bedroom but in some magic space where her reality *was* the painting. This was what she needed. Here it was possible to shut out all the horror of the past three days—indeed, the past two years. And ghosts of blond, lithe women.

She picked pastels of the subtlest, filmiest shades of blue and gray and green. The work was filled with mist, with layers superimposed on layers. Time passed as she drew her picture of Grace Point.

Much later, she surfaced. She came to reluctantly, dazed. Her shoulders were tense and her eyes ached. When she looked at the painting, she drew in her breath. At first glance, the shops and houses and ocean were simply rendered. But after a moment, the background—the backdrop against which the whole scene sat—floated up through the layers. In the mists, as real as the steeple of the Congregational Church and the piers, were the faces of babies. Their eyes were brown, like her own children's eyes. They haunted the streets of Grace Point. They were formed from the shadows and fog, the ether and spirit of Grace Point.

She stared at the painting, mesmerized. It was the best thing she had ever done. And it terrified her. *What had she seen?* Moving quickly, she picked up the canvas and, averting her eyes so that she would not have to look at it, carried it across the room. She opened the closet door, pushed aside the clothing, turned the painting against the wall, and shut the door.

The sound of voices came up from the back door.

Dan Cole sat in the Grace Point police station and waited for the phone to ring. His contact in New Haven had said he'd be calling back after lunch. Any time now.

He loosened his tie and slouched back in the chair. Police Chief Nelson's secretary looked up from her typing. He smiled, but she had already returned to her work. One-fifteen. His stomach growled. He hoped Riley remembered to bring him a sandwich when he returned.

Picking up his notebook, he scanned his latest entry. Dr. Leonard Shea, the state medical examiner, had reported that the skeletons were those of infants. Although the remains were substantially decomposed, Dr. Shea had found mummified tissue clinging to the bones, on the basis of which he had set the age of the skeletons at fifty years. The doctor had declined to speculate about the cause of death.

Nelson's secretary got up and crossed to the row of file cabinets. She was a classy number, Dan thought, wondering lazily what kept her in Grace Point. He watched in appreciation as she walked across the room. Her skirt clung to her buttocks and hip line and then fell in folds to her ankles. He would never cheat on Jenny, but that didn't mean he couldn't look at other women. She had a nice ass. High, tight. He bet she had nice legs too, but they were hidden. Between her heels and skirt, just an inch of flesh showed. She wore a cream-colored silk blouse and, over her shoulders, a woven scarf in muted colors that reminded Dan of Ireland. He recognized the costume. He knew if he went out into the street and canvassed the women passing, nearly every one would have a scarf of some kind tied around her neck or shoulders. It amazed him how, suddenly, women all wore a new fashion. Happened when he wasn't looking. One day only old ladies wore scarves, the next day every woman he saw had one. Even Jenny. Women lived in a world of secrets. He was awed by them.

Returning to her desk, the secretary switched off the computer. She was nearly out the door when she stopped and turned to Dan.

"I'm going to lunch." It was the first time she had spoken to him. "Can I get you some coffee or anything?"

"Thanks, but I'm fine. My partner's bringing me some."

She took a lot of the life out of the room with her, and he sighed. Ten minutes later, the phone rang.

Dan Cole hung up the phone. "Well, well, well," he said, breathing the words out softly. It had been Sam Riley's idea to check Barlow's background. Once again his partner had hit pay dirt.

As if on cue, the door opened and Riley entered with two take-out bags, one already stained with grease. "Here you go," he said, handing it to Dan.

The smell of fried onions and sausage seeped from the bag, but now, his hunger forgotten, Dan cleared a spot and set it on the desk.

Riley opened the other bag and took out two containers of coffee. "Black, no sugar," he said, passing one to Dan.

Dan took a sip. The coffee burned his tongue. He worked to keep his voice casual. "My friend from New Haven got back to me."

They had been partners for too long for Sam to be fooled. "Bingo?"

"Bingo."

Riley grinned. He picked up the grease-marked bag, opened it, and unwrapped a sausage-and-pepper sub.

"You gonna want this?" He washed a mouthful down with coffee. "So?"

"Looks like maybe New Haven wasn't such a swell place for Barlow to raise kids after all."

"Yeah?"

"Listen to this. About four months before the Barlows moved to Grace Point, their baby-sitter—a seventeen-year-old high school senior named Laurel Blake—accused Jake Barlow of sexually assaulting her."

"No shit."

"Absolutely."

"What happened?"

"Within a week the charge was dropped."

"The charge was dropped?"

"Right. Barlow taught English at the high school. The school board talked about a suspension, but nothing came of it."

"So what happened?"

"It died. The whole thing died almost overnight. Zoe Barlow was pregnant at the time of the incident. She had a miscarriage. Shortly after that, Jake Barlow and his family moved to Grace Point."

"Zoe?" Jane called out. "Zoe? You here? I'm dropping off Emily."

"I'm upstairs. Be right down."

"I can't stay. Elizabeth's in the car and I left it running. I'll call you tomorrow."

The back door had closed before Zoe reached the kitchen.

Zoe saw at once that Emily was overtired. There were smudges of shadow under her eyes. "Hi, honey," she said. She glanced around the kitchen; something was wrong.

"I'm hungry," Emily whined, rubbing her knuckles against her eyes.

"I'm hungry, too," Zoe said. *What was it?* "How about some spaghetti?"

"I'm hungry now. I want something right now."

"In a sec, okay, hon?" She went to the cupboard and took down a package of animal crackers. "Here. Have a couple of these while I put the water on." She opened another door to get out a jar of sauce and box of pasta. She still couldn't shake the eerie feeling. *What the hell was it?* As she reached for the sauce, her hand brushed a box of baby cereal. Then she knew. *Jesus.* Adam. He was still in the hall in the carriage. How the hell could she have been so negligent? She'd had no business painting or doing anything that could make her forget about her own children. Her stomach knotted with guilt.

She could hear Emily's petulant whine as she hurried down the hall. She sighed and quickened her step. In the dim hall light, she saw the carriage and drew in her breath. The netting was rumpled, tossed on the floor. When she bent to pick up her son, the breath went out of her lungs as sharply as if a fist had struck her.

Adam was gone.

Chapter 18

Rosalina

Even before she opened the door, Rosalina knew it was Fenris.

"What are you doing here?" she hissed in horror. "Someone will see you." She pulled him into the house. "They'll tell Joaquin. They'll—"

He put his hand gently over her mouth. "You're an exciting woman, Rosalina. I couldn't sleep last night. All I could do was think about you."

"Don't say that."

"Why not? It's true. And you, didn't you think of me, too?" His mouth twisted in a smile. "Or did you go to your priest, your Father Mallory, and ask forgiveness?"

"Why are you here? What do you want?"

"Do you have to ask, Little Rosa?"

She turned away, not answering.

"I want you, Rosa. I couldn't sleep with wanting you."

"Please," she whispered. "Go away." The smell of him, of his shaving lotion and the lingering smoke from his pipe, made her weak. She crossed the kitchen and sank into a chair, away from him.

"Is that what you want? For me to go away?" He waited.

"Yes. Please. I love Joaquin."

He crossed and knelt by her feet. He took her hand in his and ran his tongue over her finger, licking the web of skin between each finger slowly, and then, turning her hand over, he began kissing and licking her palm.

She closed her throat to keep from moaning.

"I'm not going away, Rosa. I want you too much to go away." Still on his knees, he pulled her face toward him and kissed her. She resisted for a moment and then gave in.

"I want you," he repeated.

"Not here." She whispered, as if her house had ears. "We can't stay here."

He stood and went to the door, locking it. "Are you expecting anyone?"

She shook her head, but she was terrified someone, Dolores or Helen, would come.

Even across the room, the intensity of his eyes made her drop her gaze. "Has anyone ever given you a bath, Rosalina?"

"What?"

"I want to give you a bath." He smiled. "Would you like that?"

She caught her breath. "No."

"Liar," he said, laughing.

She felt her face grow hot.

"I want to soap every inch of you. I want to touch you in places where you've never been touched. And then I want to make love to you. Like we did yesterday—and in other ways you've never dreamed of."

As he carried her down the hall and into the bathroom, she let her head rest on his shoulder. She felt sleepy and heavy.

He set her on the floor, and while the tub was filling, he began to undress her. He took her blouse off first. *Joaquin's razor was on the sink.* Then he unbuttoned her skirt; she lifted her hips so he could slip it off. *When he had kissed her good-bye that morning he had just shaved and his cheek had been smooth against her skin.* He unfastened her bra with practiced fingers. *Joaquin's washcloth hung on the bar just above her head, still wet.* Her underpants were worn, and when he took them off she was embarrassed.

When she was completely undressed, he pulled her up and looked at her. She covered her breasts with one arm. He pulled it away. "You're beautiful," he said, "so beautiful." He took off his shirt and picked her up again, setting her in the bathtub. He soaped the facecloth and washed her back and then her neck with circular strokes. His touch was tender and slow, and she shivered. As he bathed her, he crooned softly, telling her again and again how beautiful she was. She sank back against the tub and closed her eyes. Her hair floated in the water.

After a while he dispensed with the cloth, using only his hands. Slick with soap, they slid over her. His touch was rougher now as he explored her body. He pushed her legs apart and soaped between them, his fingers busy. He hurt her a little then, but she did not pull away. She was moaning, and her body began to move beneath the water.

He lifted her from the tub and, not bothering to dry her, picked her up and started back down the hall. "Where is the bedroom?"

She pointed the way. But once inside the room, she saw the bed: hers and Joaquin's. This was a line she could not cross. She could not make love with him in Joaquin's bed. "Not here," she said.

He laid her on the bed. His hands again began to explore her body, his touch rough, as it had been in the bath when he had hurt her. She pulled him to her, wanting him as she had never wanted anyone else.

She longed to sleep, to curl up in a ball like a kitten and tuck herself in the curve his body made, but Fenris was wide awake and talkative. He got out of bed and crossed to the bureau, found a pack of Camels Joaquin had left there. He lit a cigarette. Moving easily around the room, as if it were his own and not another man's, he picked up an ashtray and returned to the bed. He stretched out beside her, the ashtray resting on his chest, and blew smoke rings into the air over their heads.

She turned on her side, nestling her head in the crook of his arm, and ran her fingers over his ribs, around his nipples, playing with the springy curls of his chest hair. She slid her hand over his back—his long, beautiful back. His skin was white, as if he had never lain in the sun.

"Have you ever been to New York, Rosa?"

"No." Carefully so as not to knock over the ashtray, she traced the line of his breastbone with her forefinger.

He blew another ring and watched silently until it disintegrated. "What about Paris? Have you ever been to Europe?"

She looked up to see if he was teasing, but he was staring at the ceiling. "I haven't been anywhere. Except Fall River. I went to Fall River once." Her fingers continued their restless toying on his chest. She felt the warmth of the sun on her body as it shone high through the window. It had to be nearly noon. She began to worry again that Dolores would come by.

"You will love it, Rosa. All of it. Paris. New York. Do you like to dance?"

Her fingers fell still. *You will love it.* That's what he had said. *Will love it.* Not *would* love it. *Will.*

He set the ashtray on the table and turned to her. "Do you? Do you like to dance? I bet you do. I bet you dance the way you make love. There's another party at the Loft Saturday night. Come with me and we'll dance."

"I can't," she said.

"Why?"

She fell silent. She could not speak Joaquin's name.

"Because you're married? He doesn't have to know." He kissed her, playfully at first, then deeply.

Her fingers slid down over his stomach. He groaned and took hold of her hand in his, guiding it down. She felt him grow hard.

"Look at that," he said. "Look what you do to me. God, you excite me, Rosa. I can't get enough of you." He pulled her over on top of him. "That's it," he said. "There. This time you move while I lie back. You do the work."

She felt him moving deep inside of her. While he held his hands on her hips, teaching her, he looked up at her. "Why don't you come to the Sail Loft and move in with me?"

He smiled when he said this, but she was not sure if he was kidding.

" 'Come live with me and be my love.' "

"I can't," she whispered.

"Yes, you can. Say it." His hands pressed down on her hips, leading her in deep strokes. "Say you'll be my love."

"No. I can't."

Still in her, he rolled over so that he was on top. "Say it," he growled as he moved over her. Her breasts were covered with sweat, and he licked them with his tongue.

"Stop," she said. "That tickles."

"I'll stop when you say it. Say you'll come live with me."

"No," she giggled. It had become a game.

"Say it. Say you'll be my love." He pinned her hands down with his and began kissing and playfully biting her neck and ears and lips. "Say it." He breathed the words into her mouth, her eyelids, the hollow of her throat.

"No," she whispered back. Then, just as she came, "I will. Oh, I will," she cried into his chest.

When she woke, she was alone. "Fenris?" she called softly. The bed—the room—smelled of their sweat and of sex. "Fenris," she called again, but she knew he had gone. His name echoed in the empty house. She stretched, extending her arms high over her head and tightening her legs. She felt as spent as if she had been swimming for hours. On the underside of her arm, there was a tiny red mark where he had bitten her. She closed her eyes. When she opened them, she looked up at the crucifix on the wall behind the bed. The cross was large and finely carved. Yellow palm leaves—leaves she and Joaquin had received at St. Peter's on Palm Sunday—were tucked behind it.

"Oh, what have I done? Oh, Joaquin, my Joaquin, what have I done?" She buried her head in the pillow, away from knowledge and accusation, and wept.

When she could cry no more, she got up. Moving slowly, she dressed, then stripped the sheets from the bed. She replaced them with fresh ones and cleaned the room.

"I'm sorry, Joaquin," she whispered as she worked—as she made their bed and emptied the ashtray into the toilet and wiped the ashes clean—but the words sounded hollow. She drained the water from the tub. When it was empty, she saw the wet washcloth wadded on the bottom of the tub, and her nipples, betraying her, hardened. "No," she cried, and threw the cloth in the trash. The sight of it made her sick.

In the kitchen she prepared Joaquin's dinner. Then she practiced how she would sit when he came in. First she sat at the kitchen table, drinking a glass of lemonade. Then she went to the living room and sat on the sofa, a basket of mending beside her, needle in hand. She stretched her legs out and then tucked them under her casually. No. She was always in the kitchen when he came home, always. It was important to do everything the same. She returned to the kitchen and sat at the table waiting. But Joaquin did not come.

Light faded to dusk, but still he did not return. The hollow spot in her stomach filled with fear. Images of drowned fishermen—the Viera brothers and others—came to mind. In mounting dread, she waited for them to come and tell her that her husband was dead. It was her fault. She knew that, accepted the guilt, felt it settle on her shoulders like an old, familiar shawl.

Dusk deepened to evening, evening to darkness. No messenger came to her door. During these long hours, she did not move from her chair, not even to switch on a light. She understood now that he had not drowned. If the boat had gone down, she would have known by now.

Imperceptibly, by degrees, the sky lightened. Soon it would be dawn. Exhausted and afraid, Rosa went to bed.

"Whore."

Joaquin stood over her, swaying slightly, his fists clenched by his sides. The smell of whiskey hung heavy in the room.

"Whore." He spat the word again and she shrank back against the pillow.

"You are a whore, a *puta.* You bring filth to my bed."

"Joaquin—"

"Shut up." His face was black with fury, and for an instant she could see Victor's face, as if Joaquin wore a mask.

"Please, Joaquin. Listen to me—" Her mind

whirled frantically. She had never seen him like this.

Her words enraged him. "Shut up. Whore. *Puta.*"

"Joaquin. Please." She reached a hand to him.

He flinched from her touch. "You are just like your mother. A whore." He hit her then, so hard that her head struck the headboard. Overhead, the crucifix rocked slightly.

He stared at her. The imprint of his hand lay like a birthmark on her cheek. He stared at her as her expression turned from shock to something hard and cold and hate-filled.

"Oh, Rosa," he cried. "I'm sorry. I didn't mean to hurt you. I'm sorry."

She continued to stare at him. He no longer looked at all like Victor. The smell of stale whiskey sickened her.

"Please, Rosa," he said. "Forgive me." He sank down on the bed and buried his head against her stomach. She could feel his tears against her skin. "I don't know what happened. Rosa, I would never hurt you."

Feeding on its own galvanizing charge, the news ran through Grace Point, creating a shower of disbelief, anger, pettiness, righteousness, and—in some—smug delight that the girl had proved, after all, to be no better than her mother.

When Dominus Roderick heard that his daughter had gone to live with the writer named Fenris Boak, he felt a grim satisfaction that his expectations, fueled by years of waiting and watching, had at last been met.

He refused to talk to anyone about her. When Joaquin came to him, he said only, "She is a whore like her mother. You are better off without her." Familiar with the role of betrayed husband, he told Joaquin to exorcise Rosalina from his life just as thoroughly as he himself had done.

The day after she moved in with Fenris Boak, Rosalina stopped by the bakery to see her father.

"Get out of my kitchen," he ordered.

"Try to understand." Even as she pleaded, she wondered if she could explain her feelings for Fenris. Could her father ever understand how exciting Fenris was, how important he made her feel, and how tame, how *boring* Joaquin seemed in comparison? Trying to explain was impossible. "I love him," she finally said.

Nothing she could have said could have angered her father more. Years before, he had listened to his wife beg for him to understand that she had fallen in love with someone else.

"Evil. You are evil." Her father spat at her. "Whore." Then he turned his back and waited in silence until she went away.

Calmly, unwilling to show him how deeply he had hurt her, she wiped his spit from her cheek. But outside she wept. It was the first time since she had left Joaquin that she had cried. She thought about going to see Dolores, but her sister-in-law had been forbidden by Victor to talk with her.

She remembered how Dolores and Isabella had gone on the picnic with the sailors. Why was it all right as long as you hid your sins? Why would people accept them if you hid them or pretended to be ashamed of them? She already understood that the others were angry with her not for being unfaithful to Joaquin but because she was so open about it.

Rosa did not care.

"Are you sure?" Fenris had asked when she had gone to him. "You don't have to leave your husband for me, you know." He stared deep into her eyes when he said it, and then he kissed her, biting her lower lip, then filling her mouth with his tongue and breath. He did not say then that he would leave his wife for her, but his kisses promised everything.

The next day they drove to Boston in the green De Soto. They stayed overnight. In her mind that trip marked the real beginning of the time she belonged to him.

Chapter 19

Even before they reached Willie's, she could hear the music, could feel the throb, the heat of it. At the door, a line of tourists waited to get in. She edged closer to Fenris. "It's too crowded." She wished they had stayed in his room at the Sail Loft.

"Come on," he laughed. "Follow me." He clasped her hand in his and threaded his way into the room, weaving between the crush of bodies, pulling her along in his wake. Dozens of people called out his name as the couple made their way into the bar and toward the round table where Ben and Louise sat. Many of them reached out to grab Fenris by the hand or cuff his shoulder, and Rosa recognized several as artists and writers and students of Ben's. Over by the bar that curved along the wall, a knot of fishermen were drinking beer. Averting her eyes, she clung to Fenris.

Willie's, built out over the shore so that at high tide the water lapped beneath the plank floor with an eerie hollow sound, was the largest bar in Grace Point. The name carved in the quarterboard hanging over the front door was "The Figurehead," but no one ever called the place anything but Willie's. A deeply scarred bar ran down one side of the room, and on the opposite wall there was a bandstand shaped like a dock. Scores of mismatched tables and chairs circled a dance floor.

Harpoons and buoys and long narrow oars hung next to sepia photos of the Grace Point fishing fleets of decades past. A figurehead—a carving of a slightly bug-eyed, Roman-nosed woman with a narrow waist and armless torso, full busted, with rouged nipples poking above her ruffled bodice—crested the beam above the bar, smiling down like some lusty patron saint in benediction of her church. She was the figurehead for whom the bar had been named. Years ago, someone had tossed a beret on her head, and there it remained, dull with a veneer of dust.

Mixed in with the nautical flotsam was the jetsam of the clientele. Ribald caricatures, clever poetry, and scribbled prose covered the walls, papering them like a madman's collage. Some of them, dashed off in a drunken rush on napkins and scraps of paper, would have brought a fortune at any New York auction for the signatures alone. There were photographs of Grace Point's adopted sons and daughters, too—painters and playwrights, poets and writers.

Although women came here to dance and drink, Willie's was a man's bar. At dawn, empty and smelling of stale beer and smoke and the salty must of the sea, it seemed filled with the whispers of dead poets and drowned men.

Ben greeted them noisily, yelling at the waiter for more glasses and pushing the pitcher of beer across the table. He grabbed Fenris and kissed him on both cheeks. Pulling him down to the chair at his side, he began to talk, picking up the thread of a spirited argument they had begun earlier in the day. Rosa strained to hear what they said, but the music overpowered their words and she could only catch phrases: ". . . color . . . just color . . . juxtaposition and relationship of color. . . ."

On the other side of Ben, Louise was engrossed in conversation with a thin, lank-haired man. He was hunched forward, head bent over hands that toyed with a shot glass. Strands of dark hair fell over his forehead. Louise appeared to be trying to console him and occasionally stroked his restless hands with her broad, callused fingers. Her husband seemed not to notice. In front of the two other chairs at the table, a pair of whiskey glasses, nearly full, sat waiting for a couple to return from the dance floor.

Rosa shifted in her chair and kept smiling. After a while, to keep busy, she sipped beer, although she hated the taste of it. She felt the fishermen at the bar watching her. The smile slipped. She wanted to go back to the Sail Loft. Still deep in argument with Ben, Fenris slipped his hand beneath the table and laid it on her thigh, squeezing it once. She marveled that he could sense what she was feeling.

She drank more beer and edged closer to him.

"Damn it, Ben, what about line and pattern, rhythm and tone? You can't discount subject."

"Color *is* tone and rhythm, Boak. And as for subject, hell, a tin can on the beach can be beautiful."

Rosalina had heard Ben talk like this before. Sometimes, after class, one of the more daring students would stalk around the studio rapping a broom handle on the floor and pronounce in excited tones, "I tell you I can paint a tin can on the beach and it will be beautiful. Color. Color and light are the means of representation. Go. All of you. Go out and paint tin cans." She wondered if Ben knew the students imitated him.

A bold-eyed boy approached the table and whispered something to Louise. The sculptor laughed, shaking her long red hair back from her shoulders, then followed the boy to the dance floor. Ben did not notice. Abandoned, the lank-haired man looked stricken. For a moment, Rosa thought about slipping over next to him, maybe offering silent consolation. When he looked up at her with intense black eyes that, even drunk, missed nothing, she recognized the playwright Laurance Siebert. She smiled shyly, but Siebert did not. He refilled his glass from the bottle in front of him. His restless fingers were stained from cigarettes, his eyes pink from the bar smoke. Or exhaustion. Or despair.

"Come on." Fenris tugged her hand.

"What? Where are we going?"

He pulled her close, wrapping his arms around her. "To dance, dear Rosa. We are going to dance."

She could feel the eyes of the fishermen following them to the floor. "I don't want to. Not now," she protested. She did not look toward the bar, but she *knew* that Joaquin was there, watching.

Fenris whirled her out onto the floor, and she stumbled. Her feet felt leaden, awkward, and her heart beat fast in confusion and embarrassment. Other dancers pressed around them, and she could feel the heat coming in waves off their bodies. "I can't."

"Yes, you can. Just relax, follow me. . . . That's it. Nice and easy. . . . There you go." He sang the music softly in her ear. " 'Oh, it's a long, long time from May to December. . . .' " Gradually she relaxed.

When the song ended, she turned to walk back to the table, but he grabbed her hand.

"Where are you going, Little Rosa? We're not done yet." Holding her hand, he strode to the bandstand. The band—five sweating men in wrinkled white jackets, black pants, and scuffed shoes—watched him approach, and the bandleader, an unhealthy-looking man with a narrow mustache, leaned down. Rosa fanned her face with her hand. She could not hear what Fenris said, but she saw him hand the man a bill.

"It's hot, Fenris. Let's sit down."

"Not yet, Rosa. We've just begun." He reached up to pull the ribbon from her hair, and it fell full and hot on her neck. The music began, a liquid, Latin beat.

She froze. "I can't do this." Already couples straggled from the floor back to their seats.

"Yes, you can." He took her in his arms. "Just melt into me. Melt into me, Rosa."

She hesitated.

"Forget everyone else. Just melt into me. Pretend we are in bed. Be with me. Stay with me."

His voice mesmerized her. "That's it. . . . Yes. That's it," he whispered into her hair.

Space opened up around them as more and more dancers dropped away, giving them room, but she was only dimly aware of this. She was dizzy with the music, with her lover's whispered words. She felt the length of his leg against hers, his arm touching hers. She felt his heartbeat and the beat of the music, and both filled her blood, her brain. He dipped her back—her hair swept the floor—and then pulled her upright.

He stared into her eyes, holding her gaze with his. She abandoned herself totally to him and to the music. He no longer spoke to her. He didn't have to. His steps grew more complicated, but she did not miss a single one. They were perfectly in tune. As if they *were* in bed. And then she understood. That was what the dance was about. They were making love. She faltered, aware now of the bodies circling the dance floor, the eyes fixed on the two of them. Her cheeks flamed.

"Stay with me," he whispered, words he had whispered in bed. "Come to me, Rosa."

She no longer cared about the crowd or anything except him. She gave herself to him. They circled the floor. She felt the flow in her veins. Made bold by the music, she lifted her chin a fraction, moved a shoulder forward, arched her foot. She held the position for a beat, slowing the dance, forcing Fenris to adjust to her rhythm. He hesitated for a second and then understood. She had taken the lead. He matched his movement to hers. Triumph flashed in her eyes as she saw the surprise and then approval in his face. Measures later, he regained control, and she gave it to him, gladly.

The song should have ended, but the band kept playing, repeating the last refrain, teasing the couple along, not ready to release them yet. All eyes were on the two of them. Finally, they finished the dance with a flourish. He dipped her back so deeply that her head touched the floor. She longed for him to kiss her, but he didn't.

Applause brought her back. She heard the cheering, feet stamping, her name called out, and Fenris's.

Flushing, laughing, she skipped to her table, her hand still wrapped in his.

A touch on her shoulder stopped her. She turned and saw Jackie. "Hi, Rosa," he said.

"Jackie," she said, surprised. He looked pale. And older too, as if years, not months, had passed since the graduation. He was with a group of artists she recognized from the studio.

"You were . . . you were beautiful out there," the boy said.

"It was just a dance," she demurred, chagrined.

"I mean it," he said, stumbling a little in embarrassment. "You are beautiful."

"Thank you," she said. She wanted to say more. It was the first time any of Joaquin's family had spoken to her in the two weeks since she had moved in with Fenris. Dozens of questions flooded her mind. *Does Joaquin hate me? How is my father? Do you all hate me?* She felt achingly homesick. Fenris tugged at her hand. "Oh, Jackie . . ." she said, and then fell silent. There was nothing to say, really.

He looked at her with sad eyes. "I don't care what anyone says," he whispered. "I don't think you're a . . . well, what they say you are." Impulsively, he leaned forward and kissed her on the cheek.

Touched, she kissed him back. "Oh, Jackie—" she began again, but Fenris pulled her away before she could continue.

"The kid's right, Rosa," he said when they sat down. "You are beautiful." He turned to the others at the table. "Isn't that right? Isn't our Rosa Rugosa beautiful?"

"Beautiful," they agreed in one voice.

A laugh bubbled up in her throat, edging out the

sadness. "So are you. You are beautiful, too. Everyone is beautiful. Ben. Louise. Everyone." She felt giddy.

The band started up again. The leader looked over at their table as if he were playing only for them. The others urged them on, but Fenris just laughed. "No more dancing," he said. "Not tonight."

"A wise man," Laurance Siebert said in a rusty voice. "It's a wise man who knows enough to make a good exit and then stay the hell off the stage."

"You'd be the expert on that," Fenris said, nodding his head in a mock bow.

"Fuck you," Siebert snarled.

Before Fenris could respond, an old woman approached the table. Her white hair stood out from her head like a frenzied halo, and her deeply wrinkled skin was nut brown, as if she had spent her life unprotected from the sun. She wore a faded man's shirt that bloused out over a long cotton skirt. Strands of tiny, multicolored beads hung around her thin neck, and a half-dozen silver and stone rings shone on her fingers. She carried a staff—a branch from a hazelnut tree—and was slightly drunk. A young man, of an age to be her son, stood at her side, gazing at her adoringly.

Ben and Louise stood and embraced the old woman and then made a place for her at the table. They ignored the young man.

"My God, it's good to see you, Odessa," Ben said. "We were beginning to wonder if you had died out there on the dunes."

"Take more than the dunes to kill me, you crazy son of a bitch. I'll be dancing at your funeral."

Ben roared. He gestured around the table. "You know everyone? And of course everyone knows Odessa. Odessa Dunne, our famous Poetess of the Dunes."

Odessa turned to Laurance Siebert and took his hands in hers, stilling his restless fingers for a moment. Even though she was drunk, her eyes were bright and shrewd. "Larry, dear friend, why don't you ever listen to me? You're mad to stay here. No wonder you're dry. O'Neill himself couldn't write in this damn town. You've got to get away from the madness."

"Who told you the work isn't going well?" Siebert's tone was injured.

"Who told me? Whispers. They carry on the wind." Odessa looked around Willie's. "It never changes, this cursed town," she said. "It's like an Arab village. Buzz, buzz, buzz." She leaned toward the playwright and softened her tone. "Move to the dunes, Larry. Go back inside yourself. That's what you need to do."

"So what brought you away from your precious dunes?" Ben interrupted. "Did you run out of booze?"

She turned to the man who hovered by her shoulder. "Get me a drink, will you, dear heart?" She watched him run eagerly off. "This," she said. "This is what brings me to town." She stretched her hands out in front of her. Her fingers curled like the talons of a bird of prey, veins swollen like ancient rivers on a bed of sagging flesh. "Skin loneliness. My skin was lonely for the touch of human flesh. I'm an old woman, but age does not kill that need. I leave my precious dunes, as you call them—and so they are—so that I will be touched again. Loved again. Or what poses as love. And for touch, I gladly accept the masquerade."

So. The man at Odessa's shoulder was her lover, not her son.

"And you would be Rosalina," the poetess said. She reached out to take Rosa's fingers in hers.

Rosa shrank back. Every child in Grace Point had heard whispers of Odessa Dunne, the witch who lived in a shack out on the dunes, miles out, near the remote Coast Guard station. Rosa hid her hands in her lap and crossed her fingers. She had not done that since she was eight years old and it had been her secret sign of protection, like making the sign of the cross.

"Are you a witch?" The words were out before she could stop them.

Odessa laughed, a surprisingly lusty sound that mocked the deep lines in her skin. "I'm a woman. Some would say that makes me a witch." She leaned closer to Rosa, excluding the others. A shadow of sadness flickered across her face. "They will say that about you, child, for we are sisters, you and me. That is hard for you to believe, yes? But it is true. And once, I, too, was beautiful."

Ben lurched to his feet. "To beauty!" he pronounced, raising his glass in a toast. "To beauty and to women and to witches. Long may they weave their spell over the wretchedly mortal male!"

They all drank. When Rosa put her glass down, she saw that Louise was studying her.

"Do you know what I think, Rosalina?" the red-haired sculptress said. "Ben must paint you. Just as you danced. Yes." She drew in a breath. "Dancing and in the nude, Rosa. Oh, it would be stunning."

"I couldn't," Rosa stammered. She turned to Fenris for help, but he was nodding.

"Of course. That's great. What do you say, Ben?"

Still standing, swaying, Ben again raised his glass high in the air. Beer trickled down his arm. "I say, 'To Rosa in the nude.' " He paused for effect. "And to hell with painting tin cans!"

The others took up the words, repeating them until they became a chant that filled the room, underscored by stamping feet.

Fenris bent close to her. His lips brushed her ear and she shivered. "You know what?"

"What?"

"Right now—at this moment, dear Rosa, my Rosa—every man in this room wants to fuck you." His voice was victorious.

* * *

Summer passed in a swirl: nights spent at loft parties where there was plenty of laughter and rum; nights wrapped in twisted sheets on the big bed in Fenris's studio. Only once in those days did she see Joaquin. She passed him on the street, but he pretended not to see her, and she was shocked by how old he looked.

Of course, she no longer attended Father Mallory's mass on Sundays. Instead, Fenris took her to the dunes and read poetry to her. He assured her that his was a better way to worship.

He made her tell him stories about the town. Then he would show her how foolish the people were. The fishermen were fools for accepting the prices the icehouse owners gave them. They should band together, set the prices themselves, he said. She told him about Jackie and how Victor had destroyed the boy's violin because he would not fish. She told him about the funeral for the men who died at sea and he said the people romanticized brutality and death. She felt that she had been a child all her life and he had made her a woman.

She could deny Fenris nothing. Just once, in all the days and nights, had she said no to him. One night, drunk from rum, they had walked home from a party with a large group of artists. When they got to the studio, she saw that Cynthia, the blond model, had joined the group. Even drunk, Rosa had been stung when Fenris invited the girl to their room. They sat drinking more rum. She was tired and wanted to go to bed. "Go ahead," he'd said and tucked her in. Then he had called the model over. Suddenly, in a confused way mixed with laughter, he was hugging—kissing—them both. Stumbling over the bed, he pulled the other girl down on top so that all three were on the mattress.

He had tried to undress her then. She heard Cynthia laugh and saw her begin to strip off her clothes. "No," she'd cried.

Cynthia had left shortly after that, but Rosa could not forget the troubling memory of how the girl's hand had felt on her breasts. She vowed not to drink as much.

Fenris loved her. She knew that. And she loved him. He knew that she belonged to him. Only to him. Completely to him. Surely she had proved that.

More and more, she began to stay inside the Sail Loft. She escaped into the books Fenris gave her to read. She wept readily over the fictional heroines' pain and applauded their victories. Submerged in the pages of the books, she no longer had to think about Joaquin or her father, or Father Mallory and sin, or about the punishment for sinners. But inside, beneath all the layers, was a space she couldn't have put a name to even if she had been willing to look at it—a tight place of waiting, of limbo, of a breath held long and taut, of dread and hope and apprehension.

Chapter 20

"Fenris? Fenris, where are you?"

Rosalina threw open the studio door. Her ribs hurt from running, and she stopped inside the door to catch her breath, but she was too excited to stand still for long. Disappointment washed over her and she danced back to the hall, checking the communal bathroom and kitchen. The darkroom was empty too.

She returned to his room. His notebooks and camera were on the desk. She would die, simply die, if she couldn't share the news soon. Imagining the moment, she smiled, and her reflection smiled back. "What do you think? Isn't it wonderful? Just wonderful," she whispered to the woman in the mirror over his dresser. Then she began to dance, twirling, spinning, laughing, too happy to keep still. The miracle—the sweet, sleepy, singing miracle of it—kept her pirouetting until she was dizzy.

Delirious, she whirled across the room and fell back on the bed. Her head still spun and she giggled. She drew her knees into her chest and hugged them tightly. She could never remember being this happy. Maybe, she decided, sometimes you had to go through some pain to find happiness. Maybe everything had a price, and the bigger the gift, the higher the cost. Yes, that made sense to her. *God, where was Fenris?*

His shirt hung on the bedpost. She gathered it between her fingers and clutched it to her chest. She buried her face in it, inhaling his scent, pulling it into her lungs as if it could travel to every cell of her body. She let her head fall back against the pillow and closed her eyes, wanting him. Just the drowning, drowsy smell of him could do that. As if he were actually there on the bed with her, she felt her body grow weak.

She stood up, stripped off her skirt and blouse, her underpants and bra, all the while imagining his surprise when he returned and found her waiting nude. It would please him. She stretched out on the mattress, newly conscious of her body. She felt at once terribly fragile and incredibly strong. As she lay there, her body was undergoing miraculous changes. She touched her breasts with her fingers. They were tender and swollen. She closed her eyes and cupped them gently.

Even before she heard him, she could sense Fenris in the room. She opened her eyes. He stood in the doorway watching her. He made no move to cross to her. In the past three months, she had come to know his moods, but she could not interpret this silence. Could he already know her news?

She wanted him to sit by her on the bed. No, she wanted him to lie beside her, their bodies touching. He continued to look at her, his expression unreadable. In the past hour, she had rehearsed the scene, practicing which words she would use to tell him of the miracle. In the end, all fantasies and plans vanished and, smiling, she just blurted it out.

"Fenris. Oh, Fenris, it's happened. I'm pregnant."

He reached out for the handle and closed the door. She was sure he would come to her then, but he crossed to the desk and sat down there. Almost immediately he got up again and went to the bureau for the bottle of rum. He drank a shot in one swallow and poured more into the glass, which he carried back to the desk. He did not offer her any.

"I'm pregnant," she repeated, thinking perhaps he had not heard her.

"When did you find out?"

"This afternoon. I just came from Dr. Cook's." She moved over on the bed so that there was room for him to join her.

He stared down into the amber liquid, swirling it. "Does Joaquin know?"

The first prickling of unease spread across her body. "No. No one knows but you." She tried to cover her breasts and crotch with the shirt she still held.

"When are you going to tell him?"

"I . . . I wasn't going to."

"It was sweet of you to tell me first, Rosalina." He smiled, the patient expression of an adult explaining something to a very simple child. "Now, of course, you are going to tell your husband."

"But . . ." She hugged his shirt close to her breast. Her hands were trembling and she hid them in the folds of the fabric. "But why should I tell him?"

"Because he is your husband."

"But it isn't his."

"What are you saying, Rosalina?" The smile was gone, his voice was cold.

"It's yours. You are the father."

"How can you be sure?"

She recoiled against the pillow, as if he had slapped her. "You know I haven't slept with him since we have been together. *You know that.*" She couldn't keep her voice from trembling. She was ashamed of her nakedness now. She felt cold, exposed. She thought about putting on her clothes, but she did not want to stand nude in front of him now, did not want him looking at her with that cool expression. She pulled the sheet over her body.

He finished off the rum and got up to refill the glass. She desperately wanted him to offer her some, to be solicitous, but she couldn't ask.

"What do you want of me?" He waited, his back to her, and in the silence she heard him sigh.

She faltered, unsure. "I don't know."

He drank the rum in one swallow, then set the glass down on the bureau. He turned back to her, and they looked steadily at each other. When he crossed to the bed at last, she could have wept with relief. He sat on the edge of the mattress and took her hands in his, careful not to touch her otherwise.

He smiled again. When he spoke she could smell the rum. "Well, my Rosalina, it looks like you have a couple of choices here." He was smiling, but the expression in his eyes made her want to cover her ears. As if he knew this, he continued to hold her hands tightly. "You can tell your husband it is his—"

"No." The word was just a whimper, drawn from her.

"Or you can get rid of it."

"Get rid of it?"

"An abortion."

No. The idea was unthinkable. A sin. She could not believe he would even suggest it. She pulled her hands free from his and she lashed out, hitting him on the chest. "No. This is my baby. I want this baby. Do you understand that? I want it. It's ours. Yours and mine. I want it. Nothing else is possible." She was screaming, and her hands hurt from hitting him.

He grabbed her by the wrists. His voice was still cool, reasonable. It would have been better if he had yelled. "That's impossible, Rosa."

She let her hands go limp and leaned toward him. "It's not. We could . . . we could get married."

"Rosa." His voice was like a blade of steel now. "I am already married. You know that."

"Leave her. Marry me." She was begging now, but she didn't care. The image of the plain, worn woman in the photo flashed before her eyes. "Leave her and marry me."

"And my son—would you have me leave him too?"

"I'll give you a son." She tried to pull his hand to her stomach. If he would only feel the flesh of her belly, where deep in her their child was already growing, she would win.

"She is my wife. I told you from the beginning I was married."

Only words, she wanted to scream. *Words. Words. Only words. But you told me with your hands and your lips and your eyes and your body that you loved me.*

"But I am your woman."

He did not answer her.

"Remember? You made me your woman. How can you deny that?"

"I'm sorry if you misunderstood."

"Misunderstood? Dear God—what about this?" She threw off the sheet she had been clutching to her breasts. "What about this?" she screamed.

His eyes dropped to her breast. The tattoo marked her breast like a bruise.

"What about this? I did this for you. Would your wife do that? Would she?"

"You wanted that, Rosa. It's only what you wanted."

"That's a lie."

"Is it? You wanted my mark on you. You know you did, Rosalina."

"I didn't want it. It hurt and I hated it." The memory of the tattooing, the nightmare that she had blocked and repressed, surfaced. She remembered the trip to Boston in the green De Soto; how scared she had been, imagining in silence the pain to come. He drove confidently, one hand on the wheel, the other around her shoulders, telling her that she was the most exciting woman he had ever known.

She remembered Scullay Square and the building that housed the burlesque and liquor store, and—up over the store, up the dark stairwell—the filthy room where the tattooist, an old man with rabbit eyes that grew pinker when he looked at her, worked. She remembered, too, the smell of whiskey he exuded and the way his creepy hands shook, then miraculously grew steady when he took up the needle. And how his hand cleaned her skin with a swab of cotton, and the sharp smell of alcohol, and how his fingers lingered too long on her pale, exposed skin. And how Fenris had been watching but had said nothing. And the shock of the needle itself, the pain as he worked on her breast. She had been *proud* of the pain, a measure of her love for him. Proud that she would wear his mark on her, forever.

"I hate you," she said.

"Don't blame me for that." He reached across the inches that separated them and traced his finger over the tattoo, still not fully healed. "You wanted that. The only thing I did was understand what you wanted before you did."

"No."

"Yes, little Rosa. You wanted to be my woman. Just like you want me now."

"No."

"You don't want me?" He lay down then.

"No," she whispered, but she was the one who crossed the last few inches and arched her body to his. Her hands, not his, unfastened his belt buckle. She could not wait for him to strip. She pulled him onto her. "Damn you."

He bent his head and brushed his lips across the tattoo. "See," he said, "you *are* my woman. I knew that the first time I saw you." His clothes scratched her skin.

"Yes," she whispered. "I am. I am. And I will have our baby."

He silenced her with his lips.

* * *

Afterward, he slept. She took his hand and gently placed it on her stomach. She lay that way for a long time, his hand pressed against her belly, her hand holding his, as if they were protecting the life inside her. Her skin stung from the fierceness of their lovemaking. He still wants me, she thought. He won't leave me now. He won't leave *us* now. The worst is over. He'll take me with him when he leaves.

Chapter 21

Jackie slid into the booth until his back rested against the wall, and took a long drink of beer. The bitterness washed away the cloying sweetness of spices and fruits and sugar-rich dough. It was funny how at the end of the day even something as tempting and delicious as the smell of baking bread could become wearing. In the same way the apartment over the bakery was beginning to close in on him. It was the way Dominus sat there staring at him, as if he could bring the place to life. The baker never said this; he never asked Jackie for anything. But he'd bought a second Victrola, for the apartment, so they could listen to records each night. It had been a surprise. One day Dominus had left work early and walked over to Izzy's Secondhand and Souvenir Shop, returning with the machine. "For you," he had said that night after dinner. The gift gave Jackie responsibility he was reluctant to accept. He wasn't sure what Dominus wanted, but he felt trapped.

Two girls wandered into the bar. Summer girls. He studied them. The shorter of the two had a heart-shaped face. Freckles covered her nose. When he looked at her, he felt a yearning. If she'd been alone, he would have dared approach her, but together the girls seemed overpowering. He was afraid of their laughter. He looked away from the girl's sun-spotted cheeks and his thoughts turned back to Dominus.

Their shared love of music, at first so welcome, had become a burden in the past days, as if in the notes were hidden links that coupled them together, binding them with a power that went beyond blood. This confused him. For years, he had waited for some sign that his father loved him, or even cared for him. Like a dog cringing under the kitchen table waiting for a paltry scrap, he had hung around his father. Now, here was Dominus Roderick offering him the love and companionship his father had withheld, and he was miserable.

"Is anyone sitting here?"

Jackie looked up. The man was older, perhaps thirty. His hair was a mass of wild curls, his eyes the color of lead, of the sea and sky before a winter storm. It was the first time Jackie had seen truly gray eyes.

"No."

"Are you alone?"

"Sort of. I'm supposed to meet a friend." Not that he'd exactly call Fenris Boak a friend, and certainly not in front of his father or Dominus. He looked around the crowded bar but could not find the writer. He was relieved. Whenever he met Rosa or Fenris—frequently now that he had become friends with some of the artists who worked at the Sail Loft—he was afraid his father would find out. "Do you want to sit down?"

"Thanks. My name is Paul." The stranger reached across the table and offered his hand to Jackie. His skin was soft and smooth.

"Are you an artist?" asked Jackie. Most of the people in this bar were artists or writers spending the summer in Grace Point.

"Not me. I can't draw a straight line." The man named Paul sat down on the other bench and signaled for a beer. "Want another?"

"Sure. Thanks."

"What about you? Are you an artist?"

"No. I'm working at a bakery." He was suddenly ashamed. "What do you do?"

"I do what man is reduced to when he has neither the talent nor brains to do anything else. I teach."

Jackie studied the gray-eyed man. "I thought I'd like to become a teacher." He had never told that to anyone before.

"Don't you know what they say about teachers?"

"What?"

"Them that can, does. Them that can't, teach." He washed down the bitter words with beer and signaled for another.

Discomforted by the man's tone, Jackie twisted in the seat and tried to think of something to say. "What do you teach?" he finally asked.

"Music. I teach tone-deaf children who aren't interested how to play a song recognizable enough to please their parents. Yup, for a small sum, I can take a child and teach him to hold in his innocent, ignorant hands a splendid instrument and within a matter of hours become capable of producing sounds that would put a cat on the midnight prowl to shame."

No longer listening, Jackie recalled the hours he had spent in the music room at school. They were the happiest hours of his life. "I used to play the violin," he said. It was the first time since his father had destroyed his instrument that he had spoken of his music. He heard the hunger in his voice.

"Used to?" The gray-eyed man smiled. It was a gentle smile, and the sarcasm was gone. "You're pretty young to have already left it behind."

Jackie didn't answer.

"Didn't you like it? Is that why you stopped?"

"I loved it."

"Why did you stop?"

"My father . . ." He couldn't go on. He stared at the table. He felt diminished, as if some terrible lack in him had caused his father's actions.

Paul waited. He reached over and stroked his forefinger along Jackie's hand, running his fingertip the length of his fingers. His skin was cold from holding the glass of beer. "You have wonderful hands. Strong. Perfect for the violin."

Jackie didn't answer. The man's touch made him uncomfortable. He withdrew his hand and picked up his mug. Paul didn't seem to notice the rejection. He smiled and opened a pack of Lucky Strikes.

"Hi, Paul." A man, a regular Jackie saw frequently but did not know, stood at the booth. "We're starting a game of darts. Want to join?"

"Not now. I'm busy."

The other man swept Jackie with his eyes. "What about you? You want to play?"

Before Jackie could answer, Paul spoke. "He's busy too. We're talking." Jackie felt oddly as if Paul were protecting him, and was glad when the man went back to his dart game.

The bar was growing smokier and noiser. The two girls he had noticed earlier had gone. Paul said something, but Jackie couldn't understand him. "What?"

"I have a violin. In my room, I have a violin."

The words awoke an aching in Jackie.

"I play the cello. We could play together."

"I'm not that good. I haven't played since June." Beneath the table, he flexed his fingers, as if warming up.

"I have a feeling you're very, very good."

It had been so long. He wanted to go. He knew that. He wiped his palms along the length of his thighs. He knew, too, that he was afraid.

"What do you say? Shall we go back to my room?"

Jackie thought of Dominus. He would be sitting by the front window looking down on the street and waiting for Jackie to return. Still, there was no reason for him not to go with Paul. "Okay," he said.

They stood and made their way across the barroom. Paul looped his arm casually over Jackie's shoulders. They were almost to the door when Jackie saw Fenris.

"Where's Rosa?"

"She's tired. I see you two have met. I knew you'd hit it off. Didn't I tell you that you should get to know Jackie, Paul?"

"Knock it off, Fenris," Paul said as he led Jackie from the barroom.

The night air was still and oppressive, with not even the faintest whisper of a breeze from the ocean. Paul took a handkerchief from his pocket and mopped his neck and brow. "God, it's hot."

Even walking slowly raised a sweat. Jackie felt his shirt sticking to his back. "You should have been in the kitchen this morning. I bet it was close to a hundred. The heat was pouring off the ovens."

"We need to cool down. Come on. I've an idea," Paul said. They were at the head of the alley that ran the length of the Ocean House down to the shore. "Let's go for a swim. What do you say?" Already he began edging toward the alley.

Jackie hung back. He didn't really like to swim. All his life, his father and brothers had teased him about this, but he couldn't help it. Each moment he was in the water, he kept thinking of all the things he knew were swimming there. He had seen the bloated and stinking carcasses of sand sharks and skates washed up onto the shore more times than he cared to remember. He never swam in the ocean at night.

"Well?"

"I don't want to."

"Come on. What are you waiting for?" Paul's voice floated out of the shadows of the alleys that had already swallowed him. Reluctantly, Jackie followed. He narrowed his eyes, but nothing moved. "Paul?" Silence. "Paul? Where are you?" He was whispering. When the hand grabbed his neck, he jumped with a yelp. When he heard Paul laughing, he felt foolish.

"I didn't mean to scare you that much," Paul said. "You okay?" His hand still rested on Jackie's neck.

The man's touch was moist, and Jackie shrugged

and stepped away, but Paul did not remove his hand. Paul stepped closer. With his forefinger, he stroked the boy's jaw. "You have beautiful bones," he said softly.

"I . . . I . . . I really have to go," Jackie stammered. His back rubbed against the siding of the Ocean House. Somehow Paul had edged him to the wall. He froze. Tinglings of fear, fear of something far worse than the ocean at night, ran down his legs, weakening them.

Paul pressed against him, and Jackie could feel the man's hardness against his thigh. He closed his eyes in shame and horror. Paul kissed him. Paul's lips were as soft as a woman's. Jackie squeezed his eyes. He felt his mind go white and tried to disappear inside his head.

He heard Paul moan, a long, drawn-out, whimpering sigh, and then felt him fall away, heard the sound of his body falling in the alley. He did not dare open his eyes.

Another voice—familiar yet disguised by bitterness and loathing: "Queer—you goddamned queer."

The first blow knocked him to the ground. It was followed by a kick that doubled him over. He fell onto Paul's body. Rough hands pulled him off and, with strength fueled by fury, tossed him across the alley as if he weighed no more than a sack of dock trash. The assailant dropped on him immediately and, breathing curses, struck him again and again. Jackie felt bones break. The only sounds in the alley were his muffled sobs and the labored breathing of his attacker.

Tears flowed down his face, mingling with blood. Still—like a child afraid of seeing a nightmare—he did not open his eyes. Suddenly, the rain of blows ceased. He felt the man's hands on his arms, his legs, moving them. He wanted to protest, to curl into a ball, but he was too weak, too battered. He swam in and out of a screaming abyss. Carefully, the man stretched him on the ground, placing his limbs so that they were spread-eagled.

Jackie heard music—a sweet, flowing, liquid sound

that filled his brain and helped drown out the pain and terror. He went to the music, music so sweet he would not have dared to dream of it even in his most daring dreams. Then he screamed.

The man's heel came down on Jackie's hand with the full force of the weight and rage behind it, crushing the bones into pulp held only by skin, grinding it. At last, he lifted his eyes. They widened in disbelief and shock. It couldn't be. With measured steps, the assailant walked around the boy's body to the other side.

Jackie tried to lift his head. "No," he pleaded. "Please. Not my hands. Not my hands." They were the first words he had spoken since the beating began. He couldn't know his ruined hands were just the start of what was to come.

Chapter 22

Often Rosalina wished that she and Fenris had fled Grace Point immediately. The hostility and whispers of the town were like poison in the air. Sometimes, she was almost afraid to breathe. She could not wait for the day when she and Fenris would leave.

In the meantime, she tried to protect her unborn child. Everything she did was with the baby in mind. She stopped drinking. She slept nine hours every night, no longer going to the bars with Fenris and the other artists. During the days, she spent hours traipsing through the beach forest and went for long walks on the dunes. At the end of these walks, she would stretch out on the sand, her belly facing heaven, and soak in the sun, pulling the heat into her body and inhaling the clear, sea-washed air, as if this were a remedy for the poisonous gossip of the townspeople.

Isabella and Dolores had resented their pregnancies, grumbled about the morning sickness, the weight, the awkwardness of the final months, the swollen feet and jutting belly buttons and sore backs, the exhaustion, the stretch marks, the endless waiting. She shared none of these feelings. She loved being pregnant. She rejoiced. *Being with child.* Even the sound of those words was full. Blessed. Miraculous. Swollen with a magnificent power. Except for Fenris, she had told no one. It was still her secret, and that added to its power.

Today, on the dunes, she felt for the first time the change in the air. Although it was late August, the day was as cool as one in September. She knew that there would be a week or two like this, a foretaste of fall, and then the warm weather would return, lingering until nearly October. But this cool air was always the sign that the spell of August was broken. Sweaters came out of the backs of closets, and blankets were returned to beds. Before many more weeks, the shrubs and scrub oak would turn brown, the swamp maples would flame with crimson and orange, signaling winter and death.

She thought about Minnesota, where her new home would be. She had studied the map she had taken from the library until she knew it by heart. The capital was St. Paul. It was a good omen to have the capital city named after a saint. She had memorized the surrounding states and traced a finger over the Canadian border. She'd had no idea it was so far north. She supposed it would be cold there, lots of snow. She was surprised to see the Mississippi River ran through the southern part of the state. The state of Minnesota seemed so far away.

She kept the map in a hatbox stored beneath Fenris's bed. The box had been her mother's, and she had filled it with a number of things she had collected since she had moved in with him: a picture of Fenris with Ben Bayes that Louise had taken; a note he had pinned on her pillow one day early in the summer; a menu from the restaurant in Boston he had taken her to before she had gotten the tattoo. She could still remember the taste of that fried fish. After the meal, he had taken her for her first walk through the Boston Common.

Also in the box was an empty bottle of his aftershave. In a small envelope, there were strands of hair she had taken from his comb, and one of his handkerchiefs. She possessed the smell and sight and feel of him, secreted in this box. She was like a witch, collecting bits and pieces of her victim for bewitching.

The box also held a book of poetry by D. H. Lawrence that contained the poem about the whales. She did not understand it any better now, but when she read the part about "dreaming with strange whale eyes wide open in the waters of the beginning and the end," she thought about the baby growing inside her womb, suspended in fluid, and she felt connected to the "whales in mid-ocean, suspended in the waves of the sea." She wanted to tell Fenris but was afraid he would laugh at her and call her sentimental. Sometimes she heard him repeating things she'd told him to Ben. He would laugh, and it hurt her, but she said nothing.

She thought about all this as she lay in the sun that bathed the dunes. She could wait. The hurt, like the poison that pervaded the air of Grace Point, would evaporate as soon as they left. She rolled in the dune grass and imagined her future as Mrs. Fenris Boak. She dreamed about what they would name their child. She took up a thin stick of driftwood and wrote her name in the sand. *Rosalina Boak.* The sand was dry, and her letters faded as soon as she created them. She walked to the edge of the water and wrote the name again in the damp sand. She drew a huge heart and etched their names inside it. She walked down the shoreline, leaving a trail of their names in her wake. Fenris and Rosa. Rosalina and Fenris. Mr. and Mrs. Fenris Boak. Fenris and Rosalina Boak. She sat in the damp sand and drew a small circle and wrote their names once more, entwining the letters. Then she cupped her hands and took up some seawater and poured it over the letters and watched while they melted in a puddle that was quickly absorbed. Sometimes she felt that way when she was with Fenris, as if they were one, each possessed and absorbed in the other. The spot where she had scratched out their names was smooth now, and, without knowing what she was doing, she picked up the pencil of driftwood and etched out one last design. She drew a flower exactly like the rose that was tattooed on her breast.

* * *

Dolores was waiting for Rosalina at the Sail Loft, her face puffy from crying. She looked old. Worn. Frightened.

"Dolores, what's wrong?" Rosa reached out to touch her, but Dolores pulled away and began to cry.

"Dolores, for heaven's sake, what wrong? What's the matter? Is Tony beating you again?" She waited impatiently for an answer, but her sister-in-law was sobbing loudly now, her face buried in her hands. A terrible thought, unthinkable, struck Rosa. "It's not Joaquin, is it? Nothing has happened to Joaquin? Tell me!"

The question stopped the noisy crying long enough for Dolores to shake her head. "No. No, Joaquin's okay," she said.

"Well, what is it, then? Listen, why don't you come to Fenris's room with me?" It never occurred to her to call their shared space *her* room or *their* room. It was Fenris's studio. "Come in and sit down. I'll get you a drink. You look like you could use a drink."

"No." Dolores spoke sharply, angrily. "I don't want to be in *his* room. He's done enough damage."

"Well, what's the matter? Why are you crying?"

In fact, the flash of anger had helped Dolores to regain control, and she was no longer crying. "It's Jackie."

"What's wrong with Jackie?"

"Oh, Rosa . . ." Dolores began to cry again, this time softly. "Oh, Rosa. It's so terrible."

"What? Tell me, Dolores. What's happened to Jackie?"

"He's dead." Quickly she made the sign of the cross. "He's dead, Rosalina. Jackie is dead."

"No." *Not Jackie.* It was unthinkable that anything like that could happen. "No," she whispered.

"It's true, Rosa."

"It can't be." She felt light-headed. "I need to sit down." She reached out to lean against the wall and edged her way down the hall to Fenris's studio. He was not there, and she was surprised to find she was glad. She was afraid she was going to be sick.

"Rosa? Are you okay?" Dolores had followed her into the room.

"How? How did Jackie die?"

"He was murdered. Last night."

"But why? Why would anyone want to hurt him?"

Dolores wouldn't meet her eyes. There was more she was not telling her.

"What is it? There is something else, isn't there?"

Dolores looked at the ground. Her face turned hard.

"What is it? Tell me, Dolores."

"They're saying . . ." She stopped and looked up. Rosa was stunned by the bitterness that masked Dolores's face. "They're saying he was killed in a fight."

"Jackie? Jackie never fought." Relief flooded through Rosa. They had the wrong boy. Jackie wasn't dead.

"Oh, Rosa, they found him in the alley by the Ocean House. Everyone knows about the O House. And some of the other fishermen saw him leave Willie's with another man, one of the summer people. Now they're saying he was queer." She said the word as if it were an obscenity.

"Jackie? Jackie queer? They're crazy. Who is saying this? It isn't true. Not Jackie."

"I don't know. I mean, I'm not so sure anymore. He was hanging around with summer people. Who knows? The police are questioning all the artists now." She looked over her shoulder, as if someone else were in the room, listening.

Dolores glanced away, and Rosa knew there was more she had to tell her.

"Victor sent me."

"To me? Victor sent you to see me?"

"He says you're not to go to the funeral. They don't want you there. I'm—I'm sorry, Rosa."

Rosalina saw through the lie. Dolores had known

this would hurt her and was glad. "I can go to the church. Not even Victor can stop me."

"Don't, Rosa. Please don't go." Dolores began crying again. "They blame you."

"Me? Blame me for what?"

"Everything. Don't you see? If you had just stayed with Joaquin, none of this would have happened. Can't you see that?"

"What are you talking about? How can anyone blame me?"

"You and Fenris. If you hadn't left Joaquin, Jackie would never have met Fenris and he wouldn't have been with Fenris's friend before he died."

"What's that got to do with anything?"

"He's trouble, Rosa. Your precious Fenris Boak is trouble. Can't you see that? He's wicked. Evil."

"You sound like my father."

"Because it's true."

"Fenris had nothing to do with Jackie's death. And I am going to the funeral. No one can stop me, not even Victor."

"Don't go, Rosa. You don't belong there. You are not one of us anymore." She left without another word.

In the end, Rosalina did not go to the church. Alone —she did not want Fenris with her—she hid in a narrow street beside the rectory and watched while the Santos family filed into St. Peter's. Leona, supported by two men, led the mourners. All three seemed to lean together, their flesh and bones melding into a single shrunken body of grief. One of the men was Victor, and after a minute Rosalina saw that the other was her father. She was shocked at his transformation. His eyes were glazed—with what? Was it pain? Guilt? The other mourners followed, gray-faced with sorrow and fatigue. Girls—classmates of Jackie's from high school—were weeping as they climbed the steps to the church.

Suddenly Rosalina's grief turned to rage. *Where were you when he was alive?* she wanted to shout. *It's your fault he's dead,* she wanted to scream at Victor. *Why couldn't you let him alone? Why did you destroy him? And the rest of you, how could you stand by and let Victor hurt him so?*

She stepped out from her hiding place, no longer caring if she was seen, and walked down the street. She knew where she needed to go. She went out to the moors. Alone on the dunes, she knelt and prayed for the soul of Jackie Santos. She thought about the sweetness of him. She remembered how he had stood at the graduation and played with a purity and power that had made men weep. The wind blew through the grasses and the surf rolled in onto the shore.

She stayed in the dunes until it was dark. When she returned to the studio, Fenris was gone.

Chapter 23

The room was stripped bare—his books, his clothes, his cameras—but she could not believe that he was gone. "Fenris?" She crossed the room and pulled open the drawers of the bureau. They were empty except for the paper that lined them.

"Fenris?" Her voice was louder. There was no answer. The sound of his name rang hollowly in the Sail Loft. She ran from the studio and dashed from room to room, looking for him. For the first time, she became conscious of what she had not noticed before now. The other studios were empty. When had that happened? How could she not have noticed?

Her few belongings hung forlornly from the rod that served as a closet.

"Fenris? Fenris?" She was screaming his name now.

She went back to the hall and ran to the darkroom. Without checking to see if the red bulb above the door was lit, she rushed in. Empty. The smell of chemicals hit her. The clothesline above the sink swayed, but no pictures hung from it. The tubs of solution held no negatives, no finished pictures. All had been stripped from the room. Taking the stairs two at a time, she raced to the top floor, where Ben and Louise lived. Not bothering to knock, she flung open the door.

They were lying on the bed. Ben was resting against the headboard. Louise had propped a pillow over the footboard, and her head was plopped there, her red hair fanned out like tendrils of flame on the pillow slip.

Her feet were in Ben's lap and he was rubbing them with his huge, paint-stained hands.

"Where is he?" Rosa screamed.

The artist and sculptor exchanged looks. "He's gone," Ben said after a beat. His hands stilled on his wife's feet.

"Gone?"

"Didn't he tell you?" Louise looked at Rosalina. "No, of course he didn't. That stupid son of a bitch."

"Gone?" Rosa parroted.

Ben, uncomfortable, looked at Louise for help.

Anger flashed across the sculptor's face and she swung her feet from Ben's lap. "I told you this would happen," she said to him. "I *warned* you. Just like him to leave you to clean up his mess for him. Fenris Boak is a world-class shit." She turned to Rosalina and her voice softened. "I'm sorry, Rosa. But you must have had some idea this might happen, didn't you? After all—" The stunned look in Rosa's eyes stopped her.

"There is some explanation. There has to be." Rosa refused to believe anything else.

Louise crossed the floor and grasped her hands. "Listen, Rosalina," she began gently. "He isn't coming back. He isn't. You understand. He has gone home to his wife. He did tell you he was married, didn't he?"

Rosalina was too numb to answer.

"So you knew he would go when the summer was over."

"No. No. He wants me. Do you understand? We are going to be married."

"Oh, Rosa. Fenris would never leave his wife."

"No," she repeated. For an instant, she considered showing them the tattoo on her breast, but the look of pity in Louise Bayes's eyes stopped her. Her heart and ribs and stomach ached as if they'd been bruised. She hugged herself and bent double.

"Rosa?" Concern touched Louise's voice. "Rosa, are you all right?"

"I'm pregnant."

She could see their shock. Somehow the fact that he hadn't even bothered to tell them hurt the most. She had been so proud. That, more than anything Louise said, convinced her he had returned to his wife. She started to cry.

"Listen, honey," Louise said. "You can stay here for a few days. Can't she, Ben?"

He nodded uncomfortably.

"But then what will I do? Where will I go?"

"Home," Louise said. "You go back to your husband."

"I can't. Oh, God, what am I going to do?"

"Go home, Rosalina. Go home and begin again."

In the end she had nowhere else to go.

The house looked different to her, a stranger's house. A trespasser in her husband's home, she walked gingerly at first through the kitchen, the living room, down the narrow hall to the bedroom. It was not until she was there that she let go of the breath she had been holding. She realized then that she had been afraid she would find a sign of a woman, a sign that Joaquin had found someone else.

The place was filthy—dirty dishes in the sink, food dried on plates and cups and saucers. A nearly empty bottle of whiskey was on the counter. Soiled clothes were lumped in a heap on the bathroom floor. The bed was unmade.

Her clothes still hung in the closet. This surprised her, but it gave her hope too.

First, she changed the sheets on the bed, dusted and picked up. Dirty clothes overflowed the hamper, but there was no time for laundry today. It was quite dark out and she wondered where Joaquin was. Already she had forgotten Jackie's funeral.

She filled the kitchen sink with hot, soapy water and

began on the dishes. The water was so hot the skin on her hands turned red. The longer she worked, the better she felt. She scrubbed the kitchen floor, vacuumed, swept, polished. When the house was clean, she saw there was very little in the cupboard. She would have to buy groceries.

She moved quickly through the aisles of the store. She knew people were looking at her, she could feel their stares, but she didn't let it bother her. She had come back to Joaquin. Everything was going to be all right.

She was humming when she returned to the house. Joaquin was waiting at the table. The bottle was back out on the counter and he had poured himself a drink.

"Hello," she said. "You're home." As if he had been the one who had gone away.

"What are you doing?"

She put the bags on the counter and began taking groceries from them. "I thought we could have rice and *linguica*," she said. "Are you hungry?"

"Rosa, what are you doing here?"

"I've come home, Joaquin. I've come back home to you."

" 'I've come home, Joaquin.' Just like that. 'I've come home.' "

"I'm sorry."

"Jesus. Is that supposed to make everything all right? I'm supposed to forget everything else? You and that man. Everyone in town laughing. My own father and brother making the sign of the horns behind my back. He comes in and takes you and when he is finished he leaves you behind like a piece of garbage."

She gasped. "You know Fenris is gone?"

"Everyone knows, Rosa. You know this town. You sneeze in bed in the morning and Doc has the cold remedy waiting for you when you walk in the drugstore. He left you and now you want to come back here just like before."

"I love you, Joaquin. I'll do whatever you want."

"What kind of man is it that takes a woman back? A piece of garbage. That's what you are to me."

"You sound like your father."

"A *man*. My father is a *man*."

"Please, Joaquin. Don't you want me?"

She bent over him. He could smell the warmth of her. She touched his arm and the touch rewoke memories. "Oh, Rosa," he sighed. He did want her. And he hated himself for it.

She bent and kissed him, and when her lips touched his, a picture flashed through his mind of her with the other man. "No," he said. "Get away." He thought of her with the man, thought of what his father would say if he took her back now. These thoughts fought with the memories she had wakened. "No," he shouted.

She fell back. "Joaquin . . ."

"No." She was a devil, a witch, a *bruxa*. He hated the power she had over him. He raised his hand.

Instinctively, Rosa dropped her hands to her stomach, protecting it rather than her face.

He dropped his hand. "Oh, God," he moaned.

She faced him, her hands still cradling her belly.

"Get out. Just get out." He would not look at her. His voice was stony. "If you come back, I'll kill you. I swear it."

She went back to the Sail Loft. She lay on the bed in Fenris's studio. The pillow and sheets held the smell of him, and she buried her face in them. She did not weep. Her mind whirled frantically, an animal ensnared, but there was no escape. She could not return to Joaquin. Or to her father's house. Even if Dolores wanted to take her in, Tony would never allow it. Her hands balled into fists and she struck the pillow. *What will I do? Dear Jesus, what will I do?* She wanted to die.

And then she remembered that she was not alone.

Her fingers relaxed and she dropped her hands to her stomach. She was not alone. In the dark, she lay back and stroked her belly, whispering promises, gathering courage. "We'll be all right," she whispered. "Nothing is going to hurt us." And at last she slept.

They came for her some time after midnight. She woke to hands on her body, brutal, coarse hands that yanked her from sleep. Before she could scream, a foul-smelling rag was clamped over her mouth, cutting off sound. She struggled, whipping her head wildly from side to side, but the hand over her mouth tightened. She felt the rag against her teeth and tongue and gagged with the filth of it. She kicked, lashing out with her legs, and knew the brief satisfaction of hearing one of her attackers curse before they pinned her down. Rough hands grasped her arms and legs, lifting her. As they took her from the room, they were not gentle—never gentle—and her head and shoulders struck the door frame. She felt liquid on the skin of her face and knew it was her blood. She squirmed, desperate to be free. Sweat covered her body, and the hands of the men who held her were slippery on her skin. She writhed, and the attacker holding her head lost his grip. Her head fell to the floor, knocking her unconscious.

When she came to, she smelled sea air, heard the water. She tried to yell, but the rag they had wrapped around her mouth muffled the sound.

"Shut up, whore," one of them said.

They began to beat her. The beating was not frenzied. The men took their time, and the rain of blows upon her flesh was quite deliberate. There was something particularly ruthless about that, crueler than if they had struck her wildly. Nor were they satisfied with beating her. Grabbing a fistful of her hair, one lifted her head out of the sand and hacked at her locks.

Immediately, instinctively, she bent double, taking

most of the kicks and blows on her back and shoulders and head. She folded her arms over her stomach, protecting the baby. She felt a searing pain in her side and knew that a rib had been broken. Still they did not stop.

She was slipping to a dark place, a welcome warm place where the cruel hands lost some of their power. She felt her clothes being torn and knew fear, but that fear too was dimmed by the darkness. Encircling her, they spat at her. *Whore. Devil. Witch. Whore-devil.* The words swam in the blackness. Liquid spattered on her back. It was a moment before she understood. They were urinating on her. She felt their urine splatter on her back, her legs, her arms, her head. Her mutilated hair grew wet with it.

When they were done beating her, they left her. The tide was already beginning to come in. Dimly, she felt the salt sting the places where her flesh was ripped. At the end, before the dimness overtook her completely, she thought she recognized one of the voices. The shock cleared her head for a moment, then there was only blackness.

PART FOUR

And shake the secrets
from my deepest bones. . . .
—Theodore Roethke

Chapter 24

Zoe

An undercurrent of sound—faint, mewing sounds—ebbed and flowed through the room like waves. It was a moment before Zoe realized the sound came from her throat.

"No," she cried. "Oh, God, no."

"Zoe, honey. Please, honey. Don't." Jake was at her side. "Don't cry. It'll be all right." The strain in his voice gave the lie to his words.

She lay on the sofa in the living room, but she could not remember how she got there. She shook off the tumbler Jake held to her lips. The smell of brandy made her ill. She pushed herself up, but a wave of dizziness forced her to lie back. A heavy weight—the paralyzing, dreadful weight of terror—pushed on her chest. It hurt to breathe. In the background she heard men talking.

Daniel Cole poked his head in. When he saw that she was awake, he entered. As he approached, he dug into his pocket for a cigarette. She turned from him, burying her face in the sofa cushions. Beneath the cover of the mohair throw, her fingers tightened into a fist.

"I need to ask her some questions."

Jake moved slightly, shielding her from the sheriff's deputy. "Not just now. Give her a few more minutes."

"How's she doing?"

Jake shrugged. "She's conscious."

"You want me to send the doc back in to check on her?"

"No. She'll be all right. Just give her a little more time."

Cole hesitated. "Okay. Just a few minutes. I need to talk to her as soon as possible."

"I'm dizzy, Jake," she said after the deputy left. "So dizzy." She rubbed her forehead, her temples. Her fingers were icy.

"It's probably the shot. The doctor gave you a sedative." He tucked the mohair throw around her neck. "Just rest." With one hand he stroked her hair; he slipped the other beneath the throw, encircling hers.

"How did you get here?" she whispered.

"You called the police. They called me. You were hysterical when they got here."

She began to weep. "Dear God, Jake. Who would take Adam? Why would anyone take him? Why?"

"Easy, honey. Take it easy." His eyes watered as he held his wife. "They'll find him."

"Where's Emily?"

"At Jane Bower's. She said she'd keep Emily as long as we want. She sends her love. Says if there was anything she can do . . ."

"I want Emily here."

"I don't know, hon," Jake began. "It's better for her to stay over at Jane's, at least until things quiet down here."

"I want her here." Zoe's voice rose. "I want her where I can see her."

"Easy, Zoe. Easy."

"Now."

"After the police leave, okay? I'll get her then. Jane will keep Emily for supper and then I'll get her. You don't want her here now. Not with the house full of police."

Too weak to fight, she gave in.

Through the doorway, she saw men come and go in the hall. One officer worked on Adam's carriage. He was painting the handle with a long, slender brush. It took her a moment to realize that he was dusting it for fingerprints. Cole approached the man. The two spoke briefly; then the deputy came into the living room. This time she did not turn away.

He squatted down by the sofa so that his face was nearly level with hers. "How you doing?" Smoke from a cigarette curled up from his hand, circling his arm like a snake.

"Better. Thanks."

"I know this is difficult, but I need to ask you a few questions," he said. "Who else handles the carriage?"

"Nobody. Only Jake and me."

"No one else?"

She closed her eyes. The smoke was making her head ache.

"Sometimes Emily. Sometimes she likes to help me with it."

"Who else?" he pushed.

"No one."

"You sure? What about friends or relatives? Any grandmothers or baby-sitters? Anyone who helps with the housework?"

"She said no one else." Jake tightened his hand on Zoe's.

"Okay. Just making sure." Cole stood and motioned for the technician in the hall to come in.

The officer carried a suitcase, which he set on the table next to the tumbler of brandy. He avoided Zoe's eyes.

"I have a couple of calls to make," Cole said. "In the meantime, this is one of our men. Matt Forbes. He's going to take your prints."

"Our prints?" Zoe looked at Jake, pain and confusion on her face. "Why?"

"To help us eliminate some of the ones we got off the carriage."

"We'll take you first, Mrs. Barlow," the sheriff's man said. "It will just take a minute." He spoke softly, as if she were an invalid, but he still could not look straight at her. "It won't hurt."

He took a sheet of paper and an ink pad from his suitcase, then hesitated. "I'm going to need more light. Is there a lamp you could put on?"

Jake rose and crossed to flick on the overhead light. She closed her eyes against the glare.

Forbes reached for her hand. He was gentle, but she felt as if the bones in her fingers would break when he touched them.

After he had printed them both, he took a bottle of clear liquid and several cotton pads from the case and cleaned the ink from their fingertips. He was quick and very efficient.

"Mrs. Barlow?" Cole reappeared. "I know this is hard, but I wondered if you could take a look at the carriage."

"For God's sake, Cole," Jake burst out. "Not now."

"It's okay, Jake. It's okay." She swung her feet onto the floor and stood up. She swayed for a minute; nausea threatened. Instantly Jake was there, his arm supporting her.

"You don't have to do this now, Zoe. It can wait."

She shook off his arm and walked out to the hall.

The chrome handle was smudged with fine black powder where Forbes had worked. The blue blanket and quilted robe were still in the pram. A little rabbit, of the same material as the carriage robe, was tucked in near the bottom. To one side of the little pillow, where it had rolled, she saw Adam's pacifier. She reached out and picked it up and held it to her cheek. It smelled of Adam.

Jake tried to hold her, but she pulled away.

"Is it just as you left it?" Cole's voice was quiet.

She nodded.

"Everything?"

"Yes." Her voice broke on the word.

"I know this is hard, but can we go upstairs? To his room?"

She led the way, leaning on the banister for support as they climbed the stairs. She still held Adam's pacifier.

His room, too, was as she had left it that morning: the sheet was still rumpled in his crib; a dusting of talcum powder filmed the changing table.

"Anything missing? Any of his clothes or toys or blankets?"

It was so hard to think. "No."

"Take your time. Check the drawers."

She went through the room again, more thoroughly this time. She stopped near the crib. Paddington and Winnie-the-Pooh looked up at her with flat button eyes.

"Nothing. Nothing is missing."

She heard Cole sigh, and then, even through the cottony thickness, she understood. Whoever had taken Adam had not taken anything to keep him warm, to keep him fed, *to keep him alive.* "Oh, God," she cried.

Awkwardly, Daniel Cole put his hand on her shoulder. "Come on," he said. "Let's go back downstairs."

Sam Riley was waiting in the living room. A young woman was sitting in a chair taken from the dining room. She held a pad of paper on her lap. When Zoe and Jake came into the room, she looked up, but no one introduced her.

"We'll finish as soon as we can," Cole said. "Just a few more questions."

Zoe sat on the sofa, the pacifier still clenched in her fist, and waited for him to begin.

Slowly he took her through it all again. She replied in a monotone: how she had taken Adam out in his carriage; how he had fallen asleep and, once home, she had been reluctant to waken him; how she had left him in the carriage in the hall; how she had gone up to her bedroom to paint; how she had stayed upstairs until Emily had come home; and how she had gone to the carriage—the empty carriage. When she was finished, she looked down at her fingers. She saw traces of the fingerprint ink near her nails.

"So you left him to sleep in the hall while you went upstairs?" Sam Riley had taken over the questioning.

"Yes."

"Is that normal?"

"What?" Her mouth was so dry. "I don't know what you mean."

"I mean do you paint every day while your son sleeps?"

"No. Not usually."

"But you did today?"

"Yes."

"And how long did you leave him there alone in the hall?"

The sound of the girl's pencil scratching over paper echoed in the room.

"I don't know."

"Ten minutes? A half hour? Give us some idea."

Her head pounded. "Could I . . . could I have some water?"

Jake got it for her.

"How long was he alone in the hall?"

The words stuck in her throat. *Two hours. How could she? How could she have left him alone for two hours? Her fault.*

"Mrs. Barlow?"

"Two hours." She whispered the words. The stenographer wrote them down. Zoe felt the men looking at her. She couldn't meet their eyes.

"During that time," Riley asked, "while you were painting, did you hear any noise at all? Any sounds? A door closing? Anything?"

She shook her head. *Two hours.* Her palms were damp. She felt the stickiness of the pacifier in her fingers. It was wet with her sweat.

"So the first sound you were aware of was Jane Bower calling you and you went down to the kitchen?"

"Yes," she whispered.

Riley turned to Jake. "What about you, Mr. Barlow? Where were you during this time?"

"At the bookstore."

"All afternoon?"

She heard their voices. Questions. Answers. They did not register. *Two hours. How could she have left Adam alone for that long?*

"Yes. It's my clerk's day off and so I had to be there all day."

"Did you leave the store at all?"

Two hours. She felt ill. Lost in her guilt, she didn't hear Riley question Jake.

"No. I was there all day."

"And you were alone?"

"Except for customers. It was pretty steady."

The chief took up the questioning.

"Mrs. Barlow? Mrs. Barlow? Is there anyone you know, anyone at all who might have wanted to take your son?"

"Why? Why would anyone want to take Adam?"

"Anyone with a grudge? Were either of you married before? An ex in the picture?"

"This is a first marriage for both of us," Jake said.

"Are you in any kind of trouble? Do you owe anyone money?"

"Why are you asking us these questions? Do you think we're responsible for Adam's being kidnapped?" Zoe cried. "Why aren't you out looking for our son?"

"Mrs. Barlow," Cole said, "I'm sorry, but these are questions we have to ask. Believe me. We are doing everything possible to find your son."

"Dan?" A patrolman stood in the doorway. "Can I see you for a minute?"

They watched him leave. Jake reached for the brandy snifter. He swallowed it all.

Cole returned almost immediately. "Mrs. Barlow?"

"What?"

"What was Adam wearing this afternoon?"

"Why?"

"Please. Can you remember what he was wearing?"

She dropped her head into her hands. It was so hard to think. She was exhausted. "I don't know. I can't remember."

"Please. Try. It's important."

She closed her eyes. The pain of remembering was physical. She tried to think back to the morning. Bathing Adam. Dressing him. Only that morning? It seemed as if days had passed.

"A . . . a blue sleep suit. One-piece, cotton knit. Like terrycloth."

"Anything special about it?"

"It had snaps at the crotch. And a little patch—like a, you know, a crest—on the left side of the chest. A baseball bat with the words 'Little Slugger' embroidered underneath."

The deputy looked shaken. "Mr. Barlow, could you come out with me?"

She would not be left alone. All three went out to the kitchen. She moaned. Sam Riley was holding Adam's blue sleeper suit.

"One of our men found it," Cole said.

"Where?" The word was a whisper.

"In the alley. In a trash can in the alley."

"And Adam?" Jake was hoarse.

Dan Cole shook his head.

Chapter 25

It was after one by the time Sam Riley pulled the county sedan into Cole's driveway. Jenny had left the kitchen light on, and its glow beckoned. Dan stretched in the passenger seat. He was exhausted, but he doubted he would be able to sleep. Too much coffee. Too much adrenaline. His stomach churned. And in his mind, he kept seeing the fear and panic on Zoe Barlow's face when she saw her son's blue sleeper. He sighed and was reaching for the door when Sam stopped him.

"Nobody talks."

"What?"

"That town. It's driving me crazy. Usually, people talk. They gossip. Usually we can't kept them quiet. This town, nobody talks. And they know something. I can feel it."

"They will. We just haven't been asking the right questions."

"That's not all. . . ."

Cole waited.

"The son of a bitch is lying."

"Who?"

"Jake Barlow. He's lying through his teeth."

Dan released the door handle. "What have you got against Barlow, Sam? You've been on him since we came on the bones case."

"I don't know. Something about him." Riley switched off the ignition. "The whole thing smells." He reached across the dash and opened the glove compartment. He handed a Baby Ruth bar to his partner and took one for himself.

Chocolate on top of the caffeine was the last thing Cole needed. He unwrapped the bar and bit into it. "You don't think he's involved with his son's kidnapping, do you?"

"What kidnapping? The baby's missing. No note. No call. No ransom demand. That sound like a kidnapping to you?"

"His own baby? You think he'd take his own kid?"

"It happens. Remember that case three years ago in Providence? The couple with the six-month-old kid."

"Sampson?"

"Yeah. Right. Sampson. Half the cops in the country were looking for the baby. They took that house apart. Brought in dogs, psychics—remember that? And Sampson goes on TV and pleads for whoever took his little girl to return her. Guy was crying on the evening news."

"Two months later they find the body in a coal bin a quarter of a mile away. Turned out that he had killed the kid, right?"

"Right. Raped her, then strangled her. A six-month-old baby."

"I remember." The Baby Ruth turned sour in Cole's mouth.

Riley finished his bar and reached for another. "Your friend in New Haven," he said to his partner, "did he give you that girl's name and address? The sitter who accused Barlow?"

"Yeah. Why?"

"You got it on you?"

Dan pulled his notebook from his coat pocket and flipped it open. "Laurel Blake, 637 High Street. Why?"

Sam repeated the information, committing it to memory. He checked his watch and grinned at Cole. "Want to take a ride?"

"When?"

"Now."

Dan rubbed his eyes. They burned.

"I want to talk to this Blake girl."

"Tonight? You gonna wake her up in the middle of the night to talk to her?"

"We can be there to catch her first thing in the morning."

"Did you ever hear of the telephone, Riley?"

Sam shook his head. "I want to see her face when we ask her about Barlow. You can't see a face on the telephone."

"You really think Barlow is involved?" In an upstairs window, a light went on. Jenny was waiting for him. The bed would be warm. He sighed.

"The setup stinks. And I can't forget about the kid that disappeared six months after he landed in town. It bugs me."

"It can't wait until morning? We could grab a few hours' sleep and still be there first thing."

"You're getting old, Cole. Ya know that?"

"Shit." Dan opened the door.

"Where you going?"

Dan sighed again. "To give Jen a kiss and get some money. If we're driving down to New Haven tonight, we'll need cash for tolls and breakfast."

Chapter 26

Overnight, the news about Adam spread. The kitchen counters and table were laden with casserole dishes, pies, breads brought by neighbors and friends, the mothers of the other children at Emily's school, volunteers from the Cetacean Stranding Center.

A dozen reporters and cameramen stood vigil on the sidewalk in front of the house. One newsman had been sitting on their porch when they woke up. Jake had threatened to have him arrested for trespassing.

The silence of her home was suffocating. Jane Bower had taken Emily for the morning. Jake was at work, at her insistence. He thought they should stay together. He needed comfort, but she couldn't respond. Mixed with a sickening sense of guilt that she had left Adam alone was an incomprehensible anger at Jake.

She climbed the stairs and made their bed, then mindlessly paced about the room. From the east window, she looked out at the glistening bay. A sloop cut across the surface of the harbor on its way to the breakwater. Eighteen hours had passed since Adam was taken. Eighteen hours.

Her gaze fell to the empty alley. She had told the police about Old Joe, told them that she had seen the old man watching her house the day after the bodies had been found in the attic and again the following night. About her visit to the trailer. They had listened to her and taken notes. "We'll check it out," they had said in a way that led her to believe they thought she was blaming a hapless stranger and that they didn't think the fisherman was connected in any way to Adam's disappearance.

She was not as certain. She was haunted by the expression of rage on the old man's face when he had seen Adam in the car. *Could he have taken Adam?*

She left the room and went downstairs. In the kitchen, she resumed pacing. She thought she would go crazy with waiting—waiting for the telephone to ring, for the doorbell to chime. Waiting for some word about her son. *Could Old Joe have taken Adam?* The thought would not go away.

It was little enough, but it was all she could do. "Be right back." She tacked the scribbled message on the door, locked the house, and got in the car.

The trailer looked abandoned, but when she pulled into the yard, the two German shepherds sprang to life. Their frenzied howling brought the woman to the door.

"Shut up," she hollered at the dogs. When they continued to bark, she reached for a baseball bat that leaned against the railing and waved it at them. Everything about the woman was tired. "Shut the hell up," she swore, and swung the bat through the air. The smaller of the dogs whined and slouched back to the shade of the rowboat. The larger shepherd crouched, watching the woman.

"Hello," Zoe began. "Is Old Joe here?"

The woman set the bat down and crossed her arms. Her face was set in a stony mask. Dirt—or a bruise—smudged her cheek. "He's not here," she said. She blocked the doorway with her thick body.

"Please. It's important."

"He's not here. I told you that. Go away. We got nothing to do with you."

"Just for a minute," she said. "I just want to see

him for a minute." Zoe reached out a hand, but the woman recoiled from her touch.

"He's not here, I said."

Zoe could see beyond the woman, into the filth and neglect of the trailer. "Please."

A bolt of fear darkened the woman's eyes. "What do you want with him?"

The sentences she had prepared and practiced in the car evaporated. "My son," she said. "Someone took my baby."

The woman stared at her. A brief look of incomprehension was replaced by horror. "Go away. We got nothing to do with you or your baby."

"Just tell me. Where is he?"

"He don't tell me where he goes."

The thought of Adam inside the filthy trailer made her sick. "I'll get the police," she said. It was all she could think of to break through.

The woman sagged, as if the breath had been pulled from her body. "In there," she said. She stepped aside and pointed.

Zoe smelled the sour reek of whiskey even before she walked through the door. Old Joe lay on the torn and stained sofa, holding an empty bottle to his chest as if he were nestling a doll.

"Drunk," the woman said. "He started after you left yesterday and didn't stop until he passed out."

Zoe backed off, wanting to be away from the trailer with its stench of poverty and loss and despair. Adam was not here. She was overwhelmed with the need to go home. She had to be there in case someone called about her son. It was madness to have come here at all.

"It's her fault."

She was outside when the words stopped her. She turned back. The woman's mouth twisted with bitterness. "You can go back and tell her that. It's all her fault."

"Who? Tell who?"

"The one who sent you. Victoria Santos."

The note was where she had left it on the door. She pulled it down and entered the silent, empty house. She hadn't had time to remove her coat when the phone rang. Jake's voice was edgy with concern.

"Zoe? Where have you been? I've been trying to call you for the last half hour."

"Any news?" She could not keep the hope out of her voice.

"No. Nothing. What about you? Anything?"

"No." The word was flat. Empty.

"Do you want me to come home?"

"No, you stay there. I'll be fine."

"You sure? 'Cause if you don't mind, it helps being here. I think I'd go crazy just sitting at home, you know? Look," he continued, "I guess we better hang up. In case someone's trying to get through." He seemed anxious to get off the phone.

"Jake?"

"Yeah?"

"Have you ever heard of anyone named Victoria Santos?"

"Victoria Santos? No. Why?"

"Nothing."

After she hung up, she realized he had not asked how she was. His voice had been forced, filled with . . . what? She struggled to identify the emotion.

It came to her with a shock. *Guilt.*

She braced herself as she dialed her mother's number.

"Tory Sands Gallery."

Zoe didn't recognize the voice or the accent. British, she guessed, with a faint Jamaican undertone. A new receptionist. Tory changed employees regularly. The ones who didn't quit were fired.

"Hello. This is Zoe Barlow. May I speak to my . . . to Tory Sands, please?"

"Just a minute, Ms. Barlow. I'll see if Ms. Sands is free. May I tell her what this is in reference to?"

"Just tell her it's Zoe calling." Resentment flared. It still hurt that her mother had a separate life in which Zoe was denied any part, and it hurt that her mother's employees seemed unaware of her existence. She sighed and let it go. Old stuff. Old history.

She heard her mother's footsteps as they approached the phone, heels clicking sharply on polished oak floors. The sound elicited an immediate image of Tory, every detail restrained, tasteful, impeccable: hair streaked with gold and held back in a coil an inch above her collar; perfectly cut, raw silk suit; gold earrings, matching bracelet, a square-cut emerald solitaire on her left hand. Tory had stopped wearing a wedding band long before Zoe's father had died. Sentimental and unprofessional, she'd explained when she had placed it in her jewelry box. If it had bothered him, her father had never let on, any more than he had shown any emotion when Tory had announced her decision to return to her maiden name—for "professional reasons."

Tory's voice, sharp, impersonal, with an edge of impatience, came through the phone. Unaware she was doing so, Zoe braced herself. Protecting herself when dealing with her mother was a habit so ingrained it was second nature.

She did not cry as she told her mother about Adam. Her mother hated weakness.

"Kidnapped?" The word was spoken with disbelief and a touch of distaste. "Are you sure? Of course you're sure. Dear God, darling, this is horrid."

Zoe fought tears.

"Zoe?"

"What?"

"I hate to ask this, but does this have anything to do with Jake? Have you two split or something? I mean, could he have taken Adam?"

Weariness crept into Zoe's voice. "No. No, Mother." She heard a rustle of impatience on the other end. Tory hated to be called Mother. "Jake and I haven't split." She sank back against the counter. She could see Adam's carriage in the hall. Even from that distance, she could still see the smudges of black powder on the chrome handle. Her fingers tightened on the receiver.

"Well, don't get angry with me for asking. I mean, there was that other business."

She heard words, muffled by a palm held over the mouthpiece, as her mother talked with someone in the background.

"Please, Mother—tell me what to do. I'm so afraid."

"I'll call John Cabot."

"No." *What could her father's lawyer do?* "Could you come? Please. I need you."

There was another muffled conversation at the other end, followed by a long pause.

"Mother?"

"I'll try. I mean, if there was anything I could do by being there . . ."

What did she want from her mother? What had she expected? Comfort?

"Darling, if there was *anything* I could do," Tory repeated, "of course I'd come."

"For God's sake, Mother, Adam's been kidnapped."

"Don't swear at me, Zoe." The tone was sharp. "It's that damn house. You should never have moved there. It's bad luck. I told you that when you asked me to let you buy the house. You were the one who insisted on moving there."

Why did their conversations always end like this?

Why did she always end up feeling guilty? "Mother, listen, I have to go. I'll call later."

"Stay in touch, darling. All right? And I'll see what I can do about getting away. If you really think it will help, I'll come down."

Zoe recognized the empty promise. "No. You're right, there's nothing you can do. I'll call." She was on the verge of hanging up when the question occurred. "Mother? One more thing. Have you ever heard of a woman named Victoria Santos?"

The silence stretched on so long she thought at first that Tory had already hung up.

"Who?"

"Victoria Santos."

"No. I don't think so. No, I'm sure of it. Why do you ask?"

"Nothing." When she replaced the receiver, the hair was raised on her neck, and a chill ran like a shock through the length of her body. She knew two things. She was scared. And her mother was lying.

Dan and Sam pulled into a coffee shop just off I-95. The girl behind the counter found them a street map of New Haven.

"This is crazy," Dan said as his partner pored over the grease-stained map. He checked his watch. "We're too early. We can't go knocking on her door now. It's not even eight."

"What if she works and she leaves early? Better to wake her up than to drive all this way and miss her."

"What if she doesn't even live there anymore?" Dan repeated. "What is she now, eighteen or nineteen? Chances are she's moved out."

"There's only one way to find out." Sam folded the map and headed for the car.

Six-thirty-seven High Street was a duplex in a neighborhood that had once been what Dan's mother would have called "substantial"—single-family homes that had been converted into two-family dwellings and student apartments.

A pretty woman answered their knock. She was about fifteen pounds too heavy, and her auburn hair had the overprocessed flatness of a home-done dye job. The imprint of wrinkled sheets creased the side of her face. Sam flipped open his wallet and held out his sheriff's department ID, but Dan could tell from the weariness in her eyes that she knew they were cops as soon as she opened the door.

"We hate to bother you so early," Sam began, "but we're looking for Laurel Blake. This is the address we have for her."

The woman rubbed a hand over her eyes. "She's not here."

"Could you tell us when she'll be in or how we can get in touch with her?"

"Like I said, she's not here. She's on a trip."

Sam leaned in and smiled. Dan knew the look. He called it Sam's "No problem here, we're just your friendly local police" smile. "It's important that we talk with her."

The woman softened slightly. "What is this about?"

"Are you her sister?"

The wary look returned to the woman's face. She had seen Sam's type of charm before. "I'm her mother. What's this all about, anyway?"

"Just some questions. Laurel's not in any trouble—we just want some information."

"She's not here. She's gone on a trip."

"Do you have a number? Or the name of the place she's staying?"

She stared at Sam, then made up her mind. "Wait here." She kept them waiting on the steps and closed the door.

" 'Are you her sister?' Jesus, Sam, that was pathetic."

"Could you do any better? We're getting the number, aren't we?"

While they waited, Dan looked over the house. It had been a long time since the trim had seen a coat of paint. The foundation plantings were overgrown, their foliage a washed-out yellow-green. He would have bet a paycheck that Laurel's father, or any man, had not lived there in years.

"Looks like we should have called ahead," Dan said. "This trip's a waste of time."

The woman opened the door. Her hair was combed and she wore lipstick. She held a scrap of paper, the flap torn from an envelope. She'd scribbled an address in green ink. "Can I get you some coffee or anything?" she asked, looking at Sam.

"We'd like to, ma'am, but we've got a long drive ahead." He waited for her to give him the envelope. "Maybe you'd give us a rain check."

She handed over the address. He glanced at it, but his expression did not change. "Thanks for your help. Sorry to bother you so early."

"No problem. Don't forget that rain check on the coffee."

"Sure. I'd like that. Next time I'm in the area."

"Shit," Daniel swore as they pulled away from the curb. "A rain check, for God's sake."

"Whatever works," Sam said. "And the trip wasn't such a waste of time, after all." He handed the slip of paper to his partner. Daniel read the loopy green words. Laurel Blake could be reached at the Ship's Deck Motel in Grace Point, Massachusetts.

Chapter 27

"You've heard something?" Zoe asked. She was surprised to see the deputy at the door. He was alone. "Have you?"

The porch floorboards creaked as Dan Cole shifted his weight. "May I come in?"

"Have you found something?" She tried to read his face for clues. "Have you found Adam?"

Cole had to look away from the hope that blazed in her eyes. "Nothing yet, Mrs. Barlow."

"I see." The light died. "Yes, of course—come in." She crossed to the stove and switched on the burner beneath the pot. "Can I get you a cup of coffee?"

"If it's no trouble."

She set out two mugs and waited for him to begin, but he sat at the table in silence. While she poured the coffee, he took out his cigarettes. He fingered the pack and tucked them back in his pocket without lighting one. "Bad habit."

"Yes," she said.

"Milk and sugar?"

"Please."

She swung open the refrigerator door, but her hand froze inches from the milk carton. The gap-toothed child smiled out at her. *Missing*. The word was bold and black above the boy's face. She took out the milk.

"Have you—have you ever been involved in a case like this before?"

"A missing child?" Cole asked. He looked at the milk carton, then at Zoe. "A couple of times."

She pushed the sugar bowl toward him, avoiding his eyes. "Did you find the children? Were they okay?"

"Yes," he lied.

"Did they . . . I mean, did the people who took the children . . . did they . . ." Her voice broke. "Did they take good care of them? I mean, did they feed them and change them?"

"Yes," Cole said. "They took very good care of them." He drank the coffee. It burned his throat. He started to reach out and touch her hand but stopped himself. At the academy they had been warned about acting in any way that might be misunderstood. "Look, Mrs. Barlow, he'll be all right. Your son will be okay."

"It's just that . . . Adam's such a good baby. He seldom cries. But he's used to eating on schedule. He should have been fed four times. His skin is sensitive. If his diaper isn't changed, he gets a rash." She watched the detective sip his coffee, but she did not touch her mug. "Whoever took him didn't take any diapers or any of his things or any food. *It's been twenty hours.*"

"I'm sure they bought what they needed," Cole said reassuringly.

"Why haven't we heard anything? No one's asked for money or anything. There haven't been any calls or notes. Why would anyone take him?"

"We can only guess. In a case like this, when there's been no ransom demand, it usually turns out that it's one of two things. Either it's a domestic matter—such as an estranged spouse who takes the kid because he's been denied visitation rights—or it's someone who wants a baby and can't have one, so they kidnap one. Either way, they take good care of the child."

She looked at the milk carton and the gap-toothed boy. "Do they usually find the child?"

"The majority of the time," he lied again.

"What percentage? What percentage are found? I want to know what Adam's chances are."

"Listen, Mrs. Barlow." Daniel laid his hand on her arm. "Zoe. We aren't ready to talk about statistics yet. Okay. Adam isn't a statistic. We're going to find him."

"How?" Despair creased her face.

"We will. Trust us. We have a lead or two we're following. That's what my partner is doing right now. He's following an important lead."

"What is it?"

"I'm waiting for him to call. Let's wait until we hear from him. In the meantime, I need to ask you a couple of questions, okay?"

"Questions?"

"Your former baby-sitter, Laurel Blake. Have you or your husband been in touch with her or heard from her since you moved to Grace Point?"

Zoe stared at him.

"Mrs. Barlow?" Dan leaned forward. "Mrs. Barlow, we need to know if you have seen or heard from Laurel Blake."

"No."

"Neither of you? She hasn't called? No word?"

"I told you. No."

"And she's never called or tried to get in touch?"

"Never. Why? Why are you asking about her?"

Cole looked down at his notebook. "We went to see her."

"Laurel Blake? You went to New Haven to see her?"

"Yes. Except she was on a little vacation. She left an address with her mother." He looked directly at Zoe. "She's staying at a place called the Ship's Deck Motel. In Grace Point, Massachusetts."

"She's here?"

"We think so. My partner's checking now."

She's here. In Grace Point.

"What is it?" Dan leaned forward, searching her face.

"Nothing."

"Please, Mrs. Barlow. Help me. We're trying to find Adam. I wouldn't ask if it weren't important. What is it? You know something. Tell me what it is."

"I saw her." Her voice was a whisper.

"Who? Laurel? You're sure?"

"Pretty sure. I was walking in town with Adam. I got a glimpse of a girl. I only saw her from the back, but there was something about her—her hair . . . the way she walked. I thought it was Laurel Blake."

"When was this?"

"Yesterday. The day . . . the day Adam disappeared."

They stared at each other. Dan moved first. He shoved back his chair and got to his feet.

"We'll find her, Zoe. I promise you."

He was at the door when the phone rang.

"It's for you. Your partner." Zoe held the receiver out to him.

She never took her gaze from his face, and so she saw his eyes change color. Something darkened in their depths as he listened. He put the receiver back on the hook carefully.

"What is it?" she demanded. "Tell me. What did he say?"

Dan Cole fidgeted with his notebook.

"For God's sake, what is it?"

"Mrs. Barlow," he began. "Yesterday, when we were here, we asked your husband where he was all day. Do you remember?"

"Yes. Kind of. The doctor gave me a sedative. I can't remember much about what happened right after . . . after it happened."

"Your husband told us he was at his bookstore all day. He said he never left the store. Well, my partner just finished talking to a woman who owns the candy shop next to the bookstore. She said he wasn't there for at least an hour. She remembers because she wanted to buy a book on her lunch hour, but he wasn't there and the door was locked."

Instantly, the sign on the bookstore door—"Be Back At," with the hands on the clock face pointing to twelve and one—flashed into her mind. She remembered the sound of the phone ringing and ringing when she called to tell him to pick Emily up at the Bowers'. "There must be some mistake." *Jake had lied. To her and to the police. Jake had lied.*

"Well, we'll straighten it out. I'm heading over to the store now. I'm meeting Sam there."

She watched from the window as he walked away from her home. Three reporters stood on the sidewalk. He stopped for a minute to answer their questions. He moved his hand through the air when he spoke. She watched from behind the curtains.

Her head pounded. When Cole was out of sight, she left the window. She was sure of only one thing: Jake would never hurt Adam. No matter what the police thought, no matter what he may have done, she knew he would never do anything to hurt their son.

She washed the coffee mugs and wiped the surface of the table. *Keep busy. Keep busy. Don't think. Just keep busy.* She climbed the stairs to her room. The easel waited in the alcove. She stood in front of it, staring at the big old ceramic mug she used as a slop jar to clean the brushes in. Another jar, a bean pot, held a selection of brushes. *Keep busy. Paint. Don't think.* She picked up a tube of cerulean and unscrewed the cap. *What is Laurel doing here? Why did she come to Grace Point?* She began squeezing a dab of blue onto her palette. *Don't think. Don't think. To think is to wade in dangerous waters.* Half the tube of paint was squeezed out. She stared at the blob of intense blue. *Get hold of yourself, Zoe.* She reached for a brush and made a tentative stroke on the new canvas. Then another. And another. Mindless, repetitive bands of brittle color filled the canvas. *Jake lied. He was seeing Laurel.*

"Damn you," she whispered under her breath. "Damn you, damn you, damn you." She began to rock, and the whispered words grew into a shout. She dropped the brush and picked up her scraper razor. "Damn you," she said as she brought the blade down through the canvas. Again and again she slashed, pulling the razor through the fabric, shredding it. Her legs trembled and her skin felt hot. Still she slashed, until there was nothing left. She threw the canvas across the room. Then she flung the bean pot. Brushes flew everywhere. The pot crashed against the headboard. "Goddamn you! Goddamn you!" She threw the slop jar and it smashed against the wall. Murky water ran in streaks down the cream-colored wall. She grabbed the palette with both hands. Paint smeared on her fingers. She flung it after the jar. It stuck to the wall, then slid to the floor, leaving a broad blue stripe. She threw until there was nothing left to throw. "Liar, liar, liar!" she screamed. "Bastard—you bastard!" There was a soft background noise, but she was beyond hearing. "Why did you lie? Damn you to hell, why did you *lie*?"

Finally, she was spent. Exhausted, she slid to the floor.

It was a while before she heard the noise—a faint, muffled, frightened sound. She turned and saw Emily. The child, home from Elizabeth's, stood at the door, watching her.

Chapter 28

Rosalina

Odessa Dunne was seated at her worktable by the window. She sighed, acknowledging surrender, as she put down her pen. All morning she had been doing battle with words, and losing. It was no good when her mind was filled with so much else.

She could hear the sound of the girl's breathing from the other room. It seemed to fill the small shack, taking up space, sucking up her own space and freedom. Resentment. That was her problem. She was filled with resentment—toward the girl, toward the town, toward herself for getting involved. But she knew she could not have walked away.

Sighing again, she opened the drawer and withdrew the velvet-wrapped package. Carefully she unfolded the material to reveal the worn tarot deck. With practiced hands she shuffled the cards, then laid them out one by one on the rough surface of the table, concentrating on the spread. The sound of the girl's breathing seemed louder now. She closed her eyes and tried to ignore it, but found this was as futile as trying to shut out the crash of the surf. She drew a card from the deck. Three times since she had brought the girl to her shack, this card, the ace of cups, had turned up. There was no such thing as coincidence.

She studied the card and let its meanings wash over her. Cups. The water suit. Love, beginnings, birth, caring. There was no mistaking the message: life, love, joy, fertility. She sighed, a low sound of regret. If she could have, she would have rejected the card—too messy, too many complications. She was too old. At this time in her life, her energy and passion served only her poetry.

More sounds came from the bedroom. Carefully, the woman gathered the deck and rewrapped it in the square of rose velvet. She returned it to the drawer, and then she got up and went into the other room.

Rosalina looked around the tiny room. The sound of surf and wind leaked through the rough planks. She tried to move, and pain shot through her. The memories swept over her. Fenris. Joaquin. The pain of the blows and how she had curled up on the sand while the men hit and kicked her. Tears filled her eyes and slipped down her cheeks. Then, becoming aware of the woman standing in the doorway, she understood immediately where she was.

"Good morning," Odessa said. Without seeming to, she examined Rosa, monitoring her color, checking her eyes, noting the size of her pupils. "You're much better," she commented briskly.

"I hurt," Rosa whispered.

"You're bruised and have a few cuts," Odessa said. "At least one broken bone. But you're lucky. You'll live."

Rosa's lip trembled and she closed her eyes. Spasms of fear and despair that went far deeper than bruised flesh seized her. "I want to die."

"Why do you want to die?" The question was cool, without emotion.

She started to cry. "What will I do? What will I do? Where will I go?"

A struggle played out on Odessa's face. "Of course you have a place to go," she finally said. "You'll stay here with me."

"What will I do?" Rosa repeated. "He's gone. He went away and left me. I'm alone."

"We are all alone."

Rosalina continued to cry. "I might as well be dead."

Odessa Dunne made a disgusted noise. "Men. No man's worth dying for. I'll tell you that, child—not one man that walks the earth is worth dying over."

She came to the bed and stroked Rosalina's ruined hair back from her eyes. Her hands were gnarled and wrinkled, but the touch was firm. "Forget about dying. You will be fine. You and your baby will both be fine."

"How did you know about the baby?"

Odessa laughed. It was a wonderful laugh, as if it came bubbling out of the earth itself. "I'm a witch. Remember?"

The pain receded under Odessa's touch. Rosalina wanted her to stroke her brow forever. Her fingers were so comforting—like a mother's touch. Thinking this, she slept.

Nearly an hour passed from the moment Rosa first saw the man until he knocked on the door of the shack. She spent the time at the table, watching his progress. She'd known that they would come for her. She had been afraid of this moment every day of the two weeks she had spent at Odessa's shack. *They would not let her alone.*

The ribs of an old surfboat poked up through the sand, the only mark on the landscape. When the man drew abreast of the boat, she saw who it was. "Father Mallory!" she cried.

She hugged her arms to her chest, wincing at the reminder that although her bruises had faded to brown, she was a long way from healed. She drew back into herself.

"Make him go away," she whispered to Odessa when he knocked at the door.

"He has come to see you, not me. If you want him to go away, you tell him."

"Please." She gave a long, pleading, wild look, but the poetess did not move.

The priest knocked again. "Rosalina?" he called.

"What do you want?" she said through the wood.

"Rosalina? It's Father Mallory. May I come in?"

"No." The sound of his voice—muted through the thickness of the door—reminded her of confession. She feared him more than Joaquin or Victor or her father or any of the men who had beaten her.

"Please, Rosa. Just for a moment."

She disguised her fear with disrespect. "What do you want?"

The priest laughed softly. "I'd really like to sit down. I'm not as young as I thought, and it's a long walk. I'm thirsty, too. A drink of water would taste good."

"There is a hand pump in the hollow behind the shack. You can get water there." Her voice was harsh, unrelenting. "Then go. Go back to your church. I don't want to talk to you."

Even through the door, she could hear his sigh, hear the gritty sand beneath his feet as he shuffled on the stoop. He stood there for a long time. Finally she heard him descend the steps of the shack. She crept to the window and peered around the edge of the frame to watch the little priest draw water into the pail. When he cupped his palms and drank, dribbles of water stained the front of his cassock. Finished, he looked at the shack. Rosalina pulled back from the window. She held her breath and waited for the sound of his feet on the steps. After a while she began to breathe again. Finally she peeked out the window again. The priest had begun the walk back to Grace Point. Against the expanse of the brooding dunes, he seemed even frailer and tinier.

"Why didn't you let him in?"

Rosa jumped. She'd forgotten the poetess was in the room.

"Answer me, Rosa. Why didn't you let the old man in? You should have let him in," she said softly.

"Why?"

"It is impolite to turn away anyone who comes to the door of our shack. He was hungry and tired, and he is an old man."

"I was afraid."

"Of him? The little priest?"

Rosa stared out at the dunes. Incandescent waves shimmered above the sand, and the bones of the old surfboat appeared submerged in this ocean of heat. "Of God," she finally whispered. "Of my sins. I am damned."

The poetess snorted. "Horseshit."

Rosa sucked in a breath. "You don't believe in God?"

"I don't believe in a God who damns."

"What do you believe?"

"I believe in nature. The mother earth. That is my god." Odessa looked out the window. The priest was just a black speck bobbing across the distant sand. "He is only a man. You have nothing to fear from him. What is inside of us, inside our heart, *that* is what we have to fear."

Odessa did not wait for Rosa to answer. She picked up her shawl and took her knapsack from the peg on the wall, then reached for her walking staff.

"Where are you going?" Rosa couldn't keep the panic from her voice.

"Into town."

"Why?"

"I need to. I've been out on these dunes too long."

"Don't go. Please."

"You'll be all right, Rosalina. I'll be back tomorrow."

"I'm afraid to stay here alone."

The poetess crossed to the door. "You are afraid to stay alone. You are afraid of the little priest, a twig of a man you could knock over with one hand. You are afraid of your father and your husband and your father-in-law. You are afraid of your God. You have a lot of fears, child. It is time you began to make peace with them." She opened the door and started out.

"Wait."

Odessa stopped.

"There is one thing I want in town, something I left there. Would you bring it back for me?" She told the poetess what she wanted.

The dune shack seemed terribly empty after Odessa left. Rosalina wandered around, anxious and ill at ease. She made herself lunch and rested for a while on the bed. When she lay on her back, her stomach mounded slightly. What would she do when the baby came? Returning to the shack's front room, she sat at Odessa's worktable and stared out the window, waiting for the poetess to return.

The tarot deck lay on the table. Once, when Odessa was laying the cards out, she had asked if she could pick one. The poetess had replied, "Only if you are ready to hear and accept what is there for you."

She left the deck untouched. Outside the cabin, it grew dark, and she could no longer see if anyone might be walking toward her on the dunes. She did not light the kerosene lanterns. She sat at the table through the night, waiting for Odessa to return. At dawn, exhausted, she fell asleep.

When she woke, the first thing she saw was Odessa lying on the cot. She lay on her back, mouth open, arms spread out. Her skirt was soiled; her hair stood out in spikes, wilder than ever. Rosa stared in horror, sure she was dead.

"Odessa?" she whispered. The poetess looked unbelievably frail. Her skin hung on her frame. The veins of her neck and hands stood out in blue relief. Rosa had never seen Odessa's hands at rest before. She took up one in hers. It was cool and felt thin, fragile, like the hollow-boned skeleton of a bird. It no longer seemed possible that these hands had nursed Rosalina to health or that they had swung an ax at the woodpile, chopped vegetables, loved a man, held a pen, written poetry.

"Odessa?" she said again.

In response, the old woman snored. The sour smell of whiskey floated up from her sleeping body.

Now Rosa could see the soft rise and fall of Odessa's chest beneath the stained shirt. She giggled. The old woman had gone into town to get drunk. Gently, she let go of her hand, took up the cotton shawl from where it lay in a heap on the floor, and covered her with it.

At the foot of the cot, by the rucksack and staff, was the box she had asked Odessa to get for her. She picked it up and took it into the bedroom. She checked it quickly and, satisfied that the map and after-shave bottle and poetry book and other scraps that were all she had of Fenris Boak were still inside, she slipped it under the bed.

He would come back for her. She was sure of it.

Odessa blinked against the brilliance of the sun on the dunes. She needed to get away from the shack, to feel her feet on the sand while she wrestled with her conscience and struggled with what to tell Rosalina. As she headed toward the water, she felt the dunes give way beneath her bare feet. Others believed the sands were dead, but she knew they were alive. She felt each particle of sand shifting and realigning itself beneath the skin of her feet. That was its secret: its resiliency.

She moved unsteadily, inhaling the salt-heavy air

deep into her lungs. Her beloved dunes. She walked to the ocean's edge and waded in.

What to tell the girl? What right, if any, do I have to interfere? The surf surged and broke at her feet. Her breath became labored. She was getting too old to drink.

It was all passing so quickly. All the years—ten . . . twenty . . . fifty. The friends, the poems, the lovers. The triumphs, the foolishness. Where had it all gone? She would not have believed it could pass so quickly. *I'm tired,* Odessa thought, *a shell. Dry as an old milkweed pod. Shriveled and juiceless.* She held up her hands before her face as if offering the wasted skin as evidence. *I have been consumed. By work, by love, by life. I have nothing left to give.*

She returned to the beach. She sank to her knees, ran her hands through the sands. How many times had she bent like this? How many poems had she etched in the damp shore? No person ever saw these lines, yet she believed them to be her best. But had they been enough?

What to tell the girl?

A shadow fell on the dunes. She looked up and saw the hawk soar, wings outstretched. Last summer she had found a dying marsh hawk at the edge of the surf. She had cradled it in her lap, stroking its useless feathers and feeling beneath her fingers the beat of its heart. So frail, this hollow-boned creature, and yet to the end, its heart beat so valiantly, so violently she could feel it through the fabric of her skirt. Before it died, it turned its head, and unblinking eyes found hers. In their depths, there was intelligence she knew she would spend her whole life seeking. Now she lifted her eyes to the hawk overhead, hoping to find an answer. *What to tell the girl?*

". . . My heart in hiding stirred for a bird,—the achieve of, the mastery of the thing!"

So. *Truth.* Always Odessa had tried to seek the

freedom of truth. It would be no different now. She went in to find Rosalina.

Rosalina lay back in the bed. She tightened and relaxed her back and leg muscles. "I feel like a cat in the sun," she said.

"This feels good?" Odessa asked as she massaged warm oil over Rosa's growing belly.

"Hmmmmm," Rosa hummed. She was no longer embarrassed to be naked in front of the poetess. That her body was not dirty or evil was one of the many things she had learned from the old woman. She closed her eyes and smiled sleepily. The kick nudged her awake. She grinned and took one of Odessa's hands and held it to the spot. Their eyes met. Together they felt the baby move.

"I guess she likes it too," Odessa said. Without ever discussing it, both women called the baby "she."

Rosa felt her eyes fill with tears. "I'm glad I'm here with you." She let Odessa rub the extra oil from her skin and button her shirt closed. "I wish you were my mother," she whispered.

The words echoed. Odessa broke the silence. "No you don't."

"Yes, I do. I do." She grasped Odessa's hand and held it to her cheek.

"I wouldn't be any good as a mother. I'm too selfish. Too self-absorbed."

"No you're not. You would be a wonderful mother. I could be your daughter."

Odessa withdrew her hand. "My poems are my children, dear Rosa."

Hurt, Rosalina turned on her side.

After a minute, Odessa said, "You look like her."

"Who?"

"Your mother."

She turned back. "You knew her?"

"I still remember the first time I saw her, years ago. She was behind the counter of your father's bakery. She was beautiful. Full of light and laughter." She wiped the oil from her fingers.

"She's gone."

"Yes, I know." She took a deep breath and continued. "I mourned her when she died."

Rosalina shook her head. "You're mistaken. My mother isn't dead. She ran away when I was young. With a coastguardsman."

"Who told you she ran away?"

"My father." Bitterness hardened Rosa's voice. "My father who says I am a whore. Just like my mother."

Odessa drew another long breath and stared out the shack window, at the ocean, the sky, the lone gull dipping and soaring above the waves. "And the others? They told you the same story?"

Rosa nodded.

"Stupid people." Odessa fell silent for a long time, following the flight of the gull. She rose and went to get her tarot deck. "Take a card," she instructed.

Rosalina wanted to hide, as she had hidden from the priest, but she knew that Odessa would not be as easily put off as Father Mallory had been. She pulled a card and held it out.

Odessa studied it for a long time. Finally she gathered the cards together and wrapped them back in the square of soft velvet. "Love is stronger than hate." She seemed to be speaking to herself. "Truth is more powerful than falsehood. If we forget these truths, then we are damned."

She turned to Rosalina. "Answer me this question. The night on the beach when the men beat you and left you to die, was your father one of them?"

Rosa folded her hands over her belly and hung her head, not wanting to meet Odessa's probing gaze.

"Answer me, Rosa. Was he?"

"Yes."

"Why didn't you tell me this before?"

"I was ashamed."

"And what were you so ashamed of, dear child?"

"That I had made him hate me so much he wanted to kill me."

"Listen to me, Rosalina. Listen with your ears and heart and body. Breathe in deeply when I talk, so that you take the words and knowledge inside your body and the understanding will be part of you. You were not the cause of your father's hatred."

"He will never forgive me."

"For what?"

"My sins."

"Your sins? Shall I tell you what I think of these sins you cling to with such passion, Rosalina? I think you were guilty of being human, of being weak and foolish, of feeling your body come alive and satisfying your hunger. The sin here is not yours. You loved and you were truthful."

"I sinned in the eyes of God."

"You care too much what others think. Your God. Your Father Mallory. Your father and your friends. You have created a prison for yourself, and you will never be free as long as you give power to others."

"I can't help it."

"Of course you can help it. I will tell you something else. You are not the only one who is afraid. I know this town. When I first saw this town, nearly fifty years ago, I was twenty and my hair was thick and black and hung down to my hips. I had a different lover every week, and the artists nicknamed me Daphne." She grew quiet, lost in her memories. "I'll never forget my first sight of Grace Point. I was swept away by her beauty —the same beauty and power that has drawn me back here every summer since then.

"Do you know why I live out here in this shack on the dunes, Rosalina? It is because I am afraid that if I live in the town, I shall become it. And then I shall really know fear, because Grace Point is a town that lives in fear, that cringes and whispers and constructs lies to hide the truths, covers the secrets with violence and hatred and more lies. Your father beat you because he is afraid."

"Of what?"

"Of the truth." The old woman drew a deep breath to steady herself. "Your mother did not run away, Rosalina. She is dead. She drowned. They say it was suicide. But long ago, when she first died, they whispered that she had been killed. Some believe that your father killed her."

The words echoed in the dune shack. Rosalina sat in frozen horror on the cot. Odessa got up and started to strip off her clothes.

"Now I am going to go down to the ocean and swim and wash all the sins and the foolishness of the town from my body. And when I am done, I hope that I am strong enough to sit down and write."

Rosalina watched her go. She was dizzy with all the old woman had told her. *She's lying,* she told herself. But she feared it was all true. It was as if the knowledge had always been there, hidden away—a horrid, shameful, festering secret. Memories, long blocked, surfaced. Memories of waking in the night to the sound of her father's rage and her mother's tears.

Chapter 29

Odessa left in November.

Alone, during that winter on the dunes, Rosalina courted madness. She closed off the bedroom and slept on the cot in the living room. She kept the stove blazing so fiercely that the plank floor in front of it almost burned her bare feet each morning, but even so the corners of the shack were frigid. The cold was her constant companion. The screaming of the wind was the psalm of her days and nights. Her shack and the beach it occupied were a separate planet, as remote and naked as a moonscape. More than once she feared she would die. She wondered who would find her. The stirring of the child inside her body kept her will to live firm.

The only others she saw were the coastguardsmen who lived in the station several miles down the beach. She hid when they patrolled the stretch of beach that fronted her shack. At night, the attending guardsman reminded her of the hermit card in Odessa's tarot deck. The glow of his single lantern moved across the horizon like a phantom. She watched it from the moment it came into sight—just a pinprick of light dancing in blackness—and followed its progress past her shack and down the beach until it disappeared, extinguished by blackness.

After a while, she began to think of the light as a separate entity, not attached to the man who carried it. A dancing soul. A friend who came to visit her each night.

Even the thought of death brought no release. By her sins—unconfessed, unforgiven, indeed unforgivable—she had condemned herself and her unborn baby to everlasting damnation. She would be punished by God. Or by a stranger. Or perhaps by one of the coastguardsmen in the night.

The weeks passed, and around her, life died. The kettle-hole pond behind the cabin froze over. The fox and deer she had seen in the fall disappeared. The dusty miller and goldenrod and poverty grass curled and turned brown after the first frost. The tree swallows and marsh hens and plovers flew away to winter shelters. And while life on the great beach died, inside her the baby grew.

During that long winter, the townspeople of Grace Point spoke her name often. Mad, they called her. Why else would she spend the winter in the dunes?

Was she the wronged one, or had she wronged? Saint or sinner? Madwoman or whore? The longer she stayed out on the great beach, the more the ghost of Rosa's presence shadowed the town. And as the weeks passed, their voices changed subtly. Judgment turned to admiration, admiration was transformed to anger, and anger finally became fear. Only a madwoman, only a witch could stay alive out there. Fear gave her the strongest hold over the town. Her sin had set her free.

In January she began to find food on her steps, left like an offering. It appeared like magic. At first she thought it was from the men at the Coast Guard station. Even though she hid when they came down the beach, she was sure they saw the smoke curling from the chimney. They knew she was there.

The food was bland: canned goods, bags of flour, butter, milk. Things a pregnant woman would need. As weeks passed, the food changed. She recognized the Portuguese dishes. She did not wonder if it had been

Helen or Dolores or Isabella who had cooked for her. And when she ate the loaves of bread, she never thought about her father kneading dough in the bakery kitchen. She began to think of the food as offerings from the gods—not the God of Father Mallory, but the gods Odessa believed in. Female gods. Loving goddesses who forgave, like the earth and sea.

Three times Father Mallory made the long hike through the bitter cold to see her. Each time she refused to let him in, then peeked through the window and watched him turn slowly back. Even though she was afraid these trips to the shack would kill him, she never let him in.

As winter deepened its hold, she began to sleep as if drugged. Curled like the baby inside her, she lay beneath the blankets for hours. Many times she dreamed that she was a whale sheltering a baby whale that swam open-eyed in the fluid of her belly. Once, during a whale dream, she saw men coming for her. They carried knives, and she knew they wanted to split open her skull and take what they found inside. When she woke, her fingernails had etched bloody crescents in her palm.

Once, in March, during a night when there was a storm of such fierceness that the shack itself seemed to bend to the lashing of wind and rain, she dreamt Joaquin came. In her sleep, she heard his voice screaming at her through the howling wind. He banged on the door and called out her name. Then, cutting through the roar of the storm and the sound of his screaming, came the sound of a hammer striking a nail. She dreamed then that he was standing on the doorstep of the shack and was nailing his hand to the doorframe, while he shouted out his rage and love, despair and longing.

Unlike other dreams, this one stayed with her when she woke. After the storm died, she went to the pump. She avoided looking at the door frame. But when she returned with the pail of water, her gaze froze on the board that framed the door. She grew lightheaded with the sight of the splintered, fresh hole, as if a nail had been driven in. Afraid she would see blood, she did not look at the sand beneath the steps.

For days after that, she averted her gaze when she entered or left the shack. Then, one day, her eyes swung to the place where the hole was and she saw that the wound in the wood had turned gray and smooth, as if it had been there all along.

So passed the winter of silence and sorrow.

One morning she woke and spring had come. She opened the door and windows and let the stove grow cool. She shook off the cloak of winter sleep like an animal shedding its brumal coat. She was filled with energy, felt electric with it. Barefoot, she walked to the pond. The scent of spring was there—not the false spring of April but a true thawing. She could feel it in the earth beneath her feet. She could see it in the beach pea blossoms. A crow circled overhead and screamed. She threw back her head and called back to it. Her voice was raspy from disuse, and she was surprised at the noise she made.

Back in the shack, she brewed a cup of bitter coffee and took it to the plank table by the window. She sat for a long time gazing at the dunes and the sea beyond. Finally, when she had finished the coffee, she crossed to the bedroom and pulled the hatbox out from beneath the bed. She took it back to the table and opened it. The bottle no longer held even traces of his scent, so often had it been opened over the long winter. How many times had she looked at the pathetic few things she had to remind her of Fenris? She looked at the photo and read the note he had pinned on her pillow so long ago last summer. These things seemed to have no relation to her. They were the belongings of a stranger. She took the note, the picture, the book with the poem about the whales, the atlas page with the map of Minnesota and threw them into the firebox of the stove.

She understood now that he would never come for her.

Edgy with the strange energy that had suffused her blood and bones since morning, she picked up the empty after-shave bottle and left the dune shack. She walked toward the pond, undecided whether to bury this last trace of Fenris Boak or to throw it in the water. Her legs ached and her breath grew ragged as she lumbered across the sand, and she realized how huge she had become during the winter. Standing by the pond, her water broke.

She made it back to the cottage between the spasms of labor pain. They were monstrous, living things and overtook her like the waves that thundered onto the beach in the January storms. She screamed. She cried and shrieked and called out for her mother to help her. Believing she would die giving birth to her child, she called out a dead woman's name.

After a while, she no longer had the strength to fight the pains and so gave into them, submerging herself in them like a bodysurfer riding the waves. The sun fell lower in the sky, and the cabin grew dark.

When the knock came at the door, she was too weak to answer. The door opened and a man entered. She saw at once he was a coastguardsman and wondered if he had been one of the men who patrolled the beach to warn ships from the bars. When he spoke, she let his gentle southern accent wash over her as the pain had minutes earlier. She was glad he was not one of the local men. She could not have borne their touch.

As he lit the stove and lanterns and heated water, his movements were as efficient and as calming as a woman's. She wondered how he had known to come, but accepted his presence as another gift from the goddesses.

The pains gripped her again and she tried not to scream, but he came and sat by the bed and told her to yell. He had placed a sheet over her, but she tossed so that it slid to the floor and her pale legs and giant stomach shone whitely in the light streaming through the window. He sat and stroked her hair. He called her "ma'am."

When the time came, he helped her with the birth. In the final moments, the nameless terror she had vanquished in her winter of sleep returned. He thought she yelled because of the pain, but she was screaming with fear. She knew her baby would be born dead. Or deformed. She would not escape the wrath of God.

She slipped in and out of consciousness. Then the full, courtly voice of the guardsman pulled her to. She heard the surprise in his voice. "Well, I'll be damned," he said. "Well, I'll be damned."

She had given birth to twins.

When she woke, the man was gone. She realized she had never even asked his name. While she slept, he had moved the cot close to the wall. She felt the warmth along her ribs and breasts. Beside her, enclosed between the dune shack wall and her body, her two babies slept.

Chapter 30

Rosa sat at the kitchen table. The dunes spread before her like a calendar she had become adept at reading. The sun was higher now and reflected off the sand like beams dancing on a mirror. Every day more and more of the beach trembled to life. Soon, she knew, Odessa would be returning, and what then? There was barely room for herself and the poetess in the shack, and now there were two infants. Where would she go? What would she do?

She pushed the questions aside. Something would happen. She couldn't think of the future. Over the winter she had learned the secret of the dunes, which is this: nothing is still and nothing is permanent.

In the bedroom, the babies slept. Her babies. Her son and her daughter. A smile crossed her lips. Just thinking of them made the front of her shirt grow wet with her milk.

She adored their shallow breathing, a sound far sweeter than the wind in the beach grasses. She gloried in the incense of their bodies, more precious than the perfume of the beach pea. She delighted in their skin, more flawless than a perfect petal of the *Rosa rugosa.* She marveled over their tiny fingers, astonishing in their miniature perfection as they curled around her own in absolute trust.

She studied her infants and stroked them and took their fingers in her mouth to taste them and licked them with her tongue. When she held the babies to her breasts and fed them, their dark eyes stared directly, unblinkingly into hers and communicated words from worlds where she had never been or could not remember.

> *. . . mother whales lie dreaming suckling their whale-tender young*
> *and dreaming with strange whale eyes wide open in the waters of the beginning and the end.*

She was obsessed with them, captivated more deeply and truly than she had ever been by any man. They were her life, her reason for being. Whatever price she had paid or would be asked to pay, she would give willingly. Once she had thought that she would do anything, strike any bargain to have a child. Now she knew with equal certainty that she would do anything she had to do to protect her twins.

The winter, the isolation, the birthing of her son and daughter had changed her. She no longer cringed when the coastguardsmen patrolled past her cottage. When she thought about Fenris, she vowed that no man would ever use her again. And when she thought about Joaquin and her father, she pledged that no man would ever hurt her again.

Lost in thought, she did not catch sight at first of the man backlit by the shimmering sun who was coming toward her shack. When she finally saw him, he was just abreast of the half-buried skeleton of the trap boat. She knew at once he was not a coastguardsman, and even at a distance she could see from his height and posture that it was not Father Mallory.

Her hand flew to her hair, grown wild and long during the winter. Her shirt was still open from the babies' last feeding and stained yellow from her milk.

Her long skirt—an old one of Odessa's—was soiled and wrinkled. The man continued toward the shack.

He is coming.

She buttoned her blouse. There was not time to change into another. She closed the bedroom door, shutting her babies off from sight. Then she sank back down on the chair by the table. *Fenris? Joaquin?* She closed her eyes and tried to picture each man's face, but behind her closed lids there was only blankness, as if these months had washed away even her memory. With a patience born of the long winter on the dunes, she sat and waited.

When he drew closer, she saw that it was her husband.

Chapter 31

Zoe

It was a long time before Emily fell asleep. She hadn't let Zoe touch her. Only Jake. When he returned from work, he had found them in the bedroom, huddled on the floor. In stunned silence he'd taken in the ravaged room. Without a word he had picked up Emily, brought her downstairs to the kitchen, and rocked her until she quieted. Then he'd fed her and changed her into her pajamas.

Upstairs, moving with the careful, hunched posture of an animal, Zoe straightened out their room. She picked up the brushes and ruined canvas and broken pieces of the slop jar. There was nothing she could do about the paint blots and water splotches. The stains mocked her.

She took a shower and washed the paint from her face and hands and hair. She stayed in the shower for almost an hour, turning her face to the spray and letting the water and steam cleanse her. Back in their room, she stretched out on the bed. She heard Jake and Emily come upstairs, heard him talking to Emily as he put her to bed. She could not make out the words. His voice was low, soothing. He stayed in Emily's room for a long time.

She lay on their bed and waited. The room was dim, but she did not get up to put on a lamp. After a while, she heard Jake come out into the hall. He stopped outside their door for a moment, then went back down the stairs without speaking.

She found him in the living room, sitting in the darkness broken only by the light from the desk lamp. "How is she?"

"She'll be all right. She was frightened." His voice was even.

"Did she have dinner?"

"I found some soup in the refrigerator. And I gave her some chocolate cake someone brought. Did you eat?"

"I'm not hungry."

They were speaking in the queer, polite manner of disaster survivors before the numbness has worn off.

"Are you sure? There's more of the soup, and I saw a couple of casseroles. It will only take a minute or two to heat something."

"I said I'm not hungry."

"How about some tea? Or a drink?"

"No. Nothing."

He eyed her warily. "Would it upset you if I got something? I haven't had anything since lunch."

"No. Go ahead."

"Now you're angry."

"No I'm not."

"Yes you are. You're angry because I want to eat."

"All right. I'm angry. I mean, how can you? Just the thought of food makes me sick."

"So because you can't eat, I'm not supposed to?"

"I just don't understand how you can eat now."

"All right, I'm sorry that I want something to eat. I'm sorry that that makes me some kind of monster. Okay?"

"No. It's not okay." Her voice rose angrily. "It's not just that you're hungry. It's like you're pretending nothing is wrong."

"Well, what the hell do you want me to do? Go upstairs and trash our bedroom? And frighten Emily? Is that your idea of normal?"

"Maybe it's more normal than pretending nothing

is wrong," she shouted. "You always pretend. And we never talk about what's really going on. Well, not this time. Adam's gone." *Adam's gone and you don't even mention his name. You go on like everything is normal.*

Her voice broke. "I just don't see how you can know Adam is out there somewhere and not talk about it. I don't understand. It doesn't seem right. Unless . . ."

"Unless what?"

A stunned look crossed his face. "Good God, you don't think I had anything to do with his disappearance?" Horror darkened his eyes. "That's it. You do, don't you?" A shudder of pain shook him. He sank back into the armchair and dropped his head into his hands. "What's happening to us?" he whispered.

Zoe sat in stony silence.

"I've been afraid to mention his name," he said finally. "I thought it would make it worse for you. Remind you."

"Remind me? Do you honestly think that for even one single moment I can forget?"

"It just seemed better if we didn't talk about it."

"It's like New Haven. Exactly like New Haven. We never talked about that, either. Well, I can't pretend anymore."

"That's what this is all about, then, isn't it? What happened in New Haven? I'm still paying for that. You've never forgiven me." Seeing the bitterness in her eyes, he dropped his head against the chair back and sighed. After a minute he spoke. "I can't do this anymore, Zoe. I can't live like this. You have to decide. You can't stay on the fence. You either trust me or not, but you can't make me pay for the rest of my life for what happened there."

She didn't answer.

"Do you hate me so much? I mean, for you to believe that I could have anything to do with Adam's disappearance, you must think I'm some kind of animal."

Zoe stared at him. When she spoke, her voice was flat. "She's here, isn't she?"

"Yes."

"And you've seen her?"

"Yes."

"That's why you lied to the police, isn't it? Because you were with her when the store was closed."

"It's not like you're thinking. Laurel's here, it's true. And I've talked with her. It was her therapist's idea. She called last week and asked if she could come. Explained why. That's all."

"And you didn't think it was important enough to share with me."

"I didn't tell you because I thought it would hurt you. Reopen old wounds."

Zoe shivered suddenly, remembering Cole's visit. "How did she act?"

"What do you mean?"

"You saw her yesterday, Jake." Her voice sharpened with urgency. "How did she behave?"

"I don't know. Angry. She's furious with me—with both of us—for what she went through. She's angry that the charges were dropped."

"Oh, God."

"What is it, Zoe?"

"You better get hold of Dan Cole or his partner."

"Why?"

"Don't you see? Laurel's gone. Riley told me she left last night. After Adam was kidnapped. They haven't been able to find her."

The significance of what she was saying hit him. "You don't think . . . you *can't* think she would take Adam."

"I don't know. You talked with her. What do you think?"

He didn't answer.

* * *

It was after midnight by the time Cole and Riley had finished asking Jake questions, and it was an effort to climb the stairs to the second floor. The sight of their bedroom shocked Zoe. She had forgotten her explosion. It seemed to have happened a long time in the past, to another woman. She stood at the door and took in the damage. The carpet and the walls were stained with water from the slop jar, and paint from her palette was smeared on the floor. The shredded canvas stunned her. She barely remembered ruining it. She was ashamed that Emily had seen this.

Jake was still downstairs, turning off lights and locking up. There was nothing she could do tonight to repair the rest of the damage.

She walked down the hall to her daughter's room. The night-light in the hall cast shadows. She opened the door.

"Oh, God!" she cried. Then she screamed. "Jake! Jake! Jesus, Jake!"

He was there instantly. "What is it? For God's sake, Zoe. What's wrong?"

He came to her side, followed her gaze, and gasped, a swift intake of breath. "Oh, no. Oh, no. Dear God, no."

They stared at the empty bed, the vacant room, unwilling to believe their eyes. They reached for each other.

"I'll go call the police," Jake said.

Zoe crossed to the bed, where the outline of her daughter's head still dented the pillow. She touched the sheets, searching, hoping for a hint of Emily's warmth, but the bedding was cool to her touch. She noticed that the scraggly old blanket Emily had had since she was a baby was gone.

It couldn't be. No.

She returned to her bedroom and dressed so that she would not be in her bathrobe when Cole and Riley arrived. She felt numbed, shell-shocked. She started to go down to join Jake, when she felt the draft. It curled around her neck and bare ankles. She turned and—with a start of horror—noticed that the attic door was open. The cold curled inside her.

With dread, she walked toward the stairs to the third floor. The light was on at the head of the landing. Shivering, she started up. She had not been there in the days since Halloween. The police had combed through every carton and container, searching for clues and—although they did not say this—for any other tiny skeletons that might have been hidden there. They had searched up there again after Adam had been taken. Jake had told her that the attic was a mess, but she was unprepared. Everything had been pulled away from the walls, every box and trunk and garment bag had been emptied, as if attacked by vandals. The police had overlooked nothing.

In the middle of it all, her small body dwarfed by furniture and stacks of old clothes and magazines and books, lay Emily.

Zoe stood stock-still, staring at her daughter's motionless limbs sprawled out like a broken doll's.

"Zoe? You up there?" Jake called. She could not answer.

He came up behind her. "Zoe?"

Rooted to the spot, she did not move or answer.

Then he saw Emily and brushed by his wife to kneel by his daughter and gently pick her up, with shaking hands. He cradled her against his chest. "She's asleep. That's all. She's asleep."

The words did not register.

"It's okay, Zoe. She's just asleep." He reached over and picked up the old blanket and tucked it in Emily's arm.

"Daddy?" Emily's voice was tiny and scared.

"Emily!" Zoe cried. "You scared me to death. Did you know that?"

"Easy, Zoe," Jake said. "It's okay, Em. Mommy is

just worried. She was upset when you weren't in your bed."

"I'm sorry, Mommy. Don't cry." Emily's voice trembled.

Zoe was aware then that she was crying. She wiped her cheeks with the back of her hand. "It's okay, Em. I'm sorry I yelled at you. Daddy's right. I was just worried." She knelt beside Jake and took Emily's hand in hers. The skin was cold to her touch.

"Come on, you two," Jake said. "I think my girls had better get back downstairs where it's warm." His voice was thick.

Together they tucked Emily in. Zoe sat on the edge of the bed, rubbing Emily's forehead, while Jake went down to let the police know they were all right.

Zoe watched her daughter. "Why did you go up to the attic, Emily?"

Emily looked up at her with trusting eyes. "I was waiting for the witch to bring Adam back."

Zoe could feel the prickling of the hair rising on her arms. "There isn't any witch, honey. Adam isn't with a witch."

"If she sees me," Emily continued, "she'll take me and bring Adam back. Then you won't cry and be mad at Daddy. If Adam comes home, you'll be happy."

Zoe cupped the tear-streaked face in her hands and looked into Emily's eyes.

"Emily, I love you. It would break my heart if anything happened to you. Do you know that? I couldn't stand it if anything happened to you."

Emily didn't answer.

What have I done?

"I love you, Emily."

"More than Adam?"

"You are my only Emily. The only Emily in the whole world. If a witch came in the room now and said she would give me back Adam if she could take you, do you know what I would say?"

"No."

"I'd tell her no one in the world will ever take my Emily."

"Really?"

"Really. Oh, Em. Em, honey." Zoe hugged the child, rocking her. After a moment, one small arm reached up and curled around her neck.

When Jake returned, Emily was asleep.

"Everything okay?"

"Yes. She's fine," Zoe whispered. "I just want to stay here for a while." Emily's smooth little hand, warm now, lay nestled in hers.

So I have hurt her, as I was hurt. But no more. It stops here. We can learn. We can be healed. Jake and me. Emily and me. She stared at her sleeping child and repeated these vows. *We can change.* Tears filled her eyes. The pain, the loss of Adam washed over her. They *could* change, but could they—*would* they—ever get Adam back?

Chapter 32

Ten A.M. Forty-two hours had passed. *Forty-two hours.*

Zoe tightened her arms around Emily and fought to distance the panic.

"I'm glad you came." The words sounded stilted, formal.

"I can't stay." Tory Sands brushed invisible lint from her challis shawl.

Zoe caught the slight flicking motion. Reflexive as a tic, the gesture revealed Tory's rare display of nerves.

"I'll have to fly back by tonight at the latest," her mother continued. She had not touched her coffee. She slipped the shawl from her shoulders and folded it over the back of her chair. Even this simple gesture was graceful. She got up and crossed to the stove, accompanied by the rich rustle of silk. With arms held out to protect her clothing, she dumped the coffee grounds in the garbage and rinsed out the pot. Although she had wiped it earlier when the coffee was brewing, she swiped the countertops again, holding the sponge with the tips of lacquered fingernails. Her nail polish was translucent. Perfect white half-moons curved at the ends.

While Zoe watched, Tory tackled the food that had been brought to the house during the past twenty-four hours. Her mother found an apron—a square of white decorated with red and green rickrack that someone had given Zoe for Christmas—in a drawer by the sink. She tied it around her trim waist to protect the paisley-print skirt that matched the challis shawl. Efficiently she stored the casseroles, putting three in the refrigerator and two in the freezer. Then she lifted brownies and cakes and cookies from their pans and plates. Deftly she packaged them and then stacked them on top of the casseroles in the freezer compartment. Each time she opened the freezer door, breaths of hoarfrost escaped into the kitchen.

"Sit down. Your coffee will get cold." Zoe was exhausted just watching Tory. "I'll take care of that stuff. You don't have to do it."

Emily lay curled in her lap. The child had not left her side all morning. Gently, Zoe stroked her daughter's head. Emily lay still beneath her touch, silent except for a muffled sucking noise. She had not sucked her thumb since she was two, but Zoe did not have the heart to rule out this tiny source of comfort.

"In a minute," Tory said. She contemplated two open pans. One held a roasted turkey breast, the other a ham. Zoe knew she was deciding which one to leave out for their dinner.

"Isn't Emily late for school? Hadn't you better be getting her ready?" Tory asked.

Emily's other hand—the one not at her mouth—snaked into Zoe's grasp. The child's face burrowed into her chest.

"She's not going to go to Mrs. Lake's today." She hated the defensive tone that had crept into her voice. A frown flickered across Tory's face. An expert at reading her mother's expressions, Zoe understood.

"Jake and I decided not to send her today. We need to be together right now."

The ham went into the freezer, and Tory surveyed the kitchen with satisfaction. She squirted soap into the sink and turned on the faucet. "There are no names on any of these things," she said, sliding the pan that had held the brownies into the water. "I hope you can remember who brought what. Did you write names down as they came in?"

"Please, Mother!" Zoe shouted. "Sit down. You're driving me crazy."

Tory's back stiffened, and the French-manicured fingers withdrew from the dishwater. "I shouldn't have come."

"No. It's me. I'm sorry. I'm sorry I shouted. I'm nervous, that's all."

Tory dried her hands. Automatically she pushed each cuticle back gently with the dish towel.

"I'm glad you came," Zoe continued. "Really."

As delicately as if unclasping a strand of pearls, Tory untied the apron and set it on the counter. She crossed to the refrigerator. "Didn't I see some wine in here?"

Zoe's stomach tightened.

"I know it's still morning, but I think I'll have a glass."

Zoe knew the time. Nearly eleven o'clock now. Her mind did the math without prompting. Forty-three hours. Nearly forty-three hours since Adam had been taken. Forty-three hours and—dear God, dear God—still no trace of him. No call, no note. Only the deathly silence.

Tory held out the bottle toward her. "You sure you don't want some?"

"I'm sure." What she wanted was to be held. She wanted to lie in her mother's lap just as Emily was cuddled in her own. She wanted to feel her mother's hand stroking her hair, wanted gentle words of solace, wanted to be comforted. It seemed that she had spent her entire life longing for these things. She watched her mother pour chablis into a goblet. *Why can't it be different?*

Tory brought her glass to the table. She looked at Emily, saw the thumb in the child's mouth, saw Zoe's hand creep protectively over Emily's cheek. "Where's Jake?" she asked.

"At the police station."

Tory's eyebrow arched into a question.

Zoe paused and then continued, defiantly. "Taking a lie detector test."

"A lie detector test?"

"It was his idea." She saw her mother's eyes flick to Emily, knew that she wanted to ask more questions, but not in front of the child. Three generations. They could have been strangers. She rocked Emily gently and felt the child snuggle closer. When she looked up again, she caught Tory looking at her. Her expression was vaguely and troublingly familiar, but Zoe couldn't quite read it. She thought of all the things she wanted to say to her mother but wouldn't, the things she wanted to ask but couldn't. *What a history of silence we share,* she thought. And then—*It doesn't have to be that way.*

Tory stood up and walked to the window. She carried the wine with her. She pushed the curtain aside with one hand. "There's a reporter out there," she said.

"I know. He's the last one. Yesterday there were two or three."

"Vultures." Tory sipped her wine.

"I guess." Overnight Zoe had begun to feel differently toward the reporters. Maybe a story or a headline would reach a stranger and in turn lead to information about her son.

Tory let the curtain fall across the window. After a moment, she crossed to the refrigerator for more chablis, pouring the goblet so full that some wine spilled as she walked back to the window. She drew aside the curtain and shivered. "I never liked this town," she said in a far-off, hollow voice. "It was a mistake to come here."

"How can you dislike a town you don't even know?"

"There was always something unhealthy about it. You know what I used to think?" She took a sip of wine and continued without waiting for Zoe's response. "You know Shore Road? How it rises up and then twists? And you know if you're leaving town, there's that place, that curve, where if you look back, all of a sudden, the town is gone from view? And when you come into town that same rise is where you get the first glimpse of Grace Point. Do you know the exact curve I mean?"

Tory was whispering now. Zoe felt a chill, as if her mother were telling a ghost story.

"All those years, whenever I left the town, I always had the feeling if I turned around at exactly that spot . . ." Her voice was so low Zoe had to strain to hear her. "I believed if I turned at that spot and looked back at Grace Point, I'd be changed into a pillar of salt."

Zoe remembered then. *Damage control.* That had been the expression on her mother's face earlier. Of course. She had seen it before when an artist had appeared at an opening drunk, or a canvas had not arrived as promised—the smooth expression of someone assessing the extent of the damage even while starting to put control mechanisms in motion. That was why Tory had come to Grace Point.

"Oh, yes," Tory continued, speaking not to Zoe but to a phantom only she saw or knew. "When I left town, I was very, very careful never to look back. I never looked back."

"I didn't know you'd spent any time here," she said. *But she knew. Suddenly she knew.*

"What? Oh, yes. Once." Tory's ghostly whisper was transformed back into her normal brisk voice. "I visited it with your father. We spent a summer here."

"When?"

"I don't know exactly." The edge of impatience crept in. "About ten years after we were married, I guess."

"But you told me he only bought this place before he died." *And hadn't she just said "All those years"? What had she been remembering?*

"Did I? Well, maybe it was then." She laughed and

made a dismissive flicker with her fingers. "You know me and dates. I get confused."

Did she send you here? Tell her to leave me alone. Finally Zoe knew who *she* was. "Who is Victoria Santos?" she asked.

Tory's eyes closed. Her porcelain face seemed to sag.

Zoe set Emily down. The Halloween candy was in a wooden bowl by the sink; the sketch of the scarecrow was on top where she had tossed it after her last visit to the trailer. "Here." She handed the drawing to her mother. "Tell me who he is."

Tory barely glanced at the drawing. "I don't know."

"His name is Joe. Old Joe. And he has something to do with this house."

Tory still would not look at the sketch. "It was a mistake to come back here."

"Who is he?" Zoe was amazed at the transformation in her mother. She looked sick—sick and old and exhausted. Who was this old man who had such a hold over her mother?

"I don't know."

"Please," Zoe said. "Tell me who he is."

Tory sank into a chair. "I don't—"

"You do. You know who he is. Tell me. No more lies—I'm sick to death of lies. For God's sake, tell me who he is. And tell me who Victoria Santos is."

For a moment, Tory's face came alive with anger. Her voice was icy. "No. I'm not going to have him ruin my life, everything I worked for. All this has nothing to do with me."

"Goddamn you," Zoe said. "It does. There were four dead babies in a trunk in our attic, and my son is missing, and that man knows something about it, and you know something too, and if you don't tell me I'm going to the police."

They stared at each other, and for the first time that Zoe could ever remember, her mother looked away first.

"His name is Joaquin Santos," she said. "He is my father. And this was his house."

Chapter 33

Rosalina

The midday sun reflected off the stretch of sand with such intensity that Rosalina had to narrow her eyes against the glare. As she peered out at the approaching figure, the metallic taste of fear coated her mouth. She glanced at the door. It did not have a lock.

No man would hurt her again.

Her husband drew closer.

She searched the room frantically. The ax was outside by the woodpile. He would reach the shack before she could get it. *She could not leave the babies alone.* There was one knife, a long-bladed carving knife, the steel worn thin from use, lying by the sink. Grasping the knife, she sank back down on the chair by the table. She closed her eyes and tried to remember what she knew of Joaquin; but behind the closed lids there was only blackness, as if the months on the dunes had leached away all her memories. She hid the knife beneath the folds of her shirt.

He knocked twice, and when she did not answer, he opened the door. He stood in the open doorway but did not enter, as if already regretting that he had come.

"Hello, Rosalina." He looked around the dune shack. After a minute he said, "All winter? You stayed here all winter?"

She sat very still.

He took a step toward her, and her hand tightened on the handle of the knife. *She would not let him hurt her. Never again would she be beaten.*

He retreated. "It must have been cold," he said after a moment.

With the cunning of a fox, she followed every move. He reached back and closed the door.

She planted her feet firmly on the plank floor, tensing her legs, ready to spring.

When he saw she was not going to speak, he cleared his throat. "I've come about your father, Rosalina. He's dead."

She relaxed her hold on the knife.

"An accident." He did not tell her the rumors that swept through the town like a rogue wave. The whispers that refused to die about Jackie's death. Or that Dom's fall down the stairs had not been an accident but God's retribution for Jackie's death.

She waited.

He looked down, ashamed. "Last week."

She had not been wanted at the funeral. Just as she had not been welcome at Jackie's. At the thought of Jackie, she felt a spasm of pain.

"I'm sorry," Joaquin said.

She wanted to laugh. He thought she was grieving for her father, but she felt no grief. She remembered the night she had been beaten, thought of her mother, dead, perhaps by his hand. No, she did not grieve for Dominus Roderick. She would spit on his grave.

"Father Mallory gave the service."

She pictured the little priest doing the ritual in the incense-thick church. It had nothing to do with her.

Beneath Joaquin's shoes, beach sand grated on the shack floor as he shifted his weight from foot to foot. "The bakery . . . the house . . . it is yours now."

She took the information silently.

"You can come into town and live there," Joaquin continued.

Her fingers tightened around the knife.

"It's all over, Rosa," he said at last. "You can come back."

She stared at his hands. On the back of one was a small, round wound. Healing had begun, but the flesh was still purple. He saw her looking and pulled his hand away, hiding it behind his back. The knife forgotten, she got up and stepped toward him. He retreated until his back touched the door.

She reached behind him, taking the hand in hers. She traced a forefinger over the wound, touching it lightly, in awe. His face grew red and he tried to draw his hand away, but she would not let him. She remembered the March storm and the sound of hammering at her door. With a sense of wonder, she turned his hand over and saw the wound in the center of his palm.

"I was drunk." Again he tried to withdraw his hand, but she held it too tightly in her own.

She could not imagine Joaquin acting with such passion. She touched the mark. Then she brought his hand to her lips. She brushed her lips over the circular scar on the back and palm of his hand. Then, without thinking, she opened her mouth. She extended her tongue and drew it across his wounds.

He froze; his hand grew rigid in hers. His eyes held the look of an animal in a trap.

He remembered the night in March when he had come out to the shack, so drunk that twice he had fallen down and once had walked into the icy surf. Drunkenness had caused him to hammer his hand to the door of her shack. Drunkenness was the mask he wore to cover his rage—and his desire for Rosalina. The one fueled the other.

He hadn't been able to work for a month, but not even the pain in his hand had been able to erase the sick hunger he felt for Rosalina. For it *was* a sickness. His brother and father told him so. "You ever take that whore back, you're no son of mine," his father had said. And still he wanted her.

Rosalina, confused by Joaquin's expression, drew back. She returned to her chair, the salty taste of him still on her tongue. She heard the sound of his uneven breathing, felt it echoed in the pulse of her blood. The knife pressed against her leg, but she understood she would not need it.

Through the closed bedroom door came the sound of crying.

She knew it was her son. The other twin, the girl, seldom cried.

Joaquin stared at the door. "So," he said softly, "it's true." He looked at her in awe. "There is a baby." She should have expected the town would know. The tongues of Grace Point.

She went to the child.

When she returned, cradling her son in her arms, Joaquin had not moved. She met his gaze from across the room, and fear leapt alive in her chest. He had come to take her babies.

Never.

The knife was still on the seat of the chair. She crossed to the table and sat down, felt the reassurance of the blade beneath her thigh. She looked down at the crying infant, his face squinched tight, his mouth working. He squirmed in her arms and turned his head toward her chest, quieting.

"What is his name?" Joaquin was looking at her and then at the baby, and his eyes were naked with pain. And confusion. "Rosalina?" His voice was so low she could barely hear him. "Could I . . ." He stopped. She saw the pain in his eyes again. But behind the pain, she saw hunger. "Could I hold him?" he asked.

Her hand slid beneath her skirt and grasped the knife so tightly her fingers cramped.

"Please. I won't hurt him." She saw this was true.

He was awkward with the infant, holding it away from his chest. His hands, so sure on board his boat, were hesitant. She watched him bend his head to search the tiny face. The baby whimpered.

"What's wrong?" he asked. Alarm clouded his face, and his hands and arms stiffened.

She began to unbutton her shirt and cupped one of her swollen breasts with her hand. Then she reached for her son.

Joaquin was gaping at her breast. The baby was crying now. Joaquin backed away, still holding the child.

"Jesus," Joaquin said. He could not look away. She remembered the tattoo.

"He did that." Her husband spat. "He did that to you, didn't he?"

She took her hand from under her breast and clutched the shirt over her nakedness. "Give me my son," she said. These were the first words she had spoken since he entered the shack. Her voice was like an old woman's.

Joaquin backed against the door. His face was twisted, impossibly white with rage. "You did that for him."

"No," she said. Her baby screamed.

She reached for her son, but Joaquin pulled back, holding the infant. Panic filled her. *He had come to take her baby. He had come to take her baby.* She lurched forward, trying to wrest her son from Joaquin. At the same time, Joaquin twisted away. They each pulled at the infant, struggling. But he was too strong for her. The knife, forgotten when she unbuttoned her shirt, lay on the chair. She dashed to the table, grabbed the knife, and, raising it above her head, made for Joaquin. As she brought the blade down, slashing violently, he yelled and spun away.

The infant in his arms smashed against the doorjamb.

She recoiled in horror.

"Oh, God!" Joaquin groaned. "Oh, sweet Jesu, no!"

Rosalina's hands flew to her ears to cut out the sound. Not of screaming; the baby's cries had stopped instantly. Instead she heard the blunt sound of destruction. She cupped her palms over her ears, but she could not cut off the noise: the sound of all things being destroyed.

She did not have to see Joaquin kneel and turn the tiny body over, or meet his stricken eyes. She knew that her son was dead.

Chapter 34

Joaquin thought he was imagining things. The blood drained from his face and he shook his head, trying to clear the sound from his ears like a wharf dog shaking off flies. The wailing continued. It was coming from the other room. Rosalina did not respond. She held the tiny body of her son, blood soaking her shirt. He left her there.

He stared at the baby on the bed. It took him a minute to understand that there were two. He wanted to run—from the crying infant, from the beach shack, from Rosalina and the dead child she cradled in her arms. To run and never look back.

The baby's squalling hurt his ears. He waited for Rosalina, but she did not come. He reached over and rocked the child. At his touch, the baby stopped crying, giving him confidence. When he picked the infant up, urine seeped through to his shirt.

"Rosalina?" Even as he said her name, he knew it was hopeless. He looked around and saw a stack of folded cloths on the bureau. He put the baby on the bed and stripped off the soaked clothes. He was surprised it was a girl.

When he was finished, he carried the baby into the other room. Rosalina was still crouched on the floor. The blood had now spread to her skirt, and he was amazed that such a tiny body could contain so much blood. "Rosa?" he said.

She would not answer.

He needed a drink badly. He looked around the shack but could not find any sign of a bottle. "Rosa," he tried again. This time she looked up at him. "Rosa, who knows that you had two?"

She stared at him numbly. Her fingers fumbled with her shirt, and he watched in horror as she brought the dead infant's head to her breast. Still holding the other twin, he crossed to Rosalina and slapped her. Her head fell back with the force of his blow. He cringed at the sound of her skull striking the door frame; but when she looked at him, her eyes had cleared, and she took the body of the baby from her breast. He could have wept with relief. He got up and put the baby girl on the couch. He tried to take the boy from Rosalina, but she would not surrender him.

"Rosalina?"

She looked at him. Her eyes blazed.

"Rosa, who knew that you had twins?"

It took her a long time to answer, as if her brain had slowed down and needed to consider each syllable before she could make sense of it. He waited.

"No one," she finally replied in the eerie, old woman's voice.

"Are you sure?"

"No one knows." Like much of the dune winter, the coastguardsman who had helped at the birth was part of a dream.

Joaquin sat at the table overlooking the dunes. He did not know how long he had been looking out when he heard her begin to croon—a low, sad, mourning song. It raised the hair on his back and the nape of his neck. He turned and watched as she rocked and sang to the dead baby. She was trying to nurse it again. He watched, with the expression of a man who heard the prison gate close behind him.

He rose and crossed to his wife. "Come on, Rosalina. We're going home."

* * *

While he packed her things, she sat passively on the couch, holding her dead son. He stopped only once, when the little girl cried.

"She's hungry, Rosalina." Rosalina would not move, would not forsake the dead child to nurse the living one. He searched until he found a can of condensed milk. He dipped the tip of his finger in the milk and held it in the baby's mouth. He was amazed at the strength of her sucking, the roof of her mouth pulling fiercely against his finger. It reminded him of the ocean. Of sex.

He soon saw that she could not get enough milk that way, so he ripped a square of cloth from a sheet in the bedroom, poured condensed milk on it until it dripped, and then set it in her mouth as if she were a motherless puppy or kitten.

At last Rosalina's few things were packed, and he was ready to leave the shack.

It was a long walk back to town and would be slow going with the baby and Rosa.

He tried to take the body from her. "We will bury him before we go."

"No," she said.

"We have to, Rosa. By the pond. Where the *Rosa rugosa* grow. We can't take him back. Can't you see that?"

"No," she said.

"We have to." He grabbed her by the shoulder and reached for the baby. "Give me the damn baby, Rosa."

Her eyes changed in that instant. Later he was to know this expression well, know and dread it. But this first time it shocked him into letting go. She looked at him with dreadful, crafty eyes. "I won't leave him here. You can't make me. I will tell them that you killed him."

Their eyes locked. He turned away first, defeated.

She would not let him help her. He sat on the couch with Rosa's infant daughter. Knowing Fenris was the father, he felt no tenderness toward the baby. He watched while Rosa prepared her son. Carrying the dead baby with her, as if she did not trust Joaquin with the body, she went out to the pond and returned with a pail of water. She stripped the tiny body of the bloody clothes and washed it. While she worked, she again took up her eerie, crooning song—the lullaby of a madwoman. Joaquin resisted a fierce urge to run from the shack and never look back.

Gently, tenderly, she washed the body, dried it, then looked around for something to put it in. After a moment, she went to the pile of old newspapers beside the stove and took one. She folded the paper carefully around her son, then went to the bedroom and came back with an old hatbox. Joaquin recognized it immediately as having belonged to her mother.

She put the body in the hatbox.

When she was done, the four of them—Joaquin, Rosalina, the baby girl, and the dead baby boy—headed across the dunes to Grace Point.

They moved into the old bakery. For three days, Joaquin did not fish. He cleaned the rooms and cared for Rosalina and the baby girl. He shopped and cooked. He took down all the display cases and turned the front room into a living room. Upstairs, he made a nursery.

He had believed that his family would come to help them. But for those three days, no one came to the house. Day after day the three of them breathed and ate together. Joaquin and Rosa lay in bed, but the ghost of the boy gave them no rest.

News of their return had swept through Grace Point. The town judged them, and stayed away. The women who had made the long trip to the dune shack to leave food on the shack steps gossiped and whispered.

Through thin lips, they talked of sin. Alone on the dunes, Rosalina had been an object of Christian pity. In town, she was the object of scorn.

At the end of a week, Joaquin went to see his parents. "Come and visit us, Poppa," he begged. "See our baby. We named her Victoria. After you."

His father would not answer.

"Did she tell you that the child is yours, Joaquin?" asked his mother. She had turned sour after Jackie's death. "If you believe that, you are a fool."

"Please, Poppa," he pleaded. "Come and see us."

"Leave your father alone," Leona said. "While you live with that whore, the whole town sees our shame."

"What's wrong with you? Why can't you forgive her? The whole town doesn't care shit about who sleeps with who. Half the town sleeps around. Look at Dolores—everyone knows she fools around on Tony. What's the difference? Why is this so different?"

His mother crossed the room and slapped his face. The imprint of her palm stood out like a tattoo. It was the first time in his life she had ever struck him. "Get out," she said.

When he returned home, he tried to tell Rosalina what had happened, tried to share his despair; but she did not respond. She never spoke to him, only to her baby son.

Those first days, she kept the body, still wrapped in newspaper, in the nursery with his sister. Joaquin woke on the morning of the fifth day and found that she had put the corpse in the crib with Victoria.

It sickened him. He shook her and told her that she could not do that again. The body was beginning to decay.

She cried. "My baby is so lonely."

"Rosa. Listen to me. We have to bury him."

That afternoon, the body disappeared. He allowed himself to believe that she had buried the boy.

Sometimes, she seemed to be getting better. He

watched for the signs, clinging to them. One night, in bed, she curled in his arms. He held her and allowed himself to hope. She had been good all day. "Rosa," he began. "I need to talk to you. About the baby."

"He is very good, my baby. He never cries."

His heart sank, but he pressed on. "I mean your other baby, Rosalina."

She stiffened in his arms.

"She was crying when I got home. She was hungry and needed to be changed. That's no good, Rosalina. You have to take care of her."

She was silent for a long time. He felt her tears against his chest. "I try, Joaquin," she whispered. "I try, but when I look at her, all I see is my son."

It was the first time since the dune shack that she had so totally surfaced from her well of insanity.

Every morning when he was fishing, he tried to think of what to do. One day he decided that if she had another child she would forget her dead son. She endured his lovemaking. She lay beneath him without moving. After he was done, she went into the bathroom. He heard the water running, the toilet flush. The next morning, he saw the hot-water bottle attached to the rod over the tub, its long tube hanging down over the spigot.

Still he persisted. Each time after they made love —such a term for what they did!—he lay in the silence and listened as she washed away his sperm. After a while he no longer tried.

Weeks passed. One night, she slipped out of bed. When he followed her, he found her in the attic, crooning over the wasted body of her son. He gasped. She looked up and he saw that she would kill him if he tried to take the body away. After that, he lay back and listened to her climbing to the attic. He tried not to listen to the singing as it curled down the stairs like smoke.

Some days when he returned from fishing, he would

find his daughter—he told everyone the child was his, even began to think of her as his—wailing in her crib or playpen. Rosa would come down the attic stairs in answer to his call. "He gets so lonely all alone up there," she would say.

Days passed. Sometimes she mumbled crazily and ignored Victoria. Other times, she kept her daughter clean and well fed. These days, he allowed himself to believe she was getting better. Only a sane woman would do that, he thought.

More than once he thought about running off. But every home he had known was in Grace Point, and all he knew was how to fish. In despair, he considered going to Father Mallory. But the specter of his mortal sin, the memory of the baby's death—*murder*—prevented that. The sanctuary of the church had been taken from him. He could not be absolved. He was guilty. Guilty as sin. Guilty of sin. So he lived on the hope that somehow things would get better.

One day, two months after he had brought Rosalina home, he woke in the middle of the night to find that the sheets were cold on her side of the bed. She had been gone for a long time.

"Rosa?" he called. The room was icy with dread.

She stood in the middle of the kitchen, a bundle in her arms. With sinking heart, he saw the crafty look in her eyes.

"What have you got?" he asked.

She smiled.

"What is it?"

She crossed to the sink and unfolded the package.

He saw with horror that she held a baby.

At first he thought that she had brought the dead boy down from the attic. But two months had passed since they had come back from the dunes; this baby was newly dead.

"What have you done?" he cried in horror.

"My baby is lonely. He is used to sleeping with his twin."

For an awful instant, he thought she had killed her other baby. Then he saw that this child was a boy "Where did you get this baby?"

"In the cemetery."

"Sweet Jesu, Rosa. What have you done?"

She rocked and crooned over the dead body, singing the familiar lullaby. *Rock my sweet baby, on the treetop . . .*

He started toward her to take the body. "We have to put it back. You understand that, don't you? We have to put it back."

She ran to the corner of the kitchen and crouched down, hunched over the infant. She began to cry.

He could not bear the thought of fighting to take the body from her. "All right," he said softly. "It's okay, Rosa. I won't take it. Just tell me exactly where you got it. Tell me that, Rosa, and then you can put the baby with your son."

He walked to the cemetery by St. Peter's and almost at once—even in the moonlight—located the grave. A granite angel towered over the mound of freshly dug earth—an angel that looked down over generations of the Manuel dead. He was sick at the sight of the tiny opened casket and open grave. The Manuel baby had died four days ago, in the night in his crib. The child had been only days old. When he heard, he had gone to visit Mary and Jimmy. He remembered their grief, the way they had clung to each other, the tears that coursed unchecked down the sunburned cheeks of his friend.

Working quickly—dawn was already streaking the horizon with red—he set the coffin back in the grave and shoveled the earth on top of it. He felt as if he were burying his soul. Carefully, he smoothed the ground and set the basket of dying flowers on top of the raked earth. As he walked away, he did not look back. He would never be able to look Jimmy Manuel in the face again.

When he returned home, Rosalina was in bed. The body of the Manuel baby was nowhere in sight.

He could not sleep. He went to the bathroom and washed his hands over and over, but still they smelled of the damp cemetery earth. The dirt stayed beneath his fingernails. The knowledge that two infant bodies were in the attic pressed down on him. He longed to talk to his father or his mother, but he knew he could not. He knew only one thing: he did not have the strength to bury another empty casket in the night-shaded cemetery.

Soon it would be time to go fishing. He went into Victoria's room and leaned over the crib. Sorrow overtook him, and he was filled with terrible, shaking regret for the life he and his Rosa might have had. He reached down and touched the sleeping child. Then he left his house.

He was drunk when he returned home that night. He stood over Rosalina, shouting at her. "Enough, you crazy whore."

She looked up at him with hollow eyes.

"No more, do you hear me? You are to forget this whole business. I tried. I took you back, after everything, and I won't have any more of your craziness. You will take care of your daughter, clean my house, make my meals."

She smiled at him, the smile he had learned to hate.

"You will do as I say, Rosalina. And if you don't, I'll have them come and take you away. Do you understand, Rosalina? I'll send you to a house for crazy people and you'll never get out."

He saw by the look in her eyes that at last he had

found a way to control her. The next day, when he returned from the sea, he found that she had cleaned his house, made his meal, and cared for Victoria.

But still the people of Grace Point stayed away, as if they knew they were not wanted in the silent house of death where a man and his wife and a baby daughter lived. As if they knew it was a house peopled by ghosts.

Rosalina grew silent and sly. She wandered the streets pushing her daughter in a crow-black carriage and listening to whispers. Thus she learned what went on in town. When a baby died—so many died that summer, as if the town had been cursed—she poured rum for Joaquin. He drank thirstily. When he was drunk, she went to the graveyard. Craftier now, she closed the graves afterward.

And in the attic, two more bodies joined the others.

Chapter 35

Zoe

Zoe stared at her mother. Tory Sands. The name was a lie. Victoria Santos was her mother's real name. She felt contaminated by the secrets and lies.

If Zoe had expected Tory to be remorseful or apologetic, she saw at once she was wrong. Her mother looked up at her with defiant eyes.

"I need to know why you lied to me."

"That's all in the past." Tory dismissed the subject with a wave of her hand. "What does it matter now?"

"It matters."

"I don't expect you to understand, Zoe." Her voice was haughty. "I did what was for the best."

Zoe felt her cheeks grow pink as shame and guilt, familiar childhood feelings, rushed in. She pushed them back, refusing to be silenced as she had in the past.

"I just want to know. I want to understand. Why didn't you tell me?"

"It was for the best. I thought it was for the best."

"How? How could it be for the best?" Zoe said. "I need to understand. How could you have lied—about your mother? About who we were?"

"I did what I had to do."

"But the secrets—all of it." She could have wept. "You have robbed me of knowing who I am. And why? For what?"

"It was a mistake to come back here." Tory picked up her scarf from the back of the chair and wrapped it around her, as if suddenly chilled. "I did it for you, you know. I was protecting you."

"How can it help me to think my grandfather was dead? And what about your mother? Is she really dead, or was that a lie too?"

"You want the truth? The precious truth you are so eager to have? Well, here it is. My mother was crazy. Now you tell me this—how on earth will it help you to know that? Would you have dared have children if you knew? I spared you the horror of it. Not that you'll thank me for it."

"Did Dad know?" She waited, hands clenched.

"Your father knew me as Tory Sands. I doubt if a Yale professor would have been interested in a orphan bastard of an insane woman."

"Tell me about her," she demanded. Zoe saw the flash of panic in her mother's eyes. "Please, tell me."

After a moment, Tory sat down. "She was in and out of institutions most of my life," she finally replied, her voice as matter-of-fact as if she were reciting a grocery list.

"And your father?"

"He wasn't my real father. When I was twelve," she continued in the same flat tone, "he told me that I would grow up to be a crazy whore like my mother. He was glad when I left. I only saw him once after that. He had traced me to New Haven, where I was married to your father. He came and saw me one day when I was alone. He needed money. He'd had an accident, a fishing accident. Lost his arm in a winch. He said he would go away if I gave him money."

"Did you? Give him money?"

"Oh, yes. For a price. I made him sign the house over to me in exchange. I took the money from the gallery. Your father never knew. I told him I bought the house from someone in the gallery as an investment. After I was sure the deed was mine, I had my lawyer tell Joaquin he had to get out. It was my way of paying him back. My way to punish him for my pain."

"You made him leave his home? And you never heard from him again?"

"He called me once, and I told him if he ever tried to see me or my husband, I'd kill him. He believed me. He believed I was crazy, like my mother. I was free of him then, free of this town." She shook her head. "Except that I should have gotten rid of this house."

"Where is your mother now?"

"I haven't the slightest idea. I was notified five or ten years ago that she was being released. They were closing the state institution."

"And you never tried to reach her?"

"No."

"But she's your mother."

"I never had a mother."

But now Zoe wasn't listening. Color drained from her face. "Oh, God," she moaned. She bent over. Her stomach cramped.

"What is it?"

"This house," she said. "This was your mother's house. *Fifty years ago, she was living here.*" She felt sick. The sight of the tiny bones—tiny bodies—in the attic haunted her.

"The babies," she whispered. "The babies in the trunk . . ."

Her mother leaned across the table. Her face was rigid, her voice fierce. "Listen to me, Zoe. You are not to tell anyone any of this. Do you understand? This has nothing to do with us."

She could only stare numbly at her mother.

"This has *nothing* to do with us, do you hear? Nothing. My God. It's all in the past. Fifty years ago. Are you listening to me?"

She closed her eyes, shutting out the voice.

"It would ruin me. You see that, don't you? All I've worked for. The gallery. Everything. I won't have it all destroyed. The gallery is all I have. I want you to promise me you won't tell anyone."

"I can't."

Her mother's next words were cut off as the back door swung open and Jake walked in. Zoe looked up at her husband. He was gray and stooped with exhaustion. His eyes were pink-rimmed, and she knew he had been crying. He closed the door behind him wearily.

"Jake, what's wrong?"

He looked up at her, tears spilling from his bruised eyes. "Laurel's mother called the police." He reached out for her. "Laurel is back in New Haven."

Zoe leaned against him. "And Adam?" She was afraid to breathe.

He clung to her. She felt the weight of him on her and braced to bear it. He needed her now.

"Adam wasn't with her."

Chapter 36

Agnes Farmer could no longer ignore the smell. She headed for the shed room. "This time she goes," she muttered under her breath. "I won't stand for it anymore. No more of her stray kittens in that room." The whole house was beginning to smell of her cats. No social security check was worth that.

She knocked on the door of the spare room. "Birdy? Birdy, are you there?" It wouldn't do the old lady a bit of good to pretend. She had watched Birdy go out early that morning and had seen her return an hour later. She had been in there ever since.

"Birdy?"

Stirrings of anxiety tickled Agnes's throat. "Birdy?" she called again, this time more hesitantly.

Of course, she should have been prepared for this, she told herself as she pressed her ear against the door, against the silence. No one could live forever, especially in a room so cold you could see your breath. A wonder she hadn't kicked off years ago.

She'd have to notify next of kin, if she could find them. Tucked in the desk somewhere was a scrap of paper with the address of Birdy's only relative. Shameful the way these young people didn't care what happened to their elders as long as someone else was there to shoulder all responsibility, to clean up the mess. "Birdy?"

The drama began to play out in her mind.

That's just how I found her, Doctor. Looks peaceful

though, doesn't she? Must have died taking a nap, poor thing. Not that I would mind going like that. But here now, you must be chilled, coming out on a cold day like this. Can I get you a cup of tea? And a piece of pie? I just made one. Mincemeat. My own recipe. No, no, it's no trouble at all.

A whisper of sound behind the door broke her reverie.

"Birdy?" Irritation crept into her voice. What a start the old lady had given her. She pushed and the door to the shed room swung open. The smell of foul air rushed to greet her.

In the middle of the bed, Birdy sat.

Her gown was open and revealed withered breasts and ancient, puckered skin.

At first Agnes thought that she was holding a doll —a toy dressed in the shabby maroon and gray clothes that the old lady had knit. Then she saw it move.

"Oh, my God," Agnes breathed.

"He's mine," Birdy said. She hugged the infant closer.

"Dear God. Dear God," Agnes murmured.

"He's mine," Birdy repeated.

Agnes edged closer. "Where did you find him, Birdy? Tell me where you got him." Even as she asked these questions, headlines from the *Grace Point Sentinel* flashed through her mind. The infant that had been kidnapped. The Barlow child.

"He's mine."

Agnes edged closer. The baby seemed too still. Too quiet. She inched nearer.

Birdy drew back. "No. He's mine." Her eyes flashed with temper.

"Yes. Of course, my dear." *Dear God. Dear God. Help me.* She scanned the room, taking in the empty cans of condensed milk on the nightstand, the pint of gin, a bowl of sugar, an empty bottle lying on the pillow by Birdy's elbow. The bed sheets were badly stained, and the wastebasket was filled with soiled diapers. The smell was unbearable. She inched forward. The infant looked pale, but she thought it might be the reflection of the maroon wool next to his face. She prayed he was not dead. The room seemed even colder than usual.

She turned her attention back to Birdy. "And isn't he the handsome one," she crooned. "Just let me hold him. I won't hurt him. I promise you."

The lilting intonation had been a mistake. She saw that immediately. Birdy stared at her through narrowed, crafty eyes. "Get away."

"Please, Birdy," Agnes said in a normal voice. "Just let me help you. Let me hold your baby for a minute."

"You'll hurt my baby."

"No I won't. I'll be very careful. I promise."

The infant moved and began to cry, a weak, protesting mew.

With motions so practiced they astonished Agnes, Birdy reached for a cotton hankie that lay on the nightstand. A portion of the material had been bound in a lump, held by an elastic band. Smoothly, never taking her eyes off Agnes, the old woman uncapped the gin bottle and soaked the wad with liquor. Then she held it to the baby's mouth. His crying stopped and he sucked eagerly at the sugar-and-gin sop.

Dear God, how much of the gin has she given to the baby over the past two days? Agnes wondered. Her skin crept with dread.

"He hurt my baby," Birdy said suddenly. "He hurt my baby."

"Who? Who hurt your baby, dear?"

Birdy's face was animal in its cunning.

The infant sucked at the sop.

"Poor dear," Agnes said. "No one will hurt you. I'll go and leave you two alone. But you must be hungry. Aren't you hungry, Birdy?" She was unaware that her voice had assumed the singsong rhythm again. "I have some warm pie. And tea? Wouldn't you like that? You just wait here and I'll bring you some pie." She started backing out of the room, unaware that Birdy watched her every move with sly, knowing eyes.

Her hands were trembling when she dialed the number, and her sentences came so quickly the dispatcher had to ask her to repeat each word.

Agnes had the door open before the police were halfway up the walk.

"Thank God you're here," she said. "She's inside. In the shed room."

The toll the case had taken was written on Dan Cole's face, apparent in his hoarse voice. The pressure to find the Barlow child and to solve the mystery of the bones hidden in the attic had been relentless. The case was getting national press. And just this morning they had received news from the federal lab that one of the skeletons had a fractured skull. It didn't make sense, but this report increased for him the urgency of finding the Barlow baby.

His eyes darted around, taking in every detail. "And she has the baby?" he asked. "You actually saw the infant?"

"I sure did." Agnes Farmer's face was pink with excitement. "I tried to take it from her, but she wouldn't let me."

A third man had joined them. Agnes recognized Dr. Warner, Grace Point's only pediatrician. He carried a medical bag.

"Where is she?" Riley asked. He, too, had the beaten look of a man who has gone without sleep for several nights.

"In here." Agnes led them down the hall to the shed room.

At the door, Cole edged her aside. "We'll take it from here." She noticed then that he wore a revolver.

After a moment of silence, the deputy reached out

and turned the knob. Then he pushed the door open.

The three men did not move. "Damn," Cole swore. Agnes bobbed and ducked around the mass of their bodies until she could peek beyond.

The room was empty.

So much a part of their landscape was she that the people of Grace Point no longer noticed the woman known as Birdy when she wandered by. They were used to her as she made her thrift shop rounds, net bag at her side stuffed full of odd woolen garments, head bent toward the ground as she muttered to herself. They knew—for Agnes Farmer had told them—that she unraveled the yarn from these castoffs and refashioned it into tiny sweaters and bonnets. They smiled indulgently.

In another place, they told themselves, she would be a bag lady. They took pride that there were no homeless in their town. Grace Point cared for her own. And relieved of the burden of conscience, they passed the familiar figure on the sidewalk, but they did not see her.

Birdy. Rosa. Rosalina. The cold sang out her names. *Little Rosa. Rosa Rugosa.* It knew her names. It sang them all. *Sweet Rosa. Witch. Whore. Crazy whore. Bruchas. Crazy Rosalina.* The cold called to her. It wanted her.

She lay down. She had little flesh to cushion her bones, and the sidewalk was hard beneath her skin, but she did not mind. The cold called to her again, its siren song of death. She waited, knowing it was coming for her.

Let it come. Let it come. It had been waiting for a long, long time. No matter. She was ready now. After all the years, her baby was safe again. She curled tight.

She was so tired, she wanted to rest. *Let it come. Let it come.*

The fisherman who found her knew at once she was dead. He was nineteen years old, his name was Anthony Costa, and he was on his way to the Sunken Dory for a beer. It was the first time in his life he had ever seen a dead body. After he called the police, he was sick.

Within minutes, Cole and Riley arrived. Knowing the gesture was futile, Riley unbuttoned the old lady's soiled cardigan and felt for a heartbeat. Before he touched her skin, he saw the faded tattoo, so like a bruise, and pulled back for an instant. Dan Cole and the young fisherman also saw the mark on the puckered flesh, and they looked away as if shamed. Beneath his hand, Riley felt no pulse, no warmth.

Cole was the first to see the net shopping bag that lay on the sidewalk by Birdy's side. He inhaled but did not expel the air. Gingerly Dan picked up the bag. It was lighter than it should be, lighter than he wanted it to be. He didn't need to empty it to know that Adam was not there.

Chapter 37

They were silent on the ride back from the airport. Emily was still asleep when Jake pulled into their driveway. He got out of the car and came around and lifted their sleeping daughter out of Zoe's lap. Cradling Em in one arm, he reached out for Zoe's hand. His touch had never been gentler. The three of them walked slowly up the steps to their home, their silhouettes merging into one.

When Zoe sat in the rocking chair, Jake handed Emily over. Together they slipped her jacket off, moving carefully so as not to wake the child. Emily stirred, rubbing her face against Zoe's chest, then slipped back to sleep. The chair creaked as Zoe rocked.

"Tea or a drink?" Jake asked. He had already pulled a quart of bourbon from the cupboard.

"That," Zoe said, nodding toward the bottle.

While Jake prepared their drinks, she looked across the room at the wicker basket on the deacon's bench.

Jake handed her the drink. She tried to smile her thanks, but it hurt too much.

Although the whiskey burned her throat, she forced herself to take another sip. Jake didn't touch his. He crossed to the table and sat down. She watched as he took off his glasses and rubbed his eyes. *Is this how we will go on? One day at a time. One hour. Or can we go on at all?*

The police told them about Birdy's death—Birdy, Rosalina Santos, *her grandmother*. The things her mother had told her about their family made her head whirl. The mysteries of her childhood—her mother's unexplained coldness, the extended families her friends had but about which she felt only a child's wordless loss—all began to make sense. But she could not think about them now. Later there would be time for that. Later there would be time to sort out all the things she had silently blamed Jake for, hurts that rightly belonged in her childhood, not in their marriage.

The police had told them, too, about the ongoing search for Adam. She had seen the hopelessness in their eyes, the scheming in Tory's. *Disaster control.* Well, it was far too late for that. "The gallery is all I have," her mother had said. *You could have had me. And Jake. And Emily. A family.* She had thought the words but had not spoken them. It was too late. Her mother had never wanted a family.

And what do I have left? She looked at Jake and tightened her arms about Emily. *I have them. And hope. I mustn't give up hope.* It could feed Adam, keep him alive wherever he was. She was nowhere near ready to give that up yet.

"Hungry?" Jake broke into her thoughts.

She shook her head. Once his question would have angered her, but she realized now that this was his way of dealing with a crisis, of trying to take care of her. She slid her hand into his.

They finished their drinks in silence.

"Should we try to put her to bed?" Jake asked, nodding at Emily.

"She hasn't had supper. Maybe we should feed her first." Zoe felt a flutter of fear at the idea of letting go of her daughter. I'll have to get used to this too, she thought.

"Em," she said gently, "come on, hon. We're home. Time to wake up." She stroked Emily's hair, petting and talking to the child until she woke up.

"Hi, Em." Jake knelt by Zoe's knees, his face level with Emily's. "How's my girl? Hungry?"

Emily's hand crept to her face, and she slipped her thumb into her mouth. Zoe resisted the impulse to pull the hand away.

"Hungry?" Jake asked again. "I bet you could eat a horse."

"Where's Nana Tory?" the child asked sleepily.

"She's gone home, Em. Remember we drove her to the airport?"

Emily snuggled deeper into Zoe's arms. "Good," she said.

A wave of sorrow passed through Zoe. As if he understood, Jake embraced her, engulfing both of them in his strong arms.

When the doorbell rang, Zoe was the first to react. She handed Emily over to Jake.

It had grown dark. She flicked on the porch light and opened the door.

Jake came up behind her. Emily, asleep again, was in his arms. "Zoe? What is it? What's the matter?"

She didn't answer. She just stared at the one-armed scarecrow. Old Joe. Joaquin.

"Oh my God," she heard Jake say behind her.

Joaquin pushed the bundle at her. "It's over now," he said gruffly.

"Adam," she cried. "Oh, Adam."

"Oh God," Jake repeated in a whisper.

She cradled her son in her arms. He was cold. Instantly, she folded back the blanket, bent her face to his, heard his breathing.

Relieved of his burden, Joaquin stepped back.

"You took our son?" Jake's voice was raw with anger, threatening.

Joaquin backed away. "No. God, no. That's what you think? That I took him?" He looked at Zoe.

The chilly night air filled the entry and Zoe drew back. She nestled Adam closer, warming him with her own body. "You had better come in," she said. Up close, in the hall light, Joaquin looked much older than he had at the trailer. And worn, as if life had taken more from him than he had to give.

Joaquin hesitated, and then, after a glance at Jake, stepped into the hall. He glanced around. "She took this house away from me, you know," he said bitterly.

"Tory? My mother?" she asked.

"Victoria," he said. "She always hated me. I raised her like she was my own, and she hated me for it. Thought she was better than me." A mean, sullen expression crossed his face. Zoe had seen the same expression at the trailer when he had kicked at his dogs.

"That's why you took Adam?" Jake asked. Only the sleeping child in his arms prevented him from grabbing Joaquin.

"I told you. I didn't take him. I couldn't do that. But I never thought she would."

Zoe rocked her son, crooned to him.

"I thought she was a harmless old lady now."

"You mean Rosalina?" Jake asked.

He nodded. "Today—this morning—I saw her walkin' into an alley. She was carryin' something. I saw her lie down. By the time I got to her, she was dead. Then I saw that she had a baby. I knew it was yours." He looked again at Adam.

"I was comin' right here. Then I saw the police. I didn't want no problem with them. When I came back, you was gone. I took him home. Meg, my woman, fed him. Changed him."

He edged back to the door and turned the handle with his one hand. "So it's over."

Jake made a movement to stop him, but Zoe signaled him to let the old man go. "Thank you," she said.

"I always wanted a son." His voice was so low that Zoe didn't hear him.

"What?" she asked, but he had already disappeared into the darkness. Jake closed the door.

"Adam," she whispered. She nestled her son to her breast. Then she leaned against Jake and pulled them all tight to her—her son and daughter and husband. The wondrous circle of her family.